What Can One Man Do?

Also By Eric Rice

America at the Brink series
Our Choice: Freedom or Obedience
The Cost of Standing Up
Whatever it Takes to Win

What
Can One Man Do?

America at the Brink

Eric Rice
(Nick Turner, Book One)

Disclaimer: This novel is a work of fiction. It contemplates a 'what if' scenario in an imaginary United States, along with imaginary interactions with the rest of the countries of the world. The novel's characters and story are fictitious. Any reference to historical events, real people, or actual places are all used fictitiously. Any resemblance to those living or dead, actual events, and to any actions is entirely coincidental. I reference long-standing institutions, such as American Government entities, agencies and other public offices, both in the US and abroad. The actions of these agencies, their policies or the characters involved with or working in said agencies portrayed or implied in our tale are entirely fictitious and wholly imagined as of the point of time of publication.

Dedication

In writing a book, one faces long periods of solitude, anxiety, depression, and inspiration. Ultimately, it is a lonely business, but not one done alone. This story has been rattling around in my head for over thirty-five years. I dedicate this book to my wife, Mary Sue. She has had to listen to me pontificate about the problems of society, the solutions, and changes necessary to fix it for most of these last thirty-five years.

I am glad to have finally begun this journey. We will see where it takes us together. I have an idea, but as with any idea, the result is never quite what you think it will be. My guess is this saga will be the same. I am enjoying writing it. My hope is you enjoy it as well, but also that it opens your eyes and helps you contemplate actions and their consequences. I also hope it interests you enough to continue on this adventure to find out just who Nick Turner is, and exactly what one man *can* do. If nothing else, let's hope we all Wake up, Stand up, and learn to Think for Yourself (WST4Y).

Introduction

Never Forget. How often is this phrase used throughout history by survivors? Never Forget December 7th, the Holocaust, 9/11, or October 7th. Yet we always do. Memories fade. New generations grow up who have no direct recollection, only stories. Stories which are soon no longer retold.

The events leading up to and causing each are also forgotten. This is why we write and study history. History is a roadmap. The past is also a vision of the future. It shows us what to look for and illustrates the results we can expect if we don't learn from what has happened before.

I sit here today, in the middle of the twenty-first century, determined to do my part. I write this history, hoping it will prevent a repeat of what we've just lived through. The events, decisions, actions, and their consequences. Recognize what we didn't. Use the knowledge presented here to learn. And to act. To prevent from occurring what we had to endure. The only way to prevent history from repeating is indeed to Never Forget.

America is dead. Franklin, Jefferson, and Madison's experiment lasted longer than many expected, but not as long as it should or could have. Its destruction was remarkable, unnecessary, and complete. This was entirely our own fault. And we deserved it. Much like Adam and Eve, we failed our test, turning a blind eye to unchecked corruption. Instead, we promoted hedonism, narcissism, and self-righteousness. Allowing ignorance and propaganda to triumph over reason and common sense. We abandoned a society based upon freedom and individuality. Replacing it with indifference, dependency, and citizen malaise.

This is the saga of how and why it happened. About those who attacked it and those who sought to defend this Republic and its Constitution. Much like a tsunami wave, the collapse of the shining city and the hill on which it stood had far-reaching ramifications. Some expected and intended, many more unintended. Leading to results both catastrophic and wonderful.

Desperate times test people. When societies face desperation, the character of the people determines their ability to survive or fade into oblivion. This is about the desperate times of the United States of America. It is also a commentary on mankind. Humans are unpredictable and their actions are rarely rational.

In a country divided, questioning its founding principles, America found itself at the brink. Facing a choice to unite and recover or divide and fall.

With hindsight, it's easy to look back, to question decisions and direction. This history must be told, for we have ignored these lessons too many times in the past, repeating the same mistakes. Ignoring this maxim was one root cause of this crisis. The common people were ignorant of history. They scrubbed it from the schools. Like most societal disasters, the people in charge, who knew the history, simply ignored it. They believed they were smarter and could prevent it from repeating itself. They were wrong. Let us begin our retelling of the fate of Democracy in America.

Prologue

Lauren Bergamo struggled to load the old-fashioned 8mm film reel into the antiquated projector. She pushed her dark auburn hair out of her eyes, finally figuring out how to thread the film. The projector whirred, and the light appeared on a white screen. The footage was grainy black and white. It showed a wizened husk of a man with wispy gray hair. His voice was thin and reedy, but his eyes burned with passion, belying his ninety-nine years.

"Sir," he addressed the interviewer off camera. "Your question is what advice I would give today? It worries me young folk are no longer being taught the lessons of the Holocaust. Evil once took root, spreading like pestilence across the land. We ignored it then at our peril and we paid dearly." He held up his arm, showing a faded series of numbers tattooed on his forearm.

"This is the mark of the devil. We were not only victims, but the ones who enabled this, by ignoring the chance to stop it. He was only saying things to get elected, like any other politician, or so we told ourselves. Once in power, we assumed he would not carry out his promises. We were wrong. As we watched, our friends and neighbors, our customers and comrades, all changed before our eyes."

"We had not changed, but suddenly we were evil. The problems of society, feckless politicians, and their failed promises were all laid at our feet by the leader of their cult. Jews have been the villain in every story." He paused, leaning back in his chair, a vacant stare on his lined and wrinkled face as he remembered that time so long ago.

"Persecuted, enslaved time and time again. Expelled into exile and driven from the public square. We have soldiered on. Building and rebuilding over and over. It was different this time. This person was different. He mesmerized his followers. It was not simply exile. No, this time, it was rather more ambitious."

"Once and for all, he would eradicate the Jews. It would be his gift to the world. One must ask; how many times was someone close to him? How many times could someone have stopped him? A pistol shot, a knife to the heart or throat. A car bomb. Even gouging out his eyes with your thumbs." At this, the man lifted his quivering hands and shook his thumbs to make his point.

He said in as loud a voice as he could muster. "Why didn't anyone stop this?" Wheezing heavily, he paused before continuing.

"If you cannot remember and you are no longer taught the consequences, or the reasons it happened, how can you recognize the signs? How can you expect to stop it from happening again? Who stands to gain when this is no longer taught? The next Satan, that's who," he said, shaking his head slowly.

"Do you know, in every repressive government, they target the knowledge? In books, and from the teachers, the clergy, anyone who can lead. They make a show of threatening all who dare to challenge their authority and ability to control. I look around, not just in America, but around the world."

"What I see is an increasing distrust of history and an intolerance for anyone challenging repressive ideas. Please, do not let this happen again. Someone will come, once again, with a silver tongue, making promises, armed with the ability to wield power beyond belief. They will claim to be helping, to be solving problems, but they will enslave us once again." Once more, he paused, shaking his head.

"This time it will not be just Jews, but all who resist. We will be called into action to rise. This will only happen after atrocities and much suffering. With substantial loss of life and if, IF, we are once again ignorant, blind, and docile. Please, for the sake of my great grandchildren and their children now and in the future. Do not make them go through what I went through." He finished raising his tattooed forearm. A single tear fell from his eye down his cheek as he became distraught by his memories. The interviewer continued, saying the man would pass shortly after this filming. One of the last who had been an adult at Auschwitz, surviving the Holocaust.

Lauren sat contemplating the message of the clip. She was writing a piece about another holocaust survivor, merely a child then, who had recently passed. Her employer, the pioneer in cable news, *America's News Channel,* was asking for a story questioning the need to continue to teach the holocaust. After all, her producer had opined, there was little chance of something like that ever happening again. Times were different now. People were more civilized. Journalism, instant communications, and global oversight would never allow this to happen again.

The short film had shaken Lauren's resolve. It made her question the message her producers requested. She sat in the semi-darkness of the museum dedicated to the survivors of that tragedy and thought about the old man's request. Shaking herself out of her reverie, she packed up the film, placing it back on the shelf. She walked out of the museum, back into the light of mid-afternoon sunshine.

Sadly, his message, and this film, would be seen by few and ignored by most. But not all.

Part One

Mr. Turner Goes to Washington

"I wouldn't give you two cents for all your fancy rules if, behind them, they didn't have a little bit of plain, ordinary, everyday kindness and a little looking out for the other fella, too."

James Stewart, *Mr. Smith Goes to Washington* (1939)

Chapter 1

"Today, we received an update from Senator John Wilhelm's office. He remains in a medically induced coma. This is to allow the brain swelling from his stroke, suffered two days ago, to subside. The doctors are cautiously optimistic, reporting the swelling is lessening. They did not offer a timetable for when they thought the Senator would awaken. And certainly not when, or even if, he could resume his duties." The morning news anchor on the *New World News* network, Steve O'Leary, delivered this in a solemn voice.

He turned to his co-host Beverly James, an attractive black woman who had a suitably serious look on her face while shaking her head in concern at the news.

"Our thoughts are with the Senator's family. We're hoping for a full and quick recovery. Steve, this has to be a cause for concern for Majority Leader Fontana and the upcoming filibuster vote. The Party's majority in the Senate is now 50 to 49, with Wilhelm incapacitated. They've finally scheduled a vote to repeal the legislative filibuster, and this tragedy happens. With the vote in only a few weeks, they can't afford to lose anyone else."

"Indeed, Beverly. We're entering the fall break for Congress for the first few weeks in October. They set the vote for early November. There are other Senators to worry about with histories of medical issues. It's a stressful time for all involved. I'm sure the Majority Leader can't have this vote fast enough."

Beverly was nodding at Steve's revelation. "Hopefully, Senator Wilhelm can recover during the break and return by November. As you know, the Party claims the Opposition party has used the filibuster over and over to stop them from passing popular legislation. With their current majority and the mood of the country favoring change, this could finally be their chance to succeed," concluded Beverly in a voice full of approval at the historic opportunity.

A phone rang in the background.

Senate Majority Leader Sal Fontana lifted the remote and muted the TV in his Senate office as he answered his phone.

"Ya," he said in his pronounced New Jersey accent, listening to the voice on the other side.

"Yes, I'm watching. Yes, I realize we can't lose any more Senators, Lexi." He held the phone away as an angry female voice continued to make her point.

"I can't pull the vote forward. Senators have already made travel plans to be back in their states for town halls and other events during the fall break. Several are going on a visit to Ukraine and others to Iceland for the Climate Summit. It's only a few weeks; we'll be fine."

Sal listened intently.

"Banks?" laughed Sal in response. "Him I'm not worried about. I don't think he'll ever die." He paused as Lexi talked.

"I realize he's ninety-four. He's been waiting on this vote for decades now. Relax, we've got this. It's not my first rodeo either as leader."

Sal ended the call and unmuted the TV. He watched an administration spokesperson extoll all the great things they would accomplish, once the filibuster was gone for good.

Chapter 2

The office in the Hart building, housing half of the United States Senators, was impersonal, almost monastic in appearance. A simple desk, unremarkable chairs, a couch, and no pictures on the walls. A man sat behind the desk; his thick black hair carelessly tousled, as if he'd just rolled out of bed. Leaning back in his desk chair, he had a highlighter in one hand and papers in the other.

He was neither young nor old, clean shaven, with a slight olive complexion betraying his Italian heritage. His t-shirt, tight across his chest, displayed well-muscled arms. He was vigorously marking passages in a document with his highlighter. Wire bound briefing books covered his desk. There was barely enough room for his desk phone, Colorado State University coffee mug, his sweatpants and sock clad feet, perched on the corner.

At the sound of a knock on the door, he sat up, removing his feet from the desk.

"It's open."

In walked a man with thinning brown hair, a slight frame, wearing fashionable round tortoise-shell glasses and a pressed, tailored suit and tie.

"I hope one of those is for me. I could use a refill," he said to the man entering the office, carrying two paper coffee cups, while also cradling a couple of binders under one arm. Trying to close the door behind with his heel, he started losing his grip on everything.

The man sprang quickly from behind the desk, moving much faster than one would have expected from his six-foot four frame. He reached him just in time to catch a falling binder and to grab one coffee.

"Nice save Nick. Thanks," said the man, shifting the other binder with his now free hand.

"Didn't want to have to shampoo coffee out of the rug when I leave," explained Nick, smiling.

"I figured you needed a cup. Guess it is a refill," he said, glancing at the coffee mug on Nick's desk. He just nodded, setting the binder down on a table.

"How long have you been up?" he asked, glancing at the wall where a Murphy bed was still pulled down from its cleverly designed bookcase wall enclosure.

"I don't know, what time is it?" Nick walked to the bed, grabbed the foot rail, effortlessly lifting it back to its resting place in the wall.

"Bed made, Mom. Happy now?" His bed now looked like a wood paneled part of the wall.

"You know they hate the fact you sleep in your office, Senator," he responded as he helped Nick slide the two chairs and a coffee table in front of the now hidden Murphy bed.

"I'm happy to move in with your parents. Maybe they could adopt me? I could be Charles Bosworth Robinson IV and a half."

The man threw him a look. "Hilarious. I don't live with my parents. I live in one of their houses. There's a difference," replied the real Charles Bosworth Robinson IV.

"Sorry, my bad, Chuck," said Nick with a smirk, taking a sip of the coffee he'd brought. "Good God, man, what is this?" Nick grimaced, setting the cup down on the end table.

"Hazelnut. Wonderful, isn't it?"

"Actually, it's not." Nick walked over to the small kitchen just off the main office/bedroom of his Senate suite. Taking his empty CSU coffee cup, he started his coffee machine. It proceeded to grind and brew his third cup of this very early morning.

"Prefer my plain old Rocky Mountain Thunder dark roast. Thanks for thinking of me. Who the hell sells coffee at 4:30 in the morning?" asked Nick, looking at his watch.

"Nobody. Or at least no one whose coffee I want to drink. I brought this from home. Saw the light was on in here."

Nick nodded. "How are your parents, anyway?"

"Enjoying the Villages way more than they should," answered Chuck with an accompanying eye roll.

"Embarrassed your parents are retiring in Florida living with all those New Englanders?" asked Nick, now laughing as his coffee finished brewing.

"It's worse. Most of them are Midwesterners. Ohio, Wisconsin, Michigan. Yes, they have a villa in the south of France and a place on the lake in Tahoe and they're living in the Villages, thank you very much." Chuck sat in one chair in front of the now hidden Murphy bed.

"Not to mention a brownstone in Georgetown," added Nick. "Hey, just more for you."

"Gee thanks. If I wanted money, I'd go back to working for Goldman Sachs. You trying to tell me something?"

"Absolutely not. Clearly you have your own issues. Why else would you be here this early? I live here, so I have an excuse." Nick returned to his chair behind the desk.

"I couldn't sleep. Figured I'd get an early start too." He surveyed the piles of paper haphazardly stacked on Nick's desk. "What are you looking at?"

"I was marking up SB2520, the gun control bill." Nick was shaking his head.

"I believe you mean the 'Make Our Neighborhoods Safe with Sensible Gun Protection bill'," replied Chuck in an authoritative tone.

Nick smiled and leaned back. "What's wrong with us? Why do we do this?" He waved at the binders on his desk. "Gun control, student loan forgiveness, Supreme Court expansion, and statehood for DC and Puerto Rico. None have a chance of getting any votes from the Opposition. Where is the common sense? The compromise? Why is everything us versus them?" questioned Nick, looking at Chuck, who was now reviewing his own stack of material, listening.

"Indeed, it is. Well, you know by now how the game is played," he said, looking up. "Each time we have to push it to satisfy our progressive side. Every time we make a little progress, if slowly," finished Chuck in both a lecturing and placating voice.

"But we look like idiots to a large group of everyday Americans. Some of whom even voted for us. We keep saying we don't want to take all the guns. Guns they don't need for protection, according to us. While we also write bills defunding the police." Nick shook his head and sat in the chair opposite Chuck.

"You gotta go with the flow. It's the process. How long have you been here, nine, almost ten months?"

Nick took a long sip of his coffee, pausing before answering. "Long enough to know this isn't working. We ain't fooling anyone. How long have you worked on Capitol Hill?" countered Nick. "Twenty-five years? Does it ever matter?"

Chuck set his briefing book on the coffee table. He arranged the chair so he could see Nick without turning. "I started as a congressional aide over 25 years ago. I worked for Senator Richards for his entire time in the Senate these last 16 years. Does it matter? I like to think it does, but it is frustrating sometimes," agreed Chuck, sipping his hazelnut.

"We need to work incrementally and across the aisle to regain the trust of our voters. All of them, not just from the Party. Instead, we keep promoting and passing bills with no hope of adoption. Or worse, full of unintended consequences." Nick stood, walking to his desk, pointing to the stack of briefing books. "These just ensure further discord in Congress. There are no winners, certainly not our constituents."

Chuck rose from his chair, walking to stand in front of Nick. He was around six feet tall and had to look up at Nick. "The spirit of compromise is dead. It died on May 10, 1981, when *America's News Channel* and 24x7 cable news was born. Didn't get much rest, did you?" asked Chuck calmly, noticing his agitated state.

"No, about 3 hours. That hardly affects my views on this bill or any of the others," assured Nick, waving at the pile of binders again, filled with the various bills up for vote.

Chuck poked his finger on the pile of briefing books. "You can't get to the bottom of the pile. No matter how hard you work or how many hours, that's the job."

Nick wandered around the office, coffee in hand. "The problem is, I believe each of these bills has worthwhile pieces. They're just masked by the hundreds of pages of stupid shit in each one. Why else am I here if not to call this out? How do I find the stupid stuff if I don't spend the time reading them?

Chuck shook his head. "You can't. It's physics. There is not enough time for you to read everything. That's why the bills are a thousand pages long. No one can read all of them. You need to pace yourself, pick your battles, understand how things are done, and get with the program," he replied in a serious tone. "If you don't, you'll burn out and hate the job even more. It's a job, a thankless one sometimes, but you're one of one hundred special people elected to represent this country."

"Appointed," corrected Nick.

"You know what I mean."

Nick circled back to the desk and sat down heavily in his office supply store desk chair. "Why did you stay on after Richards died and Governor Morris appointed me to fill out the term?"

"Well, first, you asked. Since you have no experience in politics, I figured you needed all the help you could get. Plus, the Governor asked me to stay to help you."

"You mean to make sure I didn't screw up?" smiled Nick as Chuck shrugged in acknowledgment. "You're right. I have no experience in politics. After nine months, I'm not sure I'm getting much better at it."

"You're doing OK. You can't solve all the problems of the world from the junior senator of Colorado seat."

"Well, I'm lucky to have you as my chief of staff. To keep me from stepping on too many landmines. That's the reason I intentionally stayed out of the infantry," explained Nick in an ironic tone.

"Good, then we should talk about today's schedule." Chuck pointed to the window facing east into the courtyard. "Before the sun comes up. When did you get up?"

"Couple hours ago. I see Mom is back."

"Listen to me, take my advice. You can let this job consume you. It happens easily. There's always another speech or more legislation. You have half the staff you should. Way less than other senators. Let me hire some people. Your taxpayers are already paying for it. While I appreciate your desire to be hands on, delegate some tasks. Hiring more staff is not wasteful. It's actually helping your constituents," explained Chuck in a pleading tone, trying yet again to convince Nick to staff up.

"I hear you, but I don't want a bunch of backstabbing policy wonks and climbers. Can you find some regular people?"

Chuck laughed, shaking his head. "This is why you hire these policy wonks. They are the experts. They give you data and then you decide. Besides, no regular person wants to work on a senate staff. Only backstabbing policy wonks and climbers."

"Gosh, that makes me feel so much better. Glad we made this decision," complained Nick as he walked to the office closet and got his gym bag. He also grabbed a dry-cleaning bag from the closet with a suit and set it on his desk while taking a last sip of coffee.

"So that's a yes? Good, one task down. It only took nine months. Now, this is like the 100th time I've said it. You need to socialize on the Hill. You always eat lunch in the office. Have lunch with other senators or meet some lobbyists. They're not all bad. You can do this without getting in trouble or compromising your principles. When was the last time you had dinner out of the office?" asked Chuck in a tone suggesting this was a regular topic of conversation.

"Can't afford it. Have you seen what they charge for a martini in this town? No thanks," declared Nick in mock horror.

"You can afford it, just like you could an apartment. You're just cheap."

"I like what money I have. I choose not to waste it on overpriced food or lodging."

"There's an election in a little over a year, in case you have forgotten. You need to network and build up some support here and in Colorado. You need to raise more money," commented Chuck. He walked to an upright filing cabinet in the kitchen area.

Chuck opened a drawer and pulled out a couple of three-inch thick bundles of invitations wrapped in twine. "You know what these are?" he asked, holding them up for him to see. Nick merely smiled in response.

"They're invitations to parties. To embassy dinners, lobbyist lunches, hell, even to the Marine Corps ball, and some of the best socialite parties in the city. They've all gone unanswered and unattended by the tall, handsome, and *single* Senator Nick Turner of Colorado." Nick held up his hands, making the sign of the cross.

"I'm going to schedule lunches and dinners for you," Chuck raised a hand to stop Nick's protest. "No whining. This is also part of being a senator and, frankly, I don't want to find another job in a year. Neither does the rest of your understaffed and overworked team. For some reason I can't fathom, they like you," noted Chuck in a disbelieving tone.

"Fine. Go for it. Operation: get Nick out of the office can begin today."

"You think I'm kidding?" retorted Chuck, annoyed. He picked up a stack of the invitations, flipped through it and pulled out one in an attractive shade of light green. "This is the hottest ticket in town. It is the Fall Gala at Dolly Wells-Monroe's. It's a who's who and one of the few where there are even attempts to have a bi-partisan guest list. Not just anyone gets an invitation. You've ignored three since you arrived. Eventually, she'll stop inviting you. Only a select number of senators, fewer congressmen, cabinet secretaries, ambassadors, and other notables around Washington ever get *one*."

Nick sipped his coffee, smiling at Chuck's annoyed look.

"I'm going to RSVP and tell her you are pleased to accept the invitation and apologize for the late reply," announced Chuck, shaking the invitation. "We're going to throw you into the deep end of the pool and see how well you swim."

"And if I don't show?"

"The only thing worse than getting dis-invited to a Dolly Wells-Monroe party would be to RSVP and not show. This you cannot do," warned Chuck. "I am dead serious on this point. No joking."

"Then maybe you shouldn't say yes. When is it?"

"Mid-October. The Friday after everyone returns from break."

"OK."

"When was the last time you went on a date? You know the ratio of women to men in this town is like 3 to 1," said Chuck, shifting gears.

"Don't push it. Now you *are* going too far, Mom. Please don't set me up with a reporter or your cousin or whomever you have in mind," groaned Nick. "What's in the binder?" he asked, changing the subject, looking at what Chuck was reviewing.

"Actually, table that. I'm going to hit the gym for a workout and shower before you sour my day any further. We can discuss the schedule when I get back." Nick waved his arm around the spartan room. "Don't redecorate while I'm gone."

Chapter 3

Nick glanced down at the time and distance on his treadmill. He was slipping, his times getting worse and worse since coming to Washington. He rarely had time to run outdoors. Making do with a run and shower every morning at the Senate gym. Located in the basement of the Russell Senate Building, it housed the other half of the Senators. Glancing around, he was still alone at this hour. The TV was off, the only sound, his footsteps echoing as they slapped the tread. He valued this time to clear his head and process the upcoming day's events.

As he entered his last mile, the door to the gym opened. Texas Senator Federico 'Freddie' Garcia walked in wearing baggy shorts and a faded University of Texas t-shirt. He made for the stationary bike next to Nick's treadmill, draping a towel over the handlebars and glancing at the readout on Nick's treadmill.

"Still training for the Olympics?" asked Freddie.

Nick glanced at Garcia. At the pace he was running, he could hardly talk, and the earbuds in his ears should also have signaled his unwillingness.

"I get it. Can't talk and run, just being friendly," nodded Freddie.

"Almost done," gasped Nick, as he sprinted to the end of his workout and slowed the machine to a more leisurely pace.

"6.2 miles under 33 minutes? I'd say that is pretty good," said Garcia, impressed.

"Used to think I could get it under 30. Since I've been in Washington, I've lost over 2 minutes off my time," remarked Nick, removing his ear buds and toweling the sweat.

"If that's all you lose coming to Washington, you should be thankful. Anyone else in the Senate would be dead trying to run at that pace. I'm a doctor, so I should know."

"You're a cardiac specialist, right?"

"Once upon a time. Been here too long now. I wouldn't trust me with a scalpel anymore," he said a bit breathlessly as his pace was picking up on the bike.

Nick moved to a nearby leg press machine, doing a few sets of leg presses with 500lbs. "Seems like everything falls apart when you get here."

"We haven't had much chance to get to know each other, you being the enemy and all. The job can have its perks as long as you keep things in perspective," said Freddie, pedaling.

Nick laughed. "Enemy, huh? Maybe that's part of the problem. I don't think of you as an enemy. I know most of my Party colleagues assume we are at war. Not with radical Islam, terrorism, drugs, the Russians, Chinese or Iranians, but with you, the Opposition."

Garcia slowed his pace and stopped, getting off the bike. He walked over to where Nick had moved to a bench and was doing a series of different presses using dumbbells in each hand.

"Nick, it wasn't always like this. My dad was a senator. I grew up around this. It used to be honorable and decent. You could vote against someone's bill and have drinks afterwards. Not anymore. We choreograph our sound bites, television appearances, and speeches on the floor. It's all designed to keep us apart. We no longer talk to each other seeking compromise. Instead, we talk right past each other for talking heads on TV."

"Nostalgia isn't going to help us now. I have to say I expected more from our elected officials," admitted Nick. He finished his last set of presses, setting down his dumbbells on the rack and moving to the pull up station.

"Were those fifty pounds each?" asked Freddie, once again shaking his head.

"Yes."

"Showing off for me?" smiled Garcia.

"Hardly. I did seventy-five in my younger days. Seeing how most of the clientele of this gym can barely lift twenty-pound dumbbells, with both hands, I make do. Besides rotting my brain, this job is also rotting my body. You should have seen the layer of dust on those the first time I picked them up," laughed Nick.

"Maybe if you got an apartment instead of sleeping in your office, you might not work 24/7."

"I get a lot done by never leaving," said Nick at the pull-up bar.

"They've started calling you 'The Monk'," revealed Garcia as Nick chuckled. "You never leave, you never have dinner, you never have drinks. You don't even come to the gym when others are here. Plus, you avoid the cocktail party circuit. People notice stuff like this. They wonder why you're such a recluse?"

Nick stopped his pull-ups. "Is that why you came in this early? What's the matter? You guys worried I'm setting a poor example?"

"A piece of advice. Take it or leave it. Find a purpose," counseled Garcia.

Nick reached up and grabbed the pullup bar and started again.

"I have a purpose. To lookout for my constituents for another fourteen months. I can't help it if I take it seriously," responded Nick, going up and down rapidly.

"Save the patriotic shit," blurted Freddie, irritated. "I mean a personal purpose. If you don't, you'll either burnout or sellout. Only a purpose can keep you sane. Will you please stop? That's over thirty, by my count."

Nick dropped from the pullup bar. "What do you care about my sanity? I don't think you guys have a chance of flipping this seat to the Opposition. Way too many Californians have transplanted to Colorado, and they're the most progressive ones. Taking over the school boards and city councils. I don't see it going back. Trust me, once you get to Colorado, you don't leave."

"For someone here less than a year, you're pretty jaded. Have we made that bad an impression?"

Nick wiped off more sweat and walked to Garcia, now just sitting on a bike.

"Not jaded, hardened. I came in all wide eyed like Jimmy Stewart. Some may have the people first. I would even give you credit for that. Most are just here to better themselves financially. You ask why I don't do the cocktail and dinner circuit, that's why. I went to one and by the time I was done, I felt like I needed to be deloused," explained Nick, with a disgusted look on his face.

"It was nothing but backslapping and promises to make or keep for future considerations. That and about fifteen propositions. Not all from women, I might add. I felt like Dorothy in Oz, way out of my element," finished Nick. He looked at the bench press and the clock on the wall.

"Well, at least you saw through it and didn't succumb. So many people come here with high ideals and soon they get corrupted by the pleasure palaces and all the DC social life offers," admitted Freddie.

Nick wiped his towel over his face and hair. "That and the honey pots from the Chinese, Russians, and Iranians. Some probably from our allies as well. Collectively, Congress hasn't done a good job of policing its own sins nor of admitting the damage they've done. What do you think the people would say if they knew?"

Garcia shrugged as Nick continued.

"Believe it or not, it doesn't play well in the heartland when Congress people who sleep with Chinese spies keep seats on Intel committees. I realize that's in *my* party." Nick held up a hand as Garcia made to respond.

"I won't even talk about the sex, drugs, and alcohol abuse that *sometimes* get reported. People hate Congress. We're setting a very poor example," ended Nick in an accusing tone.

"There is no defense for that. I have been vocal in my calls for us to discipline our own, but leadership in both parties isn't interested. They're afraid once they open that door, money, women, men, or foreign entities have compromised most of them. It isn't right, but there isn't much we can do about it either," Freddie finished this last with almost a sigh of resignation.

"That's the problem, acceptance. I'm not anti-social. Nor am I a prude. But I hoped for better from our leaders. I just choose not to swim in that cesspool."

"Nick, this town is about who you know. Networking is key to survival, and it is a key to getting any pet projects you want done. If you truly want to be of use to your constituents, you need to play the game. Just be better at it. You can be selective. You don't have to be deloused after all of them," laughed Garcia.

"Have you been talking to Chuck?"

"Robinson telling you the same? He's a good chief of staff."

"I feel like there's a conspiracy to get me plugged in. I'll talk to him about it. He's been saying the same thing and trying to get me to go to some of these. I want to spend my time here wisely and do my best to serve out Senator Richard's term." Nick was collecting his water bottle and bag.

"Thanks for not including me in the cesspool. Congress doesn't differ much from the palace intrigues of the old European monarchies. Richards wasn't one of the good ones. He was a Party 'yes' man. He made a lot of money and directed a lot of funds to Colorado. Especially the five air force bases around Colorado Springs."

"We really didn't need three Space Force bases there. Every time we tried to close one, he'd find an excuse. You're already doing more for our country by not fighting the latest set of base cuts and consolidations. They need to happen. The pain needs to be spread. Hell, my state is losing more than any. But I'm not fighting it, because we can't afford to keep them all open," disclosed Freddie. "At least not with the funding cuts."

"Thanks, I think. As for the comparison to the palace intrigues of Europe. If my history serves me right, they spent most of their time figuring out how to kill each other and dueling to settle disagreements," stated Nick.

"Oh yeah, forgot you taught history. Yes, let's hope we aren't at the 'let them eat cake moment' in our history. It was good to get to know you a bit. If you do ever want to have dinner or a drink with a fellow non cesspool swimming Senator, let me know."

"I enjoyed this," said Nick, shaking the Senator's hand. "Maybe I'll take you up on that dinner."

"Good, not sure I can endure witnessing another embarrassing workout of yours. So pathetic to watch," said Garcia, shaking his head as he turned back to his bike.

Nick smiled as he headed to the showers.

Chapter 4

"Greg, what's on tap today?" Nick asked the young man with sandy blond hair sitting at the table in the corner of his office.

"Boss, you have a committee markup discussion first. SB2520, SB5372 and SB1091 are on the table today. Jenny, the Colonel, and Izzy plus Margie, you, me, and Chuck are in that," he said, reading from his notes.

"Let's make sure we start with guns, then voting and finish with the middle east if we still have time." Nick paced around the room, sipping his ever-present dark roast coffee.

Chuck, who was typing away on a tablet on the couch, lifted his head. "The debate on the voting rights protection bill is at the end of the week. You're in committee on the middle east tomorrow. Maybe flip them?"

"Nope, I want to give Margie a chance to make her case on the gun and voting bills. I don't want to shortchange her. Besides, if it takes too long, I might get some of the family hooch the Colonel keeps in his office tonight," revealed Nick, smiling.

Chuck wrinkled up his face. "Hooch? You mean lighter fluid? I'm not sure how you two can drink that stuff."

"Okay Mr. Hazelnut," retorted Nick. "The Colonel's family has been making fine Kentucky bourbon for over 140 years. It doesn't get much better. What else Greg?"

Greg resumed his discussion of Nick's schedule for the day. He had meetings with constituents in town for a convention. Another with the Judiciary committee. Finally, a working group session with other senators on upcoming Senate re-election activities, plus his trip to the Annex.

Nick took another long sip. "Four hours in the Annex again today?" Greg was about to reply when Chuck instead jumped in to rescue him.

"Don't pick on Greg. You know how important fundraising is in this town. Everyone has to do their part. Besides, some folks on the list today may be key to *your* election efforts."

"Senator?" Nick looked over at Greg, who was studiously looking at his notes, avoiding any further mention of the odious duty of raising money for the party. "You got a message from the Majority Leader, requesting some of your time," announced Greg tentatively.

Nick glanced at Chuck. "Did he give a hint why?"

"No sir," said Greg. "But he suggested you come by over lunch."

"I guess they've summoned me. Chuck, what've I done wrong lately?"

He looked worried. "I suspect you're about to get strong armed on these bills. Gun control, DC statehood, filibuster, infrastructure are all key pieces of legislation, and all will help the VP in her run for President next year. Most likely some stick, with maybe a little carrot. The Majority Leader's help in your election would be significant, too."

"Into the lion's den went the poor lamb."

"Just try not to piss him off, OK?" requested Chuck.

Greg was standing, having gathered his materials, and walked to Nick. "Time to move to the conference room, Senator. I'll confirm with the Leader's office you'll be there at 12:30?" Nick nodded to Greg as they walked out of the office.

Chapter 5

"Morning team," said Nick as he entered the room and took a seat in the middle of the long conference room table. He opened his notebook with its ever-present purple cover sleeve. Smiling, he looked up and down the table at his immediate staff and advisors, who all said hello back.

Greg and Chuck grabbed empty seats on either side of Nick. There were ten chairs in total. They filled most of them this morning. The room was bare except for a map of Colorado on one wall and a very large TV display in the room's corner for presentations, watching news, and press conferences.

"Senator, can we please hang some art or something? Maybe some drawings from school kids? Even a deer's head would be better than this. It's as depressing as a hospital room." An attractive early fortyish woman wearing a dark blue dress and a multicolored scarf highlighting her dark hair made the statement.

"Nice scarf Jenny. I like these walls," said Nick, waving while gesturing at the beige walls.

"Thanks, and of course you would like beige. I thought you claimed to be an art connoisseur," Jenny said with a wide smile, her pale complexion now reddening slightly at Nick's compliment.

"I am, but I won't waste good art in *here*," laughed Nick, looking around the room. "Looks like everyone is here. Let's get started."

Greg quickly outlined the agenda and then kicked off the discussion.

"First SB2520, the Make Our Neighborhoods Safe with Sensible Gun Protection bill. This is coming up for debate in the Senate first thing after the break.

Nick glanced at his senior staff gathered around the conference table. "You know my feelings on guns. I own them and I like them. You also know that in our state, we have a lot of gun owners who vote for the Party." Nick held up his hand as a young, attractive black woman seated across the table leaned forward, ready to respond.

"Hang on Margie, just a sec. I also realize we in Colorado have also had our fair share of mass shootings. Columbine, the movie theater, Boulder, and the nightclub," Nick leaned forward and put his hands on the table. "I believe there are things we can do to make gun ownership safer. My concern is I don't think any of the provisions in this bill accomplish any of the stated goals. We need to focus on solving the problem and not turn this into an ideological debate."

Chuck broke in before Margie could say anything. "Nick, that may be true, but it is an ideological debate."

"That doesn't mean we can't pass legislation with a chance of accomplishing the stated goal. OK Margie," said Nick, signaling it was her turn.

She leaned forward eagerly. Marjorie Wilson looked to still be in her late twenties, eager and full of energy.

"Senator, you know I disagree regarding the content of the bill. You knew where I stood on this when you hired me, so I'm not apologizing. I think you are missing the point."

Chuck and Jenny both sat up a little higher in their chairs. Others around the table fiddled with papers, looking down at their notes as they sensed another round of Ali-Frazier about to begin.

Nick, working to keep a grin off his face, leaned back a little in his chair and motioned for Margie to proceed.

"First, gun violence is at an all-time high. Suicides have increased, and high numbers of these are young men and women who have access to guns and use them to kill themselves. Second, no one needs an assault rifle for personal protection, nor do they need it for deer hunting. It really has no purpose other than to satisfy a need to pretend one is in the military." Nick watched Margie, her voice rising as she continued to make her points.

"Sensible things like gun locks on all guns in the home are common sense proposals to reduce accidental use by children. Reducing the size of magazines could have saved lives in several mass shootings. The criminals used magazines of 50 and 100 rounds to kill more people faster. Finally, federally mandated Red Flag laws enable law enforcement to act on reasonable requests by families and authorities to remove guns. Identifying and taking them from people who are showing mental instability or behavior that could lead to suicide or another mass murder," continued Margie quickly, surveying the others in the room.

"None of this is a wholesale gun grab, nor is it impinging on anyone's second amendment rights. We aren't stopping people from buying guns. We're just making them realize they need to be more responsible. I really don't see how any of this is going too far. We aren't asking for disarmament like New Zealand or Australia. Just common sense. I urge you to reconsider your position, especially with the election coming up. There are many in Colorado who are in favor of these laws," finished Margie righteously.

"Margie, your positions are well articulated. I applaud your passion and your commitment. Unfortunately, each of these positions directly violates the Constitution. None would withstand the Supreme Court. Hold on," said Nick. holding up a hand before Margie could speak.

"Of course, these items 'feel good' and give everyone a warm fuzzy that we are doing *something*. We would seem to be doing our part to protect fellow citizens. The reality is twofold. First, the Constitution is still the law of the land and none of these are permitted. Restricting people's rights to own guns. Then restricting their storage and use in their own home? That violates their Second and Fourth Amendment rights," said Nick calmly in rebuttal.

"Maybe the Constitution is wrong," blurted Margie.

"Margie," admonished Chuck.

"It's ok Chuck. I want everyone to feel they can express their thoughts and opinions. Criticism and pushback are fine. Margie, now it's my turn to disagree with you regarding the Constitution. Let me continue and defend my position."

Margie sat back, her body language clearly signaling an unwillingness to change.

"None, and I repeat, none of these measures are going to stop mass shootings. I'll grant you that mandating locking up guns to keep them away from children is not a bad idea. To do this federally is pure rhetoric and would never stand up in the Supreme Court."

"If it prevents even one child from getting their parents' gun and accidentally shooting themselves. Or a brother. Don't we have an obligation to do this?" pleaded Margie, on the verge of tears.

"Margie, this is where we go from good intentions to reality. Tell me. How would we enforce it? Random inspections by whom? Cops, Neighbors, Friends? Create a network of tattle tails? Besides, who's going to be snooping around someone's house enough to find out if they have their guns locked up or not? What's the worst that happens? You punish them *after* their child kills their sibling? Isn't losing the child enough punishment?" asked Nick rhetorically.

"But we have to make sure they know they're risking their children's lives by not locking up the guns. We have to keep kids from getting the guns," said Margie, emotionally.

"I agree, however, this bill has no way of enforcing this. Short of implementing surveillance in everyone's home. I hope all in this room are against that?" asked Nick, looking around the room to a chorus of nodding heads. Even Margie nodded as Jenny handed her a tissue.

"Let's look at Red Flag laws. As you know, we already have this in Colorado. Can anyone tell me what happened?"

An older man, with gray hair in a military cut, answered from the corner of the table. "Sure. Good intentions, leading to poor execution and lots of misguided application of the specifics. A few confrontations between sheriffs and citizens leading to shootouts. Frankly, it has made people less trusting of our good intentions."

"Thanks Bob. Again, the intent was good, but the execution led to unintended consequence, including legal challenges. Only the city of

Denver is still trying to enforce it. The rural sheriffs won't touch it," finished Nick.

"There are issues I agree, but how else do we discover the mentally unstable who have guns?" she interrupted.

"The Red Flag laws didn't achieve their goals in Colorado. Now we're looking to implement them as a federal law? Is that your solution?" asked Nick, shaking his head. "This is just another way for the administration to enable the seizure of guns through alternate methods. Imagine a federal database of gun owners. This is a hacker's delight. Somebody could get a hold of the state registry of gun owners and start anonymously telling law enforcement that Bart Smith beats his wife and owns a gun. That he was down at the bar threatening to kill her, or the neighbor, or anyone. We are obligating the police to pursue the tip." No one spoke as Nick continued.

"Let's assume Bart complies with their request, gives up his guns, and doesn't confront them. To clear his name, Bart must get the lawyer. He must make the case why he is *not* a risk. He has to pay to clear his name and maybe after a few years, we might even give him his guns back. This is the antithesis of innocent until *proven* guilty. Our Party is embarrassing themselves with this. This doesn't stop crime or help mental illness. They just want the guns. They know there isn't enough support to repeal the 2nd Amendment in the manner the founders provided. The solution is instead to focus on removing guns, from the 99.9% of gun owners, who are both responsible and law-abiding. The fact this made it out of committee and into a bill we're considering, *in congress,* is the true crime. Anybody have a good and lawful argument about why I shouldn't feel this way?"

No one made any effort to speak up, failing to find issue with Nick's logical explanation.

"Chuck, on good relations with your ex-wives? Think any of them might not like to turn the screws on you?" asked Nick, making a point. "How this is written, you don't even have to have a gun for this to work. Merely implying you have one, or intent, suffices to get the cops to bust down your door. Think about this people. This *is* the police state and only an authoritarian government would consider this. We are getting ready to weaponize it."

"You make it sound like everyone is going to have their guns seized. You're painting with a broad brush and ignoring any potential good," continued Margie, refusing to give up.

"Margie, even if it happens once, is this the society you want to live in? Is this what you want your legislators to be focused on? Coming up with ways to break the sanctity of your home, based on someone else's word? What's next? What about expressing opinions? Just like we are in this room. We already have a disinformation board to highlight and cancel folks for publishing what they decide is 'dis or mis - information'. Where does it stop? Guns, speech, thoughts, intent, any opposition? This is the slipperiest of slopes."

Nick looked at his staff as the explanations sank into those around the table. They hadn't contemplated this view previously, and it was apparent on some of their faces.

Margie seemed a bit deflated. "I admit to not thinking through how folks could use the Red Flag laws maliciously. I'd like to trust human nature rather than assume everyone would use it to attack an ex or a rival."

"Margie, you're young and want to believe in the good of people. You feel with your heart this is the right thing to do. In a perfect world, it would. In that world, no one would use a gun for ill purposes or leave it unlocked and loaded where a child could find it. In that world, we would have all the help needed for anyone suffering from mental illness or contemplating suicide."

Margie stared at Nick as he continued to explain.

"Unfortunately, too much of our legislation is aimed at creating this perfect world, which just isn't possible. Instead, we provide ways to use laws to punish those who choose to live differently than us. Not because they're wrong, but because we don't agree with the choices they make. We want to restrict their ability to live the way they want. Instead, we use the law to force them to live the way we want. That's not freedom. It is kings and subjects, masters and slaves, dictators and oppressed serfs," finished Nick.

"But why does anyone need an assault rifle? Surely you don't disagree. No one needs an assault rifle to hunt," said Margie, refusing to give up.

"Why is the Party against assault rifles?" asked Nick, looking around the table.

"They look like the automatic weapons our soldiers carry. And many mass shootings reported in the news involve AR-15 type weapons with large capacity magazines," answered Bob.

"Good answer. I would also add, thanks to Hollywood and video games popularizing the mass destruction from automatic weapons, we equate these with the AR-15 and others. What the Colonel could also tell you, is it's illegal to own an automatic weapon. You can't hold the trigger down and fire off a complete magazine like in the military or Hollywood movies. The only ones with fully automatic weapons are law enforcement, the military, and, of course, criminals. Nothing we pass is going to have one iota of difference in the criminals' getting weapons, automatic or otherwise." Nick looked around the room at his staff.

"What about the mentally ill? Shouldn't we be keeping them from buying an assault rifle?" asked Margie in an obstinate tone.

"You're going down the slope I just referred to," retorted Nick. "Who gets to define mentally ill? Many of my colleagues would classify *anyone* who wants to purchase a gun as mentally ill. You stop an assault rifle purchase. Instead, they buy two pistols. My point is nothing will stop people who want to get a gun. It doesn't stop criminals."

"Sure there is. Stop selling them. Make it illegal to hand them down between generations. The estate has to turn them over when the owner dies," said Margie in a righteous tone as others in the room sat quietly as the debate escalated.

Nick paused for a second, shaking his head at Margie's proposed solution. He held up his hand as Chuck made to end the conversation.

"An interesting proposal Margie. Let's consider for a second why we even have a second amendment. Trust me, it was not so a hunter could buy an assault weapon. As you know, I once taught history. One of my favorite subjects was early American history. Did you know in the Revolutionary War, most of the soldiers brought their own rifles to the army? This was because the rifle was the difference between life and death for many of these pioneers. Think about it," said Nick, as several of the people around the table suppressed smiles. He was entering professor mode again.

"Many of them lived on farms far removed from their neighbors. They used the rifle for protection, and they used it to provide game for their meals. The rifle has long been a symbol of independence. When the Constitution was being written, there were arguments on the need for a right to protect oneself, not just from enemies, but also from the government. From *us*. The second amendment was one of the first ten amendments. Why? Because the states wouldn't ratify the constitution without guarantees they could legally rise and protect themselves from another encroaching government. Just like the one they had just spent eight years overthrowing. They wanted to make sure it would be the same if the fledgling United States Government, then or now, tried to do the same."

Nick paused. Everyone present was paying attention to his lecture, so he continued.

"I believe the real reason behind the AR-15 restrictions has nothing to do with safety. At least not the safety of the people. It is rather the safety of the government as they try to take away more freedom. Just look at the bills we are discussing today. Sweeping gun control. Voting rights that don't guarantee one person, one vote. Normalizing relations with middle eastern countries whose *governments* regularly cry death to America and actively fund terrorists to carry it out. The reason we are trying to restrict access to these weapons is in case the people decide our government has gone too far. As you know, I'm a veteran, and I'm not a progressive, but I'm also not an idiot. The problem isn't the second amendment, the problem is what a very few people choose to do with the rights it provides to us."

Silence followed the end of Nick's speech, then Margie laughed.

"OK Professor Turner, wonderful speech, but you didn't answer the question. Why does someone *need* an AR-15? To save themselves from the government is conspiracy fodder."

Chuck prepared to answer, but again, Nick shook his head. "Margie, I think you missed my point. I answered the question. 1) because, until the second amendment is repealed, most likely by *our* Party, it's a citizen's guaranteed right. 2) because they want to. 3) rifles are used in less than 4% of all shootings, including years where we have mass shootings. Pistols are the primary method of gun violence. So, the argument, your argument, is we should ban these weapons because they are enabling mass shootings?" said Nick, standing.

"Statistically, guns account for very few non-suicide deaths. Yet we are fixating on restricting guns of the law-abiding. I agree any death by gun is one too many and 30,000-gun deaths by suicide are horrible. The true issue we need to address is the reason for the suicide, not the fact it was done with a gun. Two more quick points. Most of the gun deaths are in cities where the Party is in charge. Some of these we've been in charge for over fifty years. These cities have much more restrictive gun laws on the books. So why do murders and gun deaths in these cities keep rising?"

"Criminals don't obey the law," offered Jenny.

"Bingo," said Nick. "SB2520 is another useless bill that does nothing to help curb gun violence, accidental or otherwise. What it does is cause those gun owning citizens to hold on to their AR-15 that much tighter. Assuming their government is doing exactly what the founders warned against, and prepared for, by insisting on the 2nd Amendment. By restricting freedoms to the point of driving them to revolution once again. I'm not trying to be melodramatic or conspiratorial, Margie."

Nick paused after the statement.

"This and these other bills, when looked at through the eyes of Opposition and Independents, hell, even moderate gun owning Party members like me, can only lead them to think one way."

"What way is that? The safe way?" she said, still defiant.

"We're out to make them live the way we want, and if they don't, we'll force them. This has to stop, or we'll go too far one day. I fear our actions will have the most disastrous unintended consequences. Margie, in answer to your prior solution. It's not the law-abiding, gun owning citizen who is the problem. Yet these bill proposals ultimately target only one group. Those same citizens who are not causing the problems."

"Nick, you're making a pragmatic argument, but soccer moms couldn't care less about facts. They believe guns are the problem and they universally favor restrictions on having them. While your stance may be correct, from a Constitutional point of view. It sucks as a Party Senator seeking re-election," said Jenny, shaking her head with a wry smile. "Facts vs Emotions. Emotions win every time."

"Senator, I'd like to add one last point from a mental health point of view," this from another of Nick's staff, her fiery red hair pulled back in a ponytail over one shoulder.

"Go ahead, Izzy."

"As your medical issues advisor, I can confirm for you that study after study is proving many of these mass shootings and suicides show direct correlation to three things. So-called first-person shooter video games. Where primarily young men, but also increasingly young women, become immersed in the idea they are in 'battle'. Virtual Reality with their full immersion experience is making this worse."

"The second is the increasing ease of access to high potency marijuana. The combination of these two altered states. Chemically from the marijuana and the VR immersion, create alternate realities, where the young people have more control over their environment.

This has increasingly led to the inability to cope with the challenges of the real world. It is causing many to become depressed. Leading to massive opioid addiction, overdoses, and increasingly high incidents of teen and early twenties suicides."

"The third thing is the pervasiveness of social media. Online bullying, shaming, and just outright peer pressure in so many social aspects. From gender and orientation, popularity, appearance, and the fact everyone online appears to lead perfect lives compared to the reality of the viewer. This is causing our most vulnerable, the children, to process and cope with situations even fully formed and mature adults would have trouble handling," finished Dr. Isabella Culligan.

Nick sat, shaking his head. "Thanks Izzy. This just underscores my point. The gun isn't the only issue. It sucks to be a kid in today's society. And we're not helping."

Margie leaned forward, sighing. "I have to admit, you're making good points. I still think we have to do more to prevent gun violence and suicide, but maybe this bill isn't the right way to accomplish it."

"Margie, on that we can agree 100%. We need to do more to prevent suicide, especially in today's economic and political climate. I hate to use the cliche of people kill people not guns, but it's the same with suicide. *If* they want to commit suicide, lack of access to a gun won't prevent it."

"Sadly, too true," said Chuck. "We've seen it happen."

"I may not win over the soccer moms, but I may not have to convince them. Do you know what else our Party policies have done?" asked Nick. "Since the current administration has been in power, the number of guns sold has risen at 20-40% *each* year. A lot of these are first time gun buyers. Many of them are Party voters formerly against gun ownership, but they're now pro-life; their own."

His staff laughed at the unconventional use of the pro-life slogan.

"They've bought the thing they fear and hate most of all. The gun. Finally, the other statistic driven by our policies is most of these first-time gun purchasers are women. These women are afraid the police won't be there to protect them and their family. We've created a society where everyone now lives in fear. Welcome back to the Wild

West. Not something we should be proud of for sure," finished Nick, turning to Bob.

"You have issues with it, Bob?" asked Nick, looking at his military affairs advisor. Colonel Robert Sutter was an ex-Marine Lieutenant Colonel and had spent some time in the CIA before joining the private sector.

"Actually no. Your arguments are cogent, fact based, and accurate. The other fact is gun ownership has risen to over 50% of American households, because of two things. Our previous unsuccessful attempts at gun control and our *successful* efforts to defund police. Both lead to an environment of fear. The bigger question is why is it left for you, a junior senator from Colorado, with little experience in politics, to make this argument?"

"Because other senator's staff are afraid to speak the truth," said Jenny, Nick's legal affairs advisor who had spoken up earlier. Izzy also nodded vigorously, sitting next to her.

"Because this is what they *want* to pass, whether constitutional and whether it would actually work," added Izzy.

"I get it. They let their emotions, wishes, and visions of unrealistic society become their reality. They want to appease their voters and grab the guns. Lesson learned," said Margie with a smile.

"Correct. I can simplify it even more. Actions have consequences. All they think about are actions and what they want the results to be. They don't consider the actual consequences of their actions. This is a blind spot of American politics. We're so arrogant we believe any action, however noble or farcical, will have the effect we wish it to. Instead, the unintended consequences most times are far worse than the action they want to solve."

"Our well-intentioned actions on so many topics have led to consequences we're still trying to fix. I refuse to be involved in another with this bill," finished Nick, turning to Greg. "I think we blew all the time on this discussion, didn't we?"

"Fraid so boss."

"We'll shoehorn in a discussion on the voting rights bill somewhere tomorrow. Bob, I'll track you down to discuss the Middle East bill later this afternoon. Thanks everyone."

Chapter 6

After Nick's staff filed out, Chuck remained seated, looking at him.

"What?"

"Do you like being a senator?" he asked.

"Honestly? No."

"You're pretty good at it."

"Really? Personally, I think I suck. What makes you think that?"

"I've seen freshmen congresspeople come in full of ideas, gung-ho, ready to change the world. I watched as they faced the reality of Congress. They realized they are one vote, and worse, they were on the bottom of the pecking order. Which means nobody cares about what they want or say. When they figure this out, they do one of two things. If they have integrity, skill, or a conscience, they leave to do something better with their life. Something where they can make a difference. If they don't have any talent, they stay and play the game. That is how you survive and thrive in Washington," said Chuck, setting down his pen down.

Nick laughed. "Somehow, I don't think this is how the founders envisioned congressional service."

"These are the career politicians whose main purpose is getting reelected and staying as long as they can. It is extremely hard to lose a congressional seat. About the only way is to get sideways with your party, is getting caught on camera doing something stupid, or thinking you can change the way the system works. Senator Richards was not good at anything, so he became a superb politician. He made the Party leadership aware they could always count on him. I think you can sense a pattern here," hinted Chuck.

"What does that make you, since you've stayed on with me?"

"It makes me an accomplice. I enjoy the sword fights on the bills. People at my level have the exciting jobs. The Congresspeople are rarely involved in any of this. Between networking, fundraising, and being on the floor for votes. There really is no time for anything else except the occasional glad handing of constituents visiting DC."

"It's nice to be different," said Nick sarcastically.

"I can tell you one thing. There isn't another senator who could've done what you just did with Margie and everyone else in your office. That makes an impression. Look how you've turned her around these last nine months. Believe me, she is a hard core partisan. But every meeting you break more of her walls down. She's slowly thinking for herself, instead of just believing the Party rhetoric," assured Chuck, a wry smile on his face.

Nick shrugged. "I just tell it like I see it."

"I think you're selling yourself short. You don't bludgeon people to accept your view. You convince them, with their own words. Showing them they haven't considered the complete picture. Or all the consequences. The kicker is you actually accomplish what the media, candidates, and pundits can't. You change people's minds and make them feel good about it," explained Chuck.

"It's not my goal to change their mind. Just to get them to consider the common sense they so often overlook," confided Nick.

"That's such an alien view here." Chuck shook his head as Nick leaned against the wall and held his hands open, smiling.

"Like we said this morning, you are young and single, and I guess a certain type of female might find you attractive. After four or maybe five cocktails," mused Chuck, as Nick flipped him off.

"You'd be the belle of the ball at these parties. You could have your pick of the lot, something most of these old geezers would kill for. Yet you don't take any advantage of this. That's why I say you are good at this. If you can do what you do and avoid all this frivolous nonsense, then you're keeping them off guard. You're not predictable. This is glorious in an Opposition Senator and an absolute career ender in the Party," said Chuck seriously.

"Then I must be doing something right."

"Nick, the Party hates rebels. They want beholden drones, predictability, and most of all obedience. If you don't, they'll make your life miserable or they primary you out of your seat. You're a man with integrity, ideals, and unfortunately, without a party to help you achieve anything you feel passionate about."

"Is this supposed to be a pep talk? So how do you feel about it, since you're used to working for an ass kissing climber," retorted Nick, more serious than not.

"It reminds me of my first job in a senator's office. Nice and honest. He tried, but the job just consumed him. I learned a lot about what happens to you when you try to buck the system. How it fights back. You have to understand the people here didn't get here and certainly don't get to stay, by being boy or girl scouts. You're talking about 535 of the most important jobs in the country," emphasized Chuck, gesturing with his hands to make his points.

"535 people who're supposed to be serving their constituents," added Nick.

Chuck stood up. "This isn't a democracy. Nor is there a board of directors to appeal too. It's an authoritarian dictatorship. The leaders of each house wield their power like emperors. A handful of lifetime senators and representatives control this place. Their sole claim to leadership has been their ability to survive all the backstabbing and to be the best gladiator. They don't like change and the body politic spits out any who try. That happened to my first senator. He opted to retire after a single term."

"Yet you stayed and found another senator," said Nick.

"Like I said, I liked the power I had in the office, even as a newbie. I caught on early. It was the staffers who wrote the legislature with the lobbyists. It was the staffers who turned the phrases for sound bites or tweaked the bills for compromise. I had no desire to be the talent, but I found my calling as the behind-the-scenes guy. I took pleasure in knowing it was really my bill, my amendment, or my speech that made my senator look good. Better than using my Harvard MBA working at Goldman Sachs ninety hours a week." Nick listened intently as Chuck justified his purpose.

"My other alternative was to go work in Daddy's firm. That would have been suicide inducing," said Chuck with clear disdain. "So, politics is where I ended up. Plus, after two years grinding at Goldman, the Senate hours seemed like a working vacation. That gave me another advantage. While everyone else was whining at the workload, I wondered what to do with a free Sunday. It's all about perspective."

"Well, that's a strange statement. My friend, I think you're the one who needs some help," confided Nick.

"Now you sound like my father when I told him I wasn't leaving Washington to work in his firm."

"As long as they don't sell the brownstone out from under you," pointed out Nick.

Chuck laughed. "There is that minor detail. You need to head on over. Fontana appreciates punctuality. It's the union boss in him."

"Great. Sounds like my kind of guy," groaned Nick. "I've only really talked to him once. All the other times were the group meetings. What can I expect?"

"Oh, wait, it only gets better. But I won't spoil it for you," said Chuck with a grin.

Chapter 7

Nick wandered through the Capitol, nodding to a few congressmen who recognized him on his way to the Senate wing. He approached a pair of monumental doors. The ornate wooden plaque announcing the office of the Majority Leader of the Senate, Salvatore A. Fontana, New Jersey. He pulled open the heavy doors and entered the vestibule of the office. A gray-haired, thin woman with a friendly smile greeted him.

"Senator Turner, the Majority Leader will see you in a minute. He is just finishing up a meeting. May I get you any coffee or tea?"

"No, thank you, Miss…?"

"Helen Robles. Pleased to meet you, Senator," Helen replied, shaking Nick's outstretched hand.

"Please call me Nick."

Helen chuckled. "Sorry Senator, that's not how it works around here. Have a look around while you wait." Nick surveyed the vestibule with its ornate high ceilings, carved stone, and marble walls. His cold, sterile office in the Hart Building couldn't have been more different from this display of status and power. It was impressive.

He wandered over to a painting on one wall. It showed a waterfall over rolling hills at sunset. Looking closer, he saw a plaque saying it was '*Passaic Falls, Autumn*', by Thomas W. Whitley, on loan from the New Jersey Historical Society.

Leaning in to examine the painting closer, the door to the inner office opened. Out walked the rotund figure of the Majority Leader. With him was the Vice President of the United States, Alexis 'Lexi' Smythe-Thomas.

Nick stood up straighter as they approached. Lexi, in her perfectly tailored suit, skirt, and blouse, all in shades of creamy beige. She looked and walked like the former model she'd been in her youth. In her signature Louboutin high heels, she was almost a head taller than the Majority Leader. She still had to look up at Nick as she approached with an outstretched hand.

"Senator Turner, it's a pleasure to see you again. I just can't thank you enough for your bravery. I'm glad you agreed to fill out the rest of Senator Richard's term," declared Lexi, flashing her dazzling smile while grasping his hand in a firm grip.

"Madame Vice President," answered Nick, staring into icy blue eyes, noting the flawless white skin of Lexi's face. Right at sixty, she looked forty and was holding on to the last vestiges of her beauty. No frozen smiles, fake looking lips, or cheeks. Lexi was clearly doing something other than cosmetic surgery to keep her skin toned and tight. There was no doubt she had made many a man weak in the knees with her stare and smile. Nick smiled back.

"Oh, that makes me sound so old. Please call me Lexi."

Nick looked at a smiling Helen beyond the VP before answering.

"With all respect, I don't think that's how it works, Madame Vice President," replied Nick.

Lexi's smile widened as the Majority Leader let out a deep laugh.

"Son, you have a future here for sure. Come on in so we can chat. Lexi, thanks for stopping by," the Majority Leader waved his arm around. "Do you miss the place?"

"You know I do; my office is half this size and no offence, I think my decor was more appealing." Lexi waved as she walked to the door. Her secret service agents opened it as she exited, followed by several aides, who immediately began speaking to her of upcoming engagements.

"Sal Fontana, I don't think we've really met casually yet," said Sal, offering a meaty hand. Nick shook his hand and held it for a second as Sal applied extra pressure. Nick matched it until Sal released his hand.

"Nice. I see you're no fucking pansy. Good. Too many of those in our party already." This last bit delivered over his shoulder as he led the way into his office.

"Come on in, have a seat, take one by the fire," Sal said as he moved behind his ornate wooden desk, sitting down heavily in his well-worn desk chair. Nick sat in an upholstered leather chair on one side of a fireplace, with a roaring fire. Sal pointed to the fireplace framed in green marble.

"One perk of being leader, one of the few working fireplaces in the Capitol. Comes in handy because the heat in this place sucks."

Nick's eyes took in the trappings of the office of the Majority Leader of the Senate. The office decorated with what passed for artifacts given the brief history of the US, combined with modern furniture and electronics. He noticed a portrait of Woodrow Wilson above the fireplace and a towering one of George Washington on another wall. Sal noticed him staring,

"That's *the* Gilbert Stuart portrait of Washington that Dolley Madison took with her when she fled the White House from those British bastards. They burned the White House and the Capitol, you know. Fucking limeys," he said. "It's on loan from the National Gallery. Should see the favors I had to promise for that one. She didn't even save the original, it was a copy. Go figure."

There was an uncomfortable silence while Sal waited for Nick to speak. When he didn't, Sal leaned back in his chair.

"Well, Hero, I bet you're wondering why I asked you to come by today," said Sal, changing his tone from casual to more commanding.

"The thought crossed my mind."

"You know, I served in the infantry in Vietnam. Got drafted along with my twin brother," said Sal in a disgusted tone.

"We were there in 72-73. The last year of the draftees. He didn't make it. I came back and worked on the docks, wondering why I was fucking here, and he wasn't. Worked my way up through the union and eventually into the state assembly and then into fucking Congress." Nick listened without comment.

"You know, I've been here a long fucking time. I'm telling you this because I want you to know I don't mess around. Fuck with me and I can make your life miserable. Play ball and you're a made man. Hell Hero, with your background, you can practically write your own fucking ticket. At least you were smart and avoided the Army, right?" asked Sal, laughing.

"Navy and then Air National Guard, but somebody like you already knows all that," said Nick calmly. The Majority Leader's bravado and dockyard language didn't intimidate him in the slightest.

"You bet I do. Naval Intelligence, and then you up and resigned your commission. Joined the Guard to fly after that. Flew A-10's in Afghanistan, Iraq, and Syria. Who the fuck does that? You do, of course. Then the New York thing. You are a full-blooded fucking hero, just the person we need helping us," he finished as he got up, moving in front of his desk, leaning against a corner.

"How do you like Washington?"

"Well, can't say I have seen much of it, been busy working," he replied.

"And Congress?"

"It's been interesting."

"Interesting? As sausage factories go, this fucking takes the cake, and I was in Jersey politics."

"Just trying to keep my head down and do what I think is best for my constituents."

"Jesus, don't pull that boy scout shit with me. I think you've discovered by now this isn't about constituents. It's so much bigger than Colorado or New Jersey. The decisions we make have consequences everywhere. In China and India and those wimp ass Europeeeans," he said, drawing out the last syllable for further emphasis on what he thought of the EU.

Nick continued to listen, sensing Sal wasn't finished.

"The Opposition is holding us back. We spend so much time and money countering their bullshit. We've been on the cusp twice and just as we're ready to implement the changes to take the government back for the working man, something always happens. Shitty politicians, goddamn diseases, Rush fucking Limbaugh, you name it. But not this time. The prize is there. All we have to do is grab it by the balls and yank. Believe me, if anyone knows how to do that, it's Alexis Smythe-Thomas." Sal finished with a hearty laugh.

"Why are you telling me this? No offence, but I'm the junior senator from a state the Opposition hasn't won in decades. It's safe for the Party. I'm not sure what I can do to help you."

"You're a fucking Hero. Few of you are around anymore. Especially in our Party. You can do a lot. Have you given any thought about running for a full-term next November?"

"I haven't decided. As you know, I'm not a professional politician, so I'm learning on the job, so to speak," added Nick.

"Exactly. That's what makes you so appealing to us. You're grass roots, a hero, and have name recognition. Having you supporting our legislation and stumping for Lexi on the campaign trail can lead to great things."

"She still has to win the primary," commented Nick, noticing Sal dropped the excessive f-bombs when he was trying to win him over.

Sal laughed. "You're kidding, right? No one running against her in the primaries is serious. They just want jobs in her administration. If we keep the Opposition at each other's throat, they keep killing each other. She's got great polling and a magnificent smile. Hell, she's still quite a looker for her age, or any age for that matter. She is everything our last female presidential candidate was not. Attractive, articulate, smart, and probably even more ruthless. She is someone you definitely don't want to fuck with. Trust me."

"Point taken. Sounds like you guys have it all under control."

"We do, more and more every fucking day. But we need to keep recruiting new talent. You'd be a welcome addition. Joining the team has lots of perks. We can make sure you get elected to a full term with our support. Play your cards right, and there's probably a role in Lexi's administration. After that, you can write your own ticket."

"I appreciate the opportunity. Like I told you, I really am just trying to serve Colorado."

"I'll give you credit. You have the sincerity act down pat, very believable. That is a great asset to have, to survive here."

"Because it's not an act."

"How much money do you have?" asked Sal, switching gears.

"Excuse me?"

"Not personally, campaign contributions. Do you know how much we spent last cycle on average to win a seat?'"

"I'd have to ask my chief of staff. Fundraising hasn't been my focus for myself. I make the calls for the party as required," this got a grunt out of Sal. "But haven't focused on raising anything myself."

"You have $2.3 million cash on hand in your campaign coffers. Last cycle, we spent $30 million on non-contested races. $100 million on key contested races. You have a long way to go if you want to stay, Hero. You need to get started. If you aren't running, then we need to stand up another candidate and start raising money for them. We need this seat, and you need to decide in the next couple of weeks. We're happy to help, but we need to know we can count on you when the time comes."

Nick got up, as it was clear the interview was over.

"Thanks for the time and insight, Majority Leader. I'll get back to you with answers."

"Hero, you seem like a smart fucking guy and resourceful. Few people get an opportunity like this, especially after only nine months in the office. Believe me, there are many who resent you and they fucking hate your popularity. Watch your back."

"Wouldn't be the first time I've been hunted, Senator," admitted Nick, turning to go.

Chapter 8

Sal sat as Nick left his office. He reached in his desk and pulled out a fat Cuban cigar, lighting it up and taking a puff. Smoking was prohibited in the Capitol. Being Leader had its perks. Sal leaned back in his seat and stared from Washington to Wilson. "I wonder what you would think. It turned out a lot different than either of you ever thought it would," he said aloud to the portraits.

Washington seemed to stare back in disapproval. Sal always felt like Wilson had a sly smile on his face in this portrait. As if he knew exactly how he'd left the world. Sal thought back to the meeting where they chose Nick to replace the newly deceased Senator Richards. It had been in this very office, ten odd months ago.

"Governor Morris, welcome to Washington. You know Senator Banks, correct?" greeted Sal.

"Yes, I believe we've met a few times," replied the Colorado Governor. He shook the hand of the ancient and frail looking Senator who didn't attempt to raise his 94-year-old body from the chair.

"Indeed, we have," said Senator Baxter Banks of South Carolina, in a voice much stronger than his body seemed able to produce. "A pleasure to see you again, Governor. I wish it were for better reasons. We need to pick the right person to fill out Senator Richard's term, yes we do," he said in a strong southern drawl.

"I asked Senator Banks to join us for this conversation because it is an important appointment. Really fucking important," said the Majority Leader. "We need a reliable Party member, and we need them fast. After the midterms, with Richards gone, our majority is one, 50 to 49. We need to get the new senator sworn in ASAP. We have bills to pass."

Morris nodded in agreement.

"I'm well aware of the urgency and the need to pick the right person. However, as you know, I'm also facing a tough reelection and I want to use this pick to help shore up my chances. The anti-fracking legislation has hurt our state economy. A lot of my constituents were affected. Some of those were good union jobs we lost. Colorado doesn't have enough of those. I need to pick someone people can applaud me for, to help shore up confidence," said Morris, now sitting opposite Banks in front of Sal's fireplace.

Sal handed the Governor a bourbon.

"Who do you have in mind?" asked Banks.

"Congresswoman Ellis, from our Denver district. She is long serving, very progressive, black, and articulate. Nominating her would shore up both my black and women's votes. Another female Senator and a black woman makes us all look good," said Morris.

"Didn't she run against Richard's in a primary two terms ago? Against the will of the Senate leaders, specifically the Vice President when she had my job?" Morris nodded slightly in reply.

"Are you fucking nuts? Lexi would string me up by my balls if I let you nominate her. Actions have consequences and that woman screwed the wrong person with those antics. You don't cross the wishes of the VP and get a second chance. Next," said Sal dismissively, as Banks looked on with a bemused smile on his face.

"Well, if she's not good, we have several congressmen we could choose from, but they're young," said Morris, less sure of himself, figuring a black, progressive woman would have been a slam dunk.

"Come on man, this is the Senate. You cannot just elevate anyone to the position. We need an advocate; we need someone who brings something useful to the table and to the Party. These positions are the crown jewels. Lots of people will give tons to reach this pinnacle. How about your corporate donors? Anyone who can bring $10 million to our coffers, lock in a key demographic or guarantee good news coverage? Got any media moguls? Think man, think," said Sal, intentionally getting Morris flustered.

"Well, we have a sports icon who's interested in getting into politics. He thought about a run for Senate the last time a seat was up. He's very popular in the state," offered Morris timidly.

"I'm not sure that's a good idea. We need someone we can groom. Someone we can control and to whom we can offer a future in politics. Who is committed, but also impressionable," drawled Banks in his elongated syllables and mesmerizing speech patterns.

His almost 65 years of service in the Senate had seen him turn his sleepy drawl into razor sharp rebukes on key legislature. Rousing his colleagues, the press, and the public with his soaring rhetoric and oratory mastery. Even at 94, he was not someone to be trifled with.

Governor Morris stiffened a bit. This wasn't going as he'd expected. Now he was getting nervous. He had ambitions, and he wanted to do the right thing with this pick, to catch the attention of the Vice President. "Do you have suggestions?" he asked.

Sal piped up. "Yes. I believe former Governor Forrest would make an influential senator."

Morris looked uncomfortable.

"What?" asked Sal. "He was a two-term governor, a four-term congressman before that. Respected businessman and owns a string of local TV stations around the West. He isn't too old to be useful."

Morris still frowned. "Spit it out, man," said Sal impatiently.

"Uh, he's probably not the best choice. There are rumors around he has a certain predilection not widely accepted, even in today's permissive society," confided Morris.

"What the fuck are you talking about?" asked Sal angrily.

"He likes boys. Not men. Boys. There are rumors he has been traveling to Thailand twice a year because of their privacy rules. We passed him over as a choice to head a commission last year because of these rumors. Mind you, I have no proof, but I'd want a full-blown investigation before I could nominate him. And if you want this done fast….?" ended Morris.

"Shit," said Sal, pacing the room now. "We need to get this done. Who else is there? Baxter, any ideas?"

"What about Turner?"

"Turner? Turner who?" asked Sal, confused.

"Of course. Geez, why didn't I think of that?" agreed Morris, jumping to his feet, almost spilling his drink.

"I'm not following," growled Sal, getting upset.

"Nick Turner, the hero of the New York City subway terrorist attack. He's a Colorado native. Shit, is he in the Opposition?" asked Morris aloud, taking his phone out.

"I believe he teaches history at Colorado State," offered Banks.

"That's a good sign. Most professors are in the Party. Let's just hope he's not a Communist," said Sal, thinking aloud.

Morris looked at his phone. "Lifelong registered Party member. Nothing of note on the web or in our database about any issues with the law. Military veteran of both Iraq and Afghanistan. Of course, most of the info is about New York. He didn't cash in. No book deal or movie. Just went back to teaching school. This could be perfect and would really help boost my popularity if I nominated a hero," crowed Morris with excitement.

"What do you think, Sal?" asked Banks.

"Can we keep him in line? He's a neophyte."

"The entire process will intimidate him. We can keep Richard's staff intact. They can help steer things the way we want. Robinson is a good chief of staff. Reliable. We can count on him to keep him in line and to not buck the system. As long as he doesn't like little boys," said Banks, getting a chuckle from Sal as he looked at Morris.

"I'll check, but I think we're OK on that front. Have you seen his picture? The guy makes the ladies swoon," replied Morris.

"So did Rock Hudson," retorted Banks.

"Gay is not a problem, just little boys," blurted Sal. "We already have enough sanctioned perversion. We don't need more."

Morris was typing on his phone again. And getting replies.

"Alright, I think we're good. Seems he had a long-term relationship with a *woman*, but it ended during his time overseas. My staff is checking."

"Works for me," said Sal. "Do it."

Banks sat in his chair smiling and raised his glass in a toast. "To our newest Senator," as the others raised theirs in salute.

Sal puffed on his cigar, thinking back to that conversation. He certainly hadn't turned out to be a poof, but he wondered if he'd turned out to be a bit more resourceful than they bargained for. Sal could sense in their conversation, there was a lot more to young Mr. Turner than he previously thought. He sensed determination, resolve, and perhaps more. This was what worried him.

Helen buzzed him for his next appointment.

"Come on in. We have a lot to discuss," said Sal.

The other figure nodded and took a seat.

Chapter 9

Nick left the Capitol and walked across to First Street, walking south, passing the Library of Congress and the Capitol Hill club. He continued past the Opposition National Committee HQ until he came to a series of small row houses on the west side of First Street. These were owned by various lobbying firms and 'loaned' out to the parties for their fundraising activities.

It was illegal to raise money in one's congressional office. These 'houses' provided convenient locations near the Capitol to congregate to dial for dollars. Nick walked down the row and up into one of them. As he entered, an aide met him, giving him a small pile of papers, leading him down a hallway to a smallish room with a phone, a desk, and a light. The aide shut the door as he left.

Nick sat and looked at the list and sighed. For the nine months he had been here, he had religiously attended 'call time'. Raising money for the Party's reelection efforts. He looked at the call script in his hand. It looked like a car warranty telemarketer script.

"Hi, I'm Bob. Please send me your money and I'll send you not one, but two sets of steak knives. If you give me your credit card right now, we'll include a handy chopper," said Nick aloud, doing his best telemarketer impression. He sighed again, took off his shoes and set his feet on the corner of the desk. Picking up the phone, he began calling deep pocketed party donors to convince them to part with more of their money.

After two hours, Nick, who despite his disdain, was one of the better fundraisers, had actually convinced many of the donors to up their donation amounts. Most senators relied on their networks and cocktail party schmoozing to do most of their fundraising. Dialing for dollars was beneath them. Nick had no network and felt this was a better way to raise money and, frankly, it kept him from having to attend all the lobbyist meetings and dinners at night.

He was waiting on hold for Carson Williamson, a Party mega donor who was a shipping and trucking magnate.

"Senator, a pleasure to meet you," answered Carson.

"Nice to meet you, Mr. Williamson. Please call me Nick."

"Nick it is. Call me Carson. I want to tell you how proud I am of what you did in New York. I'm sure you hear it all the time, but as someone in transportation, had that attack succeeded, my businesses would have suffered greatly."

"Well, to be honest with you Carson, I didn't think. I just did what I hope anyone else would have done."

"Thank God you did. What can I do for you today, Nick?"

"As a freshman senator, it falls to me to make calls for the party. As you know, we are constantly facing challenges to our majority. The Opposition is always running excellent candidates against us to derail our plans," began Nick. He was trying to read naturally from the call script in front of him. Carson interrupted him.

"Nick, you're a United States Senator. I can't believe they have you doing this. Usually, I get calls from staffers or lobbyists to attend a gala or fund a conference. That kind of stuff."

"I'm going to be honest. This sucks," admitted Nick, as Carson let out a loud laugh.

"Because I'm appointed, and not a career politician, they encouraged me to spend a bit more time on the phones with larger donors like yourself. To introduce myself and build a network of contacts. I've got to tell you; these call scripts are just amateur. By the way, do you need some steak knives or a hand chopper?" asked Nick, in mock seriousness.

Carson was laughing so hard it took a second to talk again.

"Nick, I like you. You actually have a personality, and you don't care what you say, you say it anyway. Do you know the last time a senator actually told me the truth?"

"Couldn't even guess. I'm still waiting," said Nick drolly.

"Former Senator Johnson. He was out of office for two years before he actually broke through the training and uttered an honest opinion. They'd trained him to not say anything controversial and, heaven forbid, to not utter an honest opinion. It took him a long time to get back to normal."

"I don't think I'll be here long enough to worry about keeping my opinions to myself," laughed Nick.

"Why? You seem to be a straightforward and honest person. Exactly what we need," expressed Carson.

"Exactly why I don't expect to stay. Since we're off script, anyway, do you mind if I ask *you* a question?"

"Sure."

"Why do you give your money to the Party?"

"I give some to both, but I give way more to the Party. I'm an old-school bleeding-heart liberal, feeling sorry for the poor and minorities. Capitalism is not kind to those without an entry into upward mobility. The Party used to be the champion of the oppressed. I'm not a fan of the progressive agenda. It's probably one reason they have you calling me instead of a House member. They also probably noticed I haven't ponied up as much as before."

"What are we doing wrong? By the way, I'm no progressive either, so please be candid."

"Nick, all politicians lie. This is their one common trait. They make promises and say anything to get elected. We're not naïve on this point. My concern is their total disconnect from reality. Especially for anyone who's in a second term or longer. DC is a bubble. They've ceased to care about the average person and now serve only the corporate and political entities. The ones helping get them elected for as long as they want to serve or to set them up after public service." Nick could tell Carson was just getting warmed up.

"The Opposition isn't much better, but they're feckless when they're out of power and even more useless when they're in it. No one forces the Party to meet in the middle. No one tries to keep the Party honest. The battle isn't between opposition and party; it's within the party between left and far left. Our deficits are now so large, people don't even think about eight trillion-dollar budgets where almost half is borrowed or printed. Look at the inflation. No matter what we do, we can't seem to get it to move down. This simply cannot continue," said Carson, in a concerned tone.

"I appreciate the candor. I can't say I disagree. In my short time here, all I've seen is ass kissing and an endless merry-go-round of get more money. I hate to say it, but I'm not impressed by our elected leaders."

Carson laughed, "It is a sad situation indeed. Now you see why I'm reluctant to keep throwing good money after bad. I've already been to enough inauguration balls. If I don't get another invite, it won't break my heart."

"If you have time, one more question. How would you fix it?"

"Wow, *that* is a much longer conversation, more than we have time for now. To be perfectly honest, I'm not sure we can reverse the damage our policies have done. We were great once, so I know we have it in us, but I worry our young people don't know fortunate they are to be an American. They're no longer taught to appreciate the sacrifices made by those who came before, who made their cushy lives so easy. They don't understand true adversity and have never seen it."

"The poor, and minorities the Party claim to be looking out for, are in the same dire straits they have always been in. At some point, when you keep getting kicked, it's time to look in the mirror. To realize you have a kick me sign on your back and turn around and punch the next guy who kicks you. The Party has been kicking the minorities for decades. Taking their votes, claiming to help, and then ensuring their most reliable voting block never sees prosperity. Instead, it keeps them from advancing and from recognizing the Party isn't the solution, but rather the *problem*."

"Carson, I couldn't have said it better. In my mind, we succeeded as a country, whether party or opposition, because we all agreed the Constitution protected our best interests. We also had leaders with character. I witness it every day. None of my colleagues read bills. I see them surrounded by their aides on their way to votes. The aides tell them whether to vote yes or no. They never even contemplate the actual bill and the cause or the effect. Intended or unintended. I see how the bills are made. Congress has nothing to do with them. The meetings are between staff and lobbyists. No Congressman in sight." Nick took his feet from the desk as he spoke with passion into the phone.

"Carson, I want to believe if the common voter could see how all this works, they would revolt. But to be honest, like you, I'm worried our electorate doesn't give a crap. I don't even think they know it's the Bill of Rights enabling them to shit on their country without being locked up and thrown in jail. Maybe they should pay more attention to Russia and China. How they handle people who complain," suggested Nick, not bothering to hide his disgust.

"Senator, we are kindred souls. We waste you in this role. You care too much. Don't let it eat you alive. I'll write a bigger check, so your secret is safe with me. Do me a favor, though. I'd like to have a longer conversation about how to fix things."

"Save your money. We don't deserve it. I'd love the chance to talk longer. Then maybe we'll be worthy of a donation."

"I'll still write a *slightly* larger check. You don't know Fontana and Lexi like I do. If they heard you tell me to keep my money, it wouldn't be good for you. Trust me," Nick heard Carson laughing.

"Thanks. Do you know Martha Summers?" asked Nick. "She's next on my list."

"I've met her, but I can't say I know her. I knew her late husband. He was a straight shooter. You would've liked him. Built his business from the ground up, starting with one retail store. Now she is in the top twenty-five wealthiest. They were true partners in the business. I don't think she is a feminist, seeing as how she helped build that business with her hands too. But like I said, I don't know her beyond a few events where we shook hands and made small talk. They use their own trucks, so I never got the chance to win their distribution business," finished Carson.

"Thanks, we'll talk again soon," said Nick as they ended the call.

He cracked open a water bottle and drank half of it before making his next call. He dialed Martha Summers, the widow of the retail magnate Norman Summers. They had 1000s of discount retail stores around the world and had given billions to philanthropic causes. They were mega donors to the Party for decades, but like Carson, the amount had been diminishing in the last few years.

"Senator Turner, I have Mrs. Summers on the line now," said the assistant as the line clicked.

"Senator, a pleasure to meet you finally, if only over the phone," said a strong female voice with the barest hint of a drawl.

"The pleasure is mine, Mrs. Summers. I've spent many a day in and out of your stores through the years."

"Really? Most senators wouldn't be caught dead in one of our stores. They're full of bitter clingers as one of your fellow senators once famously labeled our primary patrons. Please call me Martha. Mrs. Summers sounds so matronly."

"Well Martha, please call me Nick and I'm not ashamed to say I still shop at your stores when I'm back in Colorado. Can't find one around here though," noted Nick with a small laugh.

"DC is too expensive, so we never built one. But we're not far away in Virginia and in Maryland outside DC. But we digress. I assume they had you call to part me from more of my money?"

"Martha, I won't bullshit you, since you are clearly on to the game we play so poorly. There's concern you haven't been as generous as in the past. It's my job to talk you out of it. Frankly, I have to say I'm not enthused about the prospect."

"I applaud your honesty, Nick. Thank you for not reading from that ridiculous call script. I don't know who drafts those, but my lowest intern in the marketing department can do better. The reason I don't give as much, and since we're being honest, is I don't like the leadership."

"My turn. Thanks for your honesty. Since we're being candid. I don't like them either," replied Nick as he heard Martha laughing on the other end.

"Nick, from what I can see, you're probably best to not say that aloud around any of them. I have watched the Vice President throughout her career. Once I even considered her a friend, when she was in the Senate. Before she became Majority Leader and then the VP. She is obsessed. Not just with power. She's a genuine believer in the progressive message. Most of them are only interested until they make enough money, then they turn away from the message. Lexi is different. She believes everything she says, and that makes her dangerous," said Martha.

"Sounds like you changed your mind about her?"

"Indeed. I don't like guns that much either, but I also don't think trying to take everyone's gun is a realistic solution. Many of my customers are gun lovers. It wouldn't make much sense for me to broadcast my support for gun control or support someone who is advocating taking everyone's gun. It's just crazy talk. Red meat for her empty-headed followers. What worries me, Nick, is I think she fully intends to implement these policies. Most politicians make promises to get people to the polls and then break all of them. With Lexi, I can only hope that happens. I'm terrified she aims to keep them, and that scares me."

"I'm guessing I'm not going to be successful with this call."

"Depends on your definition of success. Doesn't she scare you?" asked Martha, the worried tone in her voice authentic.

"Today was the second time I've met her. I don't know her personally enough to gauge whether she is just another empty promise politician or the crazy you clearly think she is. I'm a constitutionalist, so I don't agree with most of the progressive ideals and policies starting with Wilson in 1913," laughed Nick.

"Good. We need more like you if we're going to fight to stop this. I won't be giving any more of my money to the Party while the progressives are in control. I don't agree with their radical proposals and the way they've ignored every law curbing their power since they won. Ironically, the same laws they *used* to get into power. Now they don't want them used any longer. Like freedom of speech, the right to assemble peaceably, the right to dissent, or the rule of law, on things like crime or the border. Shit, I almost sound like the Opposition. Look what the progressives have done," she said with a snort.

"I like it. So how would you fix it?" asked Nick enthusiastically.

Martha paused for a second. Nick broke into her reverie. "Just so you know, I just finished with Carson Williamson. He echoed much of your sentiment. I asked him the same thing."

"Nick, the answer is really simple. The execution is hard, because so many people have given up on the election system. Rouse the sleeping giant. Inspire the lazy or cowed, the ignorant and afraid. We need to give them something to get behind. To inspire them to rise and use their voice while they still can. It may already be too late. Count me among the crazies who believe they already rigged the elections," declared Martha.

"You think there's an untapped group of voters who just need a kick in the pants to get off their asses and vote?"

"Not quite, Senator, I mean Nick, sorry. I'm saying there is a large group of either disillusioned, disinterested, or just plain ignorant people. They either don't know or care what is at risk if the Progressives enact their platform. In fact, many of them only hear 'free' this or that and it's enough to get them to support it. Or to at least not vote against it. Someone needs to wake them out of their slumber. They are going to wake up one day and have a collective epiphany about not knowing what was coming," she finished.

"Do you think that is still possible?"

Martha was chuckling. "Nick, *that* is the question. Is there anything anyone can say or do to wake these people up? These kids have tuned out because they see nothing useful coming out of the news or government. To get them to pay any attention to real impending doom, the demise of their freedoms. That requires someone or something to get them to look up from their phone porn long enough to see the truck approaching," finished Martha ominously.

"Here, I thought *I* was a cynic," said Nick facetiously.

"Sorry, I used to vent like this with Norman. I have no one to do this with anymore. You called at a low point when I was feeling sorry for myself, my country, and frankly for my grandchildren's future. I sensed a kindred soul, and once it started, I just couldn't stop. My apologies," she said in a sincere and even somewhat anxious voice.

"You know Martha, I don't understand why we need to apologize for exercising our Constitutional right to have our own opinion. I don't understand why we need to suppress and cancel everyone who has a different one. It just underscores your point about a viewpoint not being legitimate if you can't afford to have anyone disagree with you, and have others know it."

"Exactly. We are already in the authoritarian phase of our slide into totalitarianism. At some point, we won't be able to stop this any longer. Then I'm really afraid of what happens," she finished, sighing.

"I wish I could counter your statement, but I see it as well."

"We haven't had bipartisanship in years, even decades now. This is not how America has worked. Reagan looks like a saint compared to modern politicians. I look at my disdain for him and his two terms, and I now wish we had someone like him running on *either* side. I'd vote for him in a heartbeat."

"That was painful to admit, I suspect," added Nick.

"Nick, you're too young, but it didn't use to be about ideology. Everyone was looking out for the best interests of America. Internet and cable news turned it into entertainment and turned every politician into an actor and PR hack. When your exposure was the Sunday news programs, you could make tough decisions and compromise with your counterpart in the other party. Without having this effort immediately broadcast to partisans around the world. Without paid online trolls and social media activists immediately denouncing you. Or calling for your resignation or a rally in front of your house, where your wife and baby are, while you're in Washington. That's not healthy for a democracy. This is third world thuggery and as close to the brown and black shirts of Hitler and Mussolini as I have ever seen," finished Martha, her voice almost breaking at the concern she felt for her country.

"You know Martha, it is exactly this kind of impassioned speech we need in our committees. Of course, then I realized all it would do is end up with you denounced and your stores boycotted. What does that say about our current state? When someone who should be admired and celebrated for what they have accomplished in life cannot give us advice. How does it get better?" asked Nick, exasperated.

"Now I've worked you up too," she replied in a softer tone.

"Nah, I've been coming to this conclusion since I got here with such unrealistic expectations. I'm afraid I must agree with you entirely. I'm a moderate myself, one of the few remaining, if not the only one. The rest have retired, been run out of town, or simply beaten into submission," admitted Nick.

"Can you blame them? Being followed into bathrooms and recorded peeing. Having hecklers follow them as they run the Boston Marathon. Kayakers shouting all night next to your houseboat simply because you didn't agree with printing trillions of dollars. And those were Party members. What did the rest of the caucus do? Not a damn thing. Why? Because they didn't want the rabble turned on them. Nick, we're coming apart."

"I agree, but what's the alternative? There are positions of the opposition I can support, especially on the fiscal side, but a lot of the rest is crap. And our party is not moderate in any form. It's all scorched earth. The instant news cycle and the disease of social media has made governing *not* about hard choices and compromise. How do we tackle the tough topics if we can't have an honest and open discussion about the issues and the consequences? I'm ashamed by the reaction and support of our Party persecuting anyone who dares disagree. This is not what America is about," concluded Nick.

"If we had about forty-nine more like you with spines, then we might stand up to the radicals. End cancel culture, have open debate reviewing all worthy ideas. Even get the Opposition to join in this conversation and come to a consensus. I don't know if we can ever get back to this and that concerns me most," declared Martha.

"I'm not sure I have any suitable answers. As you say, we seem to have entered a phase of apathy in our country. Most people are unplugged and hunkered down. Not interested in learning anything or being educated on issues at all. Even if they see anything, it is more likely to be a take on an issue from a Hollywood gossip site than from a credible news outlet," said Nick, laughing. "Hell, listen to me. What is a credible news organization?"

Nick could sense Martha smiling on the other end of the phone. "Exactly. Where and how does someone get info they can trust?" asked Martha. "There's no such thing as a fact any longer. COVID really killed that concept and then it killed the idea of science as a function above politics."

"This lost me forever. I trusted them at the start, and I forced my company to follow their advice. I fired employees who didn't conform. When it came out the advice wasn't based on verifiable facts, that disgusted me and broke the trust I had in government. I hired all my people back and gave them bonuses to make up for the mistakes our government forced me to make. We were the first major corporation to do this. Once we broke the ice, some followed, but not all," explained Martha.

"That was magnanimous of you," noted Nick. "You made up for their mistakes."

"I was pissed. This is the one time where I wish we were authoritarian. Where we could have taken these people and lined them up against a wall. What they did was criminal and cost lives. Worse, it traumatized an entire generation of children through their fear mongering and ridiculous mandates," remarked Martha, the disgust in her tone coming through loud and clear.

"I appreciate your time and I'm glad we talked honestly with each other. It helps me understand folks like you and Carson Williamson agree with my own views that we are in big trouble. Not sure what I can do about it, but I can make sure I'm not part of the problem. I'm only one vote and one person, but we must stand up for what is right. Staying in Washington is not something I care about, so maybe my stance won't be in vain. We'll see."

"Senator, thank you for this stance. No one should expect anything less honorable from you, given your sacrifices in the wars and in New York City. You're exactly the kind of person we should be electing. You had to be appointed, because someone like you would never seek public office in today's climate."

"Sad but true. Elected office was never anything I considered, let alone aspired to," replied Nick.

"See? What would be the point of subjecting yourself to that level of vitriol for the reward of sitting in a room four hours a day raising money for idealogues like Lexi? If you ever need anything, including the money I won't send to the party, please call. I'm on your side, and I wish you well in your efforts."

"Thank you, Martha."

"My pleasure Nick. I haven't enjoyed a conversation as much as this one in an awfully long time. You've restored some hope that indeed all may not be lost."

Chapter 10

"Come on in," waved Nick, seeing the Colonel knocking at his door.

"How did your dialing for dollars go? Still the goose laying the golden eggs for the party?" remarked Bob with a laugh.

"Struck out twice this go round. Some of the big boys aren't too happy with the progressives taking over the party."

"Doesn't surprise me. They're pretty vocal about wanting to soak the rich, which presumably includes the Party mega donors. They seem to forget this sometimes. Holding out one hand for money and slapping their donors in the face with the other. Schizoid for sure," noted Bob.

"Yep. What do you have for me?"

"We have a bunch. The American Preservation Bill is an Omnibus bill that contains a bunch of funding for foreign intel operations, aid to our allies, both military and humanitarian, and aid allocated to some of our not so reliable 'friends'. The idea being to help them solve problems at home before it comes to us. We're also trying to counter the Chinese inroads being made around the world. With their investments in infrastructure, roads, ports, 5G and 6G telecommunications and internet." Bob looked up from his notes.

"How much military spending?" asked Nick.

"Not much. They cut the primary military spending budget about 5% this year, on top of about 2-3% reductions of the last few years. It's leaving us dangerously under-funded. Especially around updating antiquated equipment and extending the service life of critical components. This latest reduction is the most drastic. Estimates have China catching up on investment in the military. They continue to steal our tech and reverse engineer it faster and faster." Nick nodded, a disappointed look on his face.

"Their J-20x is now up and running and some say may even have some improvements over our F-35. Our sixth gen fighters are still years away. They're also ahead of us in lasers, cyber, space, and hypersonic advancements. Their navy exceeds ours in size and strength, even if they can't yet project power like we do. They have way more destroyers, subs, frigates, and gunboats. Our only advantage is in our aircraft carrier superiority and our ability to project air power from a longer distance. We're doing nothing to counter their overall buildup," ended Bob in a neutral tone.

"What's your feeling on the bill? You've studied it. I admit I couldn't get through 1602 pages."

"Nick, I'm probably the only staffer to read it all, and I guarantee you are the only senator who has read anything other than the top sheet summary."

Nick shook his head at the state of American lawmaking. "Alright, give me the highlights."

"China is investing heavily in Afghanistan. They have the lithium mines there, up and running. They are importing Uyghur minorities and forcing them to live in labor camps. There is a proposal funding the Afghan dissidents, but it's a drop in the bucket and won't result in any dent in the Taliban rule. Definitely not enough to counter the support of China. There's nothing in this bill regarding the Chinese human rights violations. Nothing to fund alternatives in Afghanistan to help stop their growing dependency on China," noted Bob.

"No surprise we're are going soft on the Uyghurs genocide. It was the deal the administration struck years ago to keep China from taking Taiwan, after our disastrous withdrawal from Afghanistan and the mess with Russia. Get off their backs about their ethnic minorities or face a confrontation with them over an annexation of Taiwan and lose access to their semiconductors. We had little choice. Still don't really, nothing has changed there," admitted Nick.

With nothing to add, Bob continued with his summary. "We're buying our way back into Turkmenistan and Tajikistan. We have drone bases in both. The cost is very high in terms of 'aid' and our agreement to not highlight *their* human rights violations as well."

"Great," said Nick again, shaking his head in disgust as he made notes in his ever-present purple notebook. "I need a drink. Care to share some of your family bourbon?"

"Thought you'd never ask," smiled Bob, pulling a bottle out of the computer bag leaning against his chair, heading to Nick's kitchen.

"Better make it four fingers for me. It's been a long day."

Bob returned with two glasses of bourbon.

"I love these rock ice cubes. Keeps the bourbon cold but never waters it down. Ok, ready?" Nick nodded, savoring his first sip. "The Taliban has continued hunting down any who collaborated with us during our time there. By the latest count, the estimates are as high as 100,000 Afghans who've been killed, tortured, imprisoned, or sentenced to a life of hard labor for cooperating with the Americans during the 'occupation'."

"Many of the hard labor prisoners are working in the Chinese owned lithium mines. Believe it or not, we also have $25 million in aid spec'd out for the Taliban. To help improve our joint efforts to facilitate dual citizen repatriation to the US. How this is not negotiating with terrorists is hard for me to understand," commented Bob.

"How successful have we been at destroying the equipment we left behind? It's been years. Surely, we've destroyed it all by now?"

"The latest estimate is they have five Blackhawks they've fixed and learned to operate. We believe the Iraqis taught them. As you know, we left thirty-three of them behind, supposedly rendered inoperable. We destroyed fourteen with drones and several we think ended up in China and Iran. Small arms have shown up everywhere there are terrorists. We replaced Libya as the biggest supplier of black market arms, courtesy of the stash we left the Taliban. Whenever we suspect any activities against American interests, we drone the crap out of stuff, but it's hardly making a difference," lamented Bob.

Nick just shook his head. "Unbelievable."

"Of course, the concern is, every time we kill a Taliban fighter, they send another hundred 'collaborators' to the camps and our humanitarian outfits go crazy. We've given up on any interdiction, only retaliatory strikes."

"How many years later and we're still paying for this administration's blunders in foreign policy?" fumed Nick.

"Indeed, we are," said Bob in a solemn tone.

"What about Israel and Saudi Arabia?"

"The level of aid to both countries is much reduced in this bill. It also denies the request to buy more F-35s. We're still willing to sell them old F-16's we're retiring from our National Guard fleets."

"Bob, they're called air *wings*. You Marines are all the same," said Nick in mockery, shaking his head and sipping his bourbon.

"Sorry, from our guard air *wings*. It wouldn't surprise me a bit to see us offer the A-10 to Israel when we finish decommissioning them. They're all just flying recliners, anyway," retorted Bob, sipping *his* bourbon, ribbing Nick in the endless intra-service rivalry.

Nick laughed. "Killing the Warthog makes no sense. We still need it for theaters where we own the skies. We can't produce a credible and affordable alternative for that role. You guys on the ground love us 'Hogs'." Bob raised his glass in a toast to Nick and his genuine statement about infantry love for the ugly A-10. The tank killer, and an infantryman's best friend.

"The Air Force have been trying to eighty-six it since the day they built it in the seventies. They can take such a beating and keep going. I agree, against China or Russia, the F-35 is a better platform where SAMs would be everywhere. Gotta have both stealth and standoff capability. My A-10 would have been toast in Ukraine, with neither of those," finished Nick.

"Maybe. A-10s have probably saved more infantry and Marines than anything else. My ass included. I prefer a plane I can see for close air support. Rather than an F-35, I can't. Especially when it can only stay on station for fifteen minutes before it has to be refueled. Your A-10 could hang around for hours. I'll stick with an A-10 overhead, anytime," announced Bob.

"Appreciate the A-10 love. It seems the brass didn't ask your opinion. Back to the funding. Our good buddies in the Middle East are on their own against Iran?" asked Nick.

"Yep. We know Iran has several nuclear warheads now thanks to this administration putting the nuclear deal back in place years ago. Maybe as high as a dozen. They have intermediate-range ballistic missile capability, enough to reach as far as the UK or potentially Japan. The UN sanctions we imposed did not work. The Russians and Chinese paid no attention. Clearly, the UN has lost whatever teeth they think they had," said Bob, now shaking his own head.

"No military help for our allies in the Middle East. What *are* we doing?"

"There are tens of millions allocated for every Middle Eastern country for diversity, equity, and inclusion training programs. To help them educate their populace on DEI and the importance of women's rights plus racial and gender equity," said Bob with a straight face.

Nick made a show of banging his head against the tabletop. "Has anyone in our government bothered to read the Koran? Have they studied the role of women in this religion? If so, they'd understand no amount of money is going to change their way of life or their view of women."

"None of the people writing these bills have been anywhere near the ground in these countries. It's all pie in the sky."

"Did they not learn anything from the horror stories of the poor women of Afghanistan when we left? An entire generation of women born under the Western ideas of the American umbrella. Or their eventual re-subjugation at the hands of the Taliban once we were gone? These poor women's stories made me throw up when the ones fortunate enough to get out testified at our hearings. This is all our current administration's fault. We gave them hope and walked away without a shred of guilt for what we left behind. Now we're sending them money for diversity training? Is this a cruel joke?" accused Nick.

"Fraid not, boss," answered Bob carefully.

"Whose idea was this?"

"I believe it was the Progressive Women for Change. The PW4C demanded we fund this attempt to bring these countries out of the 11th century. To convince them to see reason and allow women a rightful and equal voice in their societies," revealed Bob.

Nick sat in his chair, rubbing his temples with his fingers.

"I wonder if any of that squad have ever been to a Taliban wedding? Several of them claim to have fled this kind of life. This is the height of hypocrisy. Hell, we see the stories of the young women all the time. If they're lucky, the child bride is 15 and not 13 or 11. So much for progressive feminism. How many are in the PW4C now, fifteen, twenty?"

"I think they count thirty-seven now in the house. It's a formidable voting bloc, especially with only a six-seat majority. They get what they want and stop what they don't," answered Bob. Nick got up and started pacing, clearly frustrated.

"Nick," he said in a gentle but firm voice, "You gotta let it go. Sit down. Take a few breaths."

He stopped and looked at Bob. He'd led a platoon in Desert Storm during the first invasion of Iraq and a battalion in the second. He'd also lost men and been where Nick was now. Frustrated at the lack of resolve by the political leaders to do what was necessary to win and to stop evil. To throw young men at political objectives and ignore the realities on the ground was criminal.

"Sorry, I know you know this. I spent 20 years with these people in the Navy and Air National Guard. They're good people, simple, but no different from your average American. They just want the freedom to live their life and care for their family. We gave them a taste of this and then we cut and ran. Now it's worse than it was before 9/11 and Al Qaeda is back. We are less safe than we have ever been."

"This is true. It gets worse," shared Bob. "The latest intel reports show most of these terrorist elements are coming through the southern border. Homeland is estimating 13,000 known operatives from Iran, China, Al Qaeda, to mention only the top groups. The latest info is also pointing to them working with the Mexican drug cartels to use illegal immigrants who have cartel debt to assist in the terrorism efforts."

"Great. And we've flown and bussed them to all the lower forty-eight," observed Nick.

"They've gotten much smarter, for sure. Helping sow discord and division amongst local and federal enforcement communities. Leading to more recruitment of Americans to their cause. Using propaganda from poorly planned US airstrikes. Including the Ak Bast village strike where we killed families of the lithium mine workers and surveyors, where no ISIS was present. The Chinese made hay with that one."

"They've also been able to make inroads within former allies who now have strong anti-American, Anti-Racist League and Antifa like groups, preaching hatred of the US. They're stirring up immigrants in these countries with cries of state sponsored racism. These ARL groups are now in places like Taiwan, the Philippines, Thailand, South Korea, and every EU country agitating. These countries blame us for spreading this racial division to their shores."

"What does the bill do to stop this? More money for diversity training?" asked Nick.

"These countries get funds from the PW4C's Equity, Diversity, and Prosperity project. EDP is funding some of the ARL too."

"And the border?"

"More of the same. It doesn't look like anything is going to slow down the flow, short of us officially closing the border," suggested Bob. "And we know that won't happen soon."

Nick leaned back in his chair, staring at the ceiling. "How many do you estimate have come across in this administration? Do I even want to know the latest guess?"

"Around fourteen million, maybe as high as eighteen," said Bob.

"And the real number of illegals? Not what the press says?"

"They reported the total number at eleven million for decades. Now they have upped it to 'officially' fifteen million. Reality, from what I can get from the people in the know, closer to 40 million and maybe as high as 45 million presently here illegally."

"So, between 10 and 15% of our population? Unbelievable. No wonder unemployment is so high, and wages are still falling. Bob, this has to stop. I'm as compassionate as the next guy, but we can't be the world's salvation. Letting forty million people into a shadow economy and bleeding us dry on local, state, and federal government assistance. We need to bring them out of the shadows, but we also need to be aware they have broken our laws to get here. It is a total insult to those who came legally and went through the naturalization process. Lexi can't just wave her wand to make all these people full Americans. That is an effective way to lose at least half the population's approval forever."

"You're right. Polling says a clear majority don't favor blanket amnesty. A majority are skeptical of any at all," agreed Bob.

"America can no longer be the vanguard of freedom and goodness. We're losing our ability to guarantee global sea lanes, trade, and safety with our shrinking Navy. Just look at the issues in the Red Sea and the South China Sea. Worse, we're losing our resolve to continue to try. I know progressives see this as a plus and a better place for us as one among many, just another equal partner, in their global governance scheme. Our enemies don't see it this way. They see us weak and fractured. We have few friends remaining. Many others are happy to see us diminished. Our true enemies, the enemies of what the West has stood for, these last centuries, see this as their time to strike back. When we pull back, I fear it won't end well, and certainly not like the globalists think it will."

"No doubt. Our allies no longer trust we'll be there if they need us," agreed Bob.

"The barbarians are at the gate. Instead of defending, we're preparing to open them, thinking they come in peace. They don't play by our rules. Everything and everyone are at risk," remarked Nick.

"Well, that's a rosy picture if I ever heard one. I just came in to advise against voting for the bill. Not to get you spun up worrying about Armageddon." The Colonel sat looking into his empty glass.

"Sorry Bob."

"Nick, you know I agree. I'm sure you're hearing the same from your military contacts. We're no longer focused on winning with our military. Instead, we are more concerned with lowering physical standards for entry into the military. Of ensuring equal representation from all races, genders, and now orientations. The military is supposed to be the epitome of a merit-based organization."

Bob just looked at Nick as he nodded.

"This is simply wrong. And it is difficult to remedy. Not promoting the best, not giving the best officers the combat commands, doesn't mean you lose a contract or a football game. It means people die. I have friends who are lifers who are getting out. Check with yours. They don't trust the brass, even more than usual. What do we do if we can no longer count on our military to be the elite killing machine we need it to be?" questioned Bob, now sounding as desperate as Nick had only moments before.

"Wow, we are a couple of old hens for sure," laughed Nick.

"We're in a world of trouble, Senator. Vote No on this bill. It wastes tons of money and solves no problems. In our weakness, we're spending money on programs and policies destined to change nothing. It just looks and sounds like we're doing something while our allies and enemies shake their collective heads at our naivety."

"Will do Bob. Thanks for taking the time to read it. Thanks for the briefing and the bourbon," said Nick, smiling as Bob got up and left his office.

Chapter 11

Nick walked out of his office to stretch his legs an hour after his briefing from the Colonel. The rest of the office was quiet except for the light in Chuck's. Nick stuck his head around the open door.

Chuck's office couldn't have been more different from Nick's. Photographs of him with presidents and senators, famous Americans, and foreign dignitaries hung on every wall. For a senate chief of staff, he got around.

Every flat surface was covered in a stack of papers, briefing books, or binders. His bookshelves were overloaded, every nook and cranny filled with something. Nick always chuckled inside when he came to Chuck's office. He claimed it was organized chaos. Nick told him it was just chaos.

"9:30. Even later than usual," commented Chuck, glancing at his phone.

"It's been a hell of a day."

"What did Fontana say?"

"Well, between F bombs, he promised me a spot in Lexi's administration. If I toe the line, of course," said Nick, moving papers off a chair.

"Please tell me you said yes?"

"You'd be proud. I kept my mouth shut and didn't speak my mind. I didn't say no either," he said, sitting down.

"You didn't. Not saying anything is the same thing as saying no. Crap. Nick, start thinking like a politician. Even if you don't mean it, you say yes," said Chuck in a concerned tone, standing and coming around the desk to face Nick.

"I've always been non-committal whenever I'm asked, saying I'll review all the issues fairly."

"Which makes you public enemy number one. Especially with Wilhelm having a stroke. They didn't need you until he went down. Now they do. He can't vote in a coma, and they can't replace him unless he dies."

"Geez, you make it sound like they'll kill him so they can pass the filibuster bill if I don't go along."

"Nick, did you look at Fontana? Do you think he would hesitate to do just that in order to win? You don't survive in this town without burying a few bodies, *usually* figuratively," said Chuck, trailing off and making his point.

"Guess who walked out as I went in? The VP," said Nick offhandedly.

"Oh man, they're pulling out all the stops. Nick, now is your time. Figure out what you want in return for your vote. You have leverage. We need to use it." Chuck paused and looked at Nick.

"Fuck," said Chuck as he paced back and forth in front of Nick. He stopped and pointed a finger at him. "Don't even think about it. You'll throw everything away and they'll just bring it up again when Wilhelm is better. Or if he dies when they replace him. It will pass at some point."

Nick held up his hands. "Hey, I didn't say anything."

"But you're thinking it."

"OK, on to other glorious things. I spent my four hours dialing for dollars. What can you tell me about Carson Williamson and Martha Summers?"

"Williamson and Summers? I didn't see them on your call list?" said Chuck, confused.

"When I got there, Fontana's man gave me a new list. These guys were on it. I was a bad boy and only got to the first twenty instead of the usual quota of 40-50."

"Interesting. Both are mega donors. They have PACs, so they can spend tons more than just donations. Directing their foundations and PACs to run ads on behalf of the Party and candidates. All uncoordinated, of course," said Chuck with a smile. "How did it go?"

"It was interesting. I just told them how I saw it and what I thought needed to get done," said Nick. Chuck, still standing, shook his head, wandered over to the mini fridge and pulled out a beer for each of them.

"This was a test and a potential reward for you to vote the right way. You get these guys on your side and they could be big donors to your election campaign. How did they respond?"

"Now that you mention it," Nick said as he took a sip from his beer. "They were pretty quiet."

"I bet they were. Did you follow the script at all and get them to commit to sending any money?"

"Seemed silly. So, I just talked. They asked a few questions. Why I felt the way I did. A couple asked about me and about New York. Why I acted and what made me do it. The usual curiosity."

"Did you answer?" asked Chuck.

Nick responded by laughing, "You know me. I hate talking about myself. I quickly changed it back to them. Why do they support the Party, what are their priorities, etc.?"

"They're probably not used to that. They're used to candidates telling them what they need and how they can help."

"I think I scored some points. Chuck, they are not happy with the progressive direction of the party platform. I'm not sure they're inclined to give as much as in the past. I had nothing to do with that. They volunteered it themselves," defended Nick, as Chuck looked at him funny.

"If you screwed up, I'm sure we'll hear about it. Leadership doesn't like pissed off donors. Anything else?" asked Chuck carefully.

"Several of them want to talk again, so be on the lookout in case any of them reach out."

"Really? That is very unusual," mused Chuck. "I'll let Carla know to look for any emails from any of their organizations."

"It won't come from their organizations, but from each of them personally. Make sure it doesn't get staffed out for a reply. I want to reply to these myself if they arrive through normal channels."

"Nick, these guys are scheduled even more than you are. They have zero free time. They certainly don't write their own emails," said Chuck authoritatively, as he sat back down.

"You sure about that?" Nick held up his phone and gave it to Chuck. There were two personal texts. One each from Carson and Martha, expressing their enjoyment of the conversation, and a desire to follow up again soon for more talk at Nick's convenience.

"Son of a bitch," said Chuck, looking up and handing the phone back. "What the hell *did* you talk about?"

"The state of the country and what they would do to fix it. I spent about an hour with each one."

"You got an hour with each one?" said Chuck, whistling incredulously. "I'd hate to be their executive assistants. No telling how many hoops they had to jump through to reschedule other calls while they talked to you. Usually, you're lucky to get ten minutes of their time to go through the script," said Chuck, heading back to his desk chair.

"Oh, and we really should pass the message to the committee. They really hate the call scripts. Just being yourself would get a much better result," offered Nick.

"You forget, you're unusual. Most of these senators and house members don't know how to be themselves. In fact, they wouldn't recognize that person. They're told what to do, what to think, what to say, where to be, when to eat, pee, and drink. Without the call script, they would talk about college football or their grandkids," said Chuck, laughing.

"You forgot about being told how to vote," added Nick.

"Advised, not told," smiled Chuck.

"You know what? They should still try to be themselves. It would probably work better. I'm the golden goose and I never use the script. I usually use it as the icebreaker to say how much I hate it and the caller on the other side agrees and then we have a normal conversation. Works every time," shared Nick. "There, that is my contribution to this election cycle."

"What else is on your mind?" asked Chuck, changing the subject.

"The Dr. is in? Let me find a nickel."

"A nickel? Try $400 an hour. Hell, probably $500 in this town, but the first hour is free today."

"I spent time with the Colonel going over the foreign aid bill or whatever it is called. It's total crap, with a three-quarter trillion price tag. I can't vote for it, and Bob agrees," said Nick.

"The American Preservation bill is its name. That is certain to put you cross ways with leadership, but I sense that's not what is bothering you?"

"How do I know I'm voting the way my folks want me to? It shouldn't be how I feel, it should be how *they* feel, right?"

"Well, yes, and no. You're representing them, so they trust you to know what they need, or at least most of them," said Chuck carefully.

"Does telemarketing twenty hours a week help me do that? How does getting promised a spot in the VP's administration if I vote the way they want me to, help me do that? You know *that* is the real reason I don't do lunches with lobbyists, hit the cocktail circuit or attend dinners with the various senator groups. It's why I go to the gym and leave before anyone else gets there. I don't want to become an insider."

"Do you know why Richard's got elected and then reelected two more times?" asked Chuck.

"I have an idea."

"Because he was a party man. He supported some bills he may not have agreed with to get the same level of support for his bills. Others in his party may not have fully supported his either, but that's the way it works on the hill. It is the ultimate sausage factory. The product is edible and sometimes tasty, but no one wants to see it made," said Chuck. "Senator Richards brought lots of federal tax dollars to Colorado, supported the military, and got their support in return."

"I get it. Fontana even used the sausage factory analogy. But that was Richard's character and his desire to stay in Washington. I didn't know him, so I can't question his integrity. From what I've seen so far in the Senate, it doesn't surprise me. I'm not Richards. No, I didn't have to go through an election to win this role. And no, I would never have run for this, having no desire to compromise my principles."

"That is a bit of an unfair characterization," answered Chuck. "Look at Senator Banks. He is a guy who devoted 70 years of his life to his country. No different from serving in the military. He would argue he has had to make limitless sacrifices. Including compromising his principles again and again, to ensure the greater good was served in the long run. You should spend some time talking to him and get a unique perspective before you throw away your potential career. I believe you can do this job and keep your integrity intact."

"All I can do is vote my conscience."

"So, you really aren't interested in getting elected to a full term?" Chuck's shoulders appeared to sag in his seat as he said this.

"I didn't say that. But if I can't really do what Colorado citizens want, what is the point?"

"Maybe we should arrange some town halls and a visit back," proposed Chuck.

"Let's do it. I need to get out of here and talk to real folks back home. To get a feel for the way the people think on some of these key issues. I'm just concerned we're disconnected from the people struggling day to day to pay their rent or put food on their table. I doubt they are in favor of sending 750 billion dollars overseas."

Chuck stood up once more, gesturing with his hands. "Nick, of course they wouldn't. But they don't understand all the complex interconnections between international diplomacy and business. The push and pull. The 'official' bribes to affect behavior that ultimately benefits us in the long run. All of this is the purview of the experts in government."

Nick made a face at Chuck's praise of the government bureaucracy.

"Like it or not, we have created the most complex Rube Goldberg machine anyone could imagine. It takes hundreds, even thousands, to understand all the interconnects. Every action has a consequence. Many are unintended or unrealized until they happen. We have these armies of experts to understand all the potential consequences. Have you ever heard of the Butterfly Effect?"

"Sure, the idea a simple action has a major impact in an unintended way," answered Nick.

"Correct. Now imagine globally, we make thousands of these minor actions in a bill like the one you reference. You sometimes see us giving aid and comfort to our supposed enemies. Our experts have analyzed the probable outcomes of them doing x or doing y. Determining the probability of the outcome we want. Outweighing the chance it will go against us. These decisions are calculated."

Chuck stood, beer in one hand, gesturing to make his points.

"It may seem wasteful, stupid, and sometimes betrayal, but trust me, this is hard stuff. This is why you, as a member of Congress, aren't expected to understand and know all of this detail. Instead, you trust people like Bob to advise you on the efficacy of a proposed piece of legislation." Chuck held up his hand as Nick started to respond.

"Hang on. I know there are partisan items in every piece of legislation. This is Washington. There is too much money available to be allocated and each Congressman, at least those who want to be re-elected, will jostle and push to get their snout deeper into the trough, all for their constituents, of course," finished Chuck sarcastically.

"You just gave the most eloquent and concise description of exactly what is wrong in Congress. Not the justification of the process you think you gave me. You fully believe the Bureaucratic State is here to stay and is really in charge of our policies. We are figureheads and reliant on these bureaucrats to *tell us what to do*. Right?" asked Nick, now standing.

"I'm not sure it is that black and white, but it is the reality we face as the lone, friendly superpower in the world. We alone make global supply chains possible. Without us, it is World War I again, or maybe even further back than that. Someone must lead. It's super complex and unrealistic to think a bunch of career politicians have the knowledge of a broad series of critical subject areas to decide to support or suppress items. It's just not realistic Nick." Chuck continued, still trying to help Nick understand the impossible task faced by the US Government officials daily to keep the wheels turning. Not just at home, but globally.

Nick frowned. "I can see your point and your belief this is the only way to manage the situation. However, I reject the entire premise. It's a self-fulfilling prophecy of the Government gobbling up more and more decision-making power. Then centralizing this power and perspective in a massive government corporation unbeholden to the electorate, its shareholders. Levying taxes on people and deciding to spend this collected revenue with no consequence for poor decisions. Only subsequent decisions by the same people who get it wrong to demand more money to fix the problem they created. This is a circular cluster fuck. It will never stop unless we come to our senses," accused Nick.

"With all due respect, that is hopelessly naïve. What would you propose? Idiot Senators like Fontana deciding whether to fund plasmid DNA research for vaccines versus viral vectors or mRNA? Or instead opting to go with monoclonal antibody technologies. Who should get the bulk of the funding and why?" asked Chuck, exasperated.

"I'd have to study up on the information," replied Nick.

"Exactly. Did you get a PhD in molecular biology and genetics in between all those calls shilling for money?" interrupted Chuck. "How can you trust what you would read when each piece is written to ensure the decision the writer wants? For or against? The bureaucracy is here to stay, it is the engine running America, and ultimately the world," finished Chuck, almost pleading with Nick to see the bigger picture.

"Despite what you may think, I understand what you are saying. I have walked the production line in this sausage factory that is

American Government, and I'm frankly disgusted. I now understand why people go vegan," said Nick, now holding up *his* hand to stop Chuck from responding.

"My turn. I would ask you, who says it must be like this? Woodrow Wilson gave us this mess of a framework of experts and FDR made it a permanent reality. LBJ supercharged it and every President since has added their own 'factories' to the Bureaucratic Industrial Complex. Can you agree this is true?"

"Only in the most simplistic of views is it true," said Chuck, shaking his head.

"My question is, all these functions are ultimately local, right? The actual work is being done somewhere at the state or local level. Somebody opened their factory in a certain place. This is a local decision. What would happen if all these decisions were once again being made locally? If they left these decisions to the corporations and the local communities and states to make without sending all their revenue to Washington?" asked Nick.

"What?" responded Chuck, frustrated. "Absolute chaos and corruption if you left it to the states. This would be a disaster. Each would promise the moon, like no property taxes forever, to locate the Tesla plant in their town and on and on."

"It happens today already. That's my point. We collect tons of taxes and arbitrarily decide where to spend it regardless of where it comes from. Then we borrow tons more to spend on other pet projects. Think about it. If the money were instead collected in the states and spent in the states. If many of these national programs so fraught with waste and corruption, were suddenly shrunk and sliced into 50 state programs. They would be more efficient as each state would be obligated to serve its citizens well or risk them moving to states that did a better job. Focus on citizen satisfaction or risk them taking their business and tax dollars elsewhere. Its already begun with folks leaving mismanaged states and flocking to others." Nick paced around Chuck's cramped office, gesturing with his hands as he continued.

"Their neighbors would hold those local politicians accountable. Not some faceless bureaucrats in some Washington department who claim a seasonal puddle is a protected wetland. If we governed this way, the way the founders expected us to, then the Fed could go back to what we designed it to do. National policies like securing the border, maintaining an army, and protecting trade on the high seas," finished Nick.

Chuck walked a circle and held his hands up. "Where is this coming from? You talk to a couple of billionaires and suddenly you are dismantling 125 years of government bureaucracy? A process, I might add that won two world wars, put a man on the moon, created modern electronics, put a supercomputer in everyone's hand, built the world wide web, cured Polio and hosts of other diseases, mapped the human genome and will eventually get us to colonize other planets. Feats all spearheaded by this bureaucracy you hold in contempt," countered Chuck, beseeching Nick to see reason.

"I don't deny all of that progress. But I'm afraid to tell you, the level of innovation is diminishing as the bureaucracy gets more prevalent. Freedom allowed innovation, not bureaucracy. Capitalism enabled all of this because there was a reward to be had by those who solved the problems. Not regulations. This is why so little of this occurred outside the US. Socialism, authoritarianism and, most significantly, communism, do not and did not promote individuality. It didn't offer anyone a reason to solve a problem other than coercion. Take away the heavy hand of the state, and you free the doers, the innovators, the entrepreneurs to do their thing."

"Capitalism is also responsible for the massive gap between rich and poor, my friend," said Chuck in response.

"I don't disagree. But the alternative being proposed isn't the solution. You've listened to our Party leaders. You've heard Lexi layout the Progressive platform of her candidacy. It coerces 50% or more of the population into knuckling under if they want to continue to be employed. This isn't conducive to continuing innovation. Fear and paranoia don't create solutions. They create a desire for self-preservation. What's the end game except the destruction of our capitalistic society? There's no other path if we continue. Do you disagree?" asked Nick.

"Well, I don't have the answer, but destroying the US Government as it exists now is probably not how I'd start," said Chuck, shrugging.

"Buddy, somebody had better think about it or we are going to be looking back going WTF. Why didn't we stop this?" prophesized Nick.

"Nick, you're one man. You have to accept this is how it works."

"Do I?"

"Just promise me you won't start talking like this in public. Please?" said Chuck again in a pleading voice.

"For now. I'm hungry. Take me to one of these restaurants you keep telling me I need to try."

"Without reservations?" laughed Chuck. "Forget it. But I can find a local bistro or something in Georgetown. Am I driving as well?"

"You know I don't have a car in this city. Impossible to find a parking spot and even then, you pay an arm and a leg."

"You have a parking spot in the garage, Senator," noted Chuck as they walked out.

"Really? Did they cover that in orientation?" asked Nick, playing dumb and smiling as they headed to the Senate parking garage and the parking spot Chuck paid an arm and a leg for every month.

Part Two

Outside the Bubble

"If more government is the answer, it was a really stupid question."

Ronald Reagan

Chapter 12

A youngish man in a tailored suit stood in front of the conference room table. He was delivering a presentation displayed on the holographic screen projected in the air above the table.

"As you can see, our list of funded organizations is now over two hundred around the world. We continue to see outstanding results and a significant return on our investments," he said in accented English, looking at the elderly man at the head of the table. They were the only two in the massive room.

"Petr, I am aware of our broad reach. What I would like to know is more details about some of the activities and their success. How is our funding helping?" asked the old man, also in accented English. His betrayed the clipped cadence of the British upper classes, honed at Oxford and Cambridge.

"Of course, Mr. Pavlovich. I have slides on these efforts."

Maksim Pavlovich sighed, "Petr, I am old school, but my memory is fine. Just tell me."

"Yes sir. Through your World Harmony Society, we fund many progressive organizations who continue to drive our messages and activities. We have given many American non-profits tens of millions for this presidential election cycle. They are all instrumental in organizing ballot harvesting organizations in every state where it is legal. Also in others, where the harvesters are not allowed to bring the ballots to the polling places. In those, we are still instructing them to be involved in 'assisting' in the filling out of ballots. Finding loopholes and using them to drive turnout. Ensuring votes are being made for our preferred candidates. Of course, where harvesting is allowed, they are helping fill out the ballot or, at a minimum, observing who they are voting for in the elections; president, congress, secretary of state, attorney general, etc." Petr Novik paused, referring to his stack of printed papers, flipping pages.

"They collect all the ballots and carefully segregate them for our candidates and for those we do not support. While it is illegal to destroy the ballots of our opponents. I am told many end up 'accidentally' falling into storm drains on their way to the ballot boxes, never to be seen," smiled Petr.

Pavlovich nodded slightly in approval of these 'accidents'.

"These groups target primarily the elderly in nursing homes, poor minorities in densely populated urban cities, veterans in VA homes, and the homeless. Most of them would not vote otherwise. In some areas, they are also striving to get the young motivated to vote. Increasingly the professors are accomplishing this with the students already. Getting them involved in our causes, activism, and agitation as their civic duty."

"Excellent. We need to maximize all ways to sway voter tallies," said Pavlovich, nodding.

"We have already had exceptional success using these tactics to win Secretary of States, Attorney's General and other positions. Anywhere these roles are elected versus appointed. We now control many of the state election processes and all the elected roles in the major swing states in America," confirmed Petr as a map of the individual United States appeared on the screen.

The states where they 'owned' various of these elected positions showed different colored lines denoting each. Almost every state had at least one elected official shown as aligned to the World Harmony Society NGOs.

"Exactly what we need to ensure the culmination of our plans. Any of them getting pushback or scrutiny we can help with?" asked Pavlovich.

"The Arizona Governor, Secretary of State and election commissioner are all beholden to us. They are putting in place more and earlier mail in balloting procedures in the name of transparency and voter accessibility. They are being targeted by some lawsuits from the usual places. We are dumping money into the defense funds and reminding our judges who got them elected. Especially the ones up for reelection in the Presidential election cycle next year."

"We continue pressuring the major local newscasts and papers to keep this out of the news. All are getting some funding from one or more of our groups. I think we will prevail in keeping it obscure," explained Petr.

"If we need to buy some more TV stations or newspapers in these key districts and cities in these states, let's not let that stop us," ordered Pavlovich with a satisfied little laugh.

"Not necessary. There is enough leverage on many of them from just purchasing their debt. WHS has accrued quite a portfolio of both commercial debt on the newspapers and stations in about forty key counties in swing states."

"We've also quietly acquired all the personal debt for key officials in all these municipalities as well. Both mortgage and college loan debt for them and any children, plus any personal debt they may have as well. We have all the tools we need to *convince* them to be helpful," confirmed Petr, shuffling through his pile of notes.

"It is amazing what one can do in a capitalist society," laughed Pavlovich. "There is nothing it seems money cannot buy."

"As the Chinese have done with the Universities and research scientists in America as well," agreed Petr.

"Not to mention members of the administration's family. What about the voter ID status?" asked Pavlovich, shifting in his chair and adjusting the cardigan sweater he wore over his knit shirt. He looked the part of the kindly old grandfather, with wispy gray hair on the sides of his mostly bald head and reading glasses perched on top of his forehead. His eyes betrayed a fiery passion and intensity few could hold for more than a second.

Petr continued, "Once again, the millions we have invested in a variety of groups are paying off. Our American activist organizations successfully advocate that requiring photo IDs is disenfranchising the poor and minorities in urban settings. The university groups and various other voter participation orgs, all aimed at the twenty somethings, are getting them to rally and protest against any form of intrusive IDs as discriminatory and against social justice values."

"Finally, the civil liberties groups are working tirelessly to block any lawsuits on legal grounds. We even filed one lawsuit in Georgia, implying voter ID lawsuits were themselves perpetrating a hate crime against blacks. This, combined with some sympathetic coverage on ANC and local news, got almost 100,000 to march on the state capital demanding the legislation be dropped. It was."

Pavlovich showed his yellowed teeth in a crooked smile.

"Sir, I will add though, that private polling shows as high as 75% believe the elections are now fraudulent enough to affect the outcomes. A growing number favors voter IDs to help solve this. Including increasing calls to use biometrics. We cannot keep this up forever," he said cautiously.

"Petr, worry not. This has happened and look how we handled the various recounts, recalls, forensic audits, and digital examination requests." Pavlovich raised his hands as he explained. "We throw roadblocks up. Our officials refuse to comply with subpoenas. There are many tools to delay."

"The public in America has a brief attention span. For those who do not, we simply tie them up in litigation or we inundate their media outlets with counter propaganda. We make it look like *they* are the ones sowing doubt and trying to compromise the voting integrity. This has worked incredibly well so far." Pavlovich grabbed a small pitcher of water and poured a glass as he continued.

"How are we doing on the re-codifying *Roe* front? The conservative Supreme Court is worrisome," he asked.

Petr pulled a document from his stack. "The court has thrown the decisions back to the states. As you are aware, the conservative states have passed many individual bills to limit access. We are funding the efforts to tie these up in the courts. Preventing them from becoming law until the Supreme Court can be expanded. Then a new Roe passed by Congress, rather than overturned by judicial fiat, can be enacted."

"Planned Parenthood?" asked Pavlovich.

"Sir?" replied Petr in a questioning tone.

"Are they being affected?"

"They are still far and away the predominant organization providing abortion in America. Black abortions continue to rise, almost 1 abortion for every 1 birth now. Some attribute this to fewer young people surviving. The mortality rate amongst the 14 to 25-year-old black males in America is among the highest in the world. Between this and abortions, the black population in America is quickly declining to less than 11% and showing no signs of recovering. Within three more generations, the black population in America will resemble Native Americans in both lack of influence and abject poverty," finished Petr.

"You know Petr, Planned Parenthood was the first American organization I funded when I began this crusade. They have been faithfully doing their part to keep the population down. Preventing more poor souls from being born into disastrous and miserable lives in ghettos and slums. The charter of Margaret Sanger is coming true even if it took well over 100 years." Petr nodded slightly at this revelation.

"It was my suggestion to shift their public narrative to focus on 'women's health' rather then terminating fetuses," commented Pavlovich, thinking back to when he started using his massive wealth to remake societies.

"Indeed, it is working, sir. One out of every three births in the US is now Hispanic. With the influx of illegals across the border to the tune of 15 million or more during this administration, it will only take a decade, two at the most, before the white majority falls. Leading to a new demographic where people of Hispanic origin will be the predominant races for the latter half of the century. Along with the Indian Subcontinent and China, of course. These three will make up the dominant races."

"Good," nodded Pavlovich again. "Demographics are our friend for implementing our changes. When Lexi takes over, she will help us speed up by implementing more programs to keep the rich from getting richer on the backs of the workers around the world. We are already using our agents in the colleges to convince the youth of the stupidity and selfishness of acquiring wealth as a sign of success. It appears to be working well. Many are not saving for houses and appear to be happy working only enough to support their lifestyles. They are foregoing marriage and childbirth until much later, if they do either at all." Pavlovich looked up at Petr to continue the briefing.

"We are getting the young college educated whites to give up on following their parent's example. This should keep the US from meddling in the global governance plans," said Petr as Pavlovich nodded in agreement, reaching for his water glass. He took a small sip while holding the glass in a claw-like, bony hand.

"Anything else?"

"You had asked for a cultural update. We aim many of our efforts at politics and the big items like abortion in the US. I thought it would be good to see how some of our cultural investments are paying off."

Pavlovich just smiled, nodding.

"I am happy to report in twenty-three states in the US, elementary school children are no longer saying the Pledge of Allegiance. We continue to put pressure on the other twenty-seven using diversity and racial undertones of the pledge as the reasoning behind removing it. We are making tremendous progress in the elementary school curriculum via our control of the American teachers' unions with our various funding arms," Petr, referred to his notes as he reported more facts about the declining nature of American education efforts.

"We have an avowed Communist in the lead role at the biggest teacher's union. They are pushing against anything conservative and forcing their teachers to teach all our key disuniting programs. Critical Race Theory, pronoun idiocy, and the silliness of children being able to choose their gender. Sex education for 2nd graders and, of course, our most successful controlling scheme yet, the 'science and fear' of climate change."

"It is positively stunning to watch the fear our programs have put into the minds of every child in the US," said Petr with a smile. "We've spent the last thirty years convincing an entire generation of gullible Americans they are destroying the planet, just as the rest of the world continues to pollute at even greater rates."

"This overarching fear is allowing us to promote and drive our plans by attaching them to our twin pillars of climate change and systemic racism," concluded Petr.

Pavlovich, a broad smile on his face at the recitation of their success, spoke. "It is amazing that America and capitalism produced such advances and innovations, given their complete stupidity and lack of common sense to expose what we are promoting. Look at China, and Russia. Even the French tried stopping the American ideals of climate change and cancel culture and now the gender identity obsessions from taking root in their countries." Pavlovich shook his head disbelievingly. "In fact, they use American decline and divisiveness as the example for what NOT to allow to become popular in their countries. The American leadership of both parties is powerless to stop us. This is ultimately the soft underbelly of capitalism. It promotes individualism."

"Sir, it seems like they are slow to react and appear unable to respond to the protest activities."

"Individualism prevents them from standing up and trying to stop this. Each one of them may be thriving as the world crumbles around them. As long as it does not affect them directly, they won't stand up. Until each of them is feeling pain, nothing will change. Just as it was in Rome. Too late, they will realize their mistake."

"It seems to be almost too easy to divide them. In our wildest dreams, we never expected the people to just sit there and take it. Instead of standing up and fighting or demanding justice, they just retreated into their shells and hunkered down from the storm, expecting it to blow over," said Petr in surprise.

"I think this was a case of us not understanding the level of cultural rot. Our friends in Hollywood were much more successful at their denigration of the John Wayne and Gary Cooper values replacing them with touchy feely Hanks, Pitt, and DiCaprio. Add social media to the mix and the narcissism it has created. Freud would have a field day," laughed Pavlovich.

"Fentanyl, opioids, and the elimination of the two-parent household with no fault divorce, plus the prevalence of out of marriage children, they really never stood a chance. Affluence ruins cultures. Always has. Further, the experiment in democracy was destined to fail because they never dealt with slavery at the creation. This was a ticking time bomb. We have set it off multiple times in multiple ways. It is amazing what you can do with a bit of money, total control of the media outlets; TV, social, and movies," smiled Pavlovich.

"Indeed, sir. The silly thing is they all think it is organic and honest and naturally occurring. It is hard to remember when people around the world felt the Americans were the best at anything. They are now more ignorant than the meanest Chinese peasant."

"Some of them at least," agreed Pavlovich. "I think most of them are just being quiet and staying out of the line of fire. Remember, we cannot fall into the same trap our friends in the American media and Congress have fallen into. Believing they have captured the hearts and minds of most of the population with their leftist leanings."

"America is not yet ready for full on Socialism. Our friend Ms. Smythe-Thomas still has her work cut out for her to make that a reality. The latest generation of college aged kids will soon join their older brothers and sisters. Graduating with frivolous degrees without earning potential to match their student loan debt. Taking jobs that prevent them from building wealth or purchasing a house. Driving them into the willing arms of our progressive friends with their inclusivity, diversity, and the equity of government assistance. And the 'carrot' of forgiving their student debt."

"More of them are rightfully looking to the government to help take care of them at all stages of their life. This is the first step to destroy capitalism and the individualistic work ethic. Once this desire is no longer the primary goal of education and life, we can rewire people to think about each other first," concluded Pavlovich.

"Sir, how did you know this would work? You have spent billions of dollars over the last fifty years."

"My concern was always about the effects of one power rule on the planet. When that one power was a dispassionate capitalist society with an insatiable appetite for material. I grew concerned. I was never worried about the climate. Nature affects the planet in far greater and more immediate ways than man burning fossil fuel. One only needs to study an ice age to understand man has a miniscule impact on the planet. Man can easily make the planet uninhabitable through nuclear war, bio-engineered plague like COVID, biological mutations run amok from laboratories, or potentially Artificial Intelligence. But burning fossil fuels? Not likely, unless of course you grow to an unmanageable population," explained Pavlovich, pausing again to drink.

"Thankfully, man is prideful. In fact, I equate climate change to the Catholic Church who threw Galileo in jail for claiming, correctly, the Earth was not the center of the universe. Their entire premise of rule was based on them controlling the definition of the 'heavens'. To admit they were wrong would cost them all credibility and, more importantly, their hold on wealth and power. It is the same today with climate change. The progressives have too much invested in the hoax to admit it was all based on lies and flawed scientific analysis. To admit it is flawed would be too costly in terms of money and control. So, it must go on."

Petr nodded. "It does not seem to be in any danger of disappearing."

"What worried me more was the population. I am far more concerned with the rising standard of living and the length of life. Malthus had it right, our biggest man-made threat is population. The eradication of disease has allowed mass infant mortality to become less and less, even in places like Africa and India."

"Because of this, they have corralled the four horsemen of the Apocalypse. This is the problem. I believe the planet used pestilence, famine, war, and death from natural disaster as limiters on the ability of Earth to support its population."

"We have messed up the balance. I have made it my quest to free these four horsemen to ride again. America and their efforts to guarantee global trade have cheated the horsemen of their rewards. Once America and capitalism go, the world will fall into decline. This will lower the ability to respond to famine, to diseases and pandemics. Instead, we will fight over food and water, and lose the ability to respond to natural disaster."

"These will purge the world of billions of souls naturally and bring us back into balance. Where we can rebuild in a more communal society, one where there are no haves and have nots. Socialism only works when there is no alternative. When all must pull together, they will, or they will die," Pavlovich finished righteously.

"Sir, it is a worthy goal. Do you think we can achieve it?" asked Petr carefully.

"I do. America has indeed been that beacon on a hill, providing alternatives to socialism. As long as a successful America stood, people had alternatives and choices. Many chose that path or attempted to replicate it in their own countries. When we have fully discredited the American ideal and, trust me, we only had to start the avalanche and many of our friends have expanded the rate of destruction exponentially. Petr, it is what I live for. Without this crusade, I would long since have left this mortal world for the next," said Pavlovich with a gleam in his eye. "Thank you for the update."

"My pleasure sir" said Petr, gathering his notes and tablet and leaving the room, closing the door.

As he left, Maksim leaned back in his padded chair, deflated. Flipping up an arm on the console, he pressed a button. A concealed door in the paneled conference room slid open. A nurse came in, rolling an IV bag. She did not say a word and just walked to Pavlovich and rolled up his sleeve, revealing an IV port on a skinny arm. She connected the IV drip and left the room.

Pavlovich sat in silence as the liquid slowly entered his veins. He could feel the warmth of it as it spread throughout his body. This was his elixir of life. Twice a day he would receive a liter of this synthetic cocktail full of human growth hormone and other experimental drugs. While his body was frail and weak, his organs were not. He had already had many transplants to replace these. His mind was still razor sharp.

What he could not replace was muscle, tissue, and bones. He spent tens of millions every year funding all manner of experimental research. In molecular biology, nanotechnology, cellular growth, and cloning in hopes of one day cheating death or replacing his tired shell with a rejuvenated one. Much of this experimentation was unethical and immoral, with no regard for test subjects or failed outcomes.

For Pavlovich, this was of little relevance. He had no conscience. Not caring who was hurt or helped by his policies or actions. There were only his goals and objectives and there was only the distance between start and completion. Anything in between was just time better spent contemplating other actions. He knew what needed to be done and his only regret was he had to rely on others to complete them. He closed his eyes and rested. Thinking always of endless permutations to speed up his plans. He rarely slept.

Chapter 13

Majority Leader Fontana paced around his desk and stood in front of the fireplace, staring up at the portrait of Woodrow Wilson above it.

"Yes, I had him in here," he spoke into his phone. He glanced at the door to his office to see a middle-aged overweight man with glasses poking his head in. Fontana motioned him in with a wave of his hand.

The man walked over to the well-stocked bar, while Fontana spoke in the background.

"I don't know what Morris was thinking when he nominated him to fill Richard's term. Actually, I know. He was worried about reelection. I warned him this guy was an unknown." The man handed Fontana a drink. Fontana's voice raised as he spoke into the phone, "I've got this under control. I'll handle it."

Fontana made a face and rolled his eyes while listening. "Of course I know we need every vote to overturn the filibuster. I *am* the Majority Leader, Lexi. I do know how to do the job."

Fontana held the phone away from his ear as a loud female voice rang out. "Yes, I'll talk to you later." Fontana ended the call and stared at his phone for a few seconds. He then paced back to his office chair and took a big sip from his drink.

"The Vice President getting concerned?" asked the man, settling into one chair by the fireplace.

Fontana turned, "You know Ben, I've been in politics for forty-five years, starting on the docks. I've busted my share of heads, but I always respected those I disagreed with. They were just wrong, and I had to show them the error of their ways," he said, holding up a fist. "I miss those days."

"Wish we still had duels?" chuckled Ben Hinton, Sal's chief of staff.

"You know it. Unfortunately, there would be a lot of vacancies in our own party, not so much the Opposition. My problems are here, not with the other team."

"How did your meeting with the Hero go?" asked Ben carefully.

"I gave him the crude mouthed New Jersey union guy treatment. Usually works, especially on newbies. He didn't seem the least bit intimidated. Maybe I should have used a softer touch given his military background. I figured since he was a Pentagon desk jockey, not a grunt in the trenches, the office and meeting Lexi on the way out would awe him. That's why she called. She's peeing on her designer shoes worrying about the filibuster vote."

"Are you?"

"Of course I am. It's my job to be worried. Our majority is two, and one of those is in a medically induced coma. I need all fifty of the remaining."

"We've been trying to get this passed for years. There always seems to be a glitch," sighed Ben.

"Well, we should have it this time. How's the polling?" asked Sal.

"You want the real polls or what our friends in the media are saying?" smirked Ben.

"Real first."

"In flyover country it keeps getting worse, up to about 75% against. Jamming through the voting laws with no bipartisan support stopped them from getting the house majority back. They're still trying to force audits and recounts 11 months later. Our mail in ballot expertise and ballot harvesting helped us overcome their momentum in the mid-terms," reported Ben. "They're pretty much against everything, so nothing new there. But once the filibuster goes, we can lock in the gains and not worry about public opinion at all."

"And on our side?"

"We are slipping a bit, only 63% are in favor, some naysayers are getting through to them and as you know, EXN ratings just keep going up. That isn't helping," informed Ben.

"When the filibuster goes, we'll shut EXN down," growled Sal. "Get rid of Tommy and those radio assholes, starting with Brad Hudson. They shouldn't be allowed to preach treason every day."

"I'm not sure that is a good idea. It would be better to use our influence to get at least one of our friends in the media to say something different. They not only use the same words, they use the same sentences and even the same tone. The guests say the same things. Our blind sheep eat it up, but we ain't fooling anyone who actually thinks."

"Good thing they don't think. I don't see a problem," smiled Sal. "Sounds like they are earning their pay."

"You laugh, but I think we are playing into their hands. They keep saying the media is propaganda and just parroting our message and they would be right. Just looking at any two stations proves that."

"So? That has been going on for years, hell, for decades." Sal pulled a cigar from the desk as he finished.

"But not like they are all reading from a script provided by us. Maybe we could afford to have multiple scripts using different words to be sent to different stations," suggested Ben, shaking his head.

"Ben, we aren't providing them scripts. Let's face it, these people aren't the sharpest sticks in the pencil box," he answered, cutting the tip from his cigar and making a big show of lighting it. "They all parrot what they hear because they don't have an original thought."

"Just remember, I warned you. We're forcing more and more people to think and look at other places for different viewpoints. Eventually some of them are going to wake up and realize what we say, and the truth, are very different." Ben wrinkled up his nose as Sal exhaled a gigantic cloud of smoke.

"Ben, even if the so called 'EXcellence in News' network continues to lead the ratings and beats the networks regularly, let's be pragmatic. They hit what, four, maybe five million? So what? The networks still add up to seven or eight million. You throw in FLCN and the twelve people watching ANC and we have nine to ten million minimum. That's still twice as many as EXN. Most of our supporters don't even watch the news."

"You have a point, but it is still something we may want to tweak, just so they don't all sound like the Ministry of Truth," stated Ben in a concerned tone.

"As long as they stay the course and keep reporting what we need, we'll get to a point where it won't matter. Red state America can whine all they want when our boot is on their throat," said Sal in a menacing tone.

"Even if you mean that, and I hope you don't, it would be best to not be so obvious in your intent and plans," responded Ben, grimacing.

"Gotcha. You're the one who brought up the Ministry of Truth. I figured I would call your bet and see you with a Ministry of Love reference. I read *1984* too," remarked Sal, puffing on his cigar.

"Well, in the spirit of lying, we're telling the media and our polling friends, we need them to report our support at two-thirds minimum. It looks like we have the support we need from the public even if we don't," replied Ben, moving to a seat on the opposite side of the fireplace and further from Sal's stench.

"We just need to get it done. Have you been able to find anything on the Hero?" asked Sal, switching topics while he got up and headed to the bar. "Refill?"

Ben shook his head. "No thanks, I didn't grow up on the docks slamming whiskey shots. I'll be asleep if I have another one."

"Just as well, I'm pouring the good stuff. You sure you don't want a cigar?" asked Sal with a smile, knowing his chief of staff hated them.

"That figures. You pour the good stuff when you know I don't want to be anywhere near your stinky cigar. You know my wife hates it when I come home smelling like an ashtray."

"Get a new wife. I did," said Sal, smiling.

"I can't afford a new wife on what you pay me."

Sal offered no rebuttal.

"Back to what I found on the Hero," said Ben, looking at a tablet. "I have to say there isn't a lot out there. Only child. Unremarkable childhood, nothing special in High School. Played sports, but no scholarships. Academic or athletic. Parents are both dead, car accident. No foul play, just bad weather and part of a gigantic pile up when he just started college. State college in Texas. Naval ROTC. Two degrees, one in history, another in English. It appears he graduated in only two years. Took heavy course loads, including summer semesters. We're seeing if we can track down professors, old girlfriends, etc."

"Hmm. That takes a lot of dedication and drive. What was his hurry? He didn't show that in high school," mused Fontana.

"It gets more interesting after school. Navy commission after college just before 9/11. Served as an Intelligence officer. Eventually he attended the War College and got a Master's from Georgetown. Did both at the same time while assigned to the Pentagon for two years. Apparently, this guy now loves to study. Resigned his commission as a lieutenant commander after twelve years, but no reason given. At least nothing we can find yet. He immediately re-upped in the Air National Guard, starting as a captain," read Ben from his notes.

"Wait a minute, a lieutenant commander is the equivalent of a major in the Air Force. To get that high in twelve years is pretty rare. He goes to the War College as a lieutenant commander, gets his masters, and then leaves after flying up the ranks? Switches branches, and takes a demotion to fly for the National fucking Guard? There has to be something there," said Sal. "Find it."

Ben just nodded, referring to his notes as he went on. "He must have already known how to fly. Only had an abbreviated training course of six weeks before he deployed to Afghanistan to fly A-10s. Did eight years in Afghanistan and Iraq and never rotated home once. He was quickly promoted from captain to major, probably because he already had twelve years of service and his willingness to stay deployed."

"Made lieutenant colonel after three years of constant combat. His eight years without rotation home makes him among a handful of the longest deployed officers in the war. Most of the others are non-coms. He also did at least one tour, maybe more, in Iraq and Afghanistan when he was in the Navy, but they redacted a lot of that, as is some of his ANG record."

Sal interrupted Ben. "Redacted? Interesting. Go on."

"Resigned his Air Force commission after the surge tapped down ISIS just before we announced our pullout. He retired as a full colonel. When I asked to see past the redactions, I was politely told to fuck off."

"Really? Should have looked harder before we nominated him. Morris was just giddy at the thought of selecting the Hero and the bump in his approval. Which he got," admitted Sal.

"He has a few medals from both stints. But I suspect there is more in the redacted sections. I could see a Navy Distinguished Service Medal, a Silver Star with a V for Valor, and a couple of Purple Hearts. Not exactly sure how a Navy Intelligence officer gets top honors for valor like these, but we are checking. No luck so far. For the Air National Guard, he has at least one Distinguished Flying Cross with Valor. They show three Purple Hearts. Not sure if that is total, or three more from the guard. Lots more redactions on these medals and other hidden commendations too. That suicide bomber in New York messed with the wrong guy," said Ben with a chuckle.

"Doesn't sound like a desk jockey. But it isn't like he was a SEAL or a Delta. He was an intel geek and a weekend warrior flyboy. Doesn't make him Chuck fucking Norris," said Sal with a snort. "Plus, he got the shit stabbed out of himself in New York."

"True, but he obviously runs to the danger, and he got the Presidential Medal of Freedom with Distinction, also a rarity, for that episode," said Ben.

"Don't bring that up. We may come to regret our idiot president doing that. And further, his comments that he would have awarded it with Valor if the option existed. Thankfully, we stopped him from changing the award. As if Turner did more than the guys who went to the moon the first time," snorted Sal in obvious disgust at the mention of the current President's actions.

"Regardless, he really qualifies as a hero," said Ben, continuing to review his notes. "Funny thing is, he didn't stay in the reserves, Navy or Air Force. A full colonel in the reserves draws decent pay for their reserve duties, but he opted out. Why drop out when you make colonel faster than just about anyone? That usually means you have general's stars in your future. Why give up all that work and effort?" asked Ben in disbelief.

"I agree," growled Sal. "There has to be a reason. Find it."

Ben nodded. "After the service, he started a small consulting company, mostly management stuff, before signing up to teach history. He was a visiting professor of history at Colorado State these last few years."

"Finances?" asked Sal.

"He has good savings and 401k, and owns a house outright in Fort Collins, Colorado. Decent inheritance from his parents and a half million insurance payout, but it looks like he touched none of the money. Just sitting in investments. He has a couple million in net worth. No debt. Doesn't seem to spend his money on much. Pretty unremarkable life, really, nothing at all out of the norm. He really is a nobody if you take out his military service and heroics in New York City. He didn't even cash in on that. Turned down offers and went back to teaching. Very strange." Ben looked up from his notes.

"Shit, a real fucking boy scout. I told that asshole Morris to pick someone safe, but he was up for reelection, and he wanted the photo op with the Hero. I'll cut his nuts off if his boy doesn't play ball," growled Fontana.

"Anything you can offer him?" asked Ben.

"I dangled a spot in Lexi's administration. He didn't even flinch. Hell, eight of her primary opponents are only in the race to get in her administration; he didn't even seem to care. Remind me not to invite him to our poker games. I bet he bluffs with the best of them."

"I'll keep digging, but so far nothing we can use. If he toes the line, we could get him re-elected in a heartbeat," admitted Ben.

"We'll see. Dig into his financials. See if he has any friends. We need to find some leverage if it comes to threats. Everyone has something. He's single, find out why. Might be something there."

"Got it," said Ben, getting up to go.

"Also, dig into the military more, especially the Navy Intelligence bits. Let's get through the redactions. If he was in the Navy in the early days around 9/11, there may be something there. If you have any trouble, let me know and I'll get Haskins from the Intel committee to authorize a better look. You don't throw away a Navy career after twelve years to go fly jets for the fucking Air National Guard. That by itself should raise some flags. Find out the story. And find something sexy. Everyone has old girlfriends or, even better, boyfriends in their closet," laughed Sal, chewing on his stinky Cuban.

Ben nodded as he left the office, smelling his sleeve, getting a whiff of Sal's cigar. He headed for his office to change shirts before heading home to his wife.

Once Ben left, Sal refilled his drink and settled his bulky frame back in the chair behind his desk. He puffed his cigar and picked up his phone. Another voice answered. Without introduction, Sal started talking. "I may need some help to dig into Turner's military history. Can you do some background?" Sal listened intently for a minute before leaning forward.

"You know what? I really don't give a shit about being careful and worrying about Inspector Generals and spying on people's backgrounds. He served in the military and the taxpayers paid him. I'm the Majority Leader of those taxpayers and I want, no I need, to know what the military is hiding about him. Get me those records, got it?" commanded Sal, working himself up into a frenzy, spilling his expensive bourbon on his desk blotter as he waved his arms in disgust.

"Just get it done," he said, banging his phone down. He looked at the puddle of booze on his blotter, finally leaning over to slurp it off the desktop. "Too good to waste," he said to himself.

Chapter 14

Jean Paul Gaspard, the President of France, paced in his office, talking on the phone. He was speaking English into the phone.

"I will do what is in the best interest of the French citizens and law and order," said Gaspard in a stern tone in response to a statement from the caller. "Do not lecture me on our response. We have successfully broken them up this weekend," replied Gaspard, gesturing as he spoke. He listened intently, his face getting redder by the moment.

"*Qui pensez-vous être, me disant comment diriger mon pays?*" yelled Gaspard into the phone, slipping back into French. "I repeat, I will do what I feel is best for France. Good day, sir," he said, hanging up the phone. Gaspard paced the room while his Prime Minister, Alain Chaumont, observed, but did not speak.

Jean Paul turned to Chaumont. "Casualties from the riots this weekend?" he asked in French.

"Three dead protesters, thirteen hospitalized. We have two of our men hurt. Both should recover," answered Chaumont.

"The dead?"

"All Muslims from the quarter. One twenty-two and one twenty-nine-year-old male, both from Morocco. One seventeen-year-old French-born female. Her family immigrated from Algeria thirty years ago," recited Chaumont, reading from his phone.

"How?" asked Gaspard.

"Death and injuries occurred in the confusion when the police started using the tear gas and water to disperse the crowd."

"Damage?" asked Jean Paul, as he stood by the window looking out over the cloud of smoke hanging over northeastern Paris.

"There are fires burning in the Muslim *banlieue*. They are spreading throughout the northeastern suburbs. They won't allow the fire brigades inside to fight the fire. We are calling up the army and several tanks to escort them in. We have instructed them to fight their way in against the protestors. To protect those living there, and to keep the fires from spreading to other parts of Paris," replied Alain.

Gaspard put a hand to his forehead and pushed it through his thick, black hair. "What has happened Alain? Why now?"

"This has been a simmering tea pot for decades. No one has addressed the issues for fear of the backlash. We simply ignore them, hoping it will change or leave it to the next president. No one wants to fix it. It will be unpopular," shrugged Alain.

"This is all the fault of the Americans and their encouragement of all these racial protests. First, they export their cultural rot, and then they export their own problems to us. Well, I will not allow it," said Jean Paul, deciding, turning from the window.

"We can confirm there are financial sources in the US, but many are here in France amongst our far-left parties and in other countries in the EU. They are all funneling money to the anti-racist league organizations here. Millions of Euros," explained Alain.

"Alain, these ARL are mere fronts for the totalitarians, the communists. Cut them off. Seize their bank accounts. I will declare them enemies of the state. Set up a press conference. Anyone supporting anarchy will be considered a traitor to the Republic. The Americans are afraid of them. We are not. Protests were one thing, but now they are endangering other citizens and challenging our rule of law. We need to hold them accountable for their actions. I don't care if they are a celebrity, a billionaire, or a football star. This is not the way of France. We will warn them. This is not acceptable," declared Gaspard.

"Do you think this is wise? Announcing it, I mean. They elected us to mitigate the policies of the previous administration. We are Socialists, we should support this movement. Perhaps we just do it and not broadcast our intentions. If that was who I think it was on the phone, they wield a lot of power and have many spies and moles, and members of parliament in their pocket. If we go public, we give them a chance to rouse public opinion against our suppression plans," suggested Alain, trying to talk reason to his friend.

"I appreciate your concern and advice. These people are working in the shadows, pulling strings and funding dissent. They are doing this to drive us apart, for their benefit. We must make a stand. The longer we wait, the stronger they get. The groups they represent are not the people of France, nor are they representing the immigrants. They care not for France. They care only for their own schemes. We will not allow others to tell us what to do in France. We must stand strong. Our stance must be forceful and public. We need the common people who are cowed and afraid to know we are with them," uttered Gaspard in a forceful and patriotic tone.

"Ok, I will get the directives issued and set up your press conference," replied Alain reluctantly.

#

Two hours later, President Gaspard stood outside on the steps of the Ministry of Justice before a crowd of several thousand supporters. They had announced the rally with such short notice; the protesters were just now arriving at the back of the crowd and were being held back by the police.

Gaspard continued his speech, announcing his intentions to declare the French ARL protest orgs and several other home-grown groups agitating for racial equity, enemies of the state. He also laid out his plans to discover and prosecute any domestic and foreign entities contributing money to these organizations as accomplices in their treasonous activities to undermine French unity and society.

He implored the French citizens to come together in unity. To seek non-violent solutions to the issues of equal opportunity and equal citizenship. It was for France and its people to decide. Free from outside influence or the money of those who seek to remake France in a way not directed and not decided by French citizens.

A man stood apart, a good distance from the crowd in front of the President; a knit cap drawn low on his forehead. His dark eyes were all that showed above the upturned collar of his jacket. He stamped his feet and kept his hands in the pockets of his jacket to ward off the chill. Unlike everyone else in the crowd, who were staring at the President, this man's eyes were fixed on a man standing in the front row of the crowd.

He stood across from the podium, gently swaying back and forth. While everyone else raised their arms and cheered or clapped, the man in the front row showed no response to the speech's points, his arms hanging at his sides.

Gaspard continued his speech, reaching his conclusion. He was a charismatic speaker, able to rouse the emotions of his listeners. In closing, he laid out how he would use the army to restore order and assist the police in upholding the laws to protect *all* French citizens.

He promised to root out the outsiders and agitators, who were making the streets of Paris unsafe for all. The crowd gathered around the steps of the Ministry of Justice were cheering this decisive move by their president.

Gaspard had been a popular choice of a coalition of parties and was a little over three years into his five-year term as president. He felt he was doing the right thing for the country he loved. He was exhilarated by the response of the crowd as he led them in standing up to the agitators, finally.

Those were his last thoughts as an explosion tore through the crowd.

Chapter 15

Lexi was in her office in the Capitol when she got a call from Henry St. Cloud, the National Security Agency director.

"Henry?" she answered. "What? When? Gaspard? Oh my God. I knew things were bad there, but this is different. Of course, I'll get there as fast as we can."

They ushered Lexi into the Situation Room deep beneath the White House. The President, the CIA and NSA directors, along with Admiral Jason Kensington, the Chairman of the Joint Chiefs, and the President's chief of staff, Sam Vincent were all gathered. The US Ambassador to France, Walter Schmidt, was on a screen answering questions.

"Gaspard died instantly. There were at least 45 more confirmed dead and over 200 injured, 70 of them in critical condition. It appears to be a suicide bomber with a vest loaded with nails, shards of metal, and broken glass, designed to inflict maximum casualties. The press conference was called on such short notice, there was no time to screen everyone," stated the Ambassador in a somber tone.

Lexi glanced at the President. He was asleep in his chair. Everyone in the room was looking at her for the next step. "Walter, express our condolences to Sebastian. He takes over for now as the head of their Senate, right?"

"You are correct Madame Vice President. Sebastian Junot is in charge until they have a referendum to replace Gaspard. I suspect the Prime Minister Alain Chaumont will be the front runner," replied Ambassador Schmidt's image on the projection screen.

"Ok, let Junot and Chaumont both know we're here for whatever they need. Any chatter Rhett? Any idea who did this and why?" asked Lexi, turning to a tall man standing to one side.

Rhett Chadwick, Director of the Central Intelligence Agency, answered. "We didn't pick up any chatter of a coordinated effort before the attack. The French have been experiencing daily protests for years in this part of Paris. They escalated last weekend and Gaspard sent in the troops to break it up. Protestors died and parts of the predominantly Muslim quarter of Paris are burning as we speak. The government is laying the blame at the feet of everyone from the far-right National Rally to the French Communist parties."

Lexi stared at the handsome CIA Director. "Hardly surprising. The previous French President was adamant about preventing American cancel culture and racist protests from happening in France. This caused economic and cultural issues. They've been striking and disrupting all aspects of the economy for years now."

"Correct. This enabled Gaspard and the Socialists to form a coalition government replacing the old president. Although, in fairness, while Gaspard said more moderate things about the protests, it became increasingly clear, his stance wasn't changing fast enough for the more radical parts of the movement," noted Rhett, as Lexi frowned.

"To answer your first statement. My sources tell me Chaumont won't be asking for anything from us. Their press is in full blame mode for the protests. The media attacks are all aimed at us for interfering and exporting our racial unrest to their shores," he added.

Lexi nodded as Rhett finished.

"Henry, anything from NSA?" she asked, clearly in command.

"The funding for these protests appears to be linked to many of the same progressive organizations funding our protest, ARL, and equity organizations. The money is a combination of international support from places like Pavlovich's World Harmony Society and other NGOs. Like here, France's celebrities, sports stars, and progressive parties have expressed support for these efforts," St. Cloud looked down at his notes.

"Left-wing parties have united to advocate for full rights for the Muslim immigrants. The movement seems to have sped up in the last few weeks," answered St. Cloud.

"The measures Gaspard was announcing, has anyone confirmed or rescinded them as yet?" asked Lexi.

"No, there has been no comment, only commentary on the heinous nature of the attacks and promises to punish those who perpetrated the deeds," replied St. Cloud.

Lexi shook her head. "Gaspard was a fool to announce such harsh measures. The Muslims in Paris now number what, 15% of metro Paris' population, including the suburbs? The French have never tried to include them in society with equal rights. They should have eased these restrictions instead of sending in the army," sighed Lexi in a sorrowful tone. "He was smarter than that. Something must have set him off."

"I vote no. What was the question again?" This from the President who had awakened from his nap. He looked at his surroundings and the people gathered. "Who are we bombing?" he asked, confused.

"Mr. President, we're not bombing anyone. A terrorist bomb went off in France. It has killed their president and at least 45 more," said Lexi calmly, before Sam Vincent, the President's chief of staff, could say anything.

"President Chirac is dead? I must call Bernadette at once to express my condolences. She is a fine woman. Where is the phone?" said the President, seeing the phone and reaching for it on the table.

"Sir, not Chirac. He hasn't been president for decades. It was Gaspard, Jean Paul Gaspard," said Sam Vincent quickly.

The President paused; clarity came slowly back to his eyes. "Of course. Gaspard. I assume we've expressed our condolences? Kensington, do we need to put any forces on alert? Rhett, Henry, any chatter we need to be concerned with? I assume this was related to Gaspard calling out the army over the weekend?" asked the

President in rapid succession, clearly in touch with reality and the situation once again.

The directors quickly repeated what they'd told Lexi. "Very well. Let's monitor the situation. Schmitty, do we need to send someone to the funeral?" asked the President of his Ambassador in a much more jovial tone than the death of a fellow Head of State warranted.

"Sir, given the level of anti-Americanism here, I was even thinking of sending *my* aide," said Walter in a serious tone. "No need to risk anyone from your administration."

"Very well. Monitor things and let us know if something else happens," said the President, waving his hand across his neck, ending the call with the Ambassador. He looked at his intelligence directors and his Vice President.

"Thank you all. Let me know if anything changes. Lexi, let's get a statement out. Work with Sam and Amy to draft something. Thanks," he turned and left the situation room with his chief of staff and secret service agents trailing behind.

Lexi shook her head and grimaced, glancing at Rhett, Henry, and Admiral Kensington. No one spoke. She just shrugged as she, too, left the room.

Chapter 16

Alain Chaumont sat in his office next to the late President Gaspard's. He contemplated the events of the last few days. The protests, the suppression attempts, observing the phone call Gaspard had with the unknown person. Then, watching his friend, vaporized in an instant.

Luckily, he hadn't been present, as they had decided months ago it wouldn't be safe for both to appear in public together, for just this reason. His cell phone rang. It was an unknown number. He was tempted to ignore it, but this was his secure phone. His wife called his other cell phone.

"Allo," he answered.

"Do you know who I am?" said a mechanical voice on the phone in English.

"Yes, you are the person responsible for the death of our president," answered Alain accusingly, in perfect English.

"On the contrary, your friend chose poorly."

"So, you admit this was *your* doing?"

The mechanical laugh was sinister. "Not directly, but actions have consequences. A suicide bomber believes their actions are necessary to fight injustice. The actions of your friend led directly to his consequences. When people lose hope, they fight however they can."

"The cowardly murder of innocent civilians is hardly going to generate sympathy for the plight of the immigrants," replied Alain.

"Rumor has it you are most likely to succeed him. I will ask you the same thing I asked him. Are you willing to grant more rights to the immigrants you treat as second-class citizens?"

"Is that what you asked him?"

"More or less. I gave him a choice. Remove the army and negotiate with the leaders of the Muslim *banlieues*. Provide a path to full citizenship and the rights of a Frenchman or face the consequences of full-scale revolt. It seemed a reasonable request," said the voice.

"And if I refuse, I can assume you will unleash your suicide bombers again?"

The voice paused before answering. "Perhaps. But you have children, yes? I believe a daughter in her second year in an American college. And twin boys in prep school? Then there is your mistress, Vivienne? It would be a shame to expose this relationship on the verge of your election to president, yes?"

Alain stiffened at these threats. "If I agree, how do I know you will keep your end of the bargain?" asked Alain, cornered.

"Because we kept our end of the bargain with Gaspard. We told him what would happen if he did not do as suggested. He made the choice, not I. You have the same choice. We will be watching. In a show of good faith, we will instruct them to allow the fire brigades to enter the *banlieues* with no army escort. Then you will know we can be trusted to keep our promises. Good day, *President Chaumont*."

Alain sat staring at his phone, contemplating his choices. He didn't seem to have any. He wondered how they had threatened Jean Paul. His friend had kept his honor, but lost his life. Alain realized his honor wasn't worth *his* life.

Chapter 17

"Tell me again how this is a perk?" asked Nick, looking around at what looked like it had started life as a broom closet. The interior of the 'closet' contained two small chairs, and what looked like a secondhand leather love seat. Squeezed in the corner between the chairs was a mini fridge. Nick and Chuck sat in the two chairs with their bottles of water on top of the fridge, serving as a makeshift table.

"Having an office in the Capitol is one privilege of being a senator. Do you know what a congressman would pay to have this? They have to congregate in common rooms. And yes, this *was* a broom closet once. During the remodels, they provided space for each Senator to cut down on the back and forth between the Senate office buildings."

"Gosh, I see they spared no expense," remarked Nick, surveying his 'perk.'

"Well, you *are* the most junior member of the Senate. Believe it or not, there is actually an office smaller than this one. But it is much closer to the senate chamber, so that Senator does not want to give it up," explained Chuck with a straight face.

"What was it, a phone booth?"

"Not sure it was anything, to be honest. Anyway, today's discussion is a hearing on expanding SNAP to immigrants awaiting their asylum hearings. Making sure the EBT cards are more widely available and accepted. This would include allowing more social services organizations to distribute the SNAP cards like Planned Parenthood and various social justice groups. The purpose is to make sure no immigrants awaiting their hearings have hungry children," said Chuck.

"Your thoughts?"

"We invited them to come to the border and let them in. We sent them hither and yon with no way to support themselves except to work for slave wages. To be subjected to abuse and threats by drug dealers and shady employers. This bill at least offers them a chance to get support and food for their children," responded Chuck, shifting in his seat, as much as the cramped quarters would allow.

"So, we're correcting symptoms of a problem we created by not having a plan to manage these immigrants we allowed to enter the country because of their inhumane treatment in their home country?"

"Yep, hit the nail on the head," nodded Chuck.

"Our solution is to give them asylum. Let them loose in our country, with no safety net, no place to go other than to get on government assistance. How are they incented to get off this?"

"That's not the problem we're solving for today. We're just trying to get them a safe way to get money to buy food for their children. It polls well, and a majority of folks think it is a good thing."

"Really? Whose polls? I seriously doubt that's a true poll," retorted Nick. "What's the cost?"

"Ten billion initially, by making these asylum seekers eligible and if the estimate of six million asylum seekers is low, the funding would have to be expanded."

"How much more?" asked Nick skeptically.

"The estimates go as high as twelve million. With the recent surges of 1.5 to 2 million each of the last few years, the number could be higher."

Nick just shook his head and took a sip of water.

"How did Richards stay on top of all of this?"

"He didn't. We are doing exactly what he did. He relied on me to brief him on the things he delegated."

"But it seems like I'm not doing this justice by not digging in myself and learning more about the problems. Trying to solve the problems instead of just throwing money at symptoms," commented Nick in a dejected tone.

"You're on four committees and six subcommittees. Two of those, Judiciary and Rules, are important and highly visible, so you need to focus your time on those. Armed Services is no slouch either. These are all time-consuming," noted Chuck.

"If I don't understand the issue, how do I make the right decision?"

"Come on, Nick. We've discussed this before; it's not your job to be an expert on everything. You have to delegate, and you have to trust these people to formulate the right answers and arm you to defend the choices."

"And if I don't agree with the recommendation?"

"Then I guess we either have the wrong advisors or you are wrong," offered Chuck in all seriousness.

"Wrong?" Nick puffed up in mock anger.

"Yes, you can be wrong occasionally. It's their job to change your mind, with facts. They need to convince you so when you're in a hearing and reading the recommendations, you agree with them and can defend them against opposition. If you don't believe what you say, it shows," explained Chuck.

"I'm detail oriented. I'm not sure I can ever trust someone else's summation. In the Navy, it was my job to arm the commanders in the field. I couldn't afford to be wrong," countered Nick.

"My point exactly. You were an expert in your field telling your customer, in this case a Marine or a SEAL commander, what they should do and what they would be up against. Your advisors, me and Bob, Jenny and Izzy and all the others, we're your Intel group, and you are in the field acting on our info. We can't afford to be wrong either or you'll fire us," observed Chuck.

"Well, when you put it that way, I guess it is similar," agreed Nick, smiling.

"You can't survive here if you don't trust your staff. If you don't trust your staff, that is *my* fault and you need to fire your chief of staff," suggested Chuck with conviction.

"I'll remember that," laughed Nick.

"There's just not enough time, and with that, you need to scoot. I think I'll hang here in the broom closet for a bit and meet you back at the office after your meetings," finished Chuck.

Chapter 18

One of the smaller hearing rooms in the Capitol held the Nutrition subcommittee hearing. The subcommittee is ten senators, five from each party, arrayed in a slight semi-circle. The room contained a table with a pitcher of water and three chairs for the hearing guests.

There were a few dozen chairs in the back of the room for spectators and two cameras, one in each corner covering the whole room. On this day, eight senators were in attendance, with a few reporters and some staff in the chairs behind the witness table. A low-key hearing for a lower importance committee.

"Thank you for appearing before us today, Dr. Kozak," said Senator Newton of Washington, the Party Majority Chairman of the Nutrition subcommittee. "I'll open this hearing with a few words, followed by my colleague, Senator Langston, the ranking minority Opposition member."

"Today, we are discussing whether to feed millions of children, who, through no fault of their own, are in our country and don't know where they'll get their next meal. We welcomed these asylum seekers, many of whom have spent weeks or even months making the perilous journey. Fleeing oppression and danger to enter America," said Senator Newton in a solemn voice, as if delivering a eulogy at a funeral.

"Once here, they're released into the country to fend for themselves while they await the outcome of their asylum hearings. No safety net, no help, no compassion, just released into our communities. Their parents have no choice except to accept low-wage jobs paid a pittance, under the table by employers perfectly content in maximizing their profit. While also taking advantage of these asylum seeker's inability to report their abuse." The Senator continued, removing his glasses as if he needed to wipe tears from his eyes.

"They have fled one oppressive regime and entered the land of opportunity. Only to be thrust by an uncaring government system into another perilous situation. This is especially true of the immigrants who have the unfortunate luck to cross the Rio Grande into Texas.

Once there, the state government fights all our attempts to ease their pain. Today's bill would enable these families to qualify for Federal SNAP benefits. This would allow access to the electronic cards used for lifesaving food and medicine. Expanding this coverage and providing increased access to get the EBT cards at social services establishments gives them a chance to survive until their hearings."

"We must approve this legislation and we must get this amendment to the SNAP bill passed as soon as possible. Millions of children are starving because we care enough to accept the asylum seekers but not enough to ensure they don't suffer further once in America. I now recognize Senator Langston for five minutes," said Senator Newton, finishing his opening statement.

"Thank you, Senator Newton, and thank you, Dr. Kozak, for appearing before us. Today, we claim to have 11 to 15 million illegal aliens in the United States. This is the same amount we have supposedly claimed to have for over twenty years. According to a recent research poll, the closer estimate is 40 million and rising."

"In this administration, since we reinstated catch and release and stopped the remain in Mexico policy for asylum seekers, we've 'welcomed' twelve to as high as fourteen or even fifteen million more asylum seekers. Of these, a predominate number are children. Again, this administration has made it clear we won't stop *any* child, unaccompanied or not, from entering the US. Today SNAP benefits are used by 80 million citizens, this is a 100% increase from 2018. Admittedly, some of this is still from the various bouts of COVID and other infectious diseases that continue to wreak havoc with our economy."

"We currently spend $150 billion a year on SNAP, also a 120% increase in funding from 2018. This legislation we're discussing today would add ten million and potentially twenty-five million more recipients to the SNAP rolls. We claim it will only add 5 billion in costs. Using the current ratios, it is more likely to add 30-50 billion more, putting the total SNAP outlay closer to $200 billion for this program alone. We are creating a whole new level of dependency when our deficits are already soaring."

"This year's budget created four trillion more dollars of deficit. We cannot solve all the world's problems. We are only creating more with our short-sided policies, open borders, and continued borrowing. Borrowing more money to keep spending on illegal immigrants, while our own homeless problems expand, is not only criminal, it's the height of hypocrisy. To ignore our own citizens' needs in favor of illegals. I yield the rest of my time," finished Senator Langston.

Several reporters in the back of the room were taking notes and a few of the other senators were making their own during the speeches, including Nick in his purple notebook. The hearing continued with each side, alternating statements for the record. It was mostly grandstanding opinions for and against the bill along partisan lines.

Except for Dr. Kozak, the testifying expert witness, and Nick, no one in the room paid too much attention to anything being said by any of the Senators. The reporters in the back were mostly looking at their phones on mute. Being assigned the job of covering the Nutrition subcommittee hearings was drawing the short straw. Eventually, several of the Senators asked questions of the witness.

The Party members all focused on the humanitarian needs of these children. Predictably, the Opposition members focused on the costs of the program. Dr. Kozak answered with canned statements with little detail. Mostly in agreement with the party questions and with statistics and denials to predictions made by the opposition.

"Dr. Kozak, I'm Senator Turner, from Colorado. I'm relatively new here and haven't spent my entire career in political service. I hope you don't mind if we take the conversation in a different direction?" asked

Nick, getting a few chuckles from two Opposition Senators, and even some smiles from those in attendance in the audience.

"Ask away, Senator," said Dr. Kozak, a kindly looking older black gentleman with gray hair, beard, and mustache. He looked like the college professor he was, besides being a leading social scientist.

"I realize this bill adds significantly to the deficit. I also realize we have allowed many people to cross the border seeking asylum, so it is our responsibility to help them since we let them stay. My question is more about dependency. In your opinion, and in your experience, do people, citizens or otherwise, ever get off government assistance once they get on it?" asked Nick.

"Senator, that is a broad question. The statistics to answer that are difficult to compile and there is no evidence," answered Dr. Kozak. Nick stopped him with a raised hand.

"Dr. Kozak, my apology for interrupting. Again, forgive my newness here, but can we skip the canned politically correct answer?" said Nick in a conversational tone. "For instance, in my state, we have a high percentage of our population on government assistance. The percentage has only gone up and we now have multi-generational dependency. Again, in your opinion, is government assistance, shall we say, habit forming?"

"Senator, again statistics do not exist to answer your question," answered Dr. Kozak, raising his hands.

"Doctor, I doubt there aren't statistics that show how many families and children use our government supplied resources. I agree SNAP helps those in immediate need. My deeper concern is the ability of the recipient to give up the support and move on to self-sufficiency. Once again, can you help me out? If I were to draw an analogy, say between the meth addict and the recipient of government assistance, is it not true that both habits are very addictive and very hard to kick?"

This last statement drew a couple of exclamations from the gallery. The reporters sat a little straighter, now paying rapt attention. Several of the Senators on the panel also let out a few audible gasps.

"Senator, if you please, to mind the decorum of this hearing," expressed Senator Newton.

"No apologies, Senator. It's my time, which I haven't yielded. I'm simply asking the good doctor to render an opinion as to the addictive nature of government assistance and the dependency it creates. It's a simple clinical question. Dr. Kozak, I ask again, and I beg you to buck the trend of politically correct statements and render an honest opinion from an expert in the field. Does government assistance enable dependency and, in fact, disincentivize recipients from trying to get off the free services?" asked Nick in an earnest tone.

Before the Dr. could answer, Senator Newton interrupted once again. "While I appreciate your concern, Senator, I don't believe Dr. Kozak is required to answer a question regarding his opinion versus information supported by facts."

"Mr. Chairman, again, I may be new, but I believe I need to yield my time for you to countermand my request? I'm simply asking Dr. Kozak to answer a question, to the best of his ability based on his knowledge and experience in social science and, frankly, to just be honest. Something I think would be a refreshing change from the usual discourse in these hearings. Dr. Kozak, if you please and I will, of course, allow you to not answer if you're afraid an honest answer would materially affect your ability to appear on talk shows and cable news as a paid expert," offered Nick, in an accommodating tone.

Dr. Kozak's mahogany face darkened a bit at the implication he might not answer truthfully. It was clear he was struggling on how best to answer the question.

"Senator, at the risk of my so-called TV appearances, I'll give you my honest opinion, backed up as you say by my experience. The answer is yes. Government assistance and the expansion of ever-increasing types of benefits are indeed trapping the most vulnerable members in our society in a vicious cycle. The kinds of jobs they could and should start in, to work their way out of poverty, don't pay as much as assistance. This keeps them from taking these jobs and building up self-esteem, confidence, and skills that would allow them to contribute to society." He paused to drink from his water glass.

"While I feel your analogy is a broad sweeping condemnation of assistance as the equivalent of drug addiction, unfortunately, it is truer than not. The well intentioned good of government assistance has now morphed into a multi-trillion-dollar system of help, that for many, is too good to pass up, or give up, for hard work to provide the same benefit," pronounced Dr. Kozak with conviction, making it clear it was what he truly believed.

"Thank you, Dr. Kozak. I appreciate the *first* honest answer I have heard in nine months of these committee meetings. I yield the remainder of my time," said Nick.

There was much murmuring in the crowd and amongst the assembled senators.

"Dr. Kozak," said Senator Newton. "I appreciate your candor and willingness to indulge the very junior senator from Colorado. If I may follow up briefly in closing. Do the people who apply and receive government assistance have alternatives? If they are starving, and in this case, SNAP help is available, should they not be taking it rather than starving?"

"Well Senator, phrased that way, of course someone should take advantage of assistance rather than starve but...," Senator Newton broke in. "Thank you, Dr. I think we have already had enough of your opinions. I simply wished to have an answer to my question without further commentary and for the record. Thank you again for your time today. I adjourn this meeting."

"That should make for some choice coverage on TV tonight," said Allen McKay, an Opposition Senator from Oklahoma, seated next to Nick, leaning over to him. "I don't envy your next conversation with Fontana."

Nick looked at McKay as he gathered his papers.

"Senator, all I asked was for an honest answer. If that gets me barbequed, so be it. Perhaps we might solve some problems instead of treating only symptoms if we asked a few more honest questions and demanded a few more honest answers," shrugged Nick.

As Nick exited the committee room, several reporters immediately accosted him.

"Senator, did you really mean to imply every recipient of government aid is the same as being a meth addict?" asked an attractive, auburn-haired reporter with a perfect smile.

"Ms. Bergamo, if you took the quote in context, I didn't say those on assistance are like meth addicts. What I asked was if government assistance is as addictive as meth. There's a big difference. Once you're on assistance, much like a meth addiction, it is extremely hard to kick the habit," corrected Nick.

"But equating government assistance and meth addiction seems harsh, considering many people on assistance are there because they have no choice. Using drugs is a choice," countered Lauren Bergamo, the reporter from *America's News Channel.*

"Is it? I've spent some time as a crisis counselor and I can tell you from drug users' own experience, after the first time, drug use is rarely a choice. It is a habit. An addiction, your brain won't let you stop until you get your next fix. It is insidious and ruins lives. Government assistance can do the same thing if there is no plan to help the person receiving it kick the habit," explained Nick.

"Are you saying people should starve instead of taking SNAP, for instance? Dr. Kozak answered that question saying when faced with starvation or accepting SNAP, you would obviously choose assistance rather than watch your child starve," pointed out Lauren, looking up from her notes.

Nick stared at her cynically. Dressed smartly in her business jacket, skirt, and heels. Her attire highlighting her attractive figure and legs. So typical of the 'pretty' capitol newscasters assigned to try to get congress to say something worth more clicks or eyeballs to their network. Nick bit off his preferred retort to her question.

"Ms. Bergamo, as you also saw, Dr. Kozak, was prevented from continuing to answer the question by the committee chair. The question was whether they had other choices. I won't answer for him, but I'll provide my view. There are always choices. Programs like SNAP are there to make sure those in need do not starve. However, for instance, when SNAP funds are used to provide three meals a day, year-round for school-age children, where does it stop?"

"If there is a need, why is this a bad thing, Senator?" she pushed back.

"Where's the incentive for the parent to get a job to provide for their child? If instead the government steps in to do it for them and removes that responsibility from the parent? The government has taken over the job of the chief breadwinner in the family. It isn't an easy problem to solve, but we must address it. We already have 25% of our population getting some form of direct assistance, not counting Social Security or Medicare." Nick held up a hand as Lauren started to reply.

"These are able-bodied people in the prime of their work years. They're choosing not to work because assistance is enough to survive, if not to thrive. With our unemployment near 6%, and inflation rampant, we still have twelve million job openings with no one willing to fill them. This is a problem we've created and perpetuated by our continued policies. Paying people who could work, to not work. We need to enable them to *want* to do more than subsist off the taxpayers' funding," concluded Nick.

"Senator, does that mean you're voting against the bill?" This from another reporter, a tall skinny younger man who looked to be in his late twenties at most.

"No, Mr. Wheeler. I support SNAP and what it does. I just want to raise awareness that we should limit it in both scope and duration. We should provide ways to help families get off government assistance and become self-sufficient. We built this country on hard work, taking advantage of a free society to do anything you dream."

"That's all the time the Senator has. We have to get to other appointments," announced Chuck, magically appearing, ushering Nick away from the reporters.

As they walked away, Chuck asked Nick what caused all the commotion.

"Jesus, what did you say? This is a minor bill in a minor committee. All the sudden I'm getting texts and request to put you on the cable shows."

"I simply asked the witness to tell the truth. To stop giving us bullshit PC answers and just give his real opinion. And he did."

"Was that it? Doesn't seem that newsworthy. Or was there more?" asked Chuck, looking at Nick with a questioning raised eyebrow.

"Well, I might have said people on government assistance become addicted to it like a meth addict to drugs," admitted Nick sheepishly.

Chuck stopped and grabbed his arm. "You didn't. Did you actually say meth addict?"

"I did. I just wanted to make my point that people get addicted to government assistance and can't get off it."

"Shit, I can see the headlines tomorrow. Party Senator compares people on government assistance to meth addicts," mimed Chuck, holding up his hands in a mock headline.

"That isn't what I said."

"Did you or did you not use meth addict and government assistance in the same sentence?"

"Yes."

"Double shit," groaned Chuck, pulling out his phone.

"Maybe some people will actually get the point and realize we need to have a plan to get folks off assistance once we get them on it," answered Nick defensively. "Maybe we can have that conversation."

Chuck just shook his head. "You'll never learn. Truth is relative. Get ready for nothing but questions about why you feel all people being helped by the government are meth addicts," said Chuck.

"I'll get my two cents in, trust me," replied Nick with a determined smile.

"Ten bucks," countered Chuck.

"Bet," responded Nick, shaking his outstretched hand.

Chapter 19

"All I did was tell the truth and ask an honest question," asserted Nick as his staff stared at him in disapproval and shock.

"Nobody cares about the truth, it's all about perception," groaned Margie, shaking her head with a grimace on her face. "You know this. Think about what you say."

"If we don't tell them the truth and help them understand it, then what's the point?" asked Nick, exasperated.

"Margie is right," said Chuck. "You can talk until you're blue in the face, but they set the narrative."

"Bergamo is already doing stories on ANC about your comments. So are the others. They all say you claim those on assistance are the equivalent of drug addicts. Hooked on services enabling them 'to live a life, somewhat free from abject misery', to quote Bergamo directly," finished Margie.

"That's not what I said."

"It doesn't matter what you said or what you meant. We need to do damage control. You're on FLCN and ANC back-to-back in the 8am hour. It should give you enough of a chance to set the record straight. You need to apologize somehow for the meth addict analogy," announced Margie, looking at her phone.

"I have nothing to apologize for. I'll clarify the analogy is about addiction and how I could have used a better one, but I'm not apologizing for anything."

"You have to. Party members don't attack our social programs. It doesn't help us."

"Margie, easy," voiced Chuck, sensing Nick wasn't in the mood.

"I may be in our Party," answered Nick, attempting to stay calm. "But I'm also a human *and* a taxpayer. Answer me honestly, all of you. We had well over 1.8 million people immigrate across the border in 9 months this year, all seeking 'asylum'. Over 850,000 are children. None of them have jobs or a way to earn a living. This is the seventh year of the same numbers. Since they're officially seeking asylum, they qualify for programs other illegals 'technically' don't. Because of this, our outlay for things like SNAP is growing exponentially. Over 20% of our own citizens are on SNAP."

"It may be true, but this isn't a winning argument," observed Chuck as Margie nodded.

"Guys, this isn't a debate. It is a fact. Until we recognize this and find a way to solve it, it only gets worse. We can't keep funding these programs without ways to ensure we help folks get *off* them. What's the incentive of illegals to get off free services?"

"Be careful making sweeping statements," she cautioned.

"It doesn't even address the hold the drug cartels have on these people. Now be honest, do you want your tax dollars being spent to feed, clothe, and house people who are only here for economic reasons? Because our Party invited them?" Nick stared intently at Margie and Chuck, seated next to each other.

"When did this become about immigration? That's a much bigger issue than whether we expand SNAP. You can't solve all the problems we have," stated Chuck. Margie jumped in as he finished.

"I think it's a noble cause. They're fleeing tyranny, rape, and death. We need to do all we can to help fight human rights abuse," pointed out Margie, refusing to back down.

"Ok, fair point. Don't you think they will be subject to the same, living in squalor in Chicago, Baltimore, or El Centro? We're fooling ourselves if we think this is a noble cause. The noble cause is to bring them in legally and put them to work in a job paying taxes. Making sure the drug cartels don't set them up to deal or distribute drugs or prostitute out their children. Making them instant wards of the state doesn't set them up for success." Nobody interrupted so he continued.

"This is *our* fault. Because we did indeed invite them to come from one hell hole to live a shadow existence with no protection from our laws. They won't seek our help for fear of being deported."

"That is unnecessarily harsh," said Margie, visibly upset.

"Now it's our obligation to help the people of Honduras and Guatemala, with shit governments who prey on their citizens?"

"If they are fleeing abuse, we need to do what we can to help."

Nick looked over at Jenny sitting quietly next to him and at Chuck, who just shrugged and held his hands palm up.

"Margie, where do we stop? Shouldn't we be inviting folks from Bangladesh, Zimbabwe, Turkey, Syria, Kazakhstan, and China? Nobody oppresses their people like the Chinese. Ask the Falun Gong practitioners or the Uyghurs. Should we be sending planes to fly them in? How many? How many can we handle? Who do we turn away? You can come in but sorry, you can't. This is not a lack of compassion, this is reality. We can't take everyone. We left a bunch behind in Afghanistan. Many of whom are now dead because they helped us. Why were they less worthy than those coming across the southern border?"

"I don't have that answer, but we can help those who make the trip to the US. We have an obligation to help them," stated Margie. "They risk everything to come here. What do we do, turn them away at the end of their journey after they have paid and sacrificed?"

"Why are they coming, Margie? Risking their lives because should they be lucky enough to get here, we will take care of them. Coming as fast as they can before we close the door. They may choose to flee, but we're the ones incenting them to make the journey. Offering a life on the US government dole is better than they can do working hard in their home country."

"Exactly, that is why we have an obligation to help them," argued Margie, nodding her head vigorously.

"What's our deficit?"

"42 trillion?" answered Margie hesitantly.

"Closer to 44 trillion and over 48 next year. Less than a decade ago, it was 18 trillion. I know no one cares, but eventually it will matter. We love to spend money we don't collect, all in the name of doing good. I'll ask you one more thing, then I'll let this go."

"Is someone from Honduras or Guatemala with no ties to the US, more worthy of government funding and support than a 7th generation black family in urban Chicago, Baltimore, or Detroit? What about a 3rd generation Hispanic family in LA, Houston, or Las Vegas? Hell, a 10th generation white family in West Virginia, Tennessee, or Georgia?"

"Nick," said Jenny quietly, trying to calm him.

"Jenny, are they less deserving of government help than these new immigrants we invited with an open border? These families in the US face violence, discrimination, abuse, rape, high unemployment, poverty, meth and opioid addiction, and have for a hundred years. They've been getting help for generations and yet they still need more. Why has this not helped them get better?" asked Nick rhetorically.

"That isn't a fair comparison. They choose to not get jobs or improve their lives and to stay on government assistance. If they don't choose to improve, that's their own problem," said Margie, with conviction, crossing her arms and leaning back in her chair.

Nick smiled. "Thank you. You just made my point on the comparison between a drug addict and government assistance. They don't choose to live a shitty life; they're programmed to do it. We programmed them. We gave them crappy schooling. Even though we spend more per student than anywhere in the world."

"That may be true, but how is comparing them to drug addicts helping?" asked Chuck.

"What is the alternative? Go work in the field or in a trade. Work their way up in a warehouse or some other hard labor job where they get paid as much or less than the family can make, drawing on the plethora of government aid? This destroyed the idea of a work ethic. They have all this aid to 'help'. The one thing they need we couldn't give them. *Hope*. And how to achieve it. There are already 80 million of these people, native born in our country, without hope. Why are we importing more?"

"If not us, then who will?" said Margie, pleading with Nick to see her view of the world. "Many of these illegals aren't even eligible for most assistance, so your case against them doesn't hold up."

Chuck, seeing the look on Nick's face, made to play peacemaker, but Nick continued first.

"Margie, you are correct on that point. The purpose of today's meeting was just one more in the eventual collapse of our usual rebut to questioning services for illegals. *Our* party's tried-and-true response to the Opposition. If you take the time to look at the truth, you find that indeed, many federal programs try to exclude illegals. However, to remedy this, most of the blue states and even some of the red ones, have passed their own bills providing subsidized healthcare, education, medical care and now increasingly things like SNAP. Almost all of these are in partnership with federal funds going to these states. So, we *are* funding them through loopholes."

Margie was silent in response.

Jenny responded. "You're right Nick. California and New York lead in providing benefits to illegals. Paid for by their tax dollars and federal funds, they allocate to these. They both have the highest tax rates in the country and now the largest budget deficits," said Jenny.

Nick turned to Margie, who was sitting at the table, arms crossed. "We destroyed the Taliban in retribution for 9/11. Then we thought we could enforce our way of life on others. For their benefit, of course. In all these cases, some more than others, we tried to make democracy stick. It failed everywhere we tried. It failed because democracy comes from within, not from without. We cannot fix Mexico or Honduras or Guatemala. *They* must fix themselves and *their people* must want to do it."

"I agree," said Margie rising. "They cannot fix it there, so they come here."

Nick looked at Margie's earnest face, responding.

"Some of them want to work and they will. But it'll be subsistence and they'll make up for what they lack by having you, me, Jenny, and Chuck pay for it. This isn't xenophobia or even nationalism. This is the hard reality of preserving what we have. We need to get our own house in order before we invite others to join. Especially those who aren't ready to become fully American. If they truly want to be Americans, they can immigrate legally. Allowing open borders is a slap in the face to anyone who is and has gone through the process of legal immigration." Nick finished, got up and got a piece of pizza from the box on the conference table, took a bite and a sip from his iced tea.

"Well?" he said, looking at Chuck and then Margie.

"You make sense, but you'll never get people to sit still long enough to hear your reasoning. Nor will any of the networks let you say this," Margie said in a tone suggesting Nick had made her think. "Tommy on EXN would probably let you say this, but that would just piss off Fontana even more."

"Hey, I'll go on any show on any network willing to give me time. I'm happy to debate any talking head," he offered.

"Nick, you said it yourself. This isn't a debate. The fight is never fair. They can't let you win. They'll cut you off or quote you out of context again or simply just stop if you deviate from their points. Going on any of these shows is just going to make it worse for you," revealed Margie in resignation, looking at Chuck.

"Why are we playing defense? I'm happy to go on the shows and explain all I asked was if government assistance is addictive like drugs, and the answer is clearly it is. We aren't doing anything to help them eventually get off assistance," finished Nick.

Chuck slapped his hand against his head while Margie just leaned against the conference table with a shocked look on her face.

"Nick, you are hopelessly naïve," responded Chuck. "They won't give you the chance to make your point for precisely the reason you state. It's true."

"He's right," admitted Margie.

Nick, who was sitting once again, contemplated what Chuck had said. "You know what, this job is more depressing than watching us throw away all our gains in Afghanistan," he responded, disappointed at the prospect he wouldn't get a chance to get his point across. Pulling out a ten-dollar bill, he handed it to Chuck without a word. The others looked on, confused.

"Nick, pick battles you can win. This you cannot. They won't let you. With the filibuster vote coming up, the last thing they need is a rogue member in their caucus," revealed Chuck.

"Look guys, I am who I am. Book the shows and if EXN will have me, do it," finished Nick, heading back to his office.

Margie looked at Chuck, exasperated, as Nick left. Chuck glanced at Jenny, who had stayed silent for most of the conversation.

"You can't stop him. If he wants to commit hari-kari, he's going to do it somewhere and someplace. He might as well do it on a subject he feels passionate about," said Jenny, turning to Margie.

"Margie dear, you are young and idealistic. A product of your generation. I was once like you. I suspect even Chuck was. You're also so far from reality, I pity you," said Jenny with a wan smile.

Margie laughed uncomfortably. "You pity *me?*"

"When you realize everything you stood for, everything *they* told you was righteous and good, turns out to be nothing more than them using you to achieve *their* ends. Nick is at that point. He made the mistake of thinking he could change it as a senator. Soon, you're going to be disillusioned, disheartened, and, most of all, pissed. I sense this is already happening with Nick's help and guidance. Don't fight it. Embrace it. What I suggest is you take a stroll around the neighborhood outside the White House. Go in daylight, of course. Take someone with you, preferably a man." Jenny rose from her seat and walked around the table to sit on the edge next to Margie.

"You're going to see what reality looks like outside the bubble. What you preach and hold dear is not reality. Life in other third world countries, to quote a phrase from Thomas Hobbes, is 'nasty, brutish and short'. That's not our fault, and it is also not our problem to solve. Sadly, it is also becoming true in our own inner cities as well. Nick is right. Only the people in these countries can solve their problem. We did, and it still took hundreds of years, a war of independence and a brutal Civil War. I fear we're trending back towards the world of the 1850s, where two competing ideologies eventually led to a clash of arms."

"Jenny, I think you're just being unnecessarily bleak to support Nick's argument," responded Margie.

"Do you see compromise on the horizon? I don't. Our Party hopes to resolve this by installing a one-party rule. This may or may not solve the problem, but it is a direction, and it will force the issue. It will also signal the end of democracy as we know it. I'm not sure the opposition will remain as passive once we replace democracy. Nick knows this. So, he's bucking the system and trying to prevent it from happening. Listen to him and think about what he means, not just what he says," explained Jenny.

"You agree with putting him on the shows to commit career suicide?" asked Chuck.

"You know we can't stop him. Turn him loose. Something in my gut tells me we may be surprised," stated Jenny.

"OK. Margie, book him on *Tommy* and let's see what happens."

"Behold, a whirlwind of the LORD is gone forth in fury: it shall fall grievously upon the head of the wicked," quoted Jenny quietly.

"What was that?" asked Chuck.

"A phrase from Sunday School. It was Jeremiah, I think. Talking about how God released the whirlwind to smite the wicked," responded Jenny.

"Well, I hope God is on our side and we aren't the wicked," worried Chuck.

Chapter 20

Dolly Wells-Monroe sat in her sitting room going through the morning edition of the *Post*, sipping her tea, and nibbling on a bran muffin. She glanced at the TV. Dolly liked the anchor on the local morning show, so she chose this over the national shows for her morning noise.

She perked up at the mention of Senator Nick Turner's name and the footage of him debating ANC's rising reporter, Lauren Bergamo, after his committee hearing revelations. Dolly smiled.

She liked Turner. He was a rare breed, someone with integrity and an 'I don't give a shit' attitude. It was refreshing in this town of fake smiles and platitudes. Flicking through the pile of RSVPs for her upcoming Fall Gala, she picked one out.

"Well, well, this is a first," she said to herself. Dolly opened the return envelope to make sure it wasn't a 'declined to attend' courtesy return. Senator Turner was coming to her party.

To her knowledge, he'd attended one small cocktail party since arriving nine months before in Washington, including declining her previous invitations. This would be his debut in DC society. It thrilled her he was attending. Especially since he was making waves.

She sat back in her chair, thinking and smiling. It would be an excellent party, after all.

Dolly had built a reputation for hosting 'the Four Seasons' galas. Themed to match the season and guaranteed to be the highlight of each social season. She'd single-handedly tried to return DC society to the heyday of yesteryear's social gatherings. Parties where politics, diplomacy, glamor, and socializing were once the norm.

Partisanship and personal attacks weren't permitted. Dolly had banned certain folks from her parties for violating these rules. It didn't matter if they were a cable network president, a newspaper/astronaut publishing mogul, or the world's richest man on any given day. She'd even banned major cabinet officials.

She also removed them from future invites, without appeal. Once you crossed the current doyenne of DC, you were persona non grata. No amount of money or pleading would change her mind. Nouveau rich, especially from Hollywood, Silicon Valley, and social media moguls need not expect an invitation either. Dolly didn't consider them interesting in the slightest. It was *her* party, after all.

Because of this attention to detail, she'd accomplished the impossible. Having parties where partisan politicians put away the daggers. Pretending to be civil for the sole chance to attend and be seen as one of the in crowd.

For a few hours, four times a year, or at least when there was no pandemic, she would bring Washington back to the social heydays of the 50s and 60s. The only real problem she'd discovered was the quality of the guests in the modern era. They were nowhere near as accomplished or interesting as the stories she had heard from those last few living souls who attended the parties during the heyday.

Dolly was the daughter of an ambassador and the granddaughter of an English Earl on her mother's side. Growing up, she split time between their family estates in Virginia and England. She was educated in England and France where her father was the Ambassador to both countries in multiple administrations. Her father eventually accepted a position with a lobbying firm, returning the family to Washington when she finished school.

She quickly became one of the most eligible ladies of Washington. Courted relentlessly, she finally accepted an offer of marriage from William Monroe, whose ancestor was the fifth President of the United States, James Monroe.

They led an idyllic life, except for an inability to conceive children. They tried all science offered, including IVF treatments. It wasn't meant to be. They were otherwise a happy couple. Her husband had taken over running the family business. Paper mills scattered around the Piedmont and telecommunications tower maintenance and construction. Business boomed under his sure and steady management. Once his father passed, William sold the towers to Verizon and the mills to International Paper.

Freed from the day-to-day management of the businesses, the Monroes embarked on a six months around the world tour. Shortly after returning home, William complained of weakness. Tests revealed hemorrhagic fever, one resistant to normal treatment. He died within days. They surmised later he may have gotten the fever from handling monkeys on one of their last stops in Borneo.

Dolly found herself a very rich widow. None of it mattered to her. Devastated and rudderless, descending into depression and heavy drinking. It was Senator Bank's wife, Penelope, Penny, to her friends, who pulled Dolly out of her funk. Giving her purpose and direction, suggesting she get involved in philanthropy.

Having attended many of the parties the Banks' were famous for hosting, Penny suggested she and Dolly team up. Dolly becoming the heir apparent, as Penny could no longer continue hosting her soirees.

At first, Dolly was reluctant to take up this task. Once she became more involved in philanthropy and realized networking was the key to success, she relented, and they held a party where they both co-hosted the first of what would become Dolly's annual winter gala.

Dolly would add a spring and summer and finally a fall event, creating the now famous Four Seasons Galas. Penny regaled Dolly with tales of the old-time parties she and the Senator had attended in the Kennedy administration. Those of the Grand Dames of Washington society. She told tales of parties hosted by Susan Mary Alsop and Evangeline Bruce. Penny's favorites were those thrown by Pamela Harriman and Kay Graham, both of whom she strived to emulate. According to her, they were the best DC had ever seen.

She had listened to Penny tell tales of attending these parties where politicians from both sides socialized. Discussing business while also mingling with Nobel and Pulitzer Prize winning authors, playwrights, musicians, and scientists. Where ambassadors and even the occasional heads of state made appearances and where cabinet members and major officials, generals, admirals, and Supreme Court justices would rub elbows.

Those were the days before money, raising money, and talking about money corrupted everything. Before Washington DC became us versus them. Not that partisanship was not allowed back then. It was a time when everyone could agree, looking out for the best interests of the country, outweighed personal feelings and enmity. The losing side lost gracefully, knowing soon they would once again be on the winning side.

Such was politics in the United States and most of the free world, where no one deviated much from the middle, and all agreed the end goals were the same: peaceful coexistence and unification in the face of adversity. Penny confided in Dolly the social scene had diminished ever since JFK died. It truly died under Jimmy Carter, who had no cultured bone in his body.

It had a brief resurgence under Reagan, but by then the battle lines were drawn, with many foregoing the parties strictly on a partisan basis. After Reagan and his Hollywood friends, it disappeared entirely. Replaced by shallow partisan exhibitions of wealth, plastic surgery, and excess.

She liked to feel she was doing her part to thaw the glacial freeze DC had been dealing with since the millennial. She was now approaching forty, still holding on to her youthful looks. Flowing shoulder length wavy dark hair, dark eyes, naturally full lips, high cheekbones, and perfect skin paired with a dazzling smile. Matched with her razor-sharp wit and keen intelligence, she claimed she couldn't find a match willing to put up with her independence or, frankly, whom she found interesting enough to challenge her sensibilities.

Princes and Kings had courted her. Receiving marriage proposals from sheiks, being wooed by athletes, billionaires, Hollywood actors. Even a Hollywood actress took a swing and struck out. She never really gave them a chance. She was happy with her life and enjoyed being the new Grand Dame of DC society without the entanglement of a beau.

Dolly's parties had led to the start of several treaties for peace talks, ceasefires, and even refugee resettlements. All forged within the confines of her estate, Twin Pines. She was proud of this, and she knew most of all, Penny Banks would be proud of it too. Penny had died shortly after getting Dolly to agree to carry on, as if she knew her time was short.

She always felt honored to have spent the time she did with her. Dolly had a soft spot in her heart for Penny's widowed husband, Senator Baxter Banks. Often, he'd co-host with her, greeting guests as they arrived. He would do so for this one as well. She knew his time was coming soon too, and this saddened her.

"Miss Monroe, you must get ready for your appointments today," said her personal assistant, shaking her out of her reverie.

"Thank you, Nina. I was just daydreaming. Let's get going," said Dolly, rising and smiling as she thought about the upcoming party and her new guest of honor.

Chapter 21

Nick entered the green room at the EXN studio in Washington. In the room, it surprised him to see Dr. Kozak. He crossed the room to shake hands with him.

"Dr. Kozak, good to see you. I'm truly sorry. Who would've thought speaking the truth would cause such controversy?"

Kozak laughed heartily from deep in his ample belly. "Call me James. I have to say, I'm having a blast. It was refreshing to tell the truth. Not the stuff I usually have to recite. It may cost me in the future, but hell, maybe I'll become a talking head. I'm enjoying this."

"James, that makes me feel better. I hate the fact no one says what they feel in this town," admitted Nick, shaking his head while grabbing water from the table.

A makeup artist came in to apply some powder to their foreheads. A producer also appeared to let them know Dr. Kozak was five minutes out and Senator Turner was ten.

"Senator, not sure you've seen any of my interviews. They asked me on ANC if I felt what you did was an attempt to embarrass me because I'm black."

"What?" asked Nick, startled by his statement.

"I told them, of course not, but I just wanted to let you know the question is being asked."

"How could anything I said be construed as racist? They didn't ask me that when *I* was on ANC this morning. God damn chickens."

"I wish they could see you now. They'd have their answer. Good luck Senator, let me know if there is ever anything I can do to help," said Dr. Kozak.

"Careful, I may take you up on the offer. And it's Nick," he said, smiling and shaking his hand as the producer arrived.

"I meant it, Nick," said Kozak, as the producer led him to the studio.

Nick's phone buzzed as he waited. It was a text from Chuck, warning him to look out for a racist question. Nick quickly texted back he had heard already.

"Senator Turner, if you'd follow me, please," said a producer who led Nick into the studio on commercial break.

As Nick was being mic'd up, he shook the hand of a short stocky man with graying dark hair, in a Marine crew cut. "Senator Turner, very nice to meet you," said Tommy Charles, host of *The Tommy Charles Show*, the top-rated program on EXN and all cable TV.

"Nice to meet you as well, Tommy."

"We'll go here in a second. I won't be too tough on you since you're a virgin," confided Tommy in a snide voice.

"I think I can handle it. Give me your worst," challenged Nick, not worried in the slightest at the veiled threat.

"Careful what you ask for, Senator," added Tommy ominously as the producer counted down.

"Welcome back. I have Senator Nick Turner of Colorado with us tonight to hear his side of the story, comparing people on government assistance to meth addicts. Senator?"

"Thanks Tommy, I appreciate the opportunity to discuss what I *actually* said. As I have said several times already today, I didn't call people on government assistance meth addicts. I merely made an important analogy and one we should all be asking, is government assistance an addiction as bad as being a drug addict? Is it as hard to kick government assistance as it is to get off meth? That is an important distinction, which I think your viewers would like answered."

"Senator, the bill you were discussing would expand government assistance, SNAP, the meal program formerly known as food stamps, to illegal aliens who are in the country awaiting their asylum hearings.

During the conversation, you seemed to get frustrated with Dr. Kozak's answers. It looked as if you wanted to embarrass him by putting him on the spot," said Tommy, probing.

"That couldn't be farther from the truth. I respected Dr. Kozak before, and I now respect him even more. He was brave enough to break from the Washington congressional hearing precedent of saying a lot of words but giving no concrete answers to difficult questions. I applaud the good doctor telling the truth. Clarifying we provide gobs of assistance, with fewer and fewer hurdles, but we provide no incentives to get them to stop. That was my point. Do you not agree it's hard to stop taking it?" Nick asked Tommy.

"Of course I do, Senator, but I'm a conservative. Any incentive to keep people from taking personal responsibility is bad for the person and bad for America."

"Then we agree Tommy, and I am *not* a conservative."

"Are you frustrated with the Party narrative? Aren't you afraid you are going to make enemies in your caucus with these contrarian views?"

"Actually Tommy, I support the SNAP bill and will vote for it. My complaint is simply about the system. Where will it stop? We invited the immigrants in. We now have an obligation to support them since they can't do it themselves. Tommy, I care about my constituents. If that makes others in my caucus mad, I'm happy to debate the issues with anyone," said Nick, shrugging. "I was teaching history before I accepted this appointment and can always go back. I'm not sure how much time I have here, but I'll use it wisely."

"An honest viewpoint," said Tommy in a surprised tone.

"There was a time when the ability to immigrate was predicated on proving you had a job and family member waiting to receive you. That's how my great-grandparents came to America. You could immigrate to this country if you could prove," said Nick, raising his hand and ticking off points. "a) you would not be a burden on society, b) show you had a willingness to work and had employment waiting and c) a place to stay, usually with direct family."

"What this means is you depended on family and friends. You showed you were coming to provide value to the American workforce and to earn your own living. Not become an instant ward of the state. There was no welfare system back then. It was called personal responsibility," said Nick, raising his voice a bit.

Tommy didn't interrupt, sensing Nick had a point to make.

"Tommy, none of these are required any longer. In fact, we encourage people to come who have no family, no job, and no way to support themselves. Ensuring they are immediately a burden on society. Government assistance is a burden on society. No matter how compassionate we are, it's still a burden. It's your money and mine and everyone else's being spent, or worse, borrowed. Our children will have to figure out how to repay this debt. I'd prefer immigrants to have family, to have a job, and to rely on their family, or even their church or other community safety net rather than rely on the government. I'd also prefer they come in legally. When they come in legally, they have to meet all these criteria," said Nick. Tommy nodded, continuing to smile.

"We created the problems, and our solution is to print more money to perpetuate these programs. Welfare reform works. Every dollar of assistance we provide should be based on showing a willingness to get off the assistance as soon as possible. We've removed that incentive as well. We keep extending the programs endlessly. I'm not heartless. I believe there are folks who deserve help, but for most, it should be temporary, not permanent, and certainly not multi-generational," ended Nick emphatically.

Tommy looked surprised at Nick's statement. He fidgeted in his seat a bit. "Wow Senator, this is unexpected. Me thinks you are going to make a lot of enemies in your own party with talk like that."

"Why? Tommy, this is the problem," said Nick, throwing up his hands for emphasis. "Most of us agree we need to rein in spending. Why in the world are we continuing to throw money and assistance at illegal immigrants, with no strings attached? Money doesn't help them unless we help them get out of poverty. Getting educated, getting a good-paying job, start earning a wage, pay taxes, build meaningful skills, learn the language, and break the cycle. Right? We have the same problem with our own generational poor. How are we helping them break this cycle, too? This isn't only about illegals."

"Again, I agree completely, Senator," said Tommy with a nervous laugh. "What you say makes sense. Why is the rest of your party against this?"

"Tommy, we *are* a compassionate country. We should offer asylum to true victims. But when Central American countries hand out pamphlets teaching their citizens exactly what to say to be accepted into our programs. When they empty their prisons and send us their most hardened criminals, so *they* don't have to find funding to feed and house them. Who is at fault? At some point, the hypocrisy has to stop. Either we change our asylum rules or withhold funding from the countries. These people aren't seeking true asylum. If they are, why do we send aid to these countries if we feel compelled to take their citizens in and accept their statement their country wants to kill them? Why is it these countries make half of their GDP from money their asylum-seeking citizens make in the US? If it's so bad, why are they sending money back once they get here? This is hypocrisy of the highest order. I can only assume our media is preventing our citizens from realizing how bad this is," mused Nick, taking a breath to calm down.

"Senator, this is frankly amazing. I have to say, I have *never* heard this from a Party Senator," offered Tommy in a disbelieving tone.

"No one wants to be seen as less than compassionate by speaking against unlimited and open borders," revealed Nick. "We claim to be the party of compassion. It was no different when everyone had to put signs in their yard proclaiming support for anti-racist league groups. Because to not do it meant you were *for* racism. What has happened to our citizens and their right to have a different opinion, or even no opinion? Why does everyone have to pick a side? We have radicals on both sides. That leaves 60-70% in the middle who don't agree with the radicals in their parties. This is no longer permitted by the Party, or the media, specifically social media, setting public opinion. They now force everyone to choose. If you don't, you are called out for being neutral. We have lost the middle ground, the sane center, where common sense and compromise once ruled," finished Nick in a now calm voice.

"Senator, thank you so very much. Come to think of it, it shouldn't surprise me at your bravery, considering your track record. I'm honestly sorry we're almost out of time for this segment. That was truly enlightening and entirely pragmatic. But I'd be remiss if I don't get your thoughts on the events over the weekend."

"Tommy, a cowardly action like this does not solve any issue. Assassinating the President of France won't win any sympathy. Further, it's going to make the French government trust you less. It seems the Prime Minister is rolling back some of the more restrictive directives Gaspard put in place. This problem goes deeper than this. All I can say is violence is never the answer. Change must be organic, and it must be driven by both the oppressed and those doing the oppressing, whether out of ignorance or misguided policy. I suggest they emulate Martin Luther King. Make their cases to generate mass public support for their plight. Adopting the ways of our current anti-racist league organizations, advocating violence, destruction, coercion, looting, reparations, and threat is no way to progress," suggested Nick, shaking his head.

"Thank you, Senator. Again, pragmatic statements. Ones I hope are heeded. I hope you would come back. We'd love to have you."

"Anytime Tommy."

Nick followed the producer back to the green room.

"Senator, that was spectacular. You made some brilliant points," said the producer. "I have to tell you, we have so many people who are so careful on camera, it is refreshing to see someone be honest."

"You mean someone who isn't careful," said Nick with a smile.

"Do you have time? Tommy would like to talk to you."

"Sure, I can hang out for a minute. Can I get a cup of coffee?"

The producer showed him a machine with a variety of coffees. While it was brewing, he looked at his phone. He chuckled as he read the reaction from his chief of staff. By the time he got to the last text, it was simply a bunch of thumbs up emojis.

"Senator, thanks for sticking around," said Tommy, who came up to about mid-chest on Nick, giving him a firm handshake.

"My pleasure Tommy. Call me Nick."

"Do you mind if we go to my office, we'd have a bit more privacy? It is just down the hall here." He led the way down a hallway to a corner office in the building, looking out over part of the Washington Mall in the distance.

"Nice view" nodded Nick as he sat down in the upholstered chair across from Tommy's desk. "Better than my Senate office."

"Public service sucks," laughed Tommy. "You guys are masochists, but we love ya. Great for ratings."

"Good to be appreciated and wanted," responded Nick sarcastically.

"Which is exactly what I wanted to talk about. I have to say you are nothing like what I thought you'd be. And our interview tonight was nothing like I expected," responded Tommy in a surprised tone, smiling.

"How so?"

"Well, first, I expected a different answer to my opening statement. I figured you'd back down or try to weasel your way out of it. I wasn't expecting you to double down."

"Tommy, I'm not a politician, and I'm not a left-wing progressive going along with the party. I have a background where a spade is a spade and not a club or a diamond or a heart, no matter how you change the angle," said Nick, getting up to leave.

"I see that. We can say the residents of Colorado are well represented, even if you are Don Quixote in this town," offered Tommy.

"An educated man and here I thought you were just another blowhard on TV."

"I read the comic book."

"Uh huh, at Georgetown? Where you got a degree in the classics? They used comic books?" asked Nick.

"Did some research I see? A lifetime ago. Nobody studies the classics anymore. Well, almost no one."

"Nice to meet you. How do I get out?"

"I'll show you," replied Tommy, getting up as well.

As they walked out of the office heading to the elevator, one of Tommy's producers came up to the two of them.

"Senator," he said, nodding to Nick. "Boss, social media is blowing up. This could be our biggest segment ever," he proclaimed. Tommy looked over at Nick.

"Senator, I think we'll definitely have you back."

"Not sure having a Party Senator as your highest rated segment is a good thing for me, or for you. I guess I could commit suicide on air next time to top this. I already seem to be committing *political* suicide."

"You never know Senator. People need to be told the truth in order to be convinced they are being misled. Maybe this is the start."

"It isn't a start for me. It's just par for the course, and the way I'm wired," stated Nick as the elevator doors opened.

As the doors shut, Tommy turned to his producer, "Well, I'll be. That wasn't what I expected at all. Is the response as good as you say? We've only been off the air for 30 minutes?"

"I've never seen a response like this, seriously. It's almost all positive, especially for Turner. Your audience loves him, 'finally a politician who gets it, too bad he is in the Party' and others like 'can he change parties?' Then, of course, the usual right-wing cranks who think he is just lying to endear himself to the right before he votes to take away their guns, etc. We'll see how the overnight ratings look in the morning."

"Let's book him again and give him a bit more time. It'll help us be more bipartisan by having a Party moderate on regularly. Besides,

ANC and FLCN won't want to touch him if he keeps this up," finished Tommy.

"No doubt on that one," agreed the producer.

Chapter 22

"You were right," admitted Margie to Nick. They were sitting in his office, Nick at his desk, the rest in the various chairs.

"You really knocked it out of the park, Boss," this from Jerry, a man in his late twenties, with nerdy black glasses wearing a loose suit, white shirt, and a thin tie. He had the look of someone who spent more time behind a computer screen than in the sun.

"It looks like Tommy had the best ratings of the year for his show. Our social media accounts and other feeds show most folks found your honesty refreshing. Some said it restored faith there are some good people in Washington, to quote only a couple," said Jerry, who went by 'Jer,' most of the time.

"Good. It is always nice to see some people recognizing honesty as a virtue," nodded Nick. "Any pushback?"

"Strangely quiet on my front. No complaints or requests for meetings. Could just be because everyone is off for the next two weeks for the Senate fall break," answered Margie.

"Jer?" asked Nick.

"There are also the usual crank posts from trolls to our social media, but no more than usual. ANC is getting creamed for trying to make this about race. They're getting tons of hate mail and their ratings are so far down they're getting beaten by PBS," laughed Jer.

"Did I tell you I ran into Dr. Kozak in the EXN green room?"

"You didn't mention it," said Chuck with a why am I finding out now tone. "How was he? You probably cost him his professor's job."

"Funny thing was, he seemed almost giddy at the excitement. He also didn't appear to be too worried about it. Keep an eye out. If he gets any retaliation, I want to hear about it so we can support him."

"You bet," said Chuck with a nod.

"Nothing from leadership? I would have at least expected a slap on my wrist or a threat or something. I contradicted a lot of our Party positions. Hearing nothing is even more troubling."

"I hear you on that," agreed Chuck.

"Jenny, anything we need to do today before I head home?"

"We're in good shape on the bills. Nothing that can't wait."

"Greg, how about on your side? Anything I need to do; calls I need to follow up?" asked Nick, leaning back in his chair.

"Nope. You're all good."

"Nick, I also wanted to commend you on your response to the French situation. Given your history with suicide bombers, I think it resonated with the audience and I think your referencing MLK, and the non-violent solutions, is the correct tone," said Margie.

Nick nodded. "It's the only solution with a lasting result. Alright folks, then let's close it down early. Enjoy the time off."

Everyone filed out of the office. Only Chuck and Nick were left. "You sure you don't want me to schedule some appointments back home? Maybe raise some funds for your *own* campaign?"

"Thanks. I think I'll get on the bike and just ride around the state. I'll check in on my constituents, incognito. See what the real people have to say. Better to do this with no announcements, entourage, or press."

"Please be careful. You know there are crazies out there. You are going to the land of mass shootings; more in Colorado than anywhere else," said Chuck in a matter-of-fact tone.

"Gee thanks. Go home, Chuck," said Nick, shaking his head.

Chapter 23

The Cabinet Room of the White House was mostly full. This was the last cabinet meeting before Washington, DC, emptied for fall break. In the room were the Secretaries of the various departments, plus the Vice President, the Attorney General, and the intelligence agency directors.

The President sat at his customary spot in the middle of the table. A photographer came in long enough to take a picture of the assembled Cabinet. The President did not look healthy. His skin was drawn tightly over his face. Now well into his eighties, the vim and vigor he once displayed on the campaign trail, and in his long career in politics, no longer remained.

He'd been a compromise candidate, ascending the ultimate leadership role. Leading the country through rough times, both domestic and internationally. Continued bouts with COVID recurrences, to a disastrous withdrawal from Afghanistan, Russian incursions, Israeli wars with Hamas and Hezbollah, and terrorist attacks around the world, including US military bases.

The closest the US came to being a victim of domestic terrorism was the one Senator Turner had stopped in the New York City subway. The economy, unemployment, inflation, and his memory, combined with troubling situations around the world, were more than his aged mind and physique could handle.

His moderate stance had slowly succumbed to the unrelenting pressure of the Progressive wing of the Party. Withering press coverage and his polling favorable only when he capitulated to the demands of his aggressive progressive base. Aides and advisors from that faction surrounded him. Most of his Cabinet picks reflected the most radical elements of the Progressive wing.

Over time, his strength of resolve, to stand against policies he didn't like, crumbled. The media famously roasted him for his frequent flip flops on policy. He was also famous for going off script and contradicting his heavily managed speeches. His staff often pulled the plug on cameras and microphones to prevent further gaffes. This level of uncertainty caused confusion in the nation, its allies, *and* its enemies.

Nobody was comfortable with this situation, and everyone was on edge. Lexi was stepping in more and more often for the President. Helping keep the policies firmly articulated. As his memory and overall mental capacity diminished, the President's physicians had to resort to more powerful stimulants to allow him to address the nation. Giving ever briefer speeches on critical issues. The unfortunate result of these treatments led to extended periods of near comatose sleep.

Another unfortunate side effect of the drugs was the further decrease in his short-term memory. This led to classic symptoms of dementia and early onset Alzheimer's. He was being treated for these symptoms with another cocktail of experimental drugs, some of which left him with unfortunate side effects of their own. From incontinence to a bout with Bell's Palsy. This last keeping him out of public sight for two months, while he recovered.

The White House, now carefully stage managed any public sighting, rarely allowing him to speak. Most addresses were pre-recorded and selectively edited. They were then broadcast as if they were live sessions from the White House. He was truly a figurehead who simply followed orders. The cognitive decline had sped up of late.

Once the photographer left, the Vice President called the meeting to order, as she had been doing these last few months. She quickly went down a list of topics, occasionally glancing at the President to see if there was any reaction to anything she said. He lifted his head and turned to her when she brought up the potential for riots once they passed the bill, eliminating the legislative filibuster.

"Yes?" Lexi asked questioningly when he looked at her.

They all could see the wrinkles in his forehead as he tried to focus on the question at hand.

"Now, are we sure this is worth the effort? We're going to rile up a lot of people with that," he said in his folksy tone, once so popular with the public. "You're talking about riots. It just seems if people are going to riot, maybe this is not the best idea."

Lexi paused for a second, then responded as she would to a child. "Because we're undoing a bad thing. This is causing good things from being done by all of us. Things that will help a larger number of our citizens, Mr. President."

The President focused as he tried to process what she said.

"Lexi, it is unpopular. Is the Court going to overturn this like they have so many other things? I hate going out and having to say what we tried to do is being blocked," said the President out loud, clearly worried about getting it wrong once again.

"The courts cannot stop us this time. It's overturning a process, not a law. It is our job according to the Constitution," said Lexi, still in a quiet and non-confrontational tone as the remaining cabinet members squirmed or looked elsewhere.

"The Constitution," said the President, thinking. "A good document," he said, smacking the table lightly with a bony hand. "It's the guiding light, showing us the way in the dark cave of uncertainty and peril, leading us forward to our destiny."

He delivered this while looking in the distance with a vacant stare, quoting from a speech he'd delivered in the Senate thirty-five years ago. Ironically, he'd been arguing for the preservation of the Constitution and this same filibuster.

"That is correct, Mr. President. We're using the Constitution to remove a roadblock to progress. Backwards people, bigots, and racists are always standing in the way of progress. We need to use this effort to overcome their prejudice and ensure victory for all that is right and moral. That's why we're doing this and preparing for any unlawful demonstrations from those fighting what is right," finished Lexi.

"Carry on," nodded the President, satisfied with the explanation.

Lexi continued down her list, getting a briefing from Homeland Security on any threats they were aware of or expecting. She also heard from the FBI Director who explained they had infiltrated dozens of groups of agitators. They were in the middle of orchestrating attacks through them to expose the plots, frame the leaders, and arrest all the members of these organizations for plotting crimes against the government.

So far, there didn't appear to be any aimed at the filibuster vote itself. It seemed they were waiting for the votes following its removal. Like statehood for DC, gun bans, and more voting rights, finished the FBI Director with a prolonged cough.

"Our goal is for our agents to convince the leaders of these groups to move sooner so we can catch them before they do actual harm," he finished.

The President looked on in concern.

"Claude, you should get that cough looked at. I have a great home remedy. Hot tea with lemon, honey, and just a touch of Irish whiskey," said the President with a smile.

Some in the room gasped at the insensitivity of the statement. They all knew the FBI Director was dying of stage four lung cancer. The President knew this and had in fact earlier supported the retention of the director when others suggested he resign.

"Thank you, Mr. President. I'll try that as soon as our meeting is over," said the Director, not taking offence at the President's memory lapse.

"Good," said the President. "Lexi, where are we with making DC a state? Why hasn't it happened yet? I put you in charge of that," said the President in an accusatory tone.

"Mr. President, we're working on it. This filibuster bill will help us accomplish this sooner than later," she said, ignoring his tone.

"Good. They should have been a state a long time ago. Hawaii too," said the President.

"You mean Puerto Rico, I believe Mr. President," said Lexi.

"Right, what did I say? That's what I meant, of course. Good people the Chicano's. Reminds me when I was a young man…"

Everyone in the room rolled their eyes and let the President ramble on again. Telling his story of his run in with a so-called Puerto Rican gang in his youth. The story seemed to change in every telling. Lexi just waited patiently until he finished. They made it through a couple more briefings when the President abruptly stood, causing everyone else to rise quickly.

"I'm hungry. Anyone care to join me in the mess for a sandwich? Where's Bob?" said the President looking around for his Secret Service bodyguard. Bob came forward.

"Ah, there you are. Let's go have some lunch with the First Lady. The rest of you are welcome to join us," said the President as he walked out the side door with his nurse and Bob following.

The President's chief of staff, Sam Vincent, stood as well, torn between staying to hear what they said or following the President. As he made a move to sit and stay, from outside the door, he heard the President asking for him. Reluctantly, he turned to follow, noticing the smile on Lexi's face as he left.

No one else followed. When the door was shut, Lexi sighed. She held up a hand. "I know, I know."

"Lexi, we need to discuss it," said Secretary of State, Susanna Bangura, her light tan face showing concern, almost terror, at the latest episode of the President. "He couldn't have made a serious decision on anything today."

"They are weaning him off one drug to try a different one later this week. He'll perk up, he always does."

"Why are you so reticent?" asked Henry St. Cloud, the National Security Advisor. A snake of a man, skinny to the point of anorexia, with greased black hair, dark eyes, and wire-rim glasses. His suit hung on him. Though healthy, he looked sicker than the dying FBI Director.

"Well, let me count the ways," said Lexi sarcastically. "I want to win the election and become the first female president by the people. I don't want to be the bitch that kicked him to the curb exercising the 25th Amendment. Just so I can take the job from the rightfully elected president," snarled Lexi. "It is an optics nightmare and will give all my primary opponents something to ding me over."

"But it is the right thing to do. He can't give the order to launch nukes," said Claude, causing another coughing fit. "Sorry," he said after he finished. The Secretary of the Interior, Felicia DeNovio, handed him a glass of water.

"Javier, since Sam isn't here, what can you report?" asked Lexi, addressing the Attorney General. An impeccably dressed, handsome Hispanic man sitting at one corner of the long table. "Did you discuss with the Joint Chief's drafting an emergency powers declaration? Making me eligible to decide on using the football if Isaac and I deem the President incapable of deciding?"

Javier glanced at the gray-haired Secretary of Defense, Isaac Roth, a former Marine general, who nodded. "I did. It's within the power of the cabinet, as a precaution, short of invoking the 25th, if a majority of the cabinet agrees," said Javier.

"Why was I not consulted on this?" asked St. Cloud. "I'm the Director of National Security."

"Hank, officially you aren't a cabinet secretary. You're only here because the President invited you to attend cabinet meetings. If you like, Lexi, we can take a quick roll call to make sure we have agreement before I draw up the final document. Assuming it is never used, we will destroy the only copy after the election. No one need know we even did this as it is an emergency powers act and not required to be included in the papers of *this* president. That is my determination as the Attorney General," said Javier in a serious tone.

"What about the Football?" asked Ashley Nabors, the Director of National Intelligence.

"The second football already travels with Lexi. She'll have a card she can use. This means at least one other cabinet member will have to always travel with the Vice President in case we cannot establish a satellite link back to Isaac. They already outfitted Air Force Two with the secure communications setup to handle any of these events should we need to complete this while in the air and give the order to the Chairman of the Joint Chiefs," said Javier.

"Seems you have this all laid out," said Gustavus Edmundson, the Secretary of Agriculture. "I don't like it. The Constitution is clear and establishes the chain of command. If you want the power, invoke the 25th. Without that, I don't care what you say Javier, it's not kosher."

"Gus, I understand your concern," said Lexi in a calming tone. "These extraordinary times require us to take precautions. Let's just suppose the next set of drugs clears up his fog, and he's lucid once more. We'll look like traitors for removing him from office."

"You have a point there. I'm OK with this until we're 100% certain the President won't get better. I think if he *were* lucid, he would agree this is a prudent step," said Gwendolyn Johnson, the Secretary of Energy. She was a woman around the age of Lexi, but unlike Lexi, she was embracing going gray and wrinkly. She looked like the grandmother she was.

"Any others have concerns before we take a vote? Willa?" asked Lexi, looking down the table at the Secretary of Commerce. Wilhelmina Kreutz raised her white-haired head and stared at Lexi with her own set of icy blue eyes. There was no doubt she was the person in the room who showed her advanced age the least. Her patrician bearing speaking of the Teutonic royalty in her ancestor's background. She still spoke with a slight European accent, even though she was born in the US.

Having been schooled in the finest institutions in Europe, as would behoove any daughter of the Kreutz companies of industrial machinery, she had continued in her father's footsteps and led the company for 50 years after his death. Diversifying the company out of machinery and into services, she'd made them into one of the largest service-based companies in the world. Willa had a habit of listening, but speaking infrequently.

"My dear Vice President, I believe we skate on very thin ice. Our plans to dismantle the safeguards of our country to achieve our goals leave me worried we may regret our actions as we pursue them with such single-minded abandon. I, like Gus, do not believe we are acting in the spirit of the law. We are bending and interpreting it to meet our current circumstances. We are ignoring the unpleasant, but approved, methods of mitigating these. I am against this. As you know, though, in the minority in this cabinet, I am also against removing the filibuster."

"I would resign, but my president is currently in no state to accept it. Nor to understand the reasons I would choose to quit. Until his mind is right, I will continue to serve in his cabinet and to advocate for adherence to both his vision and to the Constitutional safeguards we all swore to protect," finished Willa, formally.

Lexi showed a tight smile in reply. "I feared you'd feel this way. I disagree and must proceed as only I think I can. To protect our fellow citizens without destroying the reputation of the man's vision you claim to be serving. I won't tarnish his more than fifty-five-year record of government service by ending it in an inglorious implementation of the 25th. Let's vote Javier."

Taking his cue, Javier stood as everyone else sat.

"There are sixteen official cabinet posts, including the DNI, but not including the VP, for obvious reasons in this vote. The emergency powers document would simply give the Vice President the same ability as the President, regarding authorizing the launch of nuclear weapons, working with SecDef and the Joint Chiefs. It takes two of the people in the cabinet for presidential decisions unlocking the use of the nuclear launch codes," explained Javier.

He started going around the room asking for votes. Gus, Willa, Wendall, from Veterans Affairs, Art, the HHS Secretary and most surprising to Lexi, Les, the Secretary of Labor, all voted against granting Lexi the emergency powers.

State, Isaac, Felicia, Silvia from Education, Rose from Treasury, Gwendolyn, Fred, from Transportation, Vance Brown the communist Secretary of Housing and Urban Development, Ashley, the DNI, and Roger from Homeland Security along with Javier, all voted in favor. This made the last count eleven for and five against.

"The votes are noted. I'll draft the document and we'll have it signed by the eleven who agreed on its implementation. As always, and perhaps most importantly in this case, if this were to leak, it's a treasonous offence. If I'm still Attorney General, I promise to prosecute this to the fullest extent. Seeking the death penalty for any who leak this decision. It's of the utmost importance to the safety of our entire nation," said Javier. No one spoke after he issued this threat.

"On that pleasant note, Henry, do we have any updates from the situation in France?" asked Lexi.

The NSA Director, still peeved he wasn't involved in the decision to give Lexi Presidential powers to launch nuclear missiles, cleared his voice. "The funeral was yesterday. Since there were no remains to speak of, they used an empty casket for Gaspard to lie in state. Chaumont appears to be the front runner to replace him. He's working in concert with Junot, the temporary president, to rescind all the draconian measures Gaspard had put in place."

"This seems to have appeased the protestors. They allowed the fire brigades into their ghettos to put out the fires and to provide medical services to the injured and displaced. Chaumont seems sincere in his efforts to use a commission to reach a path to citizenship for all the immigrants who aren't considered French citizens. This despite their being multiple generations born in France without full citizen rights. This could be an interesting development for other countries facing the same bifurcated system when the immigrants are not granted full citizenship," finished St. Cloud.

"A long time coming for sure," said Vance Brown. "The longer we wait to make our own immigrants full citizens, we risk the same explosion. We can't treat them like shit forever without repercussions."

"Indeed, we cannot," said Lexi. "Let's pass the removal of the filibuster as the President wishes, and we can right some of this injustice here too. Henry, monitor things and let us know if anything happens." St. Cloud nodded in response.

"Madame Vice President," said Rhett, "I'd like to add that Interpol is still trying to find out who detonated the bomb. While we assume it was a faction in league with the protestors, there is no one claiming responsibility. They couldn't identify any remains of the bomber, for obvious reasons. They're at a loss and have few leads to pursue. It doesn't look promising. It's doubtful we'll have any closure on this, at least not quickly."

"Thanks Rhett. Alright folks. Enjoy your break and I'll see all of you at the next cabinet meeting in a few weeks," said Lexi. "We'll hope we once again have a clear-headed commander and chief."

#

Lexi sat in her office in the Capitol. A phone in her desk drawer vibrated. She opened it, grabbing the satellite phone while also pushing a hidden button on the underside of the desk.

"Hold on," she said into the phone as the SCIF mode in her office finished engaging. When complete, she could hear the barely perceptible white noise making surveillance impossible.

"OK," she said into the phone, listening intently.

"Correct. He's getting no better."

"Yes, I believe all is proceeding as planned," answered Lexi in response to a question. She continued to listen and then nodded.

"It is done. There was some resistance from surprising places, but our threats should keep the dissenters in check." Lexi kicked off her heels, leaned back in her chair, and put her stocking clad feet up on the corner of her desk in a very unladylike fashion.

"Don't worry. We'll watch them. After the break, we'll have the filibuster vote, enact our key bills, and win the election in a landslide. At that point, we should have an uncontested path and can finally fix this broken society and then the world."

Once again, Lexi listened. She sat up quickly.

"Like I said, I have it under control," she said in a stern tone.

She listened to the other side of the conversation.

"I understand. Good day to you as well," said Lexi as she ended the call. She leaned back in the chair once again, staring at the ceiling, contemplating the call and her destiny.

#

In another room, far from the Capitol, recording equipment captured the conversation.

Chapter 24

Nick Turner parked his motorcycle in front of a diner in Durango, Colorado, got off the bike and stretched, groaning. He opened the door to the diner, surveyed the counter, and chose a stool between a couple of older guys.

"This seat open?"

"Sure," said both simultaneously.

Nick set his helmet down between his legs on the footwell of the counter and sat gingerly on the stool. The guy on his left nodded at the helmet.

"Coming far?"

"Left Montrose at dawn so I could enjoy the ride from Ouray to Durango as the sun came up. Great scenery," said Nick.

"God's country for sure," said the guy on the right. The server came up, handing Nick a menu.

"Coffee?"

"Coffee would be great, just black."

"Where you from?" asked the guy on the left.

"Fort Collins. Needed a break and decided to just go for a ride. Great time of the year to tour Colorado."

"Got that right. Leaves still changing?" asked Right.

"Just past peak over the divide. Same in Aspen and Vail. Was up there two days ago. My name's Nick." He offered a hand to Right.

"Alan and that's Roger. We just call him Junior."

"Nice to meet you both." Nick shook Junior's hand. "What do you guys recommend?"

"Well, they sell the green chili across the country, so anything with green chili," recommended Alan.

"Breakfast burrito with green chili, can't go wrong. Not riding with anyone?" Nick nodded affirmative. "Good, so only those following you will suffer," Junior said with a big smile.

Alan and Nick laughed.

"You guys' regulars?"

Before either could answer, the waitress arrived.

"Unfortunately. They take these seats every day from 8 to 10. What can I get you, hon?"

"Wanda is a real comedian," grunted Alan.

"I'd be funnier if you tipped better."

"Haha. Times are tough all over Wanda." She just gave Junior a look.

"They recommend the breakfast burrito with the green chili."

Wanda wrote up the ticket and handed it to the cook as Nick sipped his coffee.

"How are things? Been a while since I have been down here," asked Nick in a casual tone.

"Depends. Things were going really well and then the pandemics happened, crushed our tourism. This town really relies on tourists. For the train, hiking, and biking," said Junior. "Alan used to work for the railroad. It hasn't really recovered, has it?" he said, looking past Nick at him.

Alan took a long sip of his coffee before answering, "Nick, I worked on the Durango and Silverton for 35 years. Started as a summer job in high school. Did pretty much everything, maintenance, engineer, shoveled coal in the firebox, filled the steam tanks from the water tank on the route. I even spent a year as a docent, telling tourists the history. I spent my life on that railroad."

"I've taken the trip a few times. The views are spectacular, especially when you are looking down into the gorge," laughed Nick.

Alan smiled. "Folks hate that spot, freaking pee their pants."

"Got that right," Junior chimed in.

"Anyway, we were flying high. Unemployment was like 2%. The town was crawling with tourists. We even added a fourth train to keep up with demand," continued Alan, remembering.

"Then the Chinese infected the world," mumbled Junior.

"Wherever it came from, it killed tourism," Alan agreed. "A town like this can't survive a season without tourists, let alone three out of four years in a row. Even though the government tried to help, it wasn't enough. Lots of folks left town to find work in other places or headed home to their parents. I got laid off, drew my unemployment, and hunkered down. I survived. Lots of others didn't."

"COVID was tough on everyone," agreed Nick, "Both times."

"Ya, like Bezos and Gates, Musk or Zuckerberg, had it rough. They all really suffered, didn't they?" said Alan in disgust.

"What about you, Junior?"

"I was a farmer and rancher, ran a bunch of cattle, grew some winter wheat, irrigated some fields for other crops. Things were good. Fracking meant more chances to extract oil and gas. I sold some mineral rights, royalty checks were rolling in. Bought a brand new F250 with all the bells and whistles. Our oil and gas went to shit because of regulations from the Governor and then this administration after. Tourism dried up and the town just died. Restaurants closed, people lost their jobs, houses, even the college had problems," said Junior.

"That's right. Then, right after COVID, we had new taxes and spending, then more taxes. Drilling never really started again. They went to Texas, North Dakota, and Wyoming, with their Opposition governors. Nick, how long have you been here?" asked Alan.

"Born here but grew up in Texas. Been back for 15 years, spent some time in the military."

"Well, you may or may not remember, but we passed a bill with an overwhelming majority to support oil and gas," said Junior.

"Ya, we voted," added Alan emphatically. "Followed all the rules. You know majority and all that. Then the Governor didn't like the outcome. They used the state congress to overturn the will of the people and ban fracking and voila, down went the economy. What's the point of voting if they just overturn the will of the people when they don't like the outcome?" asked Alan, getting animated. "After that, it was all downhill and we've never recovered."

"That was a while ago. Has it gotten any better?"

"Some. A few people came back, some tourists have come again, but nothing like before. Half the restaurants never reopened. Hell, if that kooky guy from Barstool hadn't bailed these guys out here, this place probably wouldn't have survived." Alan glanced at a picture behind the bar.

"I noticed the sign thanking Portnoy when I came in," said Nick.

Junior nodded. "My life ain't as good as it was. Sold my truck and went back to driving my old one. Farm a bit, but I sure miss those royalty checks from the oil company, so do lots of folks. It's just not the same."

"I mean, just look around. We are in some of the most spectacular scenery in the country, just blessed. It feels like we are existing, not getting back to the way it was at all," finished Alan, raising his hands as he talked.

"What do you think we need to do to fix it?" asked Nick between bites of his breakfast. "Good choice on the burrito and the green chili has some kick as well."

"Sure does, don't it," smiled Junior.

"I don't know," stated Alan. "After what the Governor did, I have little faith in anyone. But whatever it is, it's not what we're doing now. Seems like we're paying taxes but getting nothing for it."

"Letting us drill again would be a good start. The green new deal is anything but green," opined Junior.

"Hey, that's not true," Alan interrupted. "It's green for the owners. They get lots of green from the Government."

"You said you had some wind turbines on your land, Junior?"

"I did, but now they're just sitting there. Turns out they take a lot of maintenance and upkeep, and the wind here isn't as constant as they thought. I didn't read the fine print. The amount I get is based on a percentage of the money generated, plus a tiny payment for the land. Since they aren't turning, I'm not getting much. I get to look at these ugly windmills just sitting there. Company that put them up went bankrupt. Now I can't even get the bank that owns them to pay to take them down. So much for the promise of cheap energy."

Nick continued to eat as Wanda refilled coffee cups.

"Are you ready for this?" asked Junior. "Our Party run legislature just raised our state tax to compensate for lost revenue. I'm no rocket scientist, but it seems like making more revenue from drilling for oil and gas and the money the people earn would be a much better way to raise money than destroying both and then taxing us more on less money? I call that *stupidnomics*," said Junior.

"Opposition ain't no better," said Alan. "Best you can say is they don't actively try to mess it up. They sure suck at stopping the Party."

"Hey, you voted Party, so no whining," said Junior.

"What choice did I have? The only thing the opposition is good at is losing and then whining afterwards," laughed Alan.

"Seems to me both do their fair share of whining," added Nick.

"They're all good at that and photo ops," agreed Alan, nodding.

Nick pushed away the plate and made the universal sign of giving up. "That was good, but I can't eat anymore, or I'll have to put a few more pounds of air in the tires."

They all laughed.

Wanda came by with the check. Nick handed her twenty-five dollars. "Keep the change. Best green chili I have ever had."

"Well thanks hon, I appreciate it. Will make up for these two," said Wanda, rolling her eyes. "I hope they didn't bother you."

"Seriously, Nick, how would you fix the problems?" asked Alan, ignoring Wanda.

Nick pondered while taking a sip of coffee. "Well guys, I'm not exactly sure either, but it seems to me it has to start with spending less money. And shrinking government regulation. Gotta start there."

As Nick got up to leave, they did as well. Each of them left $5 on the counter for Wanda. Nick grabbed his helmet, and they headed out to the curb together.

"Nice ride," said Junior, looking at his bike. "Indian, huh? Got something against Harleys?"

"Nope. Just liked the look. When I rode her, it felt like sinking into your favorite recliner. Of course, that was before I rode for four hours straight," said Nick, groaning.

"Hey at least it is American," laughed Alan. "What model?"

Nick looked at the maroon bike, the ivory color highlights on the tank and fenders and the tan leather saddlebags. "It's an Indian Chief Vintage, 16."

"That old? Great shape," said Alan, holding out his hand.

"Thanks for the conversation, and thanks for recommending the burrito, Junior," said Nick as he shook Junior's hand.

"Anytime, Senator. Enjoy your ride."

Nick paused, shaking Junior's hand as they both smiled.

"Guess I'm not as incognito as I thought."

Alan shook his head, "We both watch EXN, we were just talking about how you're the only Party senator I agree with anymore. 'Voila', you walked in the door."

Junior nodded. "Like some sort of magic trick."

"Well, thanks for not telling me you knew and giving me honest answers. I'm trying to do right by all of you during the time I'm in office."

"You not running for a full term?" asked Alan, surprised.

"Not sure yet," replied Nick.

"That would be a damn shame if you didn't. Few plain talking straight shooting politicians in Washington. Hell, I might even vote Party if you run," said Junior, smiling.

"That would make your daddy turn over in his grave. Sullivans haven't ever voted for the Party," said Alan.

"Well, these are strange times. Have fun, Nick, and keep standing up for us. See you tomorrow, Alan," as Junior turned and walked down the street.

"Come back anytime, you know where to find us," said Alan as he walked up the street in the other direction.

Nick got on his bike, put on his helmet, and headed out of town.

Chapter 25

Nick rode his bike out of Durango east on highway 160. It was
a beautiful day, in the 70s, sunny and clear. He passed through
Bayfield, Pagosa Springs, and then up and over Wolf Creek pass.

Stopping at the top of the pass, he took out his phone and took
a picture of the USGS plaque set in the stone wall. It stated he was
crossing the continental divide at 10,857 ft. He didn't linger as the
wind was blowing and his leather jacket was inadequate. The air was
much colder at the top of the pass than the valleys below.

He headed down toward South Fork on the east side of the divide.
With a new tank of gas, Nick continued east to Walsenburg versus
driving up through the center of the state and coming into Denver or
Colorado Springs from the West.

Rolling into Pueblo, he followed the GPS on his dashboard and
stopped at the Courtyard by Marriott hotel, just as the sun was
setting. He'd logged about 8 hours on the bike and 400 miles. His
body was feeling the effects of this; plus sitting all day long for the last
ten months in Washington meetings.

In the morning, Nick got up at dawn. Worked out, took a shower,
and did emails until mid-morning. He packed up his little overnight
bag and headed down to the front desk.

"Good morning, sir. May I help you?" Delivered from a way too
perky young lady at the desk.

"Good morning to you as well," responded Nick with a smile. "I'm
looking for a good place to get some food and a feel for what it means
to live in Pueblo. Any suggestions?"

"Absolutely. If you want the local experience and folks who'll
talk your head off, I suggest Gus's Place for food and Eilers if you're

staying until after lunchtime. Just head out down Santa Fe, over the river toward the old steel mill. East Mesa is just before you get to the mill. Turn right, Eilers is a little storefront on the south side across from St. Mary's Church. Gus's Place is further west on East Mesa under the interstate, and on the south side as well. They're two of the oldest places in town."

"Thank you. I'll check out as well."

She handed him a receipt and smiled sheepishly.

"Are you *that* Nick Turner?"

"I guess it depends on who *that* Nick Turner is?" he replied.

"The one who saved everyone in New York and is our senator?"

"Guilty as charged."

"Wow. Would you mind if I got a picture of us?" asked the girl, jumping up excitedly.

"Of course, you're a voter."

She pulled out her phone and came around to pose with him, snapping the selfie. She looked at it and grinned, showing him. He grimaced a bit when he realized he looked old enough to be her father. Doing some math in his head, he realized it was all too true.

"Thank you. This will make my mom's day. I met Nick Turner. I mean Senator, sorry."

"Not a problem, Sophia," said Nick, glancing at her name tag.

"Thank you for staying at Marriott," said Sophia as Nick left the hotel, turning back to wave.

Nick loaded his overnight bag into the bike's saddlebags, put on his helmet, and headed down Santa Fe Boulevard. It showed a typical middle American city of small bungalows in various states of upkeep.

As Nick turned right on East Mesa, he noticed an old Catholic Church on the right in the distance. He drove right past Eilers on the left. Sophia wasn't kidding. The storefront was just twenty feet wide. Essentially, a small entry area built out from the front of a house.

He continued down East Mesa, under I-25, and found Gus's on the south side of the road. Doing a U turn and parking the bike in the dirt median in front of the restaurant.

Gus's Place was an old red brick building with a green and white striped awning and signs announcing they proudly sold Budweiser. They also proclaimed they were offering something called a 'Dutch Lunch'. Nick opened the door and entered, giving his eyes a second to adjust to the low light.

As was typical of the local tavern in cities across the country, tall tables and booths were in a line along one side of the narrow building. A long bar opposite, with neon beer signs above. Nick walked up to the bar where a woman in jeans, a faded Denver Broncos super bowl T-shirt, and a Rockies ball cap greeted him.

"Hello Senator," greeted the smiling woman.

"I see word travels fast," said Nick ruefully.

"Small town. Sophia warned us you were on the way," she said with a broad smile.

"So much for being sneaky."

"No need to hide here Senator, we're all fans. I'm Janice Miller. I manage the place for the owners."

"Well Janice, nice to meet you and you can call me Nick."

"How about 'Senator Nick'?" she said, leading him to a table.

"Do you have a community table or somewhere I can sit and talk to some of your regulars?"

"Sure, the table in the back is open to anyone. It's usually filled with regulars. We have a couple in right now," said Janice, leading Nick through the dimly lit tavern to a round table in the back.

"Here you go. Jack, Emily, this is Senator Nick Turner, who's apparently slumming and needs a bite to eat," said Janice, chuckling.

"Jack, Emily, nice to meet you. Hope you don't mind if I join you," asked Nick as he shook each of their outstretched hands.

Jack was an older guy who looked like he was used to working with his hands. A few strands of gray poked out from under a well-worn John Deere cap perched high on his forehead.

"Nice to meet ya," he said in a slow drawl. He paused, like he was going to add something else, when Emily burst in with her enthusiastic "Hello" as she held on to Nick's hand. She was younger than Jack, probably in her late forties.

"Nice of you to come by." She looked around. "Where is the rest of your group, like the Secret Service and stuff?" asked Emily.

Jack answered for him. "Hon, Senators don't rate Secret Service. I *am* a bit surprised you are traveling by yourself, Senator."

"You can call me Nick, by the way. I just came back home for a quick vacation. Wanted to get on the bike and ride. Talk to folks like you, with no cameras or others around."

"When'd you get in?" asked Jack, who seemed to take the lead in making conversation while Emily looked on.

"Last night. Sophia at the Marriott directed me here to get a true taste of Pueblo along with Eilers. Two places to chat with locals. Did I say it right?" asked Nick.

"Yep, EYE-lers, lots of folks screw it up," piped in Emily.

Janice came by the table. "Senator Nick, can I get you something to drink or eat?"

"What do you recommend?" asked Nick, glancing at Jack and Emily, who were both just drinking. Jack, coffee and Emily, what looked like iced tea. "Can I buy you two an early lunch?"

"You bet. My tax dollars at work. You should have the Dutch Lunch, that's what this place is famous for," suggested Jack.

"Wait and see, you'll love it. Most get it with a beer," said Janice.

"I'm riding, so I'll pass on the beer, but get Jack and Emily what they want."

With the order placed, Nick turned back to Emily and Jack. "What's it like in Pueblo these days?"

Again, Jack paused, and Emily jumped in. "Better than they was for sure, now that we have the new plant."

"New plant?"

"Wind turbine plant," explained Jack. "They build the parts for the various turbines in a big plant south of town. Put a few people back to work. A few other renewables have opened some stuff here locally as well. As good as that is, it still is only a dent. Don't know if you know this, but Pueblo used to have one of the largest steel mills in the world. You probably saw it when you came down, if you turned on Mesa just before you got to the plant."

"I did, doesn't look like it is doing much anymore."

"Not much. A few things like barbed wire and fencing, only employs a few, nothing like the old days."

"Ya, Jack was one of the last guys laid off when they closed down the steel side for good," interjected Emily.

"They cut my pension, and I held on doing a few odd jobs surviving until I could draw my social security early. Didn't have much of a choice back then," commented Jack bitterly. "Thankfully, Pueblo is one of the few places in Colorado where the cost of housing isn't going through the roof. Our reputation as a 'dirty city' is helping that out," laughed Jack halfheartedly before continuing.

"Funny thing is, the Chamber of Commerce is trying to sell us as the 'Renewable Capital' of the country. Offering tax incentives and stuff to get these companies to come down. I guess I shouldn't laugh. It's working, and the millennials and whatever they call the next generation are coming. Buying up and fixing the houses in the old part of town. Bringing their caramel macchiato and exercise clubs."

"Jack, they're called Gen Z," said Emily with an annoyed look.

Jack shrugged. "Whatever. I call them spoiled, whiny, ignorant, and lazy. Gen SWIL. They're even worse than millennials."

Emily was preparing to respond when Nick broke in to change the subject.

"So, the economy is turning up?" asked Nick, as Janice showed up with drinks for everyone.

"For a few anyway," replied Jack. "The history of Pueblo is diverse. Once upon a time, depending on who you talk to, there were twenty-six to forty different languages spoken at the mill. We had immigrants coming to work from Japan and China, Ireland, Germany and from every southern and eastern European country. Take this place, for instance." He waved his arm. "This was originally a church in the 1890s. This part of town is called Bojon town."

"Bojon?" asked Nick.

"Bojon, used to be an insult for someone of Slavic, Slovak, Serb, or Croat descent and was considered a slur. Now we're proud of it and refer to this part of town with pride. But it's disappearing, people are dying, relatives are leaving. No one has big families anymore to carry on and, of course, the mill is gone. Used to be community pride. Nowadays, we sit here or at Eiler's and remember the past. We're the last of a dying generation, literally with this part of town."

Nick was going to ask exactly what Jack meant, but Janice arrived with platters of cold cuts, cheeses, spreads, peppers, tomatoes, onions, and loads of white bread.

"Here is our Dutch Lunch. This was a favorite of the mill workers. We'd lay out the platters and they would make their sandwiches just the way they wanted. Jack and Emily can answer questions. Enjoy!"

"This looks pretty amazing and filling," remarked Nick.

"Pretty straightforward. I'm sure you can make a sandwich," said Jack with a smile.

Nick started building his sandwich. "You were about to tell me how the older generations are dying?"

"Senator, a few years ago, once things got better with the new turbine factory. The Chamber started trying to attract more business. They suddenly decided the old slag pile from the original smelter just down the street was a problem," Jack pointed away.

"They used to melt down silver from the mines before the steel mills. The waste went into that pile. The smelter closed at the turn of the 1900s. Then the Mill took off and all the immigrants arrived. Our parents and grandparents started building their houses. Settling down on all this land, right on top of the old smelter," ended Jack as he finished building his sandwich.

"What happened?" asked Nick, suspecting he already knew.

"For decades, folks have died from various cancers in Bojon and other neighborhoods adjacent. Our parents were proud to have become Americans. Happy to work hard in the mill, in the field, and even in the mines nearby. They were hard lives, but no one complained. We just took it in stride. Shit happens. There were plenty of grandmas who made it into their 90s and even a few in their 100s," said Jack, shaking his head.

"Then all the sudden they test the land around here. The land they built their houses on a hundred years ago. And of course, what do they find? It's full of all kinds of heavy metals, asbestos, and other nasty stuff. Along comes the government with their superfund money, trying to fix the land. Sniffing the air in houses and cleaning this and that," stated Jack in disgust.

"Well, at least they're trying, Jack. You can't blame them now," countered Emily.

"Em, I sure can. What I can blame them for is not giving a shit until now. Turns out the government knew all along the land was bad. But nobody cared when it was the dumb 'Bojons' building their houses on that old slag pile. That's what bothers me. Nobody cared until they were trying to attract these new renewables companies and these millennials with all their health nut shit. So, Senator, you asked how things are, well I guess it's getting better all the time."

"Don't mind him. He has too much time on his hands, and he still hates the mill shutting down," said Emily, suddenly serious.

"Em, that ain't it, and you know it."

Nick quickly changed the subject again.

"Jack, I'm sorry to hear about all this. The government is rarely the answer I've found," agreed Nick in a conciliatory tone.

"Senator, it isn't even that, and Em is wrong. It ain't just the mill, it is hope. There just isn't any hope left. Hope for a better life, at least not here. Ya, the new plant will benefit a few and maybe the Chamber will get more here. Even get to say we are the most renewable based city in the country. But that doesn't help all of us," responded Jack in desperation.

"Why is there no hope? Seems to me that's an individual issue?" asked Nick, carefully.

"We are a proud people. I had work, we all had work, and we worked hard. Two, hell, sometimes even three shifts a day in good times. The work provided for our families. We celebrated as a community. Took care of each other in sickness and in health. We were Americans. Senator, look around, drive around and you'll see what I mean when a self-sufficient community loses the ability to take care of themselves. What you see are people with no hope, at least not here," finish Jack resignedly.

"Jesus Jack, you're even depressing me. The Senator should leave feeling good about Pueblo. What do you think of the Dutch Lunch?" asked Emily.

Nick smiled. "Emily, I work in Washington. Nothing Jack says can depress me, and this lunch is wonderful. I'm about to have seconds," Jack laughed, and Emily smiled.

"So, Jack, how do we fix it?"

"Senator, you may not like my answer. Hell, I don't like my answer."

"Shoot," said Nick, taking a bite out of his second sandwich and dribbling mustard down his lip.

"Whoops, here you go Senator," said Emily, handing him a napkin.

"How do you like that mustard?" asked Jack. "Made locally by a cousin of mine," Nick nodded as he chewed.

"Anyway, how to solve it? I was in a union. They took good care of me and my guys. They tried to help when they started shutting the plant down in waves. Just didn't have enough money to help everyone. There wasn't anything else they could do. No other jobs here. Those that could, retired and survived on reduced pensions like me. Those who couldn't, left. Foreign steel just killed us. Maybe it was the union contracts. Or it was just the greed of the owners. Maybe the government didn't do enough. Japan and Korea ate our lunch, and we were done."

"Then the government showed up. That seemed like a good idea. Folks were hurting. Lots of agencies we had never heard of before. Folks went on various forms of help and unfortunately, those who stayed never got off it." Nick nodded, not wanting to interrupt Jack.

"Don't get me wrong. We all paid taxes, unemployment was our right, same with a bit of help. The problem was, we had always taken care of each other when folks were down. We had the church, lots of churches, and we had each other. We would all band together when someone got sick and couldn't work. Nobody ever went on food stamps; it was just unheard of. We were a community who looked out for each other until someone healed or got more work."

Jack reached for his wallet, handing Nick a credit card. "You ever seen one of these?" Nick shook his head no. "Senator, this is a government issued credit card. They load it with money every month, food stamps on steroids. I qualify for things because of my age, income, etc. At first, I was against it and then I got to thinking about all the taxes I paid in my life, and I justified to myself why I should just take it. Others were, why shouldn't I get my fair share?"

Jack took the card back and put it in his wallet. "Em's got one too. But hers is because of disability. She hurt her back. So here we sit, taking up space, not contributing, eating with our government provided 'help'," said Jack using air quotes. "This is what I mean about no hope. You can walk down the streets in most of these neighborhoods and I guarantee you more than half are getting some form of government help. This ain't right."

"But if they need help, why blame the government for helping? Most would say it is the obligation of the government to do just what it is doing," said Nick.

"Nick," Jack said in a tired voice, becoming more familiar and at the same time resigned, "Look around, are we thriving? Yes, we have food, a roof, we are surviving, but what is the prospect? I don't have the answer, but I know what isn't working. Folks need, even want the help now. Once they have it, they lose something. Maybe it isn't their soul, but it is initiative at a minimum. They just cease to 'do'."

"You passed St. Mary's on your way here. It is a shell of what it once was, the center of everything, the center of community. Now it is a symbol of another time. No one has faith in *faith* anymore. No one worries about salvation; They have replaced it with a stupid credit card from the government. It may not be a drug, and lord knows there is plenty of that around, but it is just as bad. Once you are hooked, it takes too much effort to kick the habit and you just give up and figure it is your lot in life to exist and the government is your dealer. If you want to stop it, you need to get the government out of everyone's pocket, not just taxes, but so-called help too. It's killing us."

Nick took a sip from his tea and digested what Jack was saying. "Jack, I appreciate the honesty and the perspective. I have to say I have not heard it from the people. Only the lobbyist and others on the hill telling us how we need to expand all these programs so we can help more people, longer. This is the first time I have heard an argument against assistance that is not based simply on the cost in dollars." Nick took a bite out of a dill pickle spear, contemplating Jack's *solution*.

"You may not have seen it, but I got in trouble last week for saying much the same thing in a committee meeting. Equating government assistance to being a meth addict. Both addictions are equally hard to kick. You just confirmed it. You didn't see this on the news by chance, did you?" asked Nick, hoping he was not just telling Nick what he wanted to hear.

"Senator, we don't watch TV. No cable either. We come down here or Eiler's to watch the Bronco games," said Emily proudly.

"Nick, I am happy you did that. I bet that bent some people the wrong way," said Jack with a belly laugh. "I wish I had *seen* it now. What Em isn't telling you is I threw a beer bottle through the TV watching the news one night and decided there was no reason to get a new one. I may be full of shit, probably am," said Jack as he glanced at Emily, who was rolling her eyes while smiling.

"I'm sure if you walked around, many of those on help would not willingly get off it, as it *does* allow them to live today." Even Emily shook her head in agreement. "We need to provide them with hope, not handouts. I'm not saying we create bullshit jobs, but you have to give people their self-esteem. Most of them would work, they just need help. Not just training, but opportunity. We have to offer people a way to earn a living and not just give it to them. It's dehumanizing. Counter to popular belief, it is not saving them, it is instead enslaving them."

"An interesting concept, Jack," said Nick. "I can't say I don't agree with some of your argument, but the reality is what it is. We don't have enough jobs in all the right places. All we can offer is an equality of opportunity. This is the beauty of America, mobility. Look at how people have always followed the work. Even after the initial COVID lockdowns, folks started working remotely and moved from California and New York to Florida and Texas. I don't think all folks are as willing to work as you seem to think they are."

"I didn't say you would like it. But consider this: there is a percentage who would work who still have a work ethic from their parents or family. Mostly over 40 or maybe even fifty, since most millennials aren't fifty yet," said Jack sarcastically, glancing at Emily.

"Careful buster," interrupted Emily, giving Jack an evil eye.

Jack shrugged with a small grin. "I am just saying the schooling the last few decades has destroyed the family, ethics, and morality, as well as apparently the desire to work. There will be a percentage of those who would prefer to stay on the dole."

"He's right Nick. To many young kids with too much time on their hands and not working. They always seem to have enough money for food and vaping, or worse, dope," said Em in a sad voice.

Jack looked at Nick earnestly. "I'm not one of those 'get off my yard' guys. I have friends whose kids and grandkids live with them on help and have no desire to do anything. Why work when you can play? It's not a life, but they have convinced themselves it is. They don't know what they're missing because they never had it."

"At least these teenagers aren't having kids. It's too inconvenient to have a girlfriend. Requires face-to-face conversation and you can't get pregnant over texts or watching porn," laughed Jack.

"I bet you're glad you came in here today," said Emily. "Jack paints a bleak picture and highlights the worst of things. He is right, we have little hope. We're just sort of existing. But hey," Emily said brightly, "it's better than Central America, Africa, or even India."

"Em used to sit around watching Discovery and NatGeo," laughed Jack. "Basic cable costs a buck when subsidized, so we pay the extra $5 a month to get these channels. If we had a TV that is, so you see there is some good. If you're going to be on TV now, maybe we'll get a new *old* TV."

"Well, unfortunately, the only cable you'll see me on anymore is probably EXN," said Nick, shaking his head.

"Not a problem. They all suck. At least EXN is not as full of lying asses. I keep voting for the Party, but it never seems to matter. I kind of like Tommy, anyway. He's just as much of a prick to both sides," said Jack, smiling.

Janice came around and asked how the meal and the company were, while handing the bill to Nick.

"Both were excellent. This was exactly what I was looking for. Now I need to get on the bike and back on the road."

"Skipping Eiler's and the 'Bojon Initiation'," laughed Janice.

"He's smart, not drinking and riding," smiled Jack.

Nick looked at the trio, confused.

"Eiler's is famous for the Bojon Initiation. It's a shot of Slovak plum liquor you chase with a Pabst Blue Ribbon. Making you drink a PBR is punishment enough. You ain't missing anything," said Jack with a grimace.

"I guess I'll pass on that, especially since I am riding, but I'll stop by and say hello just so Sophia doesn't get in trouble," said Nick. "If I ever need to chat again?"

"Just call here. If I ain't here, they can track me down. We only live three doors down."

Nick said his goodbyes to Emily and Janice, took the obligatory selfie, and got out on his bike. He was still thinking about what Jack had to say as he did a few laps around the blocks. Surveying the houses and neighborhood, ending up at the fence outside the old steel mill. Nature was reclaiming the outer regions and even the portions that showed recent use still looked abandoned. He took a few pictures and then rode away, back to Eiler's.

Nick said hello and visited the folks there as well. The word was out. Taking a few more selfies on this visit, he never had time to quiz anyone about life in Pueblo. He ordered the 'Bojon Initiation' and took a small sip of the plum liquor and a couple of swallows of his PBR to chase it down. It was different for sure. Leaving Eiler's, he headed north toward Colorado Springs.

Chapter 26

Hamit steered his tractor trailer off I-10 just past the Ehrenberg, Arizona Port of Entry. He had just passed through the weight station and now pulled down an off ramp into the Ehrenberg Truck World terminal. The lines contained hundreds of trucks.

He pulled into one marked China World Shipping transfer, matching the container on his trailer bed. He was nineteenth in line. He'd left Long Beach early in the morning. Depending on his turnaround here, he *might* make it back in time to get in line for his next round trip.

He watched as truck after truck drove under a gantry where the container on the tractor trailer truck bed was grabbed by an overhead claw and lifted clear of the rig. The gantry then moved the full container over another truck in another line, setting the load back down on top of an empty trailer bed.

Once it was seated, that truck would drive forward on its way to deliver the load into the interior of the US. The gantry returned to repeat the process for the next truck pulling under it. The entire transfer took eight minutes.

As Hamit watched, he marveled at the whole operation. Less than three years ago, this patch of Nevada desert had been just that. Now it included massive truck terminals both east and westbound on either side of Interstate 10. He knew there were similar installations built on the Arizona side of I-8 outside Yuma, on I-40 at Topock and on the Nevada side of I-15, and I-80. Only the I-40 terminal in Topock was larger than this one. All owned and built by China.

As he slowly crawled forward, he again checked his phone logistics app to see if he was returning with a loaded container or 'dead heading' back empty. Today he was empty. Even though he'd be much lighter, he wouldn't make better time as all trucks in California were limited to traveling in the right lane of the interstate and held to strict 55mph speed limit, regardless of the posted speeds.

Hamit's truck had a speed limiter installed, allowing him to approach 58 miles per hour and no more. If he was stopped and the limiter and many other details, minor and major, weren't in place, he and his company would face stiff fines from the state of California.

His turn came. While the gantry quickly snatched his container, he looked for the light to turn from red to green, signaling his ability to pull forward. Shortly, the gantry cleared his rig with his container in its claw and he pulled forward toward the massive truck stop on the grounds of the terminal. Doing quick calculations, he realized he couldn't reach the Long Beach terminal in time to get in line today for his next load.

The Long Beach to Ehrenberg trip rarely enabled Hamit to return before the Long Beach port gates closed to entry for the evening. He preferred the Long Beach or LA to Yuma route. It was shorter and gave him the chance to get an extra run in.

Sighing, Hamit pulled into a parking spot. He got out of his rig and stretched, joints cracking. He wandered into the restaurant portion of the truck stop and took a stool next to another driver, wearing a jacket with an American flag on the sleeve.

"Hey," he said to the salt and pepper short haired driver next to him. The guy gave him a sideways glance, taking in his darker skin, dark beard, and hair.

"Hey. Coming from LA?" he asked politely.

"Long Beach. Can't make the turn, so I figured I'd eat something and catch a few z's before heading back to get in line for the morning run of the Shanghai Express. I'm Hamit," he said, holding out a hand. The driver hesitated for a second and then held out his own.

"Jake."

"Nice to meet you, Jake," replied Hamit with a smile showing perfect white teeth. He noticed a military tattoo on Jake's forearm.

"You an independent?" he asked.

"Trying too anyway. They sure are making it tough to be independent. Not even sure why I'm out here. Should head back east and drive for Walmart. You?" asked Jake.

"Do I look independent? I'm happy about the job, working for the Chinese, driving the transfers. Trying to save up enough so I can go independent," said Hamit with a snort. "At this rate, I'll never make it."

Jake laughed. "Well, at least you know you have a load every day. Me, I'm constantly working to keep my rig full. Like today, I've been sitting here all day in idle. My container was supposed to be here today, but the ship docked late, because some workers called in sick," explained Jake in disgust.

Hamit nodded in understanding. "Yep. They call it 'yellow fever' on the docks. Every week, they selected a random group to 'call in sick' to make sure the labor situation isn't fixed. The union guys are using it to squeeze concessions and more pay, or so they say. I just think it's so they can line their pockets. Nothing has changed that I can tell, and I've been making this trip for two and a half years. Ever since they opened these Chinese Truck Worlds," said Hamit.

Jake just shook his head. "I hear you. So now my container isn't arriving until noon or so tomorrow and it sets me back a day at least, which now puts my next load in Indianapolis at risk. So, now I have to make it up along the way."

"At least you can drive faster than 55," laughed Hamit.

"There is that. Do you live in California?"

"Technically no. I live in Minnesota, but for the last two years I've slept in my truck waiting overnight at the terminals or here in the Truck Worlds," said Hamit.

"Geez, man, you got a family in Minnesota?" asked Jake, concerned.

"No, I got out of Afghanistan when the US pulled out. I was one of the lucky ones. Was an interpreter with the 82nd. I was trying to get my family out, but the Taliban got them before I could," said Hamit with a sigh.

"Ah man, I'm sorry. I did three tours over there in the 10th Mountain division. What we did was a crime, leaving you and your family and all the others out to dry," said Jake in a frustrated tone as Hamit's vegetarian lasagna arrived.

Jake pointed to the waitress.

"Edna, Hamit lost his family in Afghanistan after we pulled out before he could get them out. He worked with us as a translator. Edna lost her husband," explained Jake.

"I'm so sorry for your loss. My husband always spoke highly of the translators. How you guys risked everything to help us out. Now we all see what he meant as we watch the Taliban slaughter innocent women and children." She just shook her head. "Ralph is turning over in his grave. Well, hon, I'm sorry for the whole thing. What happened to you, to me, to Jake and everyone else. Should have just left it all alone," she said, turning away to run some more food.

Jake looked at Hamit. "Lost my first family when I came back. Just too much to process. I can't really blame her. She tried. Eventually I got straightened out. Have a new wife and kid back in Ohio. It's tough being on the road so much, but the pay is good when I have a load and the way the supply chain is so fucked up, I should have job security. As long as I don't have to go into California," laughed Jake.

"I hear you," said Hamit between bites. Jake was just drinking coffee. "The AB5 bill killed the independents in California. Plus, the truck emission restrictions and all of us having to work for companies. It's no surprise there is a shortage of drivers and a backlog of goods at the ports," said Hamit, gauging Jake's reaction.

"Between the numbnuts in Washington and the idiot in California, what should we expect? These regulations, selling out to the unions, and the environmentalist wackos, it's no surprise gas is $10 a gallon and a gallon of milk is $6. These guys have no clue what their policies do. Believe me, there are plenty of trucks and truckers available to pull the loads. But owner operators can't work in California. My truck is ok and meets the standards, but a lot of the guys I meet have trucks they've owned and maintained for years, running just fine. They aren't going to buy a new rig just for the privilege of driving freight in California," said Jake, worked up.

"Right, that's why I came out from Minnesota. I'd been there working in meatpacking and dairy plants. Now that is shitty work, sometimes literally," said Hamit with a laugh, one Jake returned.

"Then I heard about the truck driver shortage. These companies offered salaries better than what I was doing. I had my commercial license to drive the rendering trucks, so I just up and went to California. Had to switch from my meatpacking union to the truckers. The only way to get the job. I guess it is ok, but lots of rules. In fact, if my union rep was here, they would probably fine me for talking to you about this," said Hamit, looking around as he finished his lasagna.

"Big brother is always watching, for sure. Listening too, especially for folks like us who still dare to work for ourselves. Even in the east coast ports, they're now putting the squeeze on the little guy. Forced unionization is picking up in the ports there. Folks are fighting it, but Washington is putting the screws to them on this too. They just can't help but meddle in our business," finished Jake.

Hamit waved at Edna for the bill. "I wish there was something we could do about it. I hate working for the Chinese making these runs. They own all the companies doing this. Even this truck stop. Hell, they could bring all of this to a halt if they called for a strike. With no independents in California, there'd be no one to pick up the slack," finished Hamit.

"Let me show you something." He pulled out his corporate ID card, which allowed him access to the ports of LA and Long Beach. He showed it to Jake. It showed his picture and serial number. There were also a series of Chinese characters along the side.

"What the?" asked Jake.

"Right, I don't know what they mean either, but all of us have them. I tried to look it up on the internet once, but it said they meant 'the sun is green and tastes like onions'."

Jake laughed loudly. "Really?"

"Right, so I tried to ask my union rep. He said he didn't know either, but the company prints the IDs, so he just does what they say. Last time I checked, this was America and we have some rights. I am a naturalized citizen. I think I have a right to know what the heck is on my ID badge," said Hamit in a demanding tone.

"Damn straight you do," said Jake, looking around. "Hey, you know there is a group of us who feel the same way you do. Let me give you a website and my cell. Take a look and tell me what you think. It's all on the up and up of course, at least on the website," laughed Jake. "If we don't do something, we're all going to end up slaves of the Chinese, just like Washington and the California Governor would like it."

"Sure, I'll look. Let's stay in touch. Hamit and Jake exchanged cell phone numbers. Let me know the next time you head this way and I'll see if we can meet again and talk," suggested Hamit.

"You got it, buddy. Thanks for your service and I'm really sorry about your family," declared Jake.

"Thanks Jake," replied Hamit as he walked out to his rig to start the journey back to Long Beach. He got in the truck, pulling out a secure smart phone. Typing in some information, including Jake's cell phone number and the website URL he had provided.

It transferred this information to the FBI database in the Hoover building in DC. They would analyze the data like similar information he'd collected these past few months running the Shanghai Express route. 'Hamit' typed a text to his wife on yet another phone saying he would be home in time for dinner as he pulled out and headed back to southern California, whistling as he drove.

Chapter 27

Nick left his hotel room in Colorado Springs at 6:30 in the morning. Colorado Springs was a military town. Besides the Army base, the Springs, as the locals referred to it, had Schriever and Peterson Air Force Base, NORAD in Cheyenne Mountain, and the United States Air Force Academy.

It was an Air Force town, but also had Ft. Carson, an army base. Many of the expeditionary forces deploying abroad originated here. Nick rolled into the cafe in the shadow of Pike's Peak, near the army base. Parking the bike, he locked his helmet on the saddlebags.

He walked into the restaurant, looking around. A hand went up in the corner. Nick walked over to a table where a man in blue air force fatigues stood up and smiled.

"Senator Turner," said the man with a smile and an exaggerated extension of Nick's last name.

"Jeff, how are you?" asked Nick as he shook his hand and gave him a quick hug.

"Fine Cap, fine," replied Jeff, using Nick's old air force call sign.

Nick laughed. "Haven't been called 'Cap' in a long time. It's good to see you. Been too long. When did you get your bottlecap?" asked Nick, using the slang term for Jeff's silver oak leaf Lieutenant Colonel insignia.

"Nick, I've been a Lieutenant Colonel for five years now. In fact, I'm on the list for full bird next year," said Jeff somewhat proudly.

"Well deserved. That's one I'll be happy to approve when it hits the Armed Services committee. You're a lifer then?" asked Nick.

"Don't know how to do anything else but fight. Besides, we just had another baby girl," announced Jeff with a huge smile.

"Oh, my God. Pam needs to get you fixed. What is that, five now?" asked Nick, with a shocked look on his face.

Jeff laughed. "Pam wishes. This is seven."

"Geez, you trying to single-handedly repopulate the US?"

"Well, you know there is nothing like being welcomed home from a long overseas tour," said Jeff with another laugh.

"I was never so lucky. That's why I never came home and just kept flying."

"Still free? Pam has some great friends," said Jeff questioningly.

"Why does everyone feel it is their mission to get me married? You sound like my chief of staff," said Nick, shaking his head. "Got a picture of the clan MacGregor?"

"I sure do." Jeff pulled out his phone and began showing Nick picture after picture of his family. Four girls and three boys ranging from 17 to less than 1-year-old. His wife was a pretty blonde, still skinny.

"A great family. Pam looks fabulous after all those kids. You're a lucky man." Nick just shook his head, somewhat envious of Jeff's situation.

"Now you know why I need to make full colonel," stated Jeff with a laugh.

"I always saw stars in your future. From the minute we met in Afghanistan."

"Who are you kidding? If you'd stayed in, you'd have been in charge by now. Way better than what we have."

"That's why I wanted to swing by and talk. When I found out you were here, it made sense," disclosed Nick.

"Did you come down from Fort Collins this morning?" asked Jeff, looking at his watch. "You must have gotten an early start."

"Nah, rolled into town last night from the south and stayed in a hotel."

"Hotel? Next time, call me. I can kick one boy out of a bunk and find you a place to sleep. Better than Afghanistan anyway," laughed Jeff.

"Boy, that is a hearty endorsement."

"What were you doing down south?"

"I decided to just ride around the state this week and speak to folks incognito and see how the regular people are doing. You know, get the pulse of real life."

Jeff laughed, nodding his head to the side. "Incognito? Cap, the waitress over there, is terrified to approach. You can't go anywhere incognito. Sometimes I wonder if you hit your head one too many times in all those ejections." He waved her over.

"Renee, this is Senator Nick Turner."

Nick got up and shook the middle-aged woman's hand. She gave him a hug. "Sorry Senator, I'm just so proud of what you did, and it's such a pleasure to meet you."

"Thank you, Renee," responded Nick.

"Can we get a couple of coffees, Renee? Just black, no cream, please?"

"Of course, Jeff."

"I come here a lot. One of the few places where Clan MacGregor hasn't been banned," he said with a smile, as Renee walked away.

"Right. Knowing you, they probably march in."

"I'm not *The Great Santini,* but it would hardly be fair to leave Pam with a troop of hellions."

Renee brought the coffees, and they ordered a couple of Denver omelets.

"It's your dime. What's on your mind?"

"Jeff, I see it from the Washington perspective. The attempts to consolidate bases, which frankly, I must admit I don't see why Colorado has five air force bases. I was in favor of consolidating Peterson's mission into Schriever and Buckley. But I got ferocious push back from the lobbyists. The Space Force is getting a ton of money and is spread all over the place. It makes no sense to me."

"Being honest, which is what I think you are expecting, not only does it not make sense, but it is also probably not deep enough. Nick, especially the Space Force. They have no goals or objectives except to expand and get more funding. That is where the pushback came from. More units equal more funding. Will it hurt? A little, but not as much as you think because most of the consolidating is for monitoring and administration, not on the line soldiers or units. It is more optics than meat."

Nick nodded. "I figured as much about Space Force, that's why I didn't fight it. Texas got hit hard as well. My concern is waste and inefficiency. You know me. I'm pro soldier and anti-leadership. That's why I quit. It required too much compromise of my principles. I know there are good people, and we need more like you, coming up from the battlefield to change the political slant. I just don't know if it is possible. Our generals and admirals are now political animals. They see the money they can make as a talking head, in a lobbying firm, or as the head of a defense contractor. They have also figured out the key to all of this is networking in Washington. To call it a swamp is an insult to a real swamp. It's more like a Superfund shithole," finished Nick in a disgusted tone.

Jeff looked somewhat startled and glanced around to make sure no one was watching. Thankfully, early on a Thursday morning, the place was mostly empty, and Nick and Jeff were in a back corner booth.

"Shit, Cap, you need to be careful saying things like that. Like I said before, for someone so smart, you are hopelessly naïve and reckless as well. That's the real reason you mustered out. You never would've been able to keep your mouth shut," said Jeff, concerned.

"Probably true. Now I'm a senator, and I'm going to do the same for the short time I have left."

"You're not going to run for a full term?" asked Jeff, dismayed.

"I don't know. It is such a cesspool. Almost everyone is a snake and a climber. I thought military ticket punching was bad. Washington is this on steroids. They all run around building power bases. Getting and giving favors. Building a base of donors so they can move up. From the House to the Senate to the Cabinet and then into the lobbying world. The one thing missing in all of this is doing a job to look out for their constituents. Maybe I *am* jaded, but man, it is nothing like I thought it would be. It is also nothing like what Franklin, Hamilton, and Madison envisioned it to be."

"Wow," uttered Jeff, looking at his watch. "7:33 and you've already ruined my day. I expect that out of a Firstie, not my senator."

"Sorry. I call it like I see it. What do *you* see?" asked Nick, pausing while Renee set down their breakfast.

"I need the truth, Jeff, not the politically correct BS I get in Washington and in the committee meetings from the generals and admirals."

"Cap, it's bad. Morale is lower than I've ever seen it," confided Jeff in a low voice, looking around. "Afghanistan started it. The debacle of the pullout. Then watching all those Afghanis get slaughtered after. Then we did nothing but send in the drones. Worst is the women. We all feel a sense of responsibility. We made the place stable for a generation of women. Made them believe they could lead a normal life of education and freedom. Then we stuck our tail between our legs and ran, leaving them all behind to be raped and tortured. Nick, it's eating at every one of us who served there. To make matters worse, our generals and leaders act as if nothing bad happened," ended Jeff, now as worked up as Nick.

"That's what I hear from others. What else is going on?"

"Frankly? It is all this diversity, equity, and inclusion crap." Jeff paused, looking around again, in between bites of his omelet, shaking his head. "I can't tell you the number of meetings and calls I've been on with superiors about DEI. They instructed us to make lists ranking our women, gay, and racial minorities and then another list with the white servicemen. They have instructed me to recommend promotions based on these, not strictly on time in grade or potential."

Nick interrupted. "I see nothing has changed on promotions based on time in grade, versus promoting on merit and potential. This has always been a problem."

"Cap, the only thing that has changed is faster promotions based on race, gender, or orientation. *These* are on afterburner. You know how bad the system has been. This just makes it worse. Bad for morale and bad for our country. I'm having great officers retire early or simply quit to go to the private sector. We're losing all the studs. You know we weed out those who can't lead, who can't command, who don't react well under pressure. We promote those who can think and make snap decisions under fire. This is why we're the best in the world. Or were. None of this matters any longer," explained Jeff.

"You're saying you are being told to promote people based on quotas instead of time served or ability to lead?" asked Nick carefully.

"Absolutely. We just had the boards for battalion promotions to Major. We submitted our lists. A black captain was fourth and a female captain was third. Both with barely three years of service as captains. When I saw the promotion list, it only showed two approvals for major this round. Care to guess who were numbers one and two?" asked Jeff.

"The woman and the black captain?"

"Bingo. I don't mind this if they promoted the other two as well. They both had more years as captains. To jump these two and not promote the others is bad for them, bad for the ones getting passed over and bad for the country. Not to mention the two who were passed over were head and shoulders above the other two, and everyone in the unit knew it. Including the two who were promoted."

"Now everyone knows they got promoted *primarily* because they're female and black to check a DEI box. That will hang over their heads for the rest of their career. The idiot politicians think they are helping. All they are doing is ruining unit cohesion and morale. It is actually *hurting* the very people they claim to be helping. Our branches of the military are all about trust and ability. Everyone knows it. You know it. Why the fuck don't our generals and admirals know it and push back? The next time we deploy to a hot spot, it's going to be bad," noted Jeff, frustrated.

"How's recruiting?"

"Ha, how do you think it is? People aren't as eager to join after what they saw in Afghanistan, Syria, Iraq, and Libya. Our last few interventions have been unsuccessful. After your little stunt in New

York, we had a minor bump, but not much since. The sad part is once again we are prioritizing gay, race based, and female recruits here too. Over the traditional midwestern farm boy and good ole boy southerners. You know, the people who love their country, believe in God, work hard, and will charge into a hail of bullets to defend it."

"Diversity is popular. You have to admit discrimination needs to be eradicated. Opening up more opportunities for all to advance equally is a good thing," offered Nick.

"I agree in every case *but* the military. I want my kids exposed to diversity. You know what it means to serve. To lead. It is not a job. It's a calling. Our usual pool of recruits is now persona non grata. I'm not sure how confident I'd be that we could win a battle against the Russians if they grab the rest of Ukraine or Poland or any of the Baltic states," said Jeff. He was getting more and more worked up as he continued to describe the environment to Nick.

Nick nodded, but didn't interrupt.

"We sure as shit couldn't stop China from taking Taiwan. Maybe we could stop Iran from taking Saudi Arabia, but Israel, forget it. The capability is suspect, and the *will* is not there. North Korea is another one. If they go into South Korea, and we don't deploy immediately, with Chinese support, the NK army will be in Seoul in two days. I only know the sitrep in the air force. I can only imagine it is worse for the ground pounders and the Marines. Cap, I don't know what we're preparing for anymore. So much of the stuff we are doing is administrative. Sitting behind consoles and computers. Our ability to put boots on the ground we can count on is getting smaller and smaller," he finished.

"I see it. Others do as well, but it just seems like we're intentionally diminishing our ability to project power. Almost like we are sorry we were the world's sole superpower and keeper of the peace. We are losing our reputation and we don't seem to care," revealed Nick.

"I know. It is frustrating. If I didn't have eight mouths to feed, I might look for a career change," said Jeff, dejected.

"Don't you dare. We need leaders like you. You've seen combat. You've led men and women into battle. If all the soldiers like you give up, we are doubly screwed."

"You mean like you did?" Jeff said this in all seriousness, looking Nick in the eyes.

"Exactly. Don't follow in my footsteps. Maybe this is my path where I can help more from here than I ever could've if I'd stayed in."

"You'd have had your second star by now easy."

"Maybe, or maybe I would have been cashiered out? We'll never know. You and I both know I wasn't cut out to follow ticket punchers. Warriors fine. Blue Falcons, forget it," sneered Nick, using a derogatory term in the air force for ass kissing officers.

Jeff laughed and took a sip of his coffee. "Used to be we dealt with Blue Falcon's, and they changed, or we made their life miserable. Now it is the only way to go. The entire upper echelon is full of them." Jeff looked at his watch. "I have to go attend another day of PowerPoint presentations on diversity. Today it will probably be how to identify and use the proper pronouns," finished Jeff sarcastically.

"Is 'numbnuts' masculine or feminine now?" asked Nick with a straight face.

"Haha Senator. What they should be teaching are your air-to-air combat tactics," said Jeff disingenuously.

"Jeff, I flew an A-10, not a fighter like you. There were no air-to-air encounters," replied Nick with a straight face.

"A huh, right Cap. Those battles never happened. Or so they advised us. I *forgot* I was supposed to forget. Must be my memory going," confided Jeff. "You'll get this one, Mr. expense account?"

"Of course, I'll use your tax dollars," smiled Nick as he and Jeff had a quick handshake and hug. "Say hello to Pam for me and tell her to take a break," ordered Nick.

"No worries there. I went to the doc after the last one."

Nick winced. "Better you than me. Good luck Jeff."

"Cap, watch your six. These guys stepped on a lot of backs to get where they are. They are not about to go down without a fight."

"They forgot how to fight. Fighting for privilege is not nearly as passionate as fighting to save one's country. Look at how the Ukrainians stood up to the Russians. I'll keep an eye out," said Nick as Jeff headed out the door.

He sat and finished his coffee, going through his phone answering emails. Renee came back up and asked him if he needed anything else. He smiled and thanked her no. She hesitated to leave for a second, and Nick looked back up.

"Something on your mind Renee?"

"Senator, I'm scared."

Nick perked up, looking around, "Scared of what, Renee?"

"No, no, not now," she said, a bit flustered. "About everything around us." She waved her arm. "I was born and grew up here. My first husband was a sergeant in the Army at Ft. Carson. He died in Iraq. My second husband is an Air Force sergeant. Guess I have a thing for sergeants," she said, smiling.

"Military men are usually pretty dependable. I can see why you're attracted to them. What has you scared?"

Renee looked around; it wasn't too busy yet. She sat down opposite Nick. "This is a military town. That's what makes us tick. Scuttlebutt travels fast. People are worried about what our focus is now. We left Afghanistan and ruined our reputation in the world. Now it's not uncommon for everyone to call us the 'Chair Force'. Cyber, Space Force, and using drones are what we seem to be concerned with. We are merging bases; we are reducing the size of Carson. Folks are genuinely concerned we're no longer worried about fighting with guns and planes. Like we think, it is all going to be a big video game in the future; you know, lasers and stuff. I'm worried Senator. I have a 17-year-old who wants to enlist, and I'm worried what kind of future he has," stated Renee.

She stood up and picked up her coffee pot. "Sorry for bothering you with this, but I want you to know people, regular people in a military town, are worried about our leaders and the decisions they make. Afghanistan tore our guts out and left us wondering why we sacrificed and if it is still worth it. That is unbelievable. Sorry," she said as she moved away to fill other cups of patrons.

Nick waved Renee back over. "Tell your son serving is an honor to our country, and to his own personal patriotism. If he stays true to those, he'll do just fine. I'll tell you, it's my job, for however long I am in the Senate, to do all I can to make sure no one's son or daughter sacrifices their life in vain. Or worse, for political purposes only. I'll do all I can to make sure that never happens again," he said, holding onto her arm. She wiped an eye. "Thank you, Senator. That helps."

She came back with the bill. Nick left her a nice tip. It was a beautiful fall day. He headed west out of Colorado Springs, up the pass and over the divide. Just riding and enjoying the scenery until he headed into Boulder late in the afternoon.

#

Nick sat in his hotel room in Boulder, reviewing the long list of emails and texts. He opened a text from Chuck. 'How is the listening tour going? Get in any bar fights yet? Need money for bail?'

He started a rude reply and stopped. Everything written, and increasingly said, was now recorded and preserved. He suddenly realized he did not differ from folks he had been talking to. Everyone was afraid to have an opinion. Even United States Senators.

"Doing fine. Enjoy the rest of the break," wrote Nick.

Sitting back, he stared at the ceiling in his hotel room. He'd been on his 'diner' tour for a week. The stories were the same. Didn't matter if they were on their way to a construction site or housekeeping staff headed to hotels. Office workers downtown and medical staff headed to the giant medical center. Nick talked to all races, orientations, sexes, and ages. He didn't ask about their party, but it was obvious by the comments.

Things were tough all over. More folks living paycheck to paycheck than ever. Crime rising even into the suburbs. Most avoided downtown because of the homeless and mentally unstable.

People were worried and felt powerless to change their own personal circumstances. There was no faith in their political leaders doing anything to help their lives get better. Most didn't recognize him with his sunglasses and three-day growth of beard.

Some folks asked why he was even asking the questions, fearing they were being targeted or their responses being recorded. This particularly worried Nick. Folks had opinions, but they were afraid to voice them. Worried they would be punished or overheard. This was the most disturbing revelation from his conversations. Fear of big brother, cancellation, and especially the US Government.

Chapter 28

Lexi slid her feet out of her heels under the table and rubbed one on top of the other. Why couldn't her signature look have been a scarf or a hairstyle instead of ridiculously high heels? Now she was expected to continue to cavort around to keep up appearances. It had kept her long legs toned, but forty-five years of heels since her teenage years were taking a toll on her feet and on her back.

Seated opposite was Holman Holliman. HH, as he was commonly called, was a scion of old money fortunes. He sat on the board of American and European banking giants, among a host of other holding companies. He looked like a typical patrician banker. Impeccably tailored European suit with perfect gray hair, fashionably styled. Expensive polished Italian shoes, Hermes tie, and a manner of utter disdain for anyone and anything others would say or do.

Seated next to HH was Ari Feldberg. He looked the part of Costello to HH's Abbott. Ari was short, overweight, balding, wearing glasses with thick lenses. He had a perpetual sheen of perspiration on his forehead. Something he patted constantly with his monogrammed handkerchief. In contrast to HH, he appeared to be wearing an off the rack wool suit with no outstanding characteristics. Looks were utterly deceiving in his case. He was as ruthless as they came.

Ari was the lead partner in an international syndicate, managing sovereign funds, and sovereign debt. These two bankers controlled or consorted with every source of international funding on the planet.

If the US passed a budget requiring them to borrow four trillion dollars, Ari and HH were the people who placed the debt into the market. Spreading it around as *they* saw fit. The dirty little secret of international banking was the perception of China owning all the

American debt. They were fine to let this be the view, but under all the facades, it was these international banking houses who controlled *all* the debt. America's, China's, Russia's, everyone's debt.

They were the real power brokers, but few realized to what extent this was true. Lexi was one of these few and only because her great-grandfather had been one of them. Even Treasury Secretaries and Fed chairmen didn't know where the debt came from or who held it all.

"Gentlemen, more tea?" asked Lexi in an uncharacteristically sweet voice. Just outside the door, a middle-aged Asian woman responded to the button Lexi had pushed under the edge of the table. "Tai, more tea please," asked Lexi in a conversational tone to her maid.

"Yes, madame," said Tai, bowing deeply.

Ari looked around the ornate study on the second floor of Lexi's five story home. Located just around the corner from the Fairmont Hotel on Nob Hill in San Francisco. "Very nice brownstone Madame Vice President," remarked Ari nervously.

"Thank you, Ari. You know I prefer Lexi in private. We just finished remodeling and modernizing the house. It took several years. It is a great location in the city, near all the best restaurants."

Tai came back in with a fresh pot of tea, scones, and biscuits. She laid these on a tray in the center of the table.

"Thank you, Tai, that will be all," said Lexi.

Tai bowed again and left the room, closing the door. Lexi pressed a different button. "I added a SCIF mode so we could speak frankly," said Lexi in response to the now audible low hum.

"What would we need to discuss so securely, Lexi?" asked HH drolly, clearly uninterested.

"Don't play coy with me HH. Capitalism has failed in America. We cannot consume and produce our way out of this. At some point, there will be a reckoning. It's up to us to figure out how to transition to a more sustainable economic reality," she asserted forcefully.

"Pass another continuing resolution to raise the debt ceiling, like you do every year. Then get your caucus to pass a budget using reconciliation. There hasn't been a federal budget passed by the

Party since they forced you to balance the budget in the 90s. The opposition has been no better. What was the last time, 2006? What's the big deal this time?" asked HH with a shrug.

"It's time to stop pretending we care about debt. We don't. We're over 40 trillion. Our debt to GDP is well into the 150% ratio. Countries have defaulted on far less," she finished.

"We all know the house of cards on which we build modern economies. We provided the cards. However, I cannot see why we need to address this. As you say, everyone either continues the way we are or it all crashes together. As long as we continue to loan money and prop up economies with faux currency, we are all fine. The deficit is irrelevant. You know as well as I it is actually over $200 trillion when Social Security and Medicare obligations are factored in. That is what, $550,000 per citizen? We can never repay it. It only crashes if someone pulls out the cards. No one in power is reckless enough to do this. It is suicidal. Correct?" asked HH, staring at Lexi intently.

"Too much of the money earned by corporations hides in low-tax countries. This must end. Even if they produce less, we need to stop it all from being offshored. This is a ticking time bomb. At some point it will go off. I would prefer it be done in a controlled manner. Controlled by me, rather than say China, or frankly, any of you," Lexi smiled wickedly.

"Lexi, this would be most unwise," counseled Ari. "You may think this is manageable, but the results and the consequences are impossible to foresee. We stand to lose much more than we could gain. How would it be any better for us? We could crash the system and hire armies to protect us. Would this accomplish anything?"

"Ari, we have tried your way. We have been trying it for well over a hundred and fifty years now. You and HH and all the others have financed both sides of every major conflict. Provided arms and funding for every major coup. Then funded the resistance and rebels who eventually overthrew the tyrants you put there in the first place. You profit from misery and mayhem. In fact, if one were philosophical, and armed with, say, a couple of major networks and cable news agencies at their beck and call, I could make the case that all the world's woes are your fault. From the colonialism and imperialism of World War I to the Fall of Russia, the bankrolling of Lenin, the rise of Hitler, Mussolini, and the Depression," Lexi sipped her tea, surveying the reaction. They waited for her to finish.

"World War II, the Cold War, Hamas, Al Qaeda. All funded by you while you also fund Israel to defend against them. And let's not forget 9/11 and now 10/7. You win no matter who wins or loses."

HH sat stoically. Ari's forehead poured sweat while listening.

"You have done the same with America. You think you have the answer in globalization and the world market. China now depends on your money. They are so hyper-financed, that should be your genuine worry regarding default. You figure you can use it to keep them from upsetting the status quo. If you lose control, you'll just wait for them to collapse and start over. Not this time. Capitalism is the problem. Most Americans now believe this. They will no longer be your willing dupes. Things are about to change. You think you're the only ones with leverage?" Lexi just smiled at the surprised faces of her guests.

"What exactly would this leverage be?" asked HH, not in the least put off by Lexi's speech.

"Seriously? We have enough debt to bring the entire world to a screeching halt. Even the mere rumor of defaulting would cause the stock markets to crash. China would be in revolt in less than a week and millions of poor would starve in two. Even if the Chinese killed twenty, forty, or even a hundred million, there are a billion more with pitchforks. They can't win. When China goes, there goes the worldwide supply chain. The Europeans revolt in two weeks and the middle class in the US in three at the most. The entire global supply chain and interconnected financial markets you have spent so many years creating would all come tumbling down." HH merely sat contemplating Lexi's speech while Ari found a dry handkerchief in his suit pocket and dabbed his damp forehead. Neither spoke.

"COVID showed you this. Something you didn't foresee or control. Look at the damage it did to the global supply chain.

You lost control. Countries started asking why they were allowing critical components to be manufactured out of their control. Putting their own livelihood at risk if a pandemic happens again? Renewed nationalism and reshoring put your model at risk. With no peasants to farm or build your yachts and G6's, even you'll be afraid of who's coming to the door," finished Lexi, leaning forward.

HH, still unruffled, on the outside, responded. "What is your point? Any of us could crash the world with little effort. What does this fix? How does this help?" Lexi smiled.

"The system is broken. It no longer works. We can do it systematically, or we can do it with a hard reset. There is a choice. You give me what I want, when I want it, and we do it the less damaging way. My way. I'll bury all of you if you screw me. You think you have the power. Working in the shadows, with mysterious phone calls, and suicide bombs, pulling the levers, making demands. Well, that ends now. I'm not afraid to burn it down, because I have a plan to bring it back," said Lexi in a forceful tone.

"Madame Vice President, I believe you are giving us way too much credit for influencing world events beyond financial matters."

Lexi laughed, and it sent a chill down their spines. "I suggest you not join any of my poker games."

Ari practically had rivers flowing down his forehead, mopping it with his now soaked handkerchief. HH looked pensive, thinking about the possibility of Lexi going through with her threat.

"What do you want?" asked HH, finally.

"Now?" answered Lexi, leaning back. "Nothing, but I expect you to seek my counsel if you are planning on funding any revolutions, toppling any governments, or perhaps killing any more leaders? I want you ready to fund my efforts to wean this country off capitalism. To do this, we are going to need funding to extend our social safety nets. Until we can normalize our population and flatten the gap between the haves and the have nots. What you get is we still consume the products from your debt funded manufacturing states while we still feed the world and allow your investments to continue growing. Don't screw me. I have the leverage now and you need to go back to your counsels, cabals, secret clubs or whatever you do and let them know of our new 'relationship'."

"Lexi, we.ve been providing stability in the world for 150 years. Human nature drove most of those conflicts and revolutions. Contrary to your accusations, we don't stoop to assassination. We merely stepped in to ensure whoever won, we'd have a modicum of control, preventing mass anarchy, and a total breakdown of the system or society," explained Ari, clearly sensing catastrophe.

"You mean like the Holocaust? The Russian Purges, Indian Famines, or the Great Leap Forward? Hundreds of millions of people dead. This was you exercising that modicum of control? I would hate to see what happens when you're not *helping,*" said Lexi.

She stared at the two men. It was clear she had won.

"This is exactly why we're going to do it my way. If you're already contemplating putting a bullet in my head, that would be most unwise. I have put a failsafe in place. Lest you forget who my great grandfather was, my last act will be to expose you and your world, to make it clear exactly what your 'modicum of control' has done to people's lives, privacy, and futures."

HH remained stoic as Lexi continued. Ari seemed to be in the middle of turning into a puddle.

"Believe me, the media would eat this up. The peasants will show up at your door first, before they start killing each other again. We are much better at cooperating than trying to scheme against each other. You get to keep pretending the world is your chess board and I get to fix America's delusions. Leading us toward a new frontier where diversity, inclusion, and equity are the core values. Once we're all rowing the same direction, we can combat climate change and save this planet while hedging our bets and colonizing others," said Lexi with fervor.

HH and Ari sat, complacent and defeated.

"Well, gentlemen, I thank you for stopping by for this delightful tea. I will see you both at the Victory Fundraiser tomorrow night?"

"Indeed, Madame Vice President, and we will convey your requests to our colleagues. I think you will find we have little choice but to agree to your demands," said HH as Ari rose as well, nodding.

"Hardly demands, simply a partnership of joint benefit," said Lexi with a smile, rising to lead them from the room and to the door.

Chapter 29

"Hey Cara," said Nick to the owner of Cara's cafe in Boulder.

"Nick!" said Cara, running up to give him a big hug.

He hugged her and stood back to look as she posed. What he saw was a very skinny woman with purple, pink, and white hair. She was wearing round rimmed glasses with lavender lenses, ripped jeans and a rainbow themed T-shirt.

"Don't you eat any of your own pie?"

"Cycling 50 miles a day. I can eat all the pie I want," said Cara with a big smile. "Here, have a seat at the counter for now and let me get you a coffee until we empty a bit."

Nick sat at the end of the counter across from the staff busily making lattes and cappuccinos for the patrons.

"Just black, right?" asked Cara, pouring a cup.

"You remembered, thanks. How's business?" asked Nick, looking around with a smile. What he saw were about fifteen tables and booths with another half dozen outdoors. On this Friday morning, all were filled, plus four of the six stools at the counter.

"It was close. If not for the PPP in the first pandemic, we would never have made it. I had to furlough some people. But as you know, we were one of the last states to ease up on the mask mandates. When Texas and Florida were wide open, they restricted us to 25% for the longest time. I burned through all my savings to keep paying folks. You know it's like a family here," she said.

Nick nodded and sipped his coffee. It was a now familiar story from his stops throughout Colorado cafes and diners.

"We eventually got back to full capacity and no masks. People started wanting to come back and then I got smacked upside the head one more time in the second one. You know, I had three stores and a small takeout cafe before the pandemics. Well, I'm back down to two again. Not because demand isn't there, but because I can't find people to hire. The state kept 'helping' people, incenting them from going back to work. At first I was all for it, but geez. It went on *forever*. I almost moved to Texas, and you know what I think of Texas politics," laughed Cara.

"I've only been in Washington a year and I can tell you they have no clue the consequences of this 'help' on the small businessperson. I tried to talk, but no one wants to listen. It's all about appearance. Who can argue with helping people in need?" shrugged Nick.

"Shit, people in need?" asked Cara, "How about people in need of a swift kick in the ass? I gotta tell you, Nick, I'm questioning my loyalty to the Party. For years as a gay activist in the LGBTQ community, I have always shouted the opposition wants to stuff us back in the closet. Only our Party cares about our needs and our rights, but I'm not so sure anymore."

"Me too, you know me. I've always been a moderate. To be honest, and don't tell anyone, but there isn't much difference between 60% of both parties in Congress. The other 40% are zealots on both sides. Nobody cares about you or me, Cara. It was truly disappointing," said Nick in a conspiratorial whisper. "Or rather, maybe they do care personally, but not enough to make waves."

"It doesn't surprise me, Nick, but it makes me worry."

He nodded. "So, things are better?"

"It's all relative. You hire people and they quit. I hire people and they don't show up." Cara just shook her head. "Let me tell you a secret I have discovered. Seems like anyone under the age of thirty has no ambition. They don't seem to care about *their* future. They don't want to work more than they have to in order to get by. To get up and be here at 7am. To work hard for 8 hours a day. And I don't know how we change that. It's really disheartening."

"Cara, sadly, I'm hearing this from all the small businesses I talk too."

"I can't hire people I can depend on. It sucks. I could be growing. I could be serving the community and providing jobs and tax revenue. But all these kids can get some type of help and live with their parents or with a bunch of their friends. They have enough to pay for high-speed internet, weed, and Doritos," said Cara as Nick laughed at the last bit.

"Doritos are still the go to munchie?" asked Nick, still laughing, as Cara nodded.

"I'm serious. They can get help to pay for their internet and phone. They can get help to pay for their food and, sometimes, pot shops can take EBT cards. Why would they get up and go work to get the same or less money after taxes than what they can get for doing nothing? Why are we doing this? It makes zero sense," said Cara, shaking her head in disgust. "You want something to eat?"

"Eggs Alejandro, of course. Fruit and pancakes as usual," said Nick with a smile.

"Let me get the order in and we can finish catching up," said Cara, heading back to the kitchen.

Nick drank his coffee and surveyed his surroundings. There were some collage paintings on the wall. Each depicting various climate destroying activities and protest efforts in clippings and photos glued to the canvas in a hodgepodge of angles and textures. Nick just smiled. Cara showed back up with coffee.

"Interesting paintings."

"Local Artist. Believe it or not, we have sold a half dozen. Hey man, it is Boulder. Austin has nothing on us for weirdness," said Cara with a laugh. "Food should be up in a minute."

"Great."

Nick looked at the patrons and saw the usual mix of couples and guys and girls together. The major difference in this case was almost all the couples were LGBTQ. Cara's was a well-known hangout in Boulder.

"Here you go, one Eggs Alejandro," said Cara.

"Looks wonderful. Can I ask you another question?"

"Of course."

"It's been a few years since we've really talked. What do you think of the status of the LGBTQ movement?"

"Funny you should ask that. Alec and I were talking about it. You remember Alec?" asked Cara.

"I think so. Tall, glasses, sandy blond hair. Used to come in on Saturday mornings like I did way back when," said Nick.

"Yep, that's him, but he is gray and a bit more rotund," laughed Cara.

"Everyone is more rotund except you."

"You still look pretty fit. Anyway, Alec thinks we have gone backward. Remember, he has been out for over 45 years. He was young during the AIDS crisis. Fought the fight, marched, sued and argued cases against discrimination. He's a lawyer. Anyway, let me bring him over. He's just reading and drinking coffee. You can get his view firsthand," said Cara, walking to the other side of a wall where she had another half dozen tables. She came back with a distinguished looking older gentleman, who had a reader and coffee in hand.

"Alec Hersh," he said, holding out his hand, his eyes widening a bit as he recognized Nick.

"Nick Turner."

"Cara, you didn't say he was our senator," accused Alec, looking at Cara, who was smiling like the Cheshire Cat.

"Don't hold it against me," commented Nick.

"No worries, Senator. Cara said you are asking for her opinion of the LGBTQ movement."

"Yep, I have my own views, but obviously, I am not part of the community. I'm interested to hear from real members versus the speakers we get at our congressional committees."

"Well, and remember, this is my opinion and I hope Cara chimes in where she disagrees. I feel like we were getting there and then it went off the rails. We have several problems. First, most of us, like most straight men and women, want to be left alone to lead our lives as we see fit. We're not interested in special treatment, just equal. For most of us, we can understand religious objection and respect that we can get a cake somewhere else versus literally making a federal case out of it," emphasized Alec.

"Amen to that," agreed Cara, smiling and nodding.

"That one hurt us, because it made it look like all we cared about was destroying Christianity. For religious people to reject their faith and their god on the altar of secular progressivism. I'm a Christian and I struggle, but I have come to terms with it personally. I would never presume to tell others how to worship. So, we looked petty there, and it went against what most of us were asking for: equal opportunity. Setback number one," said Alec as Nick nodded while eating his breakfast.

Alec continued. "The second stumble is more pervasive. You notice how most TV shows now have at least one gay character. Most times they *still* represent the worst stereotypes and don't reflect the reality of most gays being just like you and me. Normal in all ways except we are attracted to the same sex. The problem is we have a media who highlights the true minority of folks within our own communities. These are the most extreme and the most vocal, who will never be satisfied with just equality and acceptance. They want vengeance," said Alex, sighing.

"Like everything else, the media panders to the extreme. More viewers, more clicks, the crazier the better for them and the worse for our culture," said Nick.

"Senator, sadly, you are correct. Look at the war over Trans. Look at the drag queen show controversies. These are the actions of a tiny percentage of the gay community who are themselves a tiny number of the overall population. The way this is portrayed, it seems like every classroom has a drag queen story hour daily and every female bathroom is filled with transitioning males waiting to assault girls coming in to pee. Both sides are using this to create fear. This is not right and hurts all of us who just want to lead our life. We are losing all we've gained. All I fought for. All Cara fought for," said Alec, getting worked up.

"Piece of pie?" asked Cara, breaking in to give Alec a chance to calm down.

"May I buy you a piece of pie?" asked Nick.

"Rarely indulge, but I don't get to bend a senator's ear too often. How about Lemon Meringue," he said, smiling at Cara's tactics.

"Strawberry Rhubarb for me. Haven't had it in years," ordered Nick, smiling.

"OK, a couple more examples of us moving backwards. I'll try to remain calm," said Alec as Cara turned and smiled.

"I know Cara told you she is questioning the Party's commitment to our movement. The same for me. Next is the idiocy of gender fluidity. There is no worse evil concoction than the progressive driven crusade to destroy biology," stated Alec, getting animated. "I mean, what is the endgame here? What is the goal? The entire gay population is maybe 3%. Trans makes up a tiny proportion of that 3%."

"The ideas being put into the heads of young people about their gender and feelings and the ability to pick this themselves. Plus, the idea they can make this choice without the input or permission of their parents is frankly a hate crime. A hate crime against humanity. I say this as a gay man with plenty of trans friends. Adult trans friends who made this life altering decision once they were mature enough to fully understand the process, the consequences, and the irreversibility of these surgeries. Instead, it is being promoted by the Party, fully supported by the teachers' unions, the medical community and the Party controlled media. They are making it seem like anyone who is gay is in full support of this. Well, I can tell you I'm not. At all. Nor are many of my gay friends, though not all," admitted Alec, now getting upset again.

Cara brought the pie and filled the coffees while Alec continued.

"Guess what? We have children too. We understand more than most the agonizing decisions faced when one questions one's biological gender and feelings. There is no way in hell I would want my children, who are both straight by the way, even growing up with two male parents, making these decisions without my help and without counseling or consultation. This is ludicrous to think a young child has anywhere near the maturity to consider the long-term ramifications of these decisions," finished Alec, now red in the face.

"Couldn't agree more. I only have common sense to guide me. Your statement is the only one that makes *any* sense to me. I fully support anyone's right to make this decision. Let's be realistic about *when* they are mature enough to understand the ramifications it will have for the rest of their life," said Nick, seriously.

Alec nodded vigorously. "I used to think bigotry was the problem. We needed to get kids away from their parents, who were filling their heads full of racist and bigoted shit. God, were we wrong. We were too blinded to realize we were being used and our outrage was being used to destroy the very entity that could be the salvation of all of us, the family. What they are doing to children with this crap and don't get me started on all the racist shit of the so-called protestors." Alec stopped to take a bite of pie and a sip of coffee, carefully thinking before speaking again.

"All of this does one thing: it removes the parent and replaces them with the state. In the process, they have also strived to replace any faith or Christian morals and ethics with secular progressive beliefs. It's a religion, or worse, a cult, and it has lots of brainwashed zealots in the form of progressive activists. It's so seductive, like a drug. This gender dysphoria is going to ruin children for life. If they're not sure about their gender, how in the heck are they going to build stable families and raise mentally healthy children with family values, morals, ethics, and *tolerance* required to build a solid society? For all. Gay, straight, and trans," asked Alec, on the verge of tears over this conversation.

Nick reached out and put his hand on Alec's shoulder, comforting him. "You pretty much just confirmed everything I already believed to be true, but you're assuring me I am not alone. This is the testimony we need in these committee hearings in Washington. Instead, we get the authors of the books, and medical doctors who have sworn the Hippocratic oath, claiming gender fluidity is the only healthy and humane way to support children with questions." Nick glanced at Cara. "You're pretty quiet. Do you agree or have a different view?"

"Most of it. When I was young and struggling with my feelings of being attracted to women instead of men, I really could have used some guidance and counseling. It would've helped me through some rough patches. Depression, suicidal thoughts, and just general feelings of guilt. I got through it, but it wasn't easy. I still think there is a role for schools or counselors, but I agree with Alec, there is too much money associated with the junk science and no incentive to stop them from changing genders or getting on various hormone drugs. There is no money in telling them to ride it out, to monitor things, and see if they feel the same when they get older and more mature."

Nick looked from Cara to Alec.

"I think we can support these efforts. My feeling is it must be in an age-appropriate way. Transitioning is a one-way trip. If you wake up one day and realize you made a horrible mistake, what do you do then?" asked Nick.

"Nick, I could easily have been one of those kids if they had allowed this when I was young. That scares the shit outta me. My god, what a mistake that would've been. I never wanted to be a boy. I just wanted to figure out why I wasn't a *normal* girl. It gives me shivers just thinking about those poor girls and boys facing this now. With no one to guide them and tell them to weather the storm. All they have are doctors and teachers telling them to start taking puberty blockers, hormone drugs, or to consider surgery instead of wait and see, before they decide," said Cara, getting worked up as well, contemplating what could have been.

"They are just too young and immature to be making this kind of life altering choice, no matter how miserable they *think* they are. They are teenagers, after all. Teenagers do stupid shit all the time, but it rarely involves irreversible genital mutilation," said Cara, shaking her head, now visibly upset.

Nick squeezed Cara's hand as she turned to go back to the kitchen.

"Excuse me, be right back." Nick could see her wiping her eyes in the kitchen.

"She's a gem for us in Boulder. But even the LGBTQ community here is split," said Alec. "Radicals who want to burn down the system and those like us that want to enjoy the gains we have made and continue to normalize the gay choice as simply one of preference. It should have stopped at gay marriage. That was ultimately all we ever said we wanted. We had anti-discrimination laws, and we had an entire generation who had come of age acknowledging gays existed and were people just like them in every other way. Then the Progressives kept pushing. Too much money to be made in continuing the fight. They wanted payback, special treatment, and to rub people's faces in it. All of this was exactly what we were trying to convince people we didn't want. It made a mockery of everything *we* had done," said Alec as Cara came back.

"Sorry, I just haven't talked about that in a very long time."

"Senator, I saved the best for last," said Alec, looking from Cara to Nick. "But this is an example of exactly how we have allowed the progressive secular movement to use us as a tool. We have been willing dupes, supporting them with our votes even when their fiscal policies have been disastrous. When their efforts to help the marginalized and underprivileged blacks and Hispanics were downright criminal. But hey, the evil opposition are all bigots, right?" said Alec, shaking his head. "Anyway, and this one is near and dear to Cara as well. Transgender athletics."

"I was going to ask for your thoughts on that one," said Nick, eating his own pie.

"There is no greater example of things going too far than the idea, that somehow a boy who transitions to female in high school and then wins state championships running girls' races, is fair and on the up and up. This is insanity. No matter how many scientists or experts show up on cable news to say there is no difference between men and women, girls, and boys, there very much is. It is called biology.

It is wired into our DNA," said Alec, pausing while Cara filled their coffee cups.

"Think about it. Since we first walked upright, it is clear who is the hunter and who is the gatherer. The biological outcome makes man strong and woman nurturing for the perpetuation of the species. It has been clear that the women want to choose the strongest and biggest protector they can find to make a family of powerful men and women to continue the species. According to the secular progressive movement, we can now play God. We can choose to become whatever sex we want. No questions asked. It is ridiculous to think boys deciding to be girls is right or fair when competing against biological girls in sports," finished Alec.

Cara interjected at this point. "I think the solution is easy, create a separate category, run a separate race for transgendered boys and girls. If we want to support this, it cannot penalize biological girls through no fault of their own. Those girls denied scholarships and accolades of being the best at their sports against their biological rivals shouldn't suffer because of political power."

"I agree completely. Honestly, this one seems so obvious. I don't know why we are struggling with it so," said Nick.

"This is why I'm disillusioned with the Party. They say they represent me, but they don't, and this conversation has completed my epiphany. The moderate wing of the Opposition, such that it is, more accurately reflects how I live my life. That is a truly sad admission for an old gay activist like me to admit," said Alec with a rueful smile.

Nick looked at Cara. "You feel the same? About the Party?"

"Absolutely, and Alec is right. I was a state champion cross-country runner in high school. This year the top two spots in *every* girl's track and field event went to transgender girls who were biological boys. It is hard enough now to get funding and attention for women's and girls' sports. Why would a girl want to play a sport knowing there is no hope for them to win? I went to my niece's high school volleyball game. What did I see? There were two players on the opposing team that were 6'4" tall. As tall as you, Nick. They were transgender girls who had been biological males. They also play on the girls' basketball team, too. I'm sure you have heard this is an issue in the NCAA women's sports where waves of transgender girls who were males are now winning championships on college teams. The lawsuits are flooding the courts and it is not looking like common sense will prevail," finished Cara.

"We've had various committee meetings and hearings. I'm sad to say, almost all of them are doctors and PhDs, telling us how all of this is progressive and compassionate. The kicker, of course, is how it's all couched as the only way to *help* the children, often despite parental misgivings," stated Nick.

"If I had lost out on my state championship after running for 6 years of competition and missed my scholarship to Stanford because some guy decided he could beat the girls but not the boys, I think I would have been homicidal. The kicker to all this, some of these 'girls' suddenly decide they don't want to be girls after they have won the championships. How is that going to come back to haunt these women later in life? Knowing we screwed them out of life-changing accomplishments because of loopholes in legislation? You can be sure those women will not be pro-LGBTQ," said Cara. "Sorry guys, but I need to get some work done."

"Cara, it is great to see you and chat. I really appreciate both of your perspectives. It validates exactly what I've been thinking," said Nick. Cara retreated to the kitchen.

"I need to get going as well. Have a pro bono case I need to review. Nick, it was great talking with you," said Alec.

"If I need to get in touch with you?"

"Here's a card. Call any time. Thanks for the pie and the conversation. You actually give me hope."

"Great, the Senator with the least clout in Washington is making the most sense. What does that say about our government?"

"Good luck, Senator," smiled Alec, shaking his hand.

#

Nick pulled into the driveway at his house in Fort Collins, Colorado. He used the keypad to open his second garage bay and rode his bike inside. Parking it between his twenty-five-year-old Toyota Land cruiser and his vintage 1962 Corvette. His garage was just large enough for him to get the bike in between the two cars. As he stretched, he checked the two trickle chargers keeping his car batteries charged.

He unlocked the door from the garage into the house, turning off the alarm as he entered. There was a time when he didn't even lock his doors. But given his schedule and the contents of the house, his insurance company demanded he put in the alarm system. Nick turned on the lights in his kitchen. He really liked this house. It was an early 1900s bungalow in the oldest part of Fort Collins, on Mountain, a prestigious avenue the streetcar had once traveled.

The house had been added onto through the years, including an upper story. Nick had done little to it since buying it fifteen years ago. The kitchen was modern with stone backsplashes, antiqued granite counters, stainless appliances, and wide plank hardwood floors throughout. The bathrooms all had stacked stone half walls and basin sinks perched on reclaimed wood buffets. It was all beautifully restored. The few parties he had hosted as a CSU professor had earned the requisite oohs and ah's from the attendees.

Nick grabbed a Pellegrino from the fridge and walked to the living room. Art hung on every wall where there wasn't a bookcase full of hardcover books. His furniture was mostly craftsman style. Lots of wood and leather.

He sat down in a recliner and put his feet up as he sipped his water and glanced at his phone. He didn't turn on the TV perched above his stone fireplace. Pushing back the recliner, putting his hands behind his head, closing his eyes, he promptly fell asleep, back at home, finally.

He woke up, startled. The dim light streaming through the windows revealed he slept all afternoon to now dusk. The doorbell rang again. He now knew what had awakened him. Hurrying to the door, pulling it open as the figure was turning to leave. The person turned to face him. Nick's expression turned from surprise to anger.

"What the hell are you doing here?"

Chapter 30

Lauren Bergamo stepped out of the shower, drying her shoulder length dark auburn hair as she walked to the bathroom counter. Standing in front of the mirror, she contemplated her naked figure, sighing. She was still winning the battle against time, and so far, gravity, if only just.

It was a war she knew she would eventually lose. She did what she could. Extending workouts, adding yoga, and changing eating habits. She was not naïve and knew these looks were a key to both advancing and keeping her position at ANC.

While working on her journalism master's at Columbia, she had also found time to win the Miss Indiana pageant. Even making the top ten in the Miss America finals. This led to modeling opportunities. While interesting, she only modeled enough to pay her college debts. Doing a few local commercials selling mattresses and headache pills. Enough to find out she enjoyed being on camera.

Her first TV job was at an Indianapolis NWN affiliate who offered her the opportunity to do the early morning weather and traffic. She jumped at the chance, left school, and headed back to her home state.

As she toiled doing the weather and traffic in out of the way places like Indianapolis, Topeka, and Lexington, Kentucky, she contemplated what might have been, if she had stuck with modeling. She found it interesting how many former beauty queens ended up in the news business. After all, when was the last time you saw an ugly news anchor?

Her big break was a story about opioid addiction in Kentucky. How this and the fentanyl epidemic were decimating the poor in Appalachia. It won her a regional Emmy, while also getting the attention of *America's News Channel.* ANC was then still a premier source of cable news and often raided the local stations for new national talent. She moved to Atlanta and started making her mark as an investigative reporter, following stories around the globe as needed. She was determined to advance on her journalism skills and if how she looked helped, she would use it while she could.

After blowing her hair dry, she pulled it back in a loose ponytail. She was not scheduled on camera today. When not on the air, she tried to downplay her attractiveness. It was an attempt to be taken more seriously and to attract less attention from her male colleagues. Picking up her purse and phone, she thought about her recent interview with Senator Nick Turner.

Having seen first-hand the devastation of drug addiction among the poor of Appalachia, his statement about government assistance being as hard to quit as meth rang true to Lauren. But she had also seen the genuine needs of these people. Without the government's help, they would starve. The drugs made them incapable of contributing to society, or caring for themselves, in any meaningful way.

Her producers felt she got the best of him, but his answers and tone left her with a burning desire to get payback. Lauren hadn't succeeded in cable news by backing down from confrontation.

Still contemplating how to get back at Turner, she backed her red Mini-Cooper out of the underground parking garage. Her condo was in the fashionable section of Buckhead. Formerly an upscale suburb in Atlanta, it had been successful in becoming its own city. Taking half of Atlanta's tax base with it.

As a result, crime was falling precipitously in Buckhead. In Atlanta proper, the opposite was occurring, with the exit of Buckhead and its affluent neighborhoods. She made her trek to the downtown Atlanta headquarters of ANC, navigating the wild Atlanta traffic before entering the security of the underground parking in the ANC building.

Lauren acknowledged a few colleagues on the way to her desk. It was in the middle of a sea of cubicles, on one of the news floors. Years previously, they had filled all the floors with busy ANC employees. Now less than half the building was occupied by the cable station personnel.

Sitting down and waiting for her computer to finish booting up, she looked around the small office. In one corner were replicas of the two Emmys she had won, the full-size originals in her condo. The second one was a national Emmy, awarded for a story she had aired on ANC about whether there was still a need to teach high school students about the Holocaust.

She'd made the rounds of the various talk shows, promoting and defending that piece. Her research showed more global governance, faster communications, and the predominance of cell phone footage, made hiding atrocities so much harder than in World War II.

These atrocities were immediately known, with the ability to broadcast every heinous deed in Syria, Ukraine, and Gaza, as well as instant footage from school shootings in the US and other places, *as they happened*. To Lauren and her producers, it showed it was no longer necessary to keep highlighting the Jewish genocide. As if it could happen again with folks simply turning a blind eye. Her piece won accolades from the liberal media and progressive activists while earning the ire of conservatives, and the enmity of the Jewish communities, for even suggesting it was no longer necessary.

"Hey Lauren," said a man from behind her.

She turned to see her producer, Jeff Carter, standing at the doorway to her cube.

"Hi Jeff," she answered, swiveling around in her chair. "What's up?"

Jeff hid his disappointment at seeing Lauren in her sneakers, leggings, and loose sweatshirt.

"The big boss liked what you did to Turner. He appreciated you not giving up."

"Hallberg? Really?" laughed Lauren, referring to the President of the network. "Does it have something to do with the fact, 'we' conveniently forgot to include the part in our coverage where he explained how really hard it was to get off both meth and government assistance?"

"He's a big boy," shrugged Jeff, leaning on her short cube wall. "He should be used to words being twisted in Washington. I bet Fontana is loving the additional attention, just before the filibuster vote. The Opposition is eating this up.

"Don't we care EXN is broadcasting the entire footage from the committee hearing? Clearly showing we conveniently left that key point out? Or the fact Tommy had Turner on saying we twisted his words?"

Jeff smiled.

"Anything to get eyeballs. We need all the ratings we can get. Besides, our footage and everyone else, except EXN, went with the story of the 'rogue' Senator going off the reservation. EXN only plays to their partisans, anyway."

"And we don't?" replied Lauren archly.

"Our viewers rarely cross. My feeling is Fontana is going to use this to make an example of what happens when you go against the Party. Turner is going to have a short Senate tenure."

"Even if he is right?"

Jeff shrugged again.

"It's a tough town, Lauren. Facts are what we decide they are. You play by the rules, at least if you're in the Party. He criticized a key pillar of the Party faithful. That government is here to help, and more help is better than less. Anyway, the boss wants you to stay on top of this and to shadow more of his press conferences and committee meetings. Cover any more of these 'Turner Tirades'. He wants you there putting gas on the fire."

Lauren groaned. "Really?"

"Sorry. Looks like you are going to be on DC duty for a while. Screw anything up?"

"No, of course not. I go where I am told," she said, smiling tightly. She hated DC, and she hated the company apartment she stayed in when there on assignment.

Before Jeff could answer, an intern came running up out of breath.

"Mr. Carter, we have a problem. Bobbi just headed to the emergency room with food poisoning. There is no one here yet to do her news segment at the bottom of Jerry's show," said the aide, looking at his watch, "in twenty-two minutes."

"Shit," said Jeff, looking around and then at Lauren.

Lauren shook her head no.

"Come on Lauren, you can do it. Off to hair and makeup. Go. You only have fifteen minutes to get changed and down to the studio."

Lauren gave him a hateful look and ran to the elevator to head down to wardrobe to change.

Chapter 31

A man with wavy dark hair, a long angular face with dark brooding eyes, mustache, and three days of stubble stared at a monitor. The screen showed the aftermath of the explosion killing the President of France. On the desk was a half full bottle of Johnnie Walker. He sipped the scotch from his ceramic coffee cup while he moved the footage back and forth with his mouse, studying the crowd.

The video was from a security camera on a building quite a distance from the President. The cell phone footage and those of the news cameras covering the press conference at the Ministry of Justice in Paris were all equally useless in providing any clues.

This was the totality of what was available online. They simply showed a man standing in the center of the crowd in front of the President and then chaos after detonation.

A knock at the door interrupted his reverie. He minimized the video, stood, and walked to the door. Opening it carefully, upon recognizing the visitor, he opened it wide.

"Hello, Alain. Slumming?" asked the man in French, as he stepped aside to allow him to enter.

"Luc. Coffee?" he asked, staring at the coffee cup in Luc's hand and looking at his watch.

"Ha. But I can make you some if you like."

"I don't drink coffee this late in the morning. Makes me jittery," said Alain, surveying the shabby apartment. He turned to the large men standing in the hallway, nodding. One of them closed the door.

"Well, scotch in the morning keeps *me* from getting jittery," shrugged Luc. "To what do I owe a visit from the Prime Minister of France?" he asked with heavy sarcasm.

"I need your help," replied Alain Chaumont.

He returned to his desk chair, sat down facing the only other chair in the apartment, where Alain dutifully sat.

"What can I possibly offer? You have the resources of an entire nation. Not to mention Interpol."

Alain shook his head. "That is precisely why I need your help. We are getting nowhere. Somebody blew up Gaspard and then did not take credit for the deed? This defies all logic. If you pull off something like this, it is a godsend for recruiting people for your cause. Interpol is drawing a blank. I need you to find out who did this."

Luc leaned back in his chair, staring at the ceiling, not replying.

"Luc Gauthier was once the chief investigator for Interpol. A rock in a sea of corruption. I cannot trust anyone else. I need you to come back. *You* need you to come back. What else are you going to do? Sit here and drink your memories away?"

"That man is dead," responded Luc wearily.

"Then resurrect him. I need him. France needs him. I know you despise me, but Jean Paul was a friend of ours. He deserved better."

Luc stared at Alain, contemplating his statement.

"How's my sister?"

Alain stood and wandered the room, pushing his hands through his black hair. "Madeline is fine. And so are your niece and nephews. She and I have an arrangement. She likes her lifestyle and puts up with my dalliance. Besides, she is looking forward to being the first lady of France. Call her. She hasn't heard from you since the funeral."

Luc sneered at the ease with which Alain reconciled his unfaithfulness with duty and country. He had not spoken to either his sister or her husband since the funeral of his own wife and daughter almost three years prior.

"She misses you. We understand your need to grieve. I know why you resigned. Come back for your own sake and your sanity. Come back and help us. Help find Jean Paul's killer."

"Not to Interpol. It has only declined. What do they know?"

"Not much. I can give you access to all the physical evidence."

"Independent of all agencies. My terms. No questions and access to anything I need."

"Within reason, of course."

"No. My way or no way," said Luc, staring into Alain's eyes.

Alain hesitated. He saw murder there. Luc would reopen the case on the death of his family and not just the death of their president if he gave him carte blanche. He nodded slowly.

"Agreed."

"Ok, I'll start tomorrow. I'll need an office. Nowhere near the Ministry of Justice or the Prefect either. And Annie as my assistant."

"I'll arrange an office."

"And Annie?"

"I'll see what I can do," said Alain, hesitating.

Luc picked up on this. "What are you not telling me?"

Alain took a deep breath before continuing. "Luc, I was in the room when Jean Paul took a call. He said whoever was on the call was telling him how to deal with our immigrants. Jean Paul disagreed vehemently. He announced the crackdowns on the rioters, the activist funders, and the press conference on short notice just after."

"Have you told this to anyone else?"

"No."

"Why?"

"I don't want anyone to know our president was threatened."

"Do you have any theories?" asked Luc, thinking.

"No, but I suspect they are not done."

"Have you heard from them since?"

"No," lied Alain.

Luc nodded. "I don't suppose we have Jean Paul's cell phone?"

Alain shook his head. "We checked the phone records. His second to last call was untraceable."

"The last call?"

"To Juliet," said Alain. "Just before he started his speech."

Luc nodded. They stood in awkward silence.

"How will Maximilian react to this?" asked Luc with a chuckle.

"Not well. Let's not tell him."

Luc laughed outright this time. "He will find out."

"That will be my problem. You stay clear. OK?"

"I won't be the one to start any trouble. That much I can promise. Nothing else."

"Let me know what you find out. Just me."

Luc nodded.

Alain moved to the door, turning around. "Call your sister. It will do both of you good." He turned and walked out of the apartment as his security detail formed around him.

#

As the Prime Minister got into the car, a man took pictures with a telephoto camera lens from a car far down the street.

Chapter 32

Nick walked into a restaurant near Eaton, Colorado. The place was half full on a Saturday afternoon. He noticed a bunch of Harley's parked out front. He saw the group of bikers and smiled, taking a stool at the bar. Most looked like middle-aged office workers.

"Afternoon," greeted the bartender, a man in his late thirties sporting the latest hairstyle. "What can I get you to drink? You want to eat at the bar, or you looking for a table?"

"Not sure. Was just passing through. Wanted to chat with some locals. Anyone in here willing to share a table for lunch?" asked Nick.

"Let me see. Don't know those bikers. That table over there are a couple of local ranchers. Let me see if they care," said the bartender as he walked over. He said a few things with the guys at the table. They all laughed, and the bartender turned and waved Nick over.

The bartender made intros. "This is John Cross and his son David. They run a ranch near here. And this is Brian Kaufman. He's a local farmer. You want local. It doesn't get more local than these three."

"Nice to meet you, I'm Nick. Was just passing through and had heard about this place. Thought I would stop by and see how things are around here these days."

"Nice to meet ya, Nick," replied John. Nick shook hands with all of them and took a seat. "What can I get you?" asked the bartender.

Before Nick could answer. "Get him a Sawtooth, you have that on tap, right Jimmy?" Brian asked.

"I do."

"Works for me," Nick agreed.

"And some oysters," suggested Brian.

"What do you guys raise on your ranch?"

"Bison, Yak, Angus, and Hereford. Matter of fact, most of the meat on the menu comes from our ranch," offered John.

"How's business, if you don't mind me asking?"

"Not too bad. We still aren't back to as good as it was before the pandemics. We lost a lot of overseas business then. Much of it never really came back," David answered for his dad.

"David runs things," noted John. "I just make a nuisance of myself these days."

"Hardly," David said, with a wry smile. "Pops knows more about cattle than the rest of the cattleman's society combined."

"That's probably true," snorted Brian. "Course, most of the cattleman's society is no longer made up of people who actually know how to round up cattle anymore."

"Spoken like a farmer," John challenged.

"Sorry, didn't want to start a range war," laughed Nick uneasily.

Jimmy arrived with the beers and a basket of breaded appetizers. "Don't pay any attention to these guys. If they aren't on the verge of fighting, something's wrong. Ranchers and farmers are like Yanks and Rebs. And these guys are the worst."

"Stick to bar tending Jimmy," quipped Brian.

"So, what are you farming, Brian?" asked Nick.

"Rotate corn and soybean and occasionally sugar beets, if the prices look right. I have some dry land I do winter wheat on."

"Dry land?"

"Farmland without irrigation. We plant in the fall, hope for a snowy or wet winter and spring and harvest in the summer. Sometimes it works, sometimes not," said Brian, shrugging.

"And how is your business?"

"Well, let's see. Corn prices go up and down like a Yoyo. I really never know if I'm going to make or lose money from year to year. Some years I sell it all for feed to guys like John. Other years when the prices are down, I grind it for silage and sell it over the winter to the ranchers around. I do a bit of sweet corn some years. That's the only stuff that goes to stores. Then there are the soybeans. My biggest customer was China. Some years, I sold my crop before I even planted it. Not so much anymore."

"Why is that?" asked Nick.

"The pandemics spooked China. They changed their supply chain. They buy a lot of their soybean's other places now. So they don't have to rely on us. Funny how *they* seem able to change their supply chain, but we keep relying on others for our goods, and even oil now," said Brian, shaking his head. "Things have been tough the last few years. I had to sell some acreage to freaking ConAgra to pay my bills. That land had been in the family for over 125 years, but it was that or lose it all."

"Tell him about the oil," suggested David with a nod.

"You really want to get me pissed off, don't you?" said Brian.

Nick was dipping the breaded nuggets in a sauce and digging in. He wasn't sure what they tasted like. Not chicken, but not beef either. John noticed Nick eating them, and Brian and David smiled.

"What?" asked Nick, taking a sip of his excellent beer.

"You like'em?" asked John.

"Not bad. Not sure exactly what it is, though. Tastes like chicken, but its texture is more like calamari. I doubt these guys are flying in squid, so what is it?"

"Those are world famous. Karl's has specialized in Rocky Mountain Oysters for years. That's what you're eating," said David.

"Haven't ever had breaded oysters," said Nick suspiciously.

"Well, they don't come from the sea," explained John, smiling.

"Ok fellas, what am I eating?" Nick put down the second half eaten 'oyster'.

"Fried bull testicles," announced John with a straight face. "Straight from our ranch."

Nick smiled, took a sip of his beer, picked up the remaining half of his nugget, dipped it in barbeque sauce and popped it into his mouth, smiling. Brian, David, and John all laughed.

"Not bad. Actually, they taste pretty good. Better than the goat I had in Afghanistan."

"You served?" questioned John as Nick nodded. "So did David."

"I was there off and on for twenty years. Iraq too," replied Nick.

"I did a couple of tours. Marines." said David. "You?"

"Bagram and Dwyer. Flew A-10s. Before that, in Naval Intelligence in Iraq in the Green Zone and Mosul."

"We sure loved you, Hogs," said David with a grin. He turned to his dad. "These guys are almost as nuts as Marines. They fly the A-10 Warthog, ugly ass plane. It goes low and slow and absolutely shreds the Taliban and ISIS guys on the ground with depleted uranium shells about the size of a bowling pin. All the time, they are getting the shit shot out of their planes. The enemy hates the sound of the Warthog. Death from above," David finished and raised his fist to bump Nick's, comrades in arms. "We used to call in the Hogs to let them feed. No greater sound than that zip gun."

"It's a tough plane. Many a time I came back with dozens of holes in it. Nothing takes punishment like a Warthog. Except maybe a Marine," finished Nick with a smile.

"Ooh rah" answered David.

As they were finishing, a group of real bikers noisily entered the bar. Unlike the weekend warrior bikers in the corner, these guys had the look of real ones, with tattoos, scars, and bandanas. Six of them stood in the entryway, surveying the landscape.

"Shit," said Brian, looking at the bikers as they approached Jimmy the bartender. "These guys are bad news. El Fuego's. Drugs, trafficking, smuggling. They do it all," finished Brian in a low voice.

"Jimmy, we'll take some beers and a table over there," said the leader, pointing to a table near the faux bikers. "Nice outfits, ladies," said the leader to the other bikers. They ignored them. The leader just laughed as Jimmy showed up with beers. "Here you go. Come on guys, we don't want any trouble," Jimmy said, setting down the beers.

The leader looked at him. "You know why I'm here. Pay up and there won't be any trouble. How about some burgers too?"

Jimmy came by their table, asking if they wanted to order lunch.

"Hey Jimmy, we're in a hurry. Those guys can wait," yelled the biker leader, as Jimmy turned and headed to the kitchen.

"Who are those guys? Nick asked, noticing the concern."

"The leader is a guy named Nico Ramirez. He's been in and out of prison. Runs the local chapter of El Fuegos. They shake down local businesses and terrify all the illegal farm workers around the area, demanding tribute. Sheriff Greene's been trying to shut him down permanently for ages," replied David in a low voice.

"What you guys whispering about over there?" asked Nico.

Nick turned around slowly in his chair to confront Nico. All the noise in the restaurant stopped, sensing a confrontation.

"Not whispering, just deciding what to eat, once Jimmy gets back from placing your top priority order," replied Nick in a conversational tone. Out of the corner of his eye, Nick could see David positioning himself to launch in a hurry.

"Big words. I bet that pussy Indian bike is yours?" sneered Nico.

"Surprised you knew what it was. Guessing you're on a Harley?"

"Got that right." Nico turned to clink beer bottles with his crew.

"Yo, Jimmy, where are our burgers? We need some more beers," ordered Nico, losing interest in Nick for the moment.

"Coming right up," hurried Jimmy. He brought out another round of Coors to the table and headed to the kitchen to get their food.

"Why don't you guys just kick them out?"

Brian stared for a second. "Nick, where're you from? This is Colorado. We have a progressive governor, a progressive attorney general and no bail. Even when they get arrested, they're back on the street the next day. They burn down people's farms or shoot up their cars or, with the illegals, just kill someone in their family. The law means nothing to these guys. If you stand up to them, there is nothing the law can do to stop them and there is nothing it can do to protect you, either. So, people just duck and cover."

Nick just shook his head. "Even if you could give them a beat down, it doesn't matter," stated David, sensing what Nick was thinking.

Nick laughed, "Unlike you jarheads, I prefer diplomacy and I like my face the way it is." David smiled, shrugging.

"What's so funny?" demanded Nico, standing up behind Nick.

"Private joke," replied Nick, not turning to face him.

"Hey, I'm talking to you," barked Nico, putting his hand on Nick's shoulder.

Nick reached up to Nico's wrist, applied pressure, and turned as he stood up. He crumbled to his knees in pain while Nick kept pressure applied to his wrist.

"Jesus, man," gasped Nico, in pain.

"I think maybe you should get your food to go. What do you think?" asked Nick, twisting and applying a bit more pressure. David, Brian, and John were all standing, with David working his way to Nick's side of the table. He noticed one of David's legs below the knee was a prosthetic.

"Ow, OW, you're breaking my arm," whined Nico.

Nick released his hold on Nico's arm, and he slowly got to his feet. His crew was also standing. Several other patrons stood up behind Nick. The weekend bikers were also up on the other side of the room. Jimmy was ready to grab something from behind the bar.

Nico surveyed the room, having recovered his bravado. He reached to the small of his back and pulled out a knife with an 8-inch blade. "Think you're pretty cool with your kung fu moves, huh? We carve up little fuckers like you all the time."

Nick let out a big laugh. "Look at you. Calling me little? I'm 6 inches taller and outweigh you by at least fifty. If anyone is small, it's you. How big are the heels on your boots, three inches? There is nothing big about you. Get your food, pay your bill, get on your stinking Harley's, and get out of here," said Nick in a forceful tone. Nick noticed a few folks grabbing the necks of beer bottles, preparing for the inevitable bar brawl.

"Look, man, this won't end well. Even if we fight, lots of folks get hurt. You go to jail, you're the only one with a weapon in your hand.

Any move and that's attempted murder and assault. Those are some pretty serious charges," shared Nick in a conciliatory tone.

"What, you a lawyer? Figures, riding that girly bike," said Nico, tossing his knife between his hands. "I been to prison before. I'm not worried," he finished, closing in on Nick.

Nick picked up his chair and broke out two of the wooden stakes from the back like a couple of toothpicks. "If this is what you want, just remember when you wake up, you made the choice."

David moved up to the side of Nick. Nick tossed him a chair stake and broke another out of the chair.

"Well, well, soldier boy wants to play?" said Nico. "Fine by me."

Just as they were about to start swinging, the door opened with a bang, startling Nico, who jumped back.

Standing in the doorway was a large black man, about 6'2" and easily 230 lbs., wearing a black cowboy hat and a 9mm pistol on his hip. The shiny badge on his chest proclaimed him the Weld County Sheriff.

"Exactly what do we have here? Nico, is that a knife in your hands? And the rest of your crew, aren't all of you on parole? Seems to me holding a drawn weapon and threatening anyone violates your parole, let alone any other charges these good men might want to file," said the Sheriff.

"Hey, we was just defending ourselves. He assaulted me, I got witnesses," said Nico, putting his knife in his back holster.

The sheriff turned to Nick. "Is that true?" Nick shrugged.

"He put his hand on my shoulder. I interpreted it as a risk to my bodily health. I grabbed his wrist and twisted a bit. Not my fault if he is sensitive to acupressure. Not sure it qualifies as assault, but you can certainly talk to the other witnesses yourself," shrugged Nick, waving his hand around the restaurant.

"Nico, clear out, or I'll take you in for violating your parole," said the Sheriff as Nico hesitated. "NOW" he shouted. Nico threw Nick a look of pure hatred and left with his crew. Soon the sound of Harley's starting and peeling away faded.

"Thank you, Sheriff…?"

"Greene, Earl Greene."

"I have all these burgers. You guys and the Sheriff care to have a burger on the house?" asked Jimmy.

"I never turn down free food myself," replied Sheriff Greene.

"Sounds good," agreed Nick. "And bill me for the chair."

"Nah, got a million of them," responded Jimmy.

"I think we'll be going," David looked at Earl. "Sheriff, chances are Nico will try something to save face. Just want you to be aware we'll be protecting ourselves."

"I get it, take care and be safe," nodded Sheriff Greene.

"Nick, nice to meet you," said David as he, John, and Brian all made for the door.

"Likewise, thanks for the oysters," replied Nick with a smile.

Earl laughed. "They got you, didn't they?"

"Hey, I actually thought they were pretty good."

Nick and Earl took a table and chair in the corner where Jimmy brought them burgers and iced tea.

"Mind if I ask you a question?" asked Earl.

"Sure, fire away."

"What exactly would you have done if Nico attacked?"

"Put him on his ass, break a few ribs, pound a few heads. Those guys are just bullies. You stand up to them and they crumble. Heck, I probably would have disarmed him and put him on his knees again," noted Nick. "The rest of them would have caved. I've seen it before."

"No plan to pull that concealed .45 in the small of your back?"

"Good eye Sheriff, I have a concealed carry permit, if you are wondering. It's even from Colorado. Don't think I would've needed it with those clowns. But I do feel bad if it means they take it out on David and his dad."

"Don't worry about them. They won't mess with him. I'll see to it," Earl said, taking a bite of his hamburger.

"Nice burgers," said Nick, biting into his again as well.

"Uh huh, so how do you think the papers would have handled a US Senator getting in a bar-room brawl?"

"Recognized me, huh?"

"Afraid so. Actually, Jimmy did and called me once Nico started barking orders. He knew there could be trouble."

"Well then, I owe Jimmy a big tip."

"Senator, what are you doing? Hanging out in a bar that says Biker's Welcome? Going around by yourself after some of your antics? Especially in a deep red Colorado county? There are a lot of people pissed off at you. My suggestion is you think a bit more about the consequences of your decisions and consider others around you who may suffer."

"Probably right Sheriff. I didn't really consider what might happen for standing up to those punks."

"Those guys are pissants, but there are worse and much more organized groups overrunning this and other states. Senator, you guys in Washington have got to get a handle on this. I am apolitical when I wear the uniform, but I can tell you, we are being invaded. Invaded by sad and poor people who know nothing but violence and crime," said Earl between bites of his burger.

Nick responded. "I'm against the sieve that is the open border, and I'm against us sending bus and plane loads of these people to the interior of the country. But we invited them, and we have no idea what to do with them. I agree, there is no plan."

"Senator, the bottom line is we are being overrun by people who know nothing of what it means to be an American. We can't keep diluting the American morals, ethics, and entrepreneurial spirit with the influx of people who do not care to live by those rules. I'm not sure what the ultimate plan is by not enforcing our border laws, defunding police, and allowing criminals to walk or not even be prosecuted. But I can tell you, the rank-and-file American, who works and pays his taxes and hopes to leave a world and society to his children that is better than what they had, won't put up with this lawlessness much longer," said Earl, finishing his burger and leaving a $10 tip on the table.

"Sheriff, I've been on the road the last week or so. I've stopped in small local cafes and bars and pool halls just like this. Getting an earful from everyone. It doesn't matter which party or who they voted for. The people blame us in Washington and the media. I'm headed back to Washington tomorrow, with a much better feel for what regular people are feeling and what they need. I may not accomplish much, but at least now I know what I say is validated by those conversations," revealed Nick.

The Sheriff sat and stared at Nick for a few seconds.

"I need to get back to work. You guys need to get your shit together. The people may be ignorant, but they're not stupid and when their back is against the wall, I don't think Washington has a clue what people will do to stay free. Keep your gun holstered and try not to get in anymore trouble, please."

"Thanks Sheriff, I appreciate the assist and I appreciate the words of wisdom," said Nick standing up to shake the sheriff's hand.

Chapter 33

Nick returned to Washington. Reviewing bills being prepped for a vote once the upcoming filibuster vote was passed. He discussed the contents with his staff and tried to read as much of each as he could. Determined to make an informed vote and to speak from a position of knowing exactly what was *in* each one.

He gave a few interviews with several news outlets. Hoping to discuss the contents of bills and upcoming votes. All they wanted to talk about were his comments on government assistance and his attacks on the press. Eventually, he stopped accepting media requests.

Later in the day on Friday, after everyone was back to work from fall break, Nick sat in his office, hands behind his head, contemplating his bare walls. Chuck knocked and stuck his head in the doorway.

"You're going to the party tonight like we discussed? You did RSVP. It would be good for you," said Chuck, coming into the office and taking a seat.

"Ugh, I'm not really in the mood after the last few days."

"Nick, don't let it get you down. We make progress incrementally, not in big leaps and bounds."

"I just want to tell the truth. I'm not afraid to do it because I won't get invited to a cocktail party or I'm not following the proscribed path of a junior Party Senator," said Nick, frustrated.

"Even more reason to go. Washington loves the controversial. You'll be popular for sure. I think a lot of folks envy you because you stood up to the status quo, and it hasn't hurt you," remarked Chuck.

"Some of those interviews were painful. Does that count as 'hurt'?" grunted Nick. "It remains to be seen if it's hurt me or not."

"True, but you gave better than you got. Plus, you made them look like the partisan hacks they are. Those who watched saw somebody not willing to compromise his principles to earn kudos from congressional leadership or the media. You also exposed the hypocrisy of so many of these so-called experts at these committee meetings every day. That makes you standout like a Cowboy's fan at a Commander's game. They can't miss this. Being seen tonight is like being introduced to society," stated Chuck, laughing.

"Great, it sounds like I'm the prize bull at the Stock Show. Showing off to the highest bidder, so I end up on the menu at Del Frisco's. You make it sound so appealing," groaned Nick.

"Nah, have a few drinks, flirt with the pretty ladies, go home by yourself though," said Chuck seriously. "Remember, it may be 3 to 1 women to men, but we are also the STD capital of the world. Be safe."

"Do I have a curfew, Mom? You want me to text you when I get home?"

"Touché," replied Chuck. "Oh, and by the way, your suit for tonight is in your closet. It is a black-tie gala in case you forgot."

"What? No, you didn't mention that. I have to wear a tux? That does it. I'm not going," announced Nick, leaning back again.

"Too late. You back out of an RSVP to a Dolly Wells-Monroe party, and you are going to be on a shit list worse than Fontana's," warned Chuck. "Don't worry, Margie and Jenny picked it out. I am sure you'll look just fine."

"Great, that makes me feel so much better," said Nick resignedly.

Chapter 34

Dolly Wells-Monroe stood in her evening gown in the doorway of her estate, Twin Pines, as Senator Banks, assisted by his valet Hobson, came up the walk.

"Dolly, my dear, looking radiant as always. You are a goddess," said Senator Banks in his slow southern drawl, as Hobson smiled.

"Baxter, you're a scoundrel. Good to see you, Hobson," beamed Dolly, taking Bank's other arm. They steered him into the main foyer of her residence. Banks looked up as they entered and whistled.

"It is magnificent, Dolly," he said, looking up at the multi-storied ceiling of the enormous living room. Hanging from the ceiling on various length cords were silver stars and constellations of LED lights twinkling in random patterns denoting the stars. A series of lights rotated and flashed in subtle motions, illuminating patterns on the ceiling. It would indeed be a party under the stars.

Spread throughout the living room were tables of hors d'oeuvres, with bars set up in various out of the way corners. A quartet was warming up as well. Dolly and Hobson led Banks down the marble stairs into the living room.

A wide, gently curving grand staircase, decorated in lights and stars like the ceiling, led up to the expansive second-floor balcony. From there, down a wide hallway, was the large ballroom where another orchestra could be heard warming up. The ballroom would host most of the dancing. Banks hadn't been upstairs in years, even with the elevator access down another hallway from the living room.

"I want to show you the lawn," said Dolly, as they walked the length of the living room. Arriving at a twenty-foot wide opening where French doors of ornate wood and glass were pressed to the sides in accordion fashion. Exiting the living room to the solarium, then walking out to the lawn. Baxter could see a web of lights and stars strung on poles covering a large section of the immaculate turf.

The weather was cooperating, providing a cool but not cold evening with low humidity. There were dozens of tall tables and settees set up throughout the lawn under the artificial stars. Dolly looked to the side, nodding as a technician flipped switches, turning on the lights. Even in the early evening light, the effect was dazzling as the various shades of starlight replaced the daylight. Yet another ensemble set up out here. A floor of inlaid parquet formed a moderate sized dance floor under one section of the 'starlight'.

Baxter sighed as he sat. "Penny would be so proud. It's amazing. I can only imagine the upstairs ballroom is as spectacular."

"More," laughed Dolly delightfully. "I have a ceiling to work with up there."

"How many?"

"Between three and four hundred."

"The party of the season for sure," grinned Baxter in reply.

"Of course. I have a reputation to uphold. Guess who else is coming?" asked Dolly with a twinkle in her eye, her white teeth showcased against her full red lips in a mischievous grin.

"That Swiss banker who fancies you? What's his name, Duke something?" asked Banks, with a twinkle and smile of his own.

"Pshaw," replied Dolly, making a face. "NO. None other than our own Senator Nick Turner," she declared triumphantly.

"Well done. To my knowledge, he avoids these social gatherings like they were the plague."

"We are hardly the plague," answered Dolly in mock anger, throwing back her shoulders and crossing her arms under her bosom.

"He has declined several before, correct?" asked Baxter, as Dolly nodded. "I wonder what changed his mind."

"I don't know, and I don't care, as long as he shows."

"He will certainly be the talk of the party. Especially with the way he is riling up the leadership. I can tell you they are fit to be tied," shared Banks.

"I, for one, love it. We need real people here who will take a stand, however unpopular. Backing it up with facts and common sense rather than bluster or rhetoric," declared Dolly with an emphatic hand chop.

"That may be alright in the movies, my dear, but here, it is a one-way ticket to isolation and banishment. You had best enjoy our young Mr. Turner while you can. I fear he may be the butt of a few jokes by the time your Winter Gala rolls around."

"Baxter," Dolly paused, now deadly serious. "I certainly hope not. Honestly, I'm worried. Worried, we're falling further apart."

"Now dear, this is no time to be thinking these thoughts. Let's make our way back to the foyer and park me in my greeting chair. With a big drink, of course. Hobson, if you would do the honors and hoist me up, please," requested Banks.

"Of course, sir," responded Hobson, grabbing Banks' forearms and easily pulling him upright.

"Ms. Monroe, I'll get him to the foyer with a stop at the bar," Hobson said in his clipped British accent, with a wink.

"As always, thank you Hobson," smiled Dolly.

#

Later in the evening, Dolly surveyed the party. People had been arriving for over ninety minutes and the stream was now tapering off. The guests were now mingling, drinking, and dancing. She stood in one corner of the living room as the quartet played a jazz tune from Brubeck. Upstairs, she could hear the big band orchestra going full blast and the shaking of her chandeliers down the hallway showed many were enjoying themselves.

Over the course of the evening as the older and wiser crowds tired, the orchestra would be replaced by a modern DJ who would shift the music more to the taste of the twenty and early thirty- somethings who would stay to the wee hours of the morning. No one left a Four

Seasons Gala before 2am. Often a few hardy souls watched the dawn from the back lawn if the weather was hospitable.

Dolly watched as the Vice President made her way over. She automatically critiqued her outfit. Lexi wore an Alexander McQueen sheath dress off one shoulder in a pleasing burgundy color, highlighting her blonde hair, which she had pulled back and piled high atop her head.

She had on her customary Louboutin high heels, also in burgundy, matching her dress. Her makeup was tasteful and her shade of lipstick a bit too red for Dolly's taste. Lexi, over twenty years her senior, looked closer to Dolly's age than her own. Like Dolly, she was all natural, preferring exercise and skin care routines to Botox, collagen, and the plastic surgery so many in DC thrived upon.

"Dolly, my dear, what a lovely party as always," offered Lexi, leaning in and air kissing her on each cheek.

"Thank you, Madame Vice President."

"You know it is Lexi when we are socializing."

"Of course, Lexi." Dolly answered with as much of a smile as she could muster.

"I don't know how you do it. You must start planning the next one as soon as this one ends."

"Actually before. I have two going at any time. Not enough time to plan if I wait until this one is done," laughed Dolly.

"That would make sense, given the level of detail." Lexi looked up at the ceiling and around the room at the decorations. "I would say this is a success."

Dolly glanced around as well. There were people congregated everywhere. Couples were dancing in the living room and pairs sitting on the steps of the giant staircase, laughing, and eating. "It appears that way."

"And yet you seem somewhat off? Anything I can help with?"

"Hardly," replied Dolly with another laugh. "Well, I must go mingle. Is everything OK with you? Accomplishing world peace tonight?"

"Now it's my turn to laugh. Hardly," Lexi replied with a smirk.

"Enjoy yourself, Lexi. For one night, let it go and just relax," ended Dolly as she moved around the room, greeting people.

Fontana walked up to Lexi as she watched Dolly work the room. "Madame Vice President," greeted Sal, raising his newly refilled drink, smelling of bourbon already.

"Majority Leader." It was bad enough she had to work with him. She preferred not to socialize with him, too.

"Interesting party. It is a who's who of Washington and beyond. Too bad she won't let us fundraise," pondered Sal, looking around and practically licking his lips.

"That's kind of the whole point. To put the knives away for a night and relax. Go hit up Goldman Sachs or Aramco over there," suggested Lexi, pointing out two prominent business leaders.

"And get kicked out of these for life? No fucking way," uttered Sal with a look of horror before he realized she was being sarcastic.

"I thought so. Enjoy the evening," she said, walking away to say hello to the United States Ambassador to the United Nations.

"Bitch," he said under his breath, taking a sip of his drink. Spying a few cronies in a corner, no doubt disparaging some of their colleagues, he wandered over to join in.

#

Dolly walked into the foyer to check on Baxter.

As she approached, prepared to make a quip, she noticed him slumped over. She hurried over, careful in her high-heeled sandals on the slick marble. Looking down, she could see he was breathing. He was just asleep.

"Thank God," she said, holding her hand to her chest while trying to slow her breathing.

"Why are we thanking God?" asked Senator Nick Turner, standing in the doorway.

Dolly looked up, flustered. Her heart pounding from her concern over Banks. She saw Nick standing tall in her foyer with a slight smile on his face. She wasn't sure what to say. He stood there in his tuxedo, wearing a white dinner jacket instead of the traditional black, framed in a halo of light from the door. With his dark hair and eyes, he looked spectacular. Dolly regained her composure and walked to the Senator with a hand extended, smiling brightly.

Nick had watched the beautiful dark-haired woman bend over Banks and then straighten in relief. She was quite a vision. Nick told himself under his breath, he really must get out more. As she turned to him, he saw a woman, in the prime of her beauty, wearing a gorgeous dress. Her dress was a series of wonderful shades of blue with a pleated skirt, ending below her knees, displaying fabulous legs atop high-heeled sandals. He surmised this must be the hostess.

"Senator Turner, welcome. I'm Dolly Monroe."

"A pleasure to meet you, Ms. Monroe. Please call me Nick."

"You're late," Dolly cringed inside as she said aloud what she was thinking.

Nick arched an eyebrow. "I didn't know we had assigned arrival times. I would have told Albert, my Uber driver, to not take me to Chevy Chase first had I known."

"Really?" asked Dolly. "He didn't know where Twin Pine's was?"

"If he did, he gave a remarkable impression of not knowing. But hey, I got a wonderful tour of Chevy Chase, Cleveland Park, and Kalorama. If I ever want to be a DC real estate agent, I'm all set."

"Good lord. How could he be that bad?" she said with a laugh.

"Apparently, I and my Uber driver are the only people in DC who need an actual address to put in the GPS for your lovely estate," said Nick, looking around.

Dolly held a hand to her mouth. Then she bent over, laughing. Nick liked her immediately. "I never even considered putting an address on the invitation. *Everyone* knows where I live."

"Except me, clearly," a smiling Nick admitted.

"I am so sorry for the late crack. It's a wonder you made it at all. I'm surprised you didn't give up and head for Chick-fil-A."

"Uh hum. I'm sure you make a habit of visiting Chick-fil-A. I bet you don't even know where one is," accused Nick.

"Just because I clean up nice, doesn't mean I don't partake of a spicy chicken sandwich from time to time. Speaking of cleaning up nice, bold choice of tuxedo," praised Dolly with a twinkle, stepping back, eyeing Nick up and down.

"My turn for honesty. I didn't choose it. Several busy bodies in my office did. You approve?"

"I do. When you walk in, you'll see you stand out like the brightest star in the crowd. And that has nothing to do with your tux choice," grinned Dolly, laughing at her own joke.

"I'm equally impressed with your dress. You look fabulous," responded Nick, hoping he was not being too forward.

"Why thank you. You don't get out much, do you?" noted Dolly with a wide smile.

Nick paused, staring at the hostess with her dazzling smile, bright eyes, and honest banter. "No, I don't, but I know where every drive-thru in town can be found, if not Twin Pines. How would you describe your dress? I'm just curious, as I'd be at a loss and all my staff, especially the ladies, will grill me," said Nick with an eye roll.

"Senator, sorry, Nick, you are a breath of fresh air in this stuffy city. For your staff, of course," said Dolly with a mini curtsy. "My gown is Oscar de la Renta. 'Evocative of the night sky, it's cut from wispy tulle, embellished with twinkling, star-shaped sequins and underpinned by silk-blend lamé, falling to a full, softly pleated skirt'; or so I was told when I purchased it," she said, finishing with a twirl.

"Very nice," gazed Nick, appraising her. In an era where the slim and anorexic figure was in, Dolly was no skinny mini. She had more of an hourglass figure, with curves in all the right places, almost lush. The gown highlighted these. She evoked the stars of old. Ava Gardner in *The Barefoot Contessa* came to Nick's mind.

"Ha hum. Children, you have an audience," announced Senator Banks with a smile on his face, having sat quietly through their entire banter.

"Oh dear," gasped Dolly, blushing deep red, "Let's go gentlemen."

"Senator, may I help you up?" asked Nick as Banks nodded.

Dolly and Nick each took an arm and walked down into the living room as everyone watched them enter. After the unusual quiet, the roar of voices came back louder than ever. Now with something new to discuss, having watched Nick's entrance, combined with the freely flowing alcohol. The trio made their way to one of the corner bars near the open doorway to the lawn.

"Nick, what is your drink?" inquired Dolly.

"Pellegrino, I think," Nick answered, looking around the room.

"Nonsense, my dear. You cannot come to one of my parties and drink fake Italian bubbles," argued Dolly, as Banks looked on with a bemused smile on his face.

"I'll have a Macallan and soda please," Banks told the bartender. "Dolly, the usual?"

"Why yes, Baxter," Dolly said, holding eye contact with Nick, who did not look away.

"Nolet's gin, extra dry with a twist," ordered Banks.

Nick raised an eyebrow at the drink order for Dolly. "Seriously?"

"You have a problem with my drink?" asked Dolly with a small smile and an arched eyebrow of her own.

"Hardly. I'm impressed. Nolet's is one of my favorite gins. Very underappreciated, amidst all the fruit botanicals, everybody seems to distill these days," remarked Nick.

Dolly, surprised at his knowledge of European gin, visibly brightened. "I know what you mean. Gin from apples and sugar and all those funky combinations," she made a face.

"Well, if it is good enough for our hostess, I suppose it is good enough for me as well," Nick nodded to the smiling bartender.

Shortly, he handed them their martinis and Baxter his scotch.

"To a fabulous hostess and a fabulous party," toasted Nick as they clinked glasses.

"Here's to Senator Turner losing his DC social virginity. Congratulations, my dear, on being the first," said Baxter wickedly.

Nick choked on his drink at Senator Bank's statement. Dolly laughed and smiled as Nick leaned his drink forward to keep from spilling it on his white jacket as he regained his composure.

"Maybe he should have stuck with the Pellegrino," suggested Dolly to Banks in a disapproving voice.

"It appears so," agreed Banks.

"Laugh it up," croaked Nick once he could talk again.

"I will leave you kids to your mingling. Show him around Dolly. I fear I must find a place to sit. My legs are not much use any longer," said Banks as Hobson appeared at his side, as if by magic.

Dolly took Nick by the arm and steered him around the room, introducing him to a few heads of state in attendance, to CEOs and philanthropists. He met several sports team owners, a University President, a Nobel prizewinning chemist, a famous cellist and two of the premier opera singers from the Met. He also met lots of junior staffers from several congressional offices. It surprised him.

"What is it with all the junior staffers? Seems out of place," probed Nick as they headed outside to the artificial starry sky. The mini orchestra played old time waltzes as the older couples danced under the stars. Nick and Dolly stood watching them.

Before she could answer, Nick set his drink down on a table. "Miss, would you care to dance?" asked Nick, bending at the waist and offering a hand.

"Seriously? Men under 50, hell 60, no longer dance waltzes," questioned Dolly, looking up, her eyes sparkling at the thought.

"I think you'll find I'm full of surprises," hinted Nick, setting her drink down next to his, leading her by the hand to the dance floor. She did not resist.

He quickly pulled her in and seamlessly transitioned, leading Dolly as the orchestra finished a slow waltz and began a more vigorous Viennese.

Dolly's face reddened at her reaction. They wouldn't win any competitions, but she quickly followed Nick's lead as they started twirling gracefully around the dance floor. Many others moved to give them room and soon they were the only ones.

Dolly was smiling and laughing as Nick twirled her around in larger circles with the additional room. He ended the dance with a deep bend, supporting her back as he dipped her and brought her back upright. The band ended the song and the entire crowd applauded, including those who had gathered at the entrance between the living room and the lawn.

As Nick and Dolly made a deep bow. Fontana, who had joined Lexi at the edge of the living room, watching, uttered in disgust, "Figures the schmuck can dance as well."

"Indeed. Our young Mr. Turner just keeps surprising," noted Lexi as she turned to head back to the living room area. As she did, she spied Banks perched on a bar stool sipping a drink from where he had watched the festivities. "Pleasant evening, Madame Vice President, wouldn't you say?"

"As always, Baxter. Did you know Turner was coming tonight?"

"Heaven's no. He has turned down every invitation in town, including a few at the White House and even some of the military balls. Seems strange he would pick Dolly's for his coming out, don't you think?"

"I wonder what changed his mind," she said aloud, almost ignoring Baxter's statement.

"Dolly seems to have taken a shine to him," observed Banks.

"It takes more than fancy dancing to get our Dolly. Given all the proposals she's shot down, I am not sure our Ms. Monroe hasn't sworn a vow of chastity," hissed Lexi with a bit of venom.

"It isn't men she's not interested in, just marriage," he said with a sly smile. "Freshen your drink?"

Lexi turned to look at him, a bit of steel in her gaze. Baxter met hers with one of equal intensity. "Thank you."

He turned to the bartender. "Do you have any aged Negroni? I know Dolly usually has some made for these parties just for the Vice

President," asked Banks, looking at Lexi, who had her eyes fixed on Dolly and Nick as they continued to waltz.

"Of course, sir," said the bartender, pouring an Aged Negroni from a special pitcher and garnishing it with a twist. He handed the drink to Banks, who handed it to Lexi.

"To our new 'it' couple," toasted Banks with humor, knowing it would get under Lexi's skin.

"You'd like that, wouldn't you? You've been trying to find her a mate ever since Penny passed. Hell, if you were twenty years younger, I believe you would have married her already." Lexi tapped his scotch with her glass.

"Ten years, and don't think I didn't contemplate it. Penny, God rest her, would not approve. Besides, on my best day, I couldn't waltz like that," watched Banks, seeing they were now dancing once again, this time to a less aggressive waltz.

"Baxter, I don't know what you're up to and after 70 years, perhaps you should give it a rest and let the rest of us take over the Great Game," Lexi finished, making to move away.

Banks reached out a thin arm and gently grabbed Lexi's upper arm. She was startled, not used to anyone daring to touch her. Even Pete asked permission. She looked into his face to see him staring back intensely.

"Lexi, I love my country. I've sacrificed my soul frequently to advance legislation to solve our country's problems. Only to watch it have unintended consequences, leaving us worse off. I've always believed I had the best interests of the people in mind. When these occurred, I always worked to mitigate the problems WE caused."

Lexi held Banks' gaze, matching his intensity as he continued.

"I'll vote to kill the filibuster. It may be the final straw between an eternity in heaven or hell, but I promise you, we are giving you enormous power and you need to use it wisely. I fear if you move too fast and too quickly, you will wake a slumbering giant. Giants can be very unpredictable and very destructive. Do so at your own peril. Please take this advice from someone who has looked the devil in the eye and shook his hand. The price you pay is not worth the gratification you receive." He released her arm as he finished.

She looked down at him. "Baxter, when I finished with my devil, he had a satisfied smile on his face. I think my bargains will turn out just fine for me and even better for the country, which I too love. Otherwise, I wouldn't be fighting this hard to help save it from itself," she said with a smile, turning to go.

At the last second, she looked back. "Never touch me again. It will be the last thing you do, old man." She turned, still smiling, raising her hand to greet the approaching Queen of Jordan.

Banks shrank back in his seat. He felt all of his almost ninety-five years. He feared for his country in the hands of Lexi. But he also had no alternatives. The present stalemate was worse. They had to force the issue before the world took advantage of American vulnerabilities.

Banks turned back to the lawn and took a big swallow of his drink. He spied Nick and Dolly now dancing a slow dance with about a foot or so between them, like a couple of teenagers at the Prom. His hand was high on her back and hers on top of his shoulder. Banks just chuckled as he watched.

"The staffers?" asked Nick, as he and Dolly danced.

She looked at him before answering. "The only way to rebuild a social society in DC is to get the next generation involved in a social scene. Something more than texting while standing next to each other. Understanding the subtle art of conversation. Each ball, I send invitations to House and Senate offices so they can use these as rewards for their staff. Many of the Congresspeople themselves aren't even invited. They know it is a perk to have their junior staff chosen to attend. For the first couple hours of each gala, the youngsters get to mingle with the people they want to become."

"They learn the etiquette of real socializing. How to make interesting conversation, just like in the old days. In a couple hours, you'll notice the orchestra upstairs will stop playing big band hits and a DJ will replace them to play modern music so they can go back to whatever the current generation calls dancing."

Nick contemplated her strategy. "I can just see the look on the Vice President's face when a junior staffer comes up to her to discuss the dichotomy of giving the Olympics to a country where they have ethnic slaves in camps making shoes our American companies sell to our black youth for $400 a pair. Money they can only get from dealing drugs," said Nick with a disappointed smile.

Dolly ignored Nick's statement. "Actually, Lexi is one of the best. She always makes time and has the patience to help the staffers. You know why?"

"I suspect, but enlighten me. By the way, you dance marvelously. Where did you learn?" asked Nick.

"Do you always ignore the question and answer with your own, changing the subject? It is an annoying trait," she said, half seriously.

"You should talk to my chief of staff about it," laughed Nick. "He's been trying to break me of many habits like this."

"Chuck? I talk to him all the time. We're cousins," said Dolly with an impish smile.

"Why do I feel like this was some sort of huge setup?" said Nick, twirling Dolly as the song tempo changed.

"Whoa," said Dolly in surprise at the twirl, trying to keep her balance as Nick gripped her. "Let's just say we killed two birds with one stone. Chuck got you out networking and I got the hottest ticket in town for my party. I think it worked out quite well, actually."

"And Albert the driver. Was that planned?" asked Nick, turning Dolly away from a couple getting a little wild on the dance floor. Nick continued to turn her until they were once again in a safe area.

"That was close," laughed Dolly, slowly getting closer to Nick as the gap between them diminished. "No, your driver was not planned. In fact, by then I figured you had committed the ultimate sin in DC. RSVP'ing to a Four Seasons gala and then ducking it. I would have had to excommunicate you," she smiled, looking up at him.

"There sure seem to be a lot of rules at your parties," observed Nick in a disapproving tone. "More like Mother Superior than the grand hostess I hear about."

"Without rules, there is chaos and anarchy, sort of like Congress. I hope to set a good example. Now, back to your original questions about the staffers," said Dolly, following Nick's lead as they slowly glided around the dance floor.

"Oh right, I asked a question," said Nick playfully, pulling her in even closer as the song changed to a slower pace. Dolly did not resist.

"You asked why Lexi spends the time with the insignificant guests of my party," answered Dolly, trying to ignore the closeness and the increase in her heartbeat by focusing on the question.

"Lexi did not get here by looks and deeds alone. She has the best network of people who owe her favors of anyone in Washington. She collects them like a light collects moths. Much like those poor moths, many of them end up spent and dead underneath, if metaphorically."

"She is cultivating the next generation. Making them beholden to her. Teaching them to look to her to seek her counsel and approval. It would not surprise me one bit, when she gets rid of the filibuster and becomes President, one of her bills is to remove the 22nd amendment on term limits for the President. You never know, some of these staffers may be the next congress members," she finished.

"You would approve?" asked Nick, turning her slightly as he looked down into her brown eyes, with just a touch of hazel.

Dolly paused, thinking about how to answer as they continued to dance. She now had her left hand on his chest and his right hand held the small of her back. "I hope to lead by example. Returning DC to a time when both parties would actually talk to each other."

"It seems you are a one person UN, trying to bring civility back to a place determined to be uncivil," declared Nick.

The current song changed to a popular ballad. Dolly looked up into Nick's face, questioning if he wanted to continue. He just pulled her in closer. They collapsed their outstretched arms to their torsos as they gently rocked back and forth.

"Where did *you* learn to dance, Senator?"

"You're the one who dodged it earlier, you first," countered Nick, as their feet shuffled less and less.

"I grew up in Europe. Went to school in England and France. Dancing was still taught back then, and they expected women of breeding to know all the dances. I *am* the granddaughter of an Earl after all."

Nick stopped for a second in surprise. Dolly, not expecting this, continued her step, burying her sandal's heel into the top of his foot. Nick yelped and Dolly quickly brought her hand to her face in horror. He held out his hand again, and they recommenced. She put both arms around his neck as he grabbed her waist. She was laughing and burying her head in his chest. Finally, she stopped, leaned back, and looked up at him.

"I am so sorry Nick, is your foot ok?" she asked as they swayed back and forth to the slow music again.

"I am told body piercing is all the rage. Just didn't plan on starting with my foot," grimaced Nick.

Dolly blushed deep red in embarrassment. "Thank God I'm not wearing stilettos tonight," she said in a deadpan voice.

"Tell that to my foot," groaned Nick, exaggerating a limp.

"Oh, man up. We're the ones who have to wear the heels. Try that all day sometime."

"No wonder Europe has declined so rapidly; they can't even teach their young ladies how to dance properly," smirked Nick.

Dolly, with a fire in her eye, leaned back out of their embrace and slugged Nick in the stomach. Her swing was halfhearted, but she couldn't help noticing Nick's abs did not bounce in the slightest from her punch.

"Now we can add assault. I had you all wrong," remarked Nick as she returned.

"Now your turn, smartass," ordered Dolly, smiling.

"Mine was not so romantic. I'm most assuredly not the son or grandson of anyone of consequence. I learned to dance to impress a girl, like most guys. Only my girl was a professional dancer. She taught me the dances, and we practiced a lot, once upon a time," remembered Nick somewhat wistfully.

"What happened? A man who can dance is almost always a keeper. You must have worked hard to screw that one up," wondered Dolly, smiling tentatively.

"I did. My military career put an end to that. In fact, I am surprised I remembered the Viennese. I haven't danced one in at least 15 years," said Nick.

"You liked her?" asked Dolly carefully. They were no longer pressed together as they danced.

"I did, but it was my fault. Couldn't commit. Actually, wouldn't commit to her. I had no trouble committing to the military," laughed Nick ruefully. The music stopped. The orchestra said they were taking a break.

"Union orchestra," shrugged Dolly with a laugh, as they walked back toward the living room.

"Looks like our drinks disappeared."

"Apparently. Nick, it has been a genuine pleasure."

"The pleasure has been all mine, Ms. Monroe, thank you," confessed Nick, bending over to kiss the back of her hand before letting loose.

"I think we know each other enough for you to call me Dolly. I pierced your foot, after all."

"True. Don't know where we go from there," replied Nick with a smile, staring intensely into her eyes. She broke the stare after a second, blushing again.

"I would love to sit and talk longer. Later, perhaps. I've already allowed one of my guests to monopolize way too much of my time. I need to mingle." She gave him a quick hug and a kiss on the cheek. Then laughing she grabbed a napkin from the bar.

"Don't want to scare off the other ladies, now do we," admitted Dolly as she made to wipe it off his cheek.

"Can't have that now, can we? Especially on my first night out. How will I lose my virginity?" pondered Nick with a laugh.

Dolly looked him in the eye, her lips slightly parted, thinking, "On second thought, maybe I *will* leave my claim. Enjoy the evening Senator. I hope to see you again soon."

Dolly walked away, greeting guests, and making her way up the staircase to those dancing upstairs. Nick turned back to the bar.

"What do you recommend?" he asked the bartender. He pulled out a pitcher. "This is an Aged Negroni. It is equal parts: Gin, Campari and sweet Vermouth aged in an oak barrel for a month."

"I'll try it, but pour me a short one, please."

"Make it two," ordered Chuck, walking up in his more traditional tuxedo to stand next to Nick.

"You, sir, are a bastard," accused Nick with a smile.

"I saw you dancing with Dolly. It didn't seem like torture to me," replied Chuck with a broad grin.

"What's a senator to do when he can't trust his own chief of staff?" asked Nick seriously as he leaned on the bar, sipping.

"Interesting, but I think I will stick with my dry martinis."

"I like it. You can really taste the hints of oak and the way the Campari adds a taste of citrus. Very nice," expressed Chuck, saluting the bartender with a raised glass.

"Enjoying yourself?" asked Nick with a glare.

"At your expense? Always."

"How many of these have you been to?"

"Since Dolly started hosting? All of them. Before that, I'd been to a few of Senator Bank's wife Penny's galas."

"Well, I had no idea. Maybe that explains why you've been trying to get me to these since I got here. You needed a wingman."

Chuck gave Nick a sideways glance. "No offence, Nick, but you're a terrible wingman. Any woman I'm interested in would much rather be with you. Trust me. You look like a cross between Bogart and Bond in your white dinner jacket. You have Jenny to thank for that. She's the one who suggested it. She knew it would be a sea of black tuxes, and knew you would stand out anyway, but this would just make it even more evident. I thought Dolly would like you, but geez, she spent 45 minutes dancing with *you* instead of mingling with her guests. Anyone else would be written up in the gossip rags for such an egregious breach of hostess etiquette."

"But not Dolly?"

"Are you kidding?" asked Chuck as Nick shook his head. "Dolly's parties are private. If you blab, you're never invited back. Post a pic of this party and you get sued. Nobody wants to get on *her* shit list. This is the 'A' ticket of the year. Trust me. A few years ago, someone was stupid and posted some pictures and Dolly sued. Every invitation has, in tiny print, non-disclosure agreements. RSVP'ing and attending is agreeing to those terms. She barbecued the guy and soaked his company for millions. Gave it all to charity." Nick shook his head at this.

"Let's just say, if you think Lexi is the Queen of the Hill, Dolly is the Queen of the Social scene. Nobody crosses her. The only difference is she's nice," explained Chuck.

"All the kids aren't even allowed to bring their phones. It's the only time they pay attention to anyone telling them to not use a phone. Dolly's parties are *that* special. No one wants to risk being blacklisted. Plus, they're all afraid one of their friends would rat them out. I've seen nothing like it."

"Amazing, maybe she *should* be our ambassador to the UN. I can tell you one thing. I doubt Lexi can dance like Dolly," laughed Nick.

"Really? You don't know much about the VP, do you? I'll give you a dossier. If you think Dolly is a wonderful dancer, it was mostly you leading. I saw some of the first waltz. Dolly kept up. Lexi is better than Dolly and better than you. I have seen her in action. Her husband Pete is just as good. Too bad they won't retire and just join the senior ballroom dancing circuit," suggested Chuck with a laugh.

"Well, I'm here, and I'm hungry. Don't let me stop you from finding your third ex-wife."

"Working on it," said Chuck as they went their separate ways.

Nick wandered the room, speaking briefly with some senators and the odd cabinet member he knew. What surprised him was the number of people who approached him to introduce themselves and to shake his hand. Many thanked him for his heroics in New York. Some for his service to the country, and even a few for his impassioned exposure of some of the hypocrisy of Washington.

It amazed him at the variety of conversations, but even more at the genuine joy people had from talking to him. One of the Opposition Senators suggested he make a trip upstairs. See some of the junior staffers before they were too deep into Dolly's open bars.

Nick walked up the staircase. It took twenty minutes. Many couples sat on the stairs eating their small plates and sipping their drinks, talking and laughing. They rose to meet Nick as he went by.

Eventually, he reached the landing. Looking down over the railing, he glanced at his watch. It was well after midnight and yet the whole living room was a teaming mass of humanity. Folks were still dancing down below, but Nick could barely discern the music with the proximity to the ballroom at his back and the big band orchestra playing tunes from around World War II.

He turned and headed down the hallway, once again meeting younger staffers. As he entered one doorway into the ballroom, he stood, amazed at what he saw.

There had to be over a hundred, perhaps as many as a hundred and fifty, mostly young people, out swing dancing on the ballroom floor. Many were doing a jitterbug. Nick didn't know anyone even knew how to do the jitterbug any longer. It was an extremely physical dance, mostly popular in the 40s and 50s.

Nick walked in further, along a wall, to watch as one couple was putting on quite a show in the middle of the dance floor. Others swayed on the sidelines, cheering and shouting. The band was playing the *Boogie Woogie Bugle Boy*, and the dancers were going to town.

Nick watched as the man, a twenty something nerdy looking thin fellow, was twirling his partner, a pretty blonde. He was wrapping her around his body, over his head, and between his legs. It was an incredible demonstration of strength, stamina, and rhythm.

When the song ended, the crowd cheered, and the next pair moved to the middle as the band started playing *Rockin Robin*. The first couple were now off to the side, glistening with perspiration, but absolutely glowing.

If possible, the next pair displayed even more physicality. Nick knew how hard this dance was. He had done it with Heather back in the day. Remembering the exhilaration and the adrenalin of completing a well thought out routine.

Nick looked at the young Washington staffers. The guys wore rented tuxedos, and the girls were in mostly cocktail dresses. These girls weren't buying the flowing evening gowns of the red carpets. At that point, the first couple who had danced saw Nick. He was hard to miss in his white dinner jacket. She grabbed her guy and ran over.

"Senator, we are so happy to meet you. I'm Patty and this is Carl. We both work in Congressman Reiner's office. Isn't the party dreamy?" said the pretty blonde, Patty, still flushed and breathless from the dance floor. Carl held out his hand and shook Nick's.

"Pleased to meet you, Senator. We are so grateful for all you have done for the country."

Others saw them talking to Nick and started making their way over. Soon he felt like he was on the receiving line in a wedding. He met and shook the hand of most, if not all, one hundred plus of the young staffers up in the ballroom. Even those of a couple of senators, house members and their wives, husbands, or partners. At one point, he saw Dolly holding court in a corner, and she casually waved at him. He smiled and waved back.

It looked like the orchestra was getting ready to pack up and flip over to the DJ. Several of the couples pulled Nick to the dance floor and waved to the band to stop and play a few more songs. The band leader looked at Dolly, who nodded.

"Come on Senator, let us teach you the Jitterbug," said several of the couples.

"Yeah, come on Senator, learn the jitterbug," shouted Dolly from the corner, as the staffers and others turned, laughing and smiling at

Nick's predicament. Assuming he would make a fool of himself, they started shouting 'Turner, Turner, Turner'. Nick held up his hands.

"All right, all right," he said, taking off his jacket showing his suspenders. He rolled up his sleeves as he walked out on the dance floor with two other guys and three gals. His partner was a cute redhead named Cindy. She worked in the Department of Education. They all huddled together briefly. They told Nick what they would start with. Nick smiled and winked. "Try to keep up, kids," he said, grinning. He turned to the bandleader. "Can you do Benny Goodman's *Sing Sing Sing*?"

"Sure thing, Senator," said the bandleader.

The three couples spread out on the floor. Cindy and Nick looking at each other. The band kicked off the first few bars and away they went. In a short while, the steps came back to Nick. Cindy was smiling the biggest smile possible. Soon he was tossing her over his shoulders, between his legs and doing the exaggerated stops the dance was known for. Nick looked like he had done the dance a million times, and in fact, he had, if decades ago now.

They were going at it and finished with a tumble move, where Cindy rolled over his back and landed in the splits in front of him as the song ended. It had worked out incredibly well. What he did not know is the other two couples had stopped to watch once they got going.

The crowd cheered and clapped as Cindy sprang up and threw her arms around Nick and hugged him. He dodged her attempt to kiss him on the mouth, giving her a cheek. He disengaged her arms as everyone clapped. Nick found his jacket, saluting the Band Leader as he wiped an arm across his forehead. He'd worked up a good sweat.

Nick made his way toward the bar as the DJ started playing more modern music and the kids once again crowded onto the dance floor to gyrate with their hands in the air. Nick shook his head at the ability of youth to move from big band hits of the 40s to whatever this was they were playing now. It did not seem to have words, just an incessant beat.

Nick headed out of the ballroom intending to make his way downstairs, find Chuck, and assuming he struck out, convince him to give him a lift back to his office/apartment. As he moved to the hallway, he saw Dolly standing at a bar, talking to Chuck. He made his way over.

"My favorite and least favorite cousins in one place. Who'd have thunk it?" said Nick, smiling.

"Insulting our hostess is not a good idea Nick," replied Chuck solemnly, as Dolly laughed.

"I take it you too talked already, and he told you I spilled the beans?" asked Dolly, laughing more.

"I did. Nick, I have to say, I didn't know you could dance. Those were some impressive moves. Jitterbug, huh? Wow, wait until the ladies in the office hear about it," smiled Chuck.

"I haven't done a jitterbug in over 15 years. But watching those kids brought back a lot of memories. I think the last time was in Aviano, in Italy, at a dancehall just off base," noted Nick, thinking back.

"Another dancing girlfriend?" asked Dolly, wickedly.

"Hardly. I think she was a staff sergeant. Come to think of it, not an attractive one, but she could dance a mean jitterbug," laughed Nick.

"I see," said Dolly. "Drink?"

"I think I'm good for one more. Maybe I'll actually get to drink this one."

"Hey, I can't help it if you can't keep track of your drinks," claimed Dolly.

The bartender handed Dolly and Nick martinis and a scotch to Chuck. They toasted.

"Cheers to operation, get Nick out," proclaimed Chuck, as he and Dolly got a laugh at Nick's expense.

"You two are off the Christmas list," said Nick. "Speaking of that, how is finding your next ex-wife going?"

"Well, let's just say there are lots of candidates and leave it at that," confided Chuck with a sly smile.

"Hey, I bet Dolly has a lot of friends. Surely she can help you," Nick suggested, glancing at Dolly.

Dolly had a frown on her face. "I think I'm out of that business," mumbled Dolly evasively.

Nick looked from one to the other. "OK, what's up? Did you two get married before you figured out you were cousins or something?" asked Nick.

Chuck laughed. "Hardly, besides we are very distant cousins. No, Dolly *did* set me up with my second wife."

"I've been trying to make it up to him ever since," lamented Dolly.

"It wasn't your fault. Half her family was in the looney bin. How were you supposed to know she was as bat shit crazy as the rest of them?" said Chuck in an ironic tone.

"I said I was sorry," repeated Dolly, biting her lower lip in a pout.

Nick laughed. "I'll have to hear the complete story on this one sometime."

"I'll have to be a lot drunker and since I drove, I've been limiting my drinks," noted Chuck.

"Good, then you can drop me by the office."

"You aren't going back to work after the party, Senator? That is above and beyond the call," said Dolly, looking startled.

"Oh no, nothing like that," answered Chuck, laughing. "Cuz, the good senator sleeps on a pullout bed in his Senate office."

"You're kidding, right?" asked Dolly, as Nick shook his head. "No wonder you never go out and just eat drive through. This town is fun, Nick. You just need to make a little effort. We're not New York or Paris, but it is not like we're in LA or Dallas, for God's sake," she finished, wrinkling her face.

"Well, maybe now that I'm no longer a social virgin, I can leave the convent more," agreed Nick.

Chuck looked shocked for a second, looking from Nick to Dolly.

"Don't worry, Chuck, it is an inside joke. Maybe Nick, maybe," stated Dolly with a knowing smile.

"I'll wait by the stairs. Thank you as always for a wonderful party," said Chuck, giving her a hug and a kiss on the cheek. He walked toward the staircase, leaving Nick and Dolly alone.

Nick took her hands in his own. "I can see why you have the reputation you do. The party was fabulous. The company even better. Who would ever have thought I'd get to do a Viennese Waltz and a Jitterbug at this party? I think it would be a good time for me to leave. I'm going to be unable to move in the morning." He turned his head, showing her he still had the remnants of her lipstick on his cheek, and smiled.

"Nick Turner, you are a special man, I can sense it," proclaimed Dolly, holding a hand on his cheek. She leaned in and gave him a kiss on the lips and when he didn't resist, she lingered for a second longer than a courtesy kiss. "Whoops," she said as she used a finger to wipe the lipstick off his mouth. "Sorry."

"Why are you apologizing? Thank you for the invite. I promise I won't duck them any longer. Good night, Dolly." He gently squeezed her hand before turning and walking down the staircase with Chuck toward the door.

She stood by the railing and sighed, watching him wind his way through the crowd. Dolly hadn't felt these feelings in a very long time. She sighed heavily again, disappointed he didn't even look back. Just as she was about to turn, as he went up the steps to the foyer, he glanced up, caught her eye, and smiled. Then he was gone. Smiling, her heart beating like a schoolgirl, she turned back to her other guests.

#

Senator Banks sat in a comfortable chair in Dolly's living room. He loved to observe the people and the interactions as they played out during the party. Baxter watched the scene between Nick and Dolly on the upstairs balcony. He could see the delight on Dolly's face as Nick turned to look up at her on his way out the door. Baxter smiled.

"Well, Penny, my dear," he said to himself. "I've done what I can. Now nature must take its course. I'll join you soon, but not yet. I must finish one last task."

As he finished his inner dialogue, Banks glanced up to see Dolly making her way down the stairs. He motioned to Hobson to help him up as she approached.

"Dolly, it was wonderful as usual. Penny is smiling down at you."

"Thank you, Baxter. I'm glad she would approve. I'm trying to do her parties justice," she said, kissing Bank's cheek. She watched as Hobson led him slowly up the stairs and out the front door of the estate.

Dolly had a fleeting vision of his funeral, row after row of chairs filled with well wishers with a military officer delivering the eulogy. This pained her heart, realizing soon, time would deprive her of not just Penny, but also Baxter Banks.

She turned to survey her living room full of revelers, smiling. As long as she had the Galas, she'd never be alone. Thinking about Nick turning to smile up at her, she greeted guests and made her way to a nearby bar in the living room for a nightcap.

Chapter 35

Nick sat in the Armed Services committee meeting room, listening to the Chairman of the Joint Chiefs, Admiral Jason Kensington, provide updates on the status of the military's latest initiatives.

"Senators, I can report we have seen a 23% reduction in carbon emissions in our military bases around the country. We've successfully implemented wind and solar alternative energy resources. Substantial progress is being made in electrifying a significant number of our trucks."

"We continue to work to make ourselves less dependent on fossil fuels, reducing our dependency and improving our ability to respond to challenges in a more eco-friendly and sustainable manner. Our goal is removing reliance on supply chains which could be affected in the event of conflict," said Admiral Kensington, referring to a fancy infographic showing these reductions in pie and graph charts.

"Further, we're also pleased to report our progress in efforts to cleanse the military of those we believe could respond to the dog whistle of the white supremacists undermining our mission. We've rotated many of these soldiers out of the military entirely the last few years, not offering re-enlistment opportunities."

"All levels of leadership are ensuring mandatory diversity and inclusivity training while removing the former patriarchal, white dominated view of the command structure. We are actively mentoring and fast tracking our soldiers and sailors of color to make our overall command structure more reflective of our society. Our recruiting efforts have shifted to be more diverse and inclusive. They are working to expand the appeal and opportunities for women and people of all sexual preferences. A military career is no longer limited to a narrow and potentially bigoted minority of our society," finished Admiral Kensington in an almost righteous tone.

"The Chair recognizes ranking Opposition member, Senator Garcia of Texas," said Colin Fitzpatrick of Massachusetts, the Chairman of the Armed Services Committee.

"Thank you, Mr. Chairman. Admiral, I have reviewed the military budget proposal for next year. While I understand the desire to control costs, how do you explain reducing our annual expenditures when it appears China is upping theirs by at least 20%?"

"Senator, China is spending a large portion of that budget on ships and planes and maintaining their much larger standing army. They do not have the level of technology we do. They are spending lots of money on prototype airplanes and on expanding their naval capabilities. We do not feel any of these are a threat in terms of new technology or in an area where the threat level is greater than previously. As for our own budget, the administration asked us to reduce our budget by 3%. This has led to a few base closures or consolidation efforts. We are also reaping the benefits of our climate change initiatives, lowering our overall fuel costs to help reduce our budgets as well," said Admiral Kensington, looking at his notes.

"Further, we are expanding our expenditures for both the Space Force and our cyber warfare capabilities. We feel both will give us a technological advantage in the future and neither are resource intensive, rather technology based."

Senator Garcia leaned forward in his chair. "Admiral, forgive me for being skeptical. For more than the last decade, we have attempted to use our standoff capabilities, namely drone technology, to kill our enemies. While this appears to be successful, there is never a shortage of replacements and terrorist attacks have been on the rise, not falling. We have been fortunate so far to not have any foreign terrorist attacks on our soil. That has to do more with Senator Turner and his personal heroics than it is to anything our military or intelligence agencies have accomplished," noted Senator Garcia, looking at Nick and nodding.

"Meanwhile, we have seen heinous terrorist attacks in London, Italy, Israel, Germany, Sweden, Spain, Portugal, on several cruise ships, our own ships and bases attacked across the world, and now the assassination of the President of France. In many of these attacks, some of our own equipment has been used," fumed Garcia, looking at his own notes as he continued.

"Many of our allies blame us and our disastrous Afghanistan surrender for both arming and emboldening our enemies. While also causing irreparable damage to our reputation and a reticence in these countries to share or accept intelligence, let alone any help. Yet you tell me, we are making progress, going green and purging our ranks of the very warriors we need. How is this making us safer?"

"Senator, the world is a dangerous place. It is true. As you said, we have not had a successful foreign terrorist attack on our soil. What we have had is a rise in home-grown terrorist activities, and in mass shootings, by predominately white supremacist groups. We know they have been recruiting from and targeting fellow citizens in and out of our armed forces. This is the current threat, and this is what they focused us on purging and ensuring we are not enabling through advanced military training," lectured the Admiral.

"It is important to note, while the actual attacks get coverage, the ones foiled by either our military intelligence or the efforts of our intelligence services do not. It would be short sided to assume we are unsuccessful in suppressing most terrorist activities against us around the world. Finally, I would also add, that our efforts to purge extremism from the military is not in any way related to religion or anyone's personal religious beliefs," finished the Admiral in a forceful tone, showing his disdain for the Senator's implied statements.

Garcia interrupted with a laugh. "Sir, we are not on ANC, so please spare us the trope of white supremacy being our biggest domestic threat. Have you looked at Chicago? Pick any weekend. 25-50 killed, 50-100 shot. Almost none are white. Are these all *black* supremacists? Yes, we have had mass shootings by mentally ill people. Have some visited white supremacist websites, yes, but the total mass shootings in the last few years amount to *two* weekends of shootings in Chicago."

"And that does not include Baltimore, New York, DC, Detroit, LA and on and on. You are the Chairman of our military. What are you going to do about the Chinese navy passing 1000 ships while we have fallen below 400? I want to know why the Chinese now have 100 submarines, while we're now below 65? I want to know how the hell we're going to protect Taiwan or Lithuania or Latvia or Poland or God forbid Israel, when our enemies realize we are both too weak to respond and lack the will. The latter seems to be a given, considering where our priorities are. The former is my concern today. Your job is not to give into the administration. Your job is to tell us what you need, not tell us what we want to hear," said Garcia, finishing emphatically.

"Senator, I can assure you, we lack neither the will nor the ability to counter threats to America around the world," replied Kensington.

Garcia shook his head at the parsing of the words by the Admiral.

"We face many threats, both domestic and foreign. It is our job to recommend the correct courses of action and to educate you and your colleagues so you can approve the budgets," said the Admiral.

"I noticed you said America. You did not say our allies," responded Garcia. He was going to continue when the Chairman interrupted. "Senator Garcia, your allotted time is expired," said Senator Fitzpatrick. A visibly frustrated Garcia sat back in his chair. The fleetingness of smiles crossed the Admiral's face as he looked down at his notes.

Each of the Senators took their time and asked the Admiral questions, the Party senators asking questions designed to give the Admiral the opportunity to tout the diversity, inclusion, and climate initiatives. The Opposition senators continued the theme of Senator Garcia, trying to pin the Admiral down on the true readiness of the soldiers and sailors. To understand the true nature of the equipment, the support of allies, and the overall status of America in the world with the ever-diminishing ability to project power.

Finally, as the most junior member of the committee and the final questioner, it was Nick's turn. The pool reporters in the room straightened up and started listening, wondering if they would get another of 'Turner's Tirades' as they were now called by the press pool.

"The Chair recognizes the Senator from Colorado, Senator Turner. You have five minutes." Not wasting any time with platitudes, Nick jumped right in.

"Admiral, I would remind you, my fellow senators, and all our citizens of the reason our military exists. As General Douglas MacArthur said in his farewell speech at West Point, speaking to the cadets, '*Through all this welter of change and development, your mission remains fixed, determined, inviolable. It is to win our wars … You are the ones who are trained to fight. Yours is the profession of arms, the will to win, the sure knowledge that in war there is no substitute for victory, that if you lose, the nation will be destroyed, that the very obsession of your public service must be Duty, Honor, Country'.*"

"Duty, honor, country. Not diversity, equity, inclusion and climatism. These are admirable traits, in our business and in our own daily life. However, our average citizen's life's aim is not to protect our country and all its citizens, which, if I am not mistaken, is the *sole* reason we have a military. I would like to know how diversity, inclusion, and climate activism are making us better at achieving this goal? Remember, there is no diversity, inclusion, or carbon emission scorecard on which to score more points than say the Chinese or any of the 1100 terrorist groups the FBI and CIA list as wanting to do us harm," finished Nick.

Kensington looked bored at Nick's lecture, looking down at his notes and ignoring what Nick was saying. He had a much different body language with Nick than the respect he had shown all the prior senators. He continued undeterred, having also noticed the Admiral's disrespect.

"In fact, none of these things the Admiral speaks of as successes today have improved our ability to beat the Chinese, Russians, or terrorists one iota. **Not a single thing**," emphasized Nick, clearly stating each word. "I would argue, they are making us weaker and less able to protect our own borders, let alone project the power our allies need and count on us to do. Sir, you have one job, and I have heard nothing today that says you are performing this job in a way to improve the safety of our citizens," accused Nick emphatically.

"I'm sorry Senator, was there a question?" asked the Admiral in mocking tone, clearly annoyed at Turner's accusations. Several of the Senators of both parties looked up at his tone. Turner may have been new, but this was still the Senate. Some looked to Senator Fitzpatrick.

Senator Fitzpatrick spoke up, "I would remind the Admiral…," Nick interrupted.

"It's okay, this is nothing new from him, trust me," said Nick with disdain and an audible chuckle, causing Kensington's face to redden.

"Admiral, I believe you have already delivered all of your canned comments. Spare us a replay," said Nick calmly. "By your own statistics, we are woefully behind the Chinese in artillery and naval forces. We are out manned and outgunned on almost every statistic by the Chinese, except our vaunted airpower. If we are pushed far enough away, our airpower is of little use, and it is of no use to the Taiwanese if we cannot support them with boots on the ground."

"Again, Senator, I cannot see the questions in your statements," said the Admiral in a terse tone but seemingly under control again.

"Again, *Admiral*, I congratulate you on your 23% reduction in emissions for our bases and the promotion of many soldiers and sailors because of your diversity quotas and inclusive policies. My only question is, can we see the promotion lists for captains, majors, and Lieutenant Colonels for, say, the last 5 years? We, of course, vote on the Colonels and above here in the Senate. I have tallied these up as well. I am impressed by the number of diverse and inclusive officers we are promoting. If you would please provide the actual promotion lists, I would appreciate it," asked Nick.

The Admiral, obviously surprised, paused. "Ah, I'm not sure
if those are available for distribution," he said, turning to an aide
next to him.

"Why not Admiral? It should be a simple task. As you know more
than most, I also served and have been on and have seen these very
lists. They are published to the commanders each promotion cycle,
and are used to decide and grant the promotions," noted Nick.

"I know how our promotion systems work, Turner," replied
Kensington angrily, for the first time losing his cool. "I just don't
know if or why you would want to see them?" he finished flustered.

The other senators murmured at Kensington's rude comment
to Nick, but he continued. "Admiral, I certainly hope we have
not foresworn all ideas of merit being a reason for promotion. As
someone who has seen combat, you follow your leaders because
you know the American military is supposed to be a meritocracy.
Where promotions are based on ability, not simply because of ticket
punching, and certainly not on the color of one's skin nor of their
gender," continued Nick.

"I believe we have Constitutional Amendments that require all
of us to adhere to this rule. The last place in the world we need
affirmative action is in the military where we need the best promoted,
regardless of how they look, or God forbid, whether they have a
healthy appreciation of the Constitution or a love of the country.
Tell me, Admiral, how have the recruiting quotas been filled since
Afghanistan? Are you still getting plenty of volunteers from the
Southern and Midwestern states? People who love God and country,
who go to church, are demonstrably Christian, and will charge
into battle to fight and die for their country?" inquired Nick as
Kensington glared hatefully while saying nothing.

"I can answer this question for you. For the last seven years,
we have in fact failed to meet our quota. This number has fallen
off precipitously since the Afghanistan withdrawal and since this
administration made it clear, they deem anyone who is white,
Christian and from the south as more likely a white supremacist than

a good recruit. Is it not true that you have been providing signing bonuses to recruiters and recruits who are in fact not white, not male and not from predominately red states? Again, a rhetorical question, since we both know the answer to this question is, you do."

Kensington continued his disdainful glare as Nick continued.

"Also, while you take what you can get in a volunteer army, I don't doubt these recruits will and can be made into excellent warriors. But as MacArthur said, 'There is no substitute for victory.' Victory is obtained by recruiting and accepting the best candidates the country has to offer. Not by turning them away because of political optics."

Nick raised his voice as he reached his concluding point.

"I look forward to seeing the original versions of these promotion lists. To prove white soldiers, rated higher than others, *as combat leaders*, are not being passed over to promote people of color or women solely to fill quotas and make you look more diverse and inclusive. That violates the Constitution and should be prosecuted, if found to be true. Furthermore, we owe it to our soldiers and sailors and their parents, to ensure they are being led into battle by those best equipped to complete the mission and keep their sons and daughters *alive*," said Nick in a commanding tone, looking at the admiral as he delivered his last sentence. "I yield back my time."

"This concludes today's hearings. Admiral Kensington, thank you for your appearance today. This session is adjourned," said Senator Fitzpatrick, before anyone could ask to be recognized.

The senators picked up their notebooks and binders. Nick stayed seated, holding his purple notebook in his hand. The Admiral gave Nick a look full of contempt as he gathered his things, leaving with his aide. Nick responded with a smile.

"Know the Admiral?" asked Freddie Garcia sitting on the edge of the curved table where their seats were.

Nick looked up from his reverie. "A long time ago. I served under him some of my time when I was in the Navy."

"He's come a long way. He was more junior than any other Joint Chief, only three stars, and he'd only had the third star for six months when he was selected. Of course, being selected as a Chairman, he got an immediate promotion and a fourth star," said Garcia.

"No surprise. If you look up Blue Falcon in the military slang database, his picture should be there representing the Navy," added Nick ruefully.

Garcia laughed. "I forgot that one. It fits."

"Right, you served in the reserves. He's a total fraud," said Nick.

"It's a brilliant question. Don't let up. Make them give you the lists. Do you know something?" questioned Garcia.

Nick nodded, "I have a couple of buddies still in and they have told me they know for certain, white captains and majors are being passed over while they promote officers of color or women above them."

"It also stigmatizes the black, Hispanic, and female officers. Now they carry the burden of whether they earned their promotion. This is exactly the same problem we have seen for generations with affirmative action in the colleges. It means well on paper, but unfairly labels the recipient for life. It's bad enough in the business world, but it will get you killed on the battlefield if we don't give the best leaders the promotions to lead. That bit of doubt in your commander leads to a breakdown of the unit cohesion. These woke generals and admirals have forgotten what it means to be in battle with only your buddy next to you. Without trust, we fail. I know this is happening and I don't expect to see the actual lists," finished Nick.

"You never know, I agree with you on this one," offered Freddie.

"We are all closer on most issues than we think. There're just a few puppeteers who refuse to let us act on our own," Nick replied, as he got up.

Garcia shook his hand and left the Committee room.

Nick picked up his purple notebook and headed out the door.

Senator Fitzpatrick waited there to ambush him.

"What kind of stunt are you pulling? We don't need any grandstanding with the filibuster vote coming up," said Senator Fitzpatrick.

"Want to complain? Go on EXN again and trash us, but keep it out of the official record. You're cutting your own throat. You know how hard folks work to get here?" asked Fitzpatrick, fuming, spittle flying from his mouth as Nick stared back calmly.

"Their whole lives sometimes and you just skip all that, get here and show your gratitude by shitting allover us. Shut up, fill out the term of a real senator, and enjoy your pension when you're done. Don't screw up things for which you have so little understanding as seen by your petty complaints," finished Fitzpatrick, not bothering to hide his disgust with Turner.

"And a pleasant day to you too, Senator. Clearly, we have a difference of opinion," replied Nick as he walked away.

"You're not much of a team player, are you, son?" asked the Senator to Nick's retreating back.

Nick stopped and turned slowly, looking at the Senator in such a way, he took a step back.

"Senator, a team has a common goal. They have each other's back. The teams I'm used to aim to do good, not harm. Is that the goal of our team?" asked Nick.

"Turner, there are winners and losers and believe me, it is better to be on a winning team than a losing one. It can be lonely sitting on the bench. You need to decide if you want to play or not," replied Fitzpatrick.

Nick turned without answering and continued walking toward the Capitol atrium out into the sunshine of midday.

#

In his ornate office near the Senate Chamber, Majority Leader Fontana muted his feed of CSPAN2.

"Shit, shit, shit," he said, kicking his trash bin across the room. "Goddamn baby. I'm gonna string Morris up by his balls and roast him for picking this guy. I really don't need this right now," he said out loud, turning his trash can right side up.

He walked over to his bar, put a couple of ice cubes in a rocks glass, grabbed his bottle of Makers, and poured in a splash. "Fuck it," he said, as he filled the glass half full. Taking a slug, he glanced up at the portrait of Woodrow Wilson hanging in the office.

"You had it easy, pal." Fontana jumped as both the cell phone and a satellite phone on his desk rang simultaneously.

He set down his drink, glanced at his iPhone, picking up the Sat phone.

"Ya," he answered. "Of course, I saw it," he said into the satellite phone. "What am I going to do about it? I'm gonna fucking kick his ass is what I'm gonna do," said Sal as he listened intently, "Of course I know we need his vote, ya, ya ya…alright I'll try the velvet hammer, but you had better be ready to implement plan B," Sal sipped his drink and listened intently.

"How much notice do you need?" he asked. "OK, I'll talk to him and let you know so we can decide. This is all fucking Morris' fault. He needs to pay. Got it." Sal hung up the phone and stood sipping his drink, thinking intently. He glanced back up at Wilson. "Ok, maybe it wasn't easy, but you got away with murder buddy," he said, tossing back the rest of his drink. He picked up his iPhone to return the other call.

Chapter 36

Chuck joined Nick as he walked out of the capital toward the Hart building. He said nothing, waiting for Nick to start the conversation.

"Don't keep me waiting. Let the lecture begin," declared Nick, waiting for his chief of staff to rebuke his actions.

"What prompted that? It was a simple task. Listen to his comments. Ask a few questions. We all know special interest, money, and personal priorities corrupt the Senate. The military brass is no different. Making a speech on CSPAN2 isn't going to change that. Even if any of the networks pick it up, you'll get coverage for 2 minutes, not change anything, and ensure you're now officially a malcontent."

"That about sums it up. My trip to Colorado just underscored it. Chuck, we're not doing anything to help the people. Whether we're in the majority or the opposition is, it's the same. More money for special interest, crazy policies, and the people get little or nothing," said Nick as they walked into the Hart building, heading for the stairs to his office.

"The sad part is the people aren't even mad anymore. They know the government is ineffective and they just assume we're all rich crooks. They don't think voting matters anymore, mostly thanks to our antics with mail in voting. What does that say?"

"Boss, passion is good. Let's just try to direct it in a way to help. Now you just look like a whiner, even if you are right. No one cares," said Chuck, wheezing. "Can we maybe take the elevator next time? I'm neither young nor fit."

"Sorry," Nick replied as they entered his office, with Chuck trailing behind, trying to catch his breath. Nick's assistants managing the front lobby handed him a small stack of call notes. Nick glanced at them as he headed down the hall to his office.

"Senator?" called out Margie as he walked by her open office door. Nick stuck his head in the office.

"We need to catch up. The shows are asking for comments and bookings tonight and this weekend. We need to figure out a strategy," suggested Margie as Nick grimaced.

"I guess they watch CSPAN2?"

Margie replied with arched eyebrows. "Of course they do. I wish you'd give me some warning before you poke the hornet's nest. I also got a nasty call from the Party comms director asking me to put a muzzle on you until the filibuster vote is over."

"Sorry, I'll swing by in a few." Nick continued walking to his office, where he was met at the door by Greg.

"Couldn't resist, could you?" asked Greg, smiling.

"Hey, honesty is supposed to be the best policy, right?" insisted Nick with a laugh as Chuck closed the door behind the three of them. Nick glanced at Chuck and Greg. Neither were laughing at his joke.

"Geez, and I thought the opposition was a tough crowd." Nick got water from the fridge. He threw one to Chuck. Greg already had a cup of coffee in his hand.

"Nick, this is not a joking matter," Greg said, concerned, looking at Chuck. "Can't you talk some sense into him? You are the father figure, after all."

"I don't think I can take him behind the woodshed. I'd be the one in the ER. I *have* tried to reason with him."

"Guys, come on. Was there anything I said or asked that was incorrect? Besides, Kensington is a sanctimonious SOB."

"That's not the point," said Chuck.

"Yes, it is. And if it isn't, then it should be. Everyone talks about a Great Game or the Potomac Two Step or whatever other terms there are for gritting your teeth and voting for bad legislation in order to get yours passed later. This isn't right. We need to tell the truth and we need to ask for the truth in return."

"Do you really think it is going to matter? It is just going to make it hard for you to get any of *your* agenda done while you're here." Chuck uttered this in a fatherly tone, trying to impart wisdom.

"If this is what it takes to get things done, then I guess the only thing we'll get done is to point out the hypocrisy of how nothing substantial gets done and why," fumed Nick.

Chuck just sighed and shrugged. "They'll just isolate you. You won't get a platform to even complain. This is how this works."

"The Majority Leader wants to meet with you, of course," said Greg, breaking in. "As soon as you can. I set it up for Tuesday afternoon. I said you had meetings with constituents until them. That's as close to the vote on Wednesday as I could get. Care to give us an idea about how you intend to vote?" asked Greg, trying to change the direction of the conversation.

Nick wandered over to his couch and sat down heavily, ignoring the question. "Would you guys like to hear about my trip?"

"Is that what brought this on?" asked Chuck, pacing the office. "You can't get sentimental. There are many people hurting, but you can't save them all. The Senate is macro politics, not micro. You can't drill down to the individual; Consider the much larger picture."

"Do I? The 'macro' picture comprises lots and lots of little 'micros'. They're called people. Every macro decision we make affects all those micros."

Chuck pointed his hand at Nick. "Don't make me out to be the bad guy. I'm right and you know it. We cannot get bogged down on the individual issues or we get nothing done."

"That's my point. What if we're making things worse instead of helping? I spent days riding around the state, stopping in towns, eating in diners, trying to have honest conversations with locals. Hearing what mattered to them and what their lives are like."

"There are people suffering everywhere. Chuck is right. It's good to keep these folks in mind, but we have to keep our eye on the bigger picture, not just in Colorado but across the country. Even the world," offered Greg.

"Guys, I get it. We are important. We make big decisions that affect lots of people in broad ways." Nick held up his hand as both Chuck and Greg started to object.

He got up and walked over to the fridge to get another water. "You know I didn't know what to expect, but what I saw and heard was not it. There are a lot of folks out there leading a hard life, with little, but they're not desperate, they're not giving up either. They're just resigned. I spoke to a couple of old timers on social security who had been through good times and bad. Busts and booms. They gave me some sage advice when I asked them how to fix things." Nick stopped, taking a drink.

"I bet they did," speculated Chuck.

"I think you'd be surprised. These were guys who worked with their hands, in factories and in fields. They said first, stop trying to fix things. You just cause more problems. People will fix their own problems, but you have to give them tools and opportunities to do it." Nick paused again. "That little tidbit is the best solution I've heard. We need to stop trying to fix things and get back to basics. They all pretty much say *we* are the real problem, here in the Senate, in Congress, in the Presidency, the media, etc."

"Of course they do. We're an easy target. Change is easy to talk about and much harder to do," explained Chuck.

"I thought so too. As I was riding, I thought about it. It really isn't hard at all. We just need to look outside the box."

"Not following," said Greg, as Chuck chimed in with, "me neither."

"Let's look at it from their point of view. They have no idea what getting rid of the legislative filibuster means. They only know the laws being passed aren't helping them. Taxes are going up, police funding is going down, housing, utilities, and food costs are rising. Open borders and immigrants coming to Colorado stress the welfare systems and crush low skill wages. Inflation, welfare, opioid addiction, and suicide are all on the rise," recited Nick, his voice rising as he explained what he heard, wandering around the office, talking with his hands.

"All of them were sick and tired of the government sticking their hand into these issues. Forcing schools to take the lead on stuff best left to families and parents," noted Nick, sitting on the edge of his desk.

"All agreed education has always been the key to getting ahead for them and their children and grandchildren. This education is now more concerned with gender studies, critical race theory, climate change, wokeism, and celebrating immorality. I expected this from a Weld County pool hall, but not from an LGBTQ couple or a Boulder professor."

"Interesting," mused Chuck, contemplating the message Nick was delivering.

"The other thing was, they all think the media and the government are not helping because they keep giving airtime to the small fringe groups. This is causing more people to be angry and less accepting of those who want to tell them how to lead their life." Nick stopped, taking a long pull from his water bottle.

"Boulder is not Berkeley or San Fran. I think the militant LGBTQ groups would beg to differ with your comments from their brethren. I'm not sure you want to be standing up making those points," suggested Chuck.

"You mean *our* agitators? The ones our allies in the media celebrate and make more significant by giving them time on air?" asked Nick.

"It is the problem with our coalition. One issue voters tend to not play well with others," explained Chuck. "Antifa is a perfect example. We support and use them when it is convenient, but we can't control them. Even when we win, they keep burning down Portland."

"And Minneapolis, Oakland, Detroit and...," added Greg.

"Guys, that is exactly the point they were making. No one is standing up to these mobs. The public is fed up and even more so with the media, who keep amplifying their issues. None of it helps them and, most times, it hurts them. Because the places they work, if they do have jobs, will fire them if they dare to disagree or express an opinion." Nick paced, clearly frustrated.

"We don't control how the media portrays these issues. Trying to point that out is also not a good idea. They control the megaphone. They control when you get to use it. Without them on our side, our message is a whisper," said Chuck, quietly explaining to Nick.

"Chuck, the media controls the narrative. Look at the corporations. They are terrified of the woke mobs. Their reaction to any complaint is to fire the offender and promote the complainer. People aren't stupid. They see this. They see us supporting these tactics. This is not only not helping relations between races, sexes, and genders, but creating a feeling of everyone against everyone. The assumption is they can complain and get some benefit if they're part of an aggrieved group. Groups we and our media created, support, and amplify. This is exactly the opposite of the help we think we're giving. The people are depressed. They feel like they cannot say *anything* for fear of persecution," revealed Nick. "It was very disheartening to think the public feels this way. And blames us, the Party."

Chuck stared at Nick for a second as Greg shifted in his chair.

"I can see how a week of listening to that would have caused you to be perturbed at the testimony of the Admiral. But what you said and did is of little importance in the eyes of most of the other ninety-nine senators. It has absolutely no impact on the people you just said are 'depressed'."

"That's pretty harsh," answered Greg, defending Nick.

"Greg, it's ok. He is entitled to his opinion. Chuck, that's actually good, because I don't give a shit what the other ninety-nine senators care about. All I care about is our country and its people," announced Nick.

"So, what? Now you wanna change parties to the Opposition?" asked Chuck angrily, getting red.

"Easy boy. No. I want to take back control of the Party. I want moderates in the party to band together and work with moderates in the Opposition on joint legislation that helps our country and prevents the radical right and progressive left from being in control."

"Well Pollyanna, you came to the wrong place. Because like it or not, the Progressive left is in charge, and they won't give up power. We must get what we can. The days of compromise are long gone. There was a civil war in the Party and the Progressives won."

"That doesn't mean we shouldn't be trying to fix things as much as possible," retorted Nick.

"We are. Incrementally. This is all you can do from the junior senator of Colorado perch. Did you actually talk to anyone who voted for the party on your little trip? Sounds to me like you just attended CPAC," said Chuck, exasperated.

Nick laughed, "Seems like it doesn't it, but yes, the only place I went where it was obvious the folks voted for the opposition was in Weld County. I think a few of the folks in some of the other places were reluctantly for the Party. Former union members, and stuff like that. I was a bit surprised, like you. The people aren't happy with the radical turn. They feel like the Party is now a leftist quasi socialist party and the moderates of Colorado I spoke to are not having any of it."

"That *is* disturbing. I can only assume the folks you talked to aren't representative. I'll have to ask Jer to do some more polling in the state. We aren't seeing what you experienced," admitted Greg.

"Don't get me wrong. They may not be happy with us, but the good news is, the opposition is so inept in Colorado, they have nowhere to go. All the Californians bringing in their progressive ideals keeps us in the majority. I'd say Colorado is almost solid blue now," stated Nick. "We aren't in any danger of losing our senate seat. However, holding your nose and voting for us is hardly what I'd call enthusiastic support."

"Maybe, maybe not. Sounds like new math, addition by subtraction. Since you were alone, maybe folks were a little more candid? You said a few of them recognized you. Did that change the conversation?" asked Chuck.

Nick laughed. "Only in that pool hall. They knew who I was and pummeled me with their dislike of our party rule. Many of them were out of work. Oil field workers, welders, and truck drivers. All guys who lost high paying oil jobs thanks to the moratoriums on fracking. From what I can tell, Morris will have his hands full trying to get re-elected next time. Him they definitely dislike."

"You got that right," nodded Chuck. "I hear he is getting an earful from Fontana for nominating you to this role."

"Glad to help."

"Let's talk about what you can expect from Fontana," counseled Chuck.

"Right, so what happens now?" asked Nick.

"Good news is they still need your vote on the filibuster, so they won't completely cut you off. We need to be careful and rebuild some trust. Right now, you're a loose cannon. They hate unpredictability more than anything. We need to find a way where you can continue to highlight the things you don't like, but still be effective. With the Senate split, it is a fine line to walk, but you may get some reform as the leverage for voting for the Party agenda."

"The parts of the agenda I don't agree with. What about that? Do I just have to toe the line?" asked Nick.

"What's the alternative? Throwing away your vote for nothing but a statement? This town is about trust and relationships. I get it. You don't like the way we make the laws and the tradeoffs and how so much of it helps a few a lot more than the many, but Nick, that's the way it works now. You aren't Harry Potter, and you cannot wave your wand to fix all this."

"And here I thought I was the Chosen one," said Nick, waving an imaginary wand as he walked around the office, staring at a blank wall for a few seconds. "You know, I think I have just the piece of art to hang on this wall."

Chuck threw his hands up in exasperation. "Have you heard a word I have said?"

"Yes. You know, when I was sitting in those diners listening to those real people. People who lost jobs or loved ones or watched their neighborhoods decline. Seeing their kids turned into drug addicts or worse, indoctrinated drones spouting propaganda they learned from their teachers. I reached a low point."

"Nick, welcome to the Senate. Being a senator is solving things in increments. A little progress here, a little there and yes, you must support things you don't believe in or that may hurt some segment of the population. But you weigh it against the greater good. There are winners and losers, and you're on the team making those decisions. Somebody must do it and you have one of those seats. You have a duty, no different from when you were flying A-10s or stopping a terrorist in a subway," ended Chuck in a solemn tone.

"Now I'm a warrior senator? You appealing to my patriotism?"

"I guess I am. Think of the Senate as an elite special forces unit, 100 of the best and the brightest," proposed Chuck with a sarcastic tone. "Or at least in their own minds."

"Please stop before I get sick," countered Nick. "I need to play their game, hold my nose and vote their way to do some good."

Chuck just shook his head in an affirmative nod.

"I'm sorry Chuck, I didn't intend to make your life miserable, Greg, same for you. If you want to quit, I understand. I wouldn't hold it against either of you."

"Nick, we all hitched our wagon to you. I think I can speak for Greg and the rest of the staff. We have your back," assured Chuck as Greg raised his coffee mug in salute and agreement.

"Alright, then prepare for battle."

Chapter 37

Nick sat in a studio in Washington. It was in a house rented out by the various networks for senators, house members, and others to do their remote shots for various shows. Nick sat mic'd up, waiting for his next appearance.

This one would be the morning show on one of the major networks. He'd already done the other networks and cable, including the top-rated morning show from EXN. Nick prepared to answer the same inane questions and plastered a smile on his face as the countdown began on the monitor in front of him.

"Good morning, Senator," said the smiling face of a black woman on the monitor.

"Good morning to you as well, a pleasure to be here," lied Nick.

"Senator, as you know, the Defense Appropriations bill is up for a vote, and you clearly had some tense words with the Chairman of the Joint Chiefs in the committee hearing. What prompted your response? You made some accusations regarding the ongoing efforts of the military to increase diversity and inclusion and to do their part to help combat climate change."

"Monica," answered Nick, "our military forces exist for one reason: to keep us safe and to win when they are engaged. My concern is the readiness of our forces to do that."

"Are you questioning the patriotism of our recruits because we recruited them for diversity and inclusion, meaning women and gays?" asked Monica in a concerned tone.

Nick laughed, "Of course not. In fact, I've served with people of all races and orientations. They are every bit as patriotic as any other soldier or sailor who volunteers to serve. What worries me even more is the idea that we must 'make up'," said Nick, making air quotes, "for years of supposed discrimination in the armed forces based on race, sex, and now sexual orientation. The ultimate result is still the same. When we deploy, our sole mission is to succeed at the objective. We need to prepare for and deliver on that goal, with the best available force we can field."

"But Senator, there are very few black generals, and admirals and few that are openly gay," said Monica.

"Today's proportions are about 60% white, 15% black and 25% Hispanic. It's about 80% male and 20% female. Same for racial percentages in the upper ranks. Keep in mind, it takes over twenty-five years to get your first star and you must make the military your career."

"Senator, thank you for making my point. This discrimination has been going on for decades."

Nick tried to keep his face neutral at Monica's response.

"The military, like athletics, is supposed to be meritocracy. You field the best team. Just like Tom Brady kept playing and winning super bowls, it was because he could and because he was the best option for a team. The military is *supposed* to work the same way. You promote those who prove themselves in combat. You promote those who have proved their ability to lead, to make life and death decisions at a moment's notice," explained Nick.

"We try not to promote those who cannot do this consistently. This is the beauty of our military. We promote those who are best equipped to lead troops in combat. We are not perfect at this by any means, but anything less and the result is people die."

"But you cannot argue minorities and women are underrepresented in the upper ranks?" pressed Monica.

"Mostly, our meritocracy has worked well for the last few hundred years," answered Nick. "Where it has failed is in the last 50, maybe 60 years. A military which takes its orders from a civilian leadership will always have friction. But this is good friction."

"Unfortunately, our top military leaders no longer represent our best combat leaders. Their mission is no longer to win wars. Their mission is to practice politics. This is a major reason we haven't won a war in the last 80 years. Politics and political leaders *in our military* have combined to manage our military endeavors for political gain, not for victory. We win the battle and lose the victory. Money, both in terms of budgets, and the money all these leaders stand to make from the networks they build while serving in Washington and on your media channels, is the main reason we fail to achieve victory. A second and probably bigger problem is *you*," accused Nick.

"Excuse me?" asked Monica, clearly surprised.

Nick smiled. "The media aren't concerned with just facts. You're not concerned with context. You're only concerned with the current news cycle and how being for or against a particular military activity improves your ratings or your standing with or against the administration, depending on who is in power and who you favor."

"Senator, I must disagree. We cover the news. This focuses us on facts, and we make sure the public knows these, regardless of who they may embarrass," defended Monica righteously.

"Monica, I'm not here to win friends, nor am I here to build my network. My goal is not to get a talking head job on a media channel, a cushy job lobbying the very people I once commanded, as so many of our military commanders do these days."

"Senator, those are some sweeping accusations against our military leaders' motives."

Nick shrugged on camera. "I admit, I am painting with a broad brush. For this, I apologize to the warrior generals and admirals. They know who they are. My statement won't offend them and instead they'll applaud my willingness to say it. They can't for fear of reprisal. The important thing is the men and women who serve under these generals and admirals know about whom I am talking. In terms of the commanders you will follow into hell and the ones you would like to send there," said Nick, shaking his head.

"Senator, those are some strong words and pretty negative opinions of our military leaders and the media. Frankly, I think you're wrong on both counts," proclaimed Monica in a serious tone.

"It is your first amendment right to disagree with my opinion. Monica, war is hell. It is brutal. Many we fight do things you cannot imagine in your worst nightmare. To defeat them takes determination and bravery you also cannot imagine. It's not for the meek. It's not for the unpatriotic and it's not something that should be subject to racial, sex, or gender quotas. What I heard is we are no longer promoting our officers based solely on merit. Instead, the specter of affirmative action is creeping into our military. If we promote based *solely* on race, gender, or orientation. In order to achieve some percentage of representation based on people who have never stared down an enemy in their life. There will come a time when our military no longer functions as we need it to."

"Senator, why is it wrong asking for more black and Hispanic and female generals and admirals? They represent a larger and larger portion of our population. Yet our command structure is very lopsided in terms of white male dominance," implored Monica.

Nick stared into the camera for a second, trying to remain calm.

"Monica, first, our army is all volunteer. We do not get an equal proportion of people who want to join our military from all races, sexes, and orientations. Second, I think I already answered you, but let me try one more example. This is the reason I asked the Admiral to provide me the lists of captains and majors being promoted."

"Let's say there are four people on the list to be promoted to major. The first two are white males. The next two are a black male and a Hispanic woman. They are all qualified to make the jump, but their commanders have stack ranked them based on *ability and readiness* to lead larger groups, which is what a promotion to major entails."

"What I suspect, and in fact know, but want to confirm, is the black male captain and the Hispanic woman captain, number 3 and 4 on the list are both being recommended for promotion to major and the two white male captains, ranked by their actions 1 and 2 are going to have to wait for the next cycle," said Nick as he stared earnestly into the camera. Monica stared back silently trying to follow his story.

"In your mind Monica, this is perfectly fine?"

"Absolutely Senator. You yourself said they were qualified. How does it hurt to promote them faster over their white counterparts, who, you say, will get their promotion, just later? Seems reasonable to me to right decades of unfair treatment in our military," responded Monica, falling into Nick's rhetorical trap.

"Here is what is happening, Monica. The same thing that has happened to generations of blacks attending ivy league schools because of affirmative action. They are now tagged *for the rest of their careers* with the stigma of people never knowing if they got their promotion by earning it, or because they were black, brown, female or LGBTQ or worse, filling a quota requirement. Once this starts, you have created the worst possible scenario in a military command structure: *doubt*. The soldiers and sailors know. They know who the best leaders are. They also know when injustice occurs. You have ruined unit cohesion by promoting officers on something other than pure merit," said Nick with conviction.

"But Senator," broke in Monica. "We *must* become more diverse. If it means a few white officers have to wait on promotions in favor of advancing blacks, Hispanics, and LGBTQ, it is a small price to pay."

"You may not understand this, Monica, but this is a terrible situation. Here was the Chairman of our armed forces standing in front of Congress telling me this very scenario is alive and well and being implemented and, in fact, accelerating. This is the road to ruin. While we are getting more diverse and inclusive, lessening our standards for combat, lowering the physical requirements across all branches, including the SEALs, for God's sake. Our enemies are doing exactly the opposite. The Chinese and Russians and the terrorists are not worrying about diversity and inclusion in their armed forces. Their forces exist for one reason. To kill their enemies, namely us. And lately they are succeeding," concluded Nick.

"Senator, I'm sorry, but to me, this sounds like you are against diversity and inclusion. You are also disdainful of the efforts of the military to go green, doing their part to help all of us defeat climate change," said Monica in a superior tone.

"Monica," said Nick with a smile. "Anyone who knows me knows I'm all in on diversity. I believe we need to be color blind in all aspects of life. In the military, there is only one thing that matters: personal merit. We live in a world where we're measured by our actions. All of us."

Monica looked disgusted. "Well Senator, words are actions, too."

"Indeed, they are. Here are some that matter for the military. The best person, regardless of color, gender, or orientation, should be judged based solely on their actions. Any other measurement is not objective and is hard to defend. If that makes me a racist or whatever phobe or ism you choose to call me, well, I'm a big boy. Your sticks and stones really don't hurt." Nick paused for a second, deciding how to respond, before throwing caution to the wind, and ending his statement with, "because frankly, I don't care."

"Senator, this is a surprising position of a Party Senator and certainly puts you at odds with our leadership at a crucial time when we need to count on every vote."

"*Our? We?*" asked Nick at Monica's slip up.

"The Party, yes," clarified Monica.

"Uh huh, I thought I heard you right the first time. I'm not sure how listening to my own constituents puts me at odds with my fellow Party members? I'm confident I'm representing their views. Maybe the others should get out to theirs more often and not in scripted town halls or photo ops, but one on one with no aides or security. It might surprise them what they hear. I was," finished Nick.

"Thank you, Senator, that is all the time we have," answered Monica tersely, clearly no longer hearing what Nick was saying.

"Thank…," said Nick as the red light disappeared on his monitor before he could finish his closing. "You," he said aloud to his empty studio room. Nick pulled off the mic and the earpiece and left the studio to walk back to his office.

As he walked, nodding to the occasional greeting, he contemplated the end of his nascent senatorial career, seemingly over before it even got started. He smiled. A great weight had been lifted. He realized he really didn't give a shit any longer. He'd serve out his term and leave all this behind him. This made him ecstatic. He whistled as he walked, thinking about taking a certain person out for a spicy chicken sandwich.

Part Three

The Vote

"In Republics, the great danger is, that the majority may not sufficiently respect the rights of the minority."

James Madison

Chapter 38

Nick walked through the Capitol. He'd spent the day meeting with constituents and avoiding reporters who just wanted to discuss his comments from last week.

He patiently explained his positions to his constituents and why he felt they were in the best interests of both them and the country. It surprised him when even the most ardent opponents voiced support after hearing his reasoning. They got it. Too bad he couldn't have this type of conversation with *every* potential voter.

Nick had finished meeting with Chuck and Greg, preparing for upcoming committee meetings and votes. He thought about stopping by Margie's office to get his latest verbal rebuke. He'd been making his communications director's life miserable lately with his antics.

Looking at his watch, he left and headed to the Capitol in the brisk mid-November air. He now stood in front of the Majority Leader's suite, once again admiring the large ornate doors.

"Hello Senator Turner," greeted Helen Robles, the Majority Leader's executive assistant.

"Hello Ms. Robles," replied Nick, smiling.

She smiled brightly as well. "The majority leader is ready to see you. Just go on in."

"Thanks."

Nick knocked and opened the door to the inner office of the leader. Once again, there was a fire in the fireplace and Woodrow Wilson towered overhead. Sal Fontana lifted his bulk from behind his desk and walked to Nick.

"Turner. Have a seat. Can I get you a drink? I'm having one."

"A small one, Senator, thank you."

Sal filled two glasses with ice and poured a couple fingers of dark liquor in each glass.

"You sure can dance. I saw you at Dolly's party," he said, wandering back to Nick, handing him a glass. He took the seat opposite him in front of the fire.

"Have to say it has been a few years, and I felt it in every muscle. I'm not as young as I once was," said Nick with a laugh.

"Ain't that the truth?" grunted Fontana.

"Thanks." Nick took a small sip. It was very good scotch.

Seeing Nick's reaction, Sal piped up, "It's 21-year-old Balvenie Scotch, pretty fucking smooth, isn't it?"

"Very."

"A gift from the President, when I became leader."

"A thoughtful gift. I'm honored to share it with you." Nick held out the glass, nodding slightly.

Sal swirled the cubes in his glass and looked Nick in the eyes. "What the fuck was that stunt with the Admiral?" asked Sal in his familiar New Jersey union boss tone.

"Honestly, growing pains and frustration at the pace of change. As a vet, after our debacles in Afghanistan, and failing to fight terrorism in Nigeria, Yemen, and Saudi Arabia. Having our military focused on diversity, inclusion, equity and climate change instead of figuring out how to kill terrorists seems a bit out of touch with reality," offered Nick in a disgusted tone.

"Next time you get frustrated, just fucking call someone. We don't need this kind of negativity. We can arrange a private meeting to discuss these priorities, or shit, call a closed-door meeting of the Armed Services committee to go over plans. This was just a public status meeting, to give him a chance to advance positions we support as a caucus. You embarrassed him and you cast doubt on positions which are very important to a substantial part of our base."

"Sorry Senator, but I couldn't sit there and let him mislead our committee and those few in the country paying attention," said Nick. "Like our allies, who don't trust us to have their back."

"Son, you are a slow learner for someone who is supposed to be so bright. You just said it yourself. How many people were watching CSPAN2? Eight, fifteen, fifty?"

"Well, of those fifty, six of them were networks. As you saw."

"You did fine until you got to RBS. Did you really have to stick it to Monica? She already thinks we aren't doing enough, or fast enough. Then you tell her she is the problem and is making the country less safe? Not smart, my boy. Now you put us in a position of having to disavow your comments. We don't need this right now."

"I understand, but again, I have to stick to my convictions," advised Nick, sipping his scotch. "Disavow away."

"You understand the importance of this vote?"

"More than you know," Nick replied, looking at Sal over his glass. Sal levered himself out of the chair to stalk around his office.

"We've been trying to get this filibuster removed for years, decades even. The Opposition have used this time and time again to fuck us and stop progress. We're now on the cusp of finally removing this roadblock to progress. The filibuster is a relic of the past. A way to ensure change is prevented by a minority of senators."

Nick calmly watched Fontana hover in front of him. "Senator, are you not concerned removing the filibuster could come back to bite us? If we're ever in the minority again?" asked Nick. "It already did with the Federal Judges and with the Supreme Court. We made it possible for the prior president to turn the court conservative."

"True, but this is why we need to get rid of the legislative filibuster. We can pass laws to regain that majority on the court and then we can fix the problems the Opposition have caused all these years. It's true, we used the filibuster effectively when we were in the minority, but the Opposition is about to be in the minority on a fucking permanent basis," crowed Fontana triumphantly.

"Really? We have 51 to 49 in the senate and a six-seat majority in the house. This doesn't seem like a sure thing to me," doubted Nick.

"Leave the fucking leadership questions to us and trust that we know what is best for the party. We wouldn't do this if we thought we'd be in the minority again soon. Passing this is finally going to allow us to make some long overdue moves on gun control, the supreme court, and adding states," said Sal, talking with his hands and marching back and forth.

"It will give us the ability to get truly universal healthcare and re-codify *Roe*. We can roll back all the southern state's bans on abortion. So many things we can do with our majority once we get rid of this shit," intoned Sal in the baritone voice he used to project in the senate chamber.

"What does national polling say? The reason I ask is I spent a week back in Colorado, just talking to folks."

"Fuck the polls. Besides, they'll come around once folks get help from this legislation we're passing," assured Sal.

"Senator, my constituents don't favor killing the filibuster. In fact, they don't trust us, or the opposition either."

"Nick," growled Sal. "Fuck the people. They're stupid, lazy, and narrowminded and have no idea of the big picture. And so easily swayed. Franklin had it right when he said we shouldn't trust the people to vote on important things. It's why we're a Republic and not a true Democracy. Do you really think they even know how the filibuster is used as a weapon to keep money out of their hands?"

"That may be true, but to many of them, they know enough to see that removing the filibuster means we can pass whatever we want without opposition and with no collaboration or compromise. We didn't win 100 to 0. We are 51 to 49 and we are potentially disenfranchising half the country. Is that really wise?"

Sal walked around his desk and sat down heavily. "I hear you. You need to trust that all 51 of us have the best interests of the country at heart and we'll certainly listen to the other 49 senators. We still need to win local elections. I know the public will get on board once they see what we pass and how it helps them," pointed out Sal, switching from Union boss, too kindly old grandfather mode.

"Do we represent our state, Senator? Or ourselves?"

"Fuck this Mr. Smith shit. You are a member of *my* fucking Party caucus. You are part of *our* Party. The Party recommends we pass this bill, remove the fucking filibuster, and pass the fucking legislative agenda we ran on to keep this majority. They expect us to fucking do this," said Sal, getting louder and more animated as he morphed back into his true persona. "It is your duty as the appointed stand in for Senator Richards. I could count on him to follow our lead. Governor Morris appointed you to fill out his term, honor his memory, and carry on his good work."

Nick rose from his seat and stood in front of Sal's desk. Towering over the seated Fontana, he said in a calm voice, "I respect Senator Richard's memory. I take my role seriously to fulfill the rest of his term, representing my fellow citizens of Colorado. I don't agree with all of what you say, but I also don't disagree with all of it either. My sole concern is the long-term repercussions of removing the filibuster and how it will neuter the minority, whomever it may be in the future. Many of our colleagues today, only a few years ago, are on record saying we should preserve the filibuster at all cost. What has changed?" asked Nick questioningly.

Sal leaped from his chair. "What is at stake is the unwillingness of a single fucking Opposition Senator to grow a set of fucking balls and work with us to pass groundbreaking legislature that will make capitalism more fucking compassionate, providing more help and assistance to those in need. That is what has fucking changed," Sal finished this by stabbing his letter opener into the top of his desk where it stood, quivering just like his voice. "Senator, do we have your vote or not?" commanded Sal.

"Thank you for the drink and enlightening conversation. You'll have my answer tomorrow on the floor," responded Nick calmly.

"Hero, you are playing a very dangerous game. Don't fuck with us. You don't want us as enemies. You can do so much, you are young, you can go so far. Hell, you could be in this seat one day. Use your head, think of your future, and don't do anything stupid. Think it through carefully. Talk to Robinson. He understands the consequences of screwing the caucus. I implore you to see reason." This last delivered almost as a plea, very unusual coming from the normally brusque Majority Leader. A hundred and eighty degrees from his demeanor only 30 seconds before.

"I always consider all my actions and their consequences, Senator. Good evening," concluded Nick.

Nick turned to leave, exiting the office while pulling the door shut behind him. Sal stood for a minute. Going back to his bar, he poured a full glass and promptly tossed it back. Walking back to his desk, he took out the satellite phone. He dialed a number and simply said, "Go". Staring into the fire, sipping his drink, he considered how he had failed.

Chapter 39

Lexi leaned back in her leather chair in her Capitol office next to the Senate Chamber. Fontana sat in a chair in front of the Wilson desk. Standing in a corner of the office was Mel Arenson, Lexi's chief of staff, a thin man of medium height, bald on top with gray hair on each side.

"Well, where do we stand?" asked the Vice President.

"I don't know. We need to assume Turner is a no," Fontana said from his chair in an exasperated voice.

"Shit, how did you let this happen Sal?" asked Mel, in a questioning tone.

"Mel, if I recall, you were in favor of Governor Morris appointing him when it was suggested," he answered, staring daggers at him.

"I was, but it was your job to take this neophyte and keep him in line. Couldn't your guy rein him in?" asked Mel. As Sal prepared to answer, Lexi interrupted.

"Alright boys, what's done is done. What next?" inquired Lexi.

"We vote, we give him his five minutes of fame and maybe he'll surprise us. When he votes, if he goes against us, we fucking destroy him, simple as that," snapped Fontana.

"Maybe, maybe not. He could be useful as a poster boy for what happens when you buck the trend. We can't make him a martyr," disagreed Mel.

"I assume he's not going to run for a full term?" asked Lexi.

"Don't know where he would get money if we don't help him? He's only got a few million and we would primary him if he ran," explained Fontana.

"We have any suitable candidates? We can't afford to have this seat flip," questioned Mel.

"I got it under control. Don't worry about the Senate. You just make sure you keep up the good work on the mail in ballots," growled Fontana.

"Once we get through this, do we have the bills ready? We need to get them out there and passed before we get into the primaries and campaign season," offered Lexi.

"Yes, we already have bills ready to pass in the House and fast track in the Senate," acknowledged Sal.

There was a sound throughout the office, followed by pages calling the Senate to order. "Well, here we go gentlemen, let's go make history," said Lexi as she rose to enter the chamber followed by Senator Fontana.

After they left, Mel got on his phone. "OK, be ready. I'll let you know. We won't have a lot of notice," he said to the person on the other end of the call.

Chapter 40

The senate chamber was filled. Senators sat at their desks and rotated to the rostrum to deliver their five-minute speeches in favor of keeping or removing the legislative filibuster. The gallery above the Senate, normally filled with the visiting public, was today full of press and guests of the Senators. Very few of the public were in attendance in the chamber for this monumental debate and vote.

For the last two decades, the Party majorities in the Senate had slowly whittled the filibuster into ineffectiveness. First the judges and then the Supreme Court. Both moves came back to haunt them when the Opposition regained control in both branches. Nominating hundreds of conservative federal judges to lifetime appointments. Finally, the short sidedness of the Party allowed the Opposition to use the lack of a judicial filibuster to turn the Supreme Court 6-3 conservative.

Removing the legislative filibuster would do the same for Congress. Allowing the House and Senate to pass bills with as small a majority as 1 in the house and a tie in the Senate with the Vice President to cast the deciding vote. With a six-vote lead in the house and two in the Senate, the Party was counting on keeping their caucus in line long enough to pass key legislation to solidify their majority for the foreseeable future.

Fontana like his predecessor Majority Leaders, had invoked the nuclear option. Removing cloture and the requirement for a 60-vote majority to pass the removal of the legislative filibuster. Now all that was needed was a simple majority of senators today to remove it once and for all.

Throughout the morning, the Senate chamber resounded with soaring rhetoric not heard since the heady days of debate on the Civil

Rights Act of 1964. Then the southern Party Senators had filibustered the legislature for 75 days, trying to keep the southern blacks from being given full voting rights.

It was ironic that now this same Party wanted to remove this legislative tool in order to remake society. Nick sat at his desk, listening to the arguments for and against. The Opposition pointed out the worst-case scenarios. Repealing the bill of rights, seizing guns, censoring the press, and preventing people from having alternative opinions.

Adding new Party leaning states to assure a permanent Party majority. Implementing deficit ballooning plans like universal healthcare, free college tuition, forgiving all student loan debt, and mandating the end of all fossil fuels, regardless of economic impact.

For every doomsday pronouncement, the Party senators got up, and either softened the possibility such as shredding the bill of rights or turned all the Opposition negatives into compassionate improvements to help the poor, the middle class, and all those struggling.

They highlighted the flattening of society to penalize the uber rich and transfer their wealth into the social programs. Programs to help lift all up instead of allowing a few to control massive amounts of wealth built on the backs of the laborers.

Listening to the Party Senators, an uninformed listener, would agree their view of the future was much more appealing than the Opposition's predictions of Armageddon. Since most regular people fit into the uninformed listener category, the polling did in fact approve of the Party's preferred outcome, removing the filibuster.

As Nick's name was approaching, he made his way to the well of the Senate chamber in preparation.

"The chair recognizes the Senator from Colorado. Please limit your speech to five minutes," said Lexi, presiding over this vote as the President of the Senate, a role of the sitting Vice President.

Nick stood tall behind the rostrum, with no notes or supporting material, facing his colleagues in the Senate and the audience above and around in the gallery.

"Madame President, my esteemed colleagues, and fellow citizens, I currently sit at a desk once occupied by the late Senator Margaret Chase Smith of Maine. In her day, freshmen senators were to be seen and not heard. I know there are those who wish this were still the general rule," said Nick, getting a few laughs from the assembled senators and gallery above.

"Order, please," shouted Lexi, banging her gavel.

"In Mrs. Smith's Day," continued Nick, "Joseph McCarthy, a colleague of hers, was implying widespread infiltration of the government by communists. When she pressed him to show proof of his allegations, McCarthy could not provide compelling information to prove his accusations or to convince her of the truth of his argument. Yet Senator McCarthy continued his attacks in this very chamber. She watched as none of her more senior colleagues, from either side of the aisle, dared to challenge his statements. Mrs. Smith, unable to stay quiet, rose to deliver a speech, now known as the Declaration of Conscience."

"I can find no better way to describe today's situation than the opening words she uses to describe it in **1950**. I quote: *I would like to speak briefly and simply about a serious national condition. It is a national feeling of fear and frustration that could result in national suicide and the end of everything that we Americans hold dear. It is a condition that comes from the lack of effective leadership either in the legislative branch or the executive branch of our government. I speak as briefly as possible because too much harm has already been done with irresponsible words of bitterness and selfish political opportunism. I speak as simply as possible because the issue is too great to be obscured by eloquence. I speak simply and briefly in the hope that my words will be taken to heart. Mr. President, I speak as a Republican. I speak as a woman. I speak as a United States Senator. I speak as an American.*"

"She went on," said Nick, '*The United States Senate has long enjoyed worldwide respect as the greatest deliberative body in the world. But recently that deliberative character has too often been debased to the level of a forum of hate and character assassination. I think that it is high time for the United States Senate and its members to do some real soul searching and to weigh our consciences as to the manner in which we are performing our duty to the people of America and the manner in which we are using or abusing our individual powers and privileges. I think that it is high time that we remembered that we have sworn to uphold and defend the Constitution. I think that it is high time that we remembered that the Constitution, as amended, speaks not only of the freedom of speech but also of trial by jury instead of trial by accusation,*' finished Nick, looking out over his colleagues, many of whom were paying attention on this momentous occasion.

"Take a minute to think about this. Mrs. Smith was railing against the unfounded accusations of McCarthy, *a member of her own party.* Specifically, his personal attacks and defamation. There are parallels to our time where people are afraid to express an opinion. Or rather, to have one that is counter to the narrative we promote. What we are discussing, in removing the filibuster, is akin to removing the Bill of Rights. Instead, we would hand the protections and right to determining who should and should not be persecuted, not to a set of laws we all agreed to be ruled under, the Constitution, but to a majority, in this case, our Party in this Congress."

"This is the tyranny of the majority that Franklin and Madison feared and from which George Mason sought to protect us, demanding a Bill of Rights be added. The filibuster is there to protect us from the popular, from mob rule. As we all know, what is once popular quickly falls from favor, and can turn out to be not only unpopular, but dangerous. If we are to do away with the filibuster, does it matter whether the minority is 1 or 49 Senators? The dissenting voices shall be silenced, one and all."

"Only a few years ago, my Party was in the minority's position, voicing an opinion, not unlike every minority party. That doing away with the filibuster would be counter to the founder's intentions. The idea of democratic government is one of collaboration and compromise. With bills and laws decided by both a majority and a vocal and participatory minority," stated Nick, once again surveying the audience, gauging their response. Those in the gallery leaned forward. There was no sound other than the occasional wheezing from Senator Banks in the front row, close to Nick.

"We have allowed money, power, and perception to corrupt our democratic republic. Shouting from the rooftops, claiming our opponents opposing our opinion are enemies of the republic, for daring to differ. We progressed from trying to convince our opponents with facts and persuasion to deciding it is no longer necessary to debate or defend our own opinions."

"It has now spread to the everyday life of citizens. If you dare to hold an opinion counter to the fanatical public position, it is not only right, but expected, that you need to be ruined, shamed in the public square and, if possible, prevented from earning a livelihood. To leave you broken and powerless, a casualty for all to see the consequences of daring to differ publicly with the dictates of the majority." Nick paused, standing tall and alone, in front of his colleagues in the Senate chamber.

"Once again, I return to Mrs. Smith and her speech and her plea for a Declaration of Conscience. She highlighted these most basic of American principles, I quote." *Those of us who shout the loudest about Americanism in making character assassinations are all too frequently those who, by our own words and acts, ignoring some of the basic principles of Americanism. The right to criticize. The right to hold unpopular beliefs. The right to protest. The right of independent thought. The exercise of these rights should not cost one single American citizen his reputation or his right to a livelihood nor should he be in danger of losing his reputation or livelihood merely because he happens to know someone who holds unpopular beliefs. Who of us does not? Otherwise none of us could call our souls our own. Otherwise thought control would have set in. The American people are sick and tired of being afraid to speak their minds lest they be politically smeared 'Communists' or 'Fascists' by their opponents. Freedom of speech is not what it used to be in America. It has been so abused by some that it is not exercised by others. The American people are sick and tired of seeing innocent people smeared and guilty people whitewashed.'* Nick paused for a second.

"Think about these words. I can neither write nor say any more accurate than what Mrs. Smith spoke…in 1950!"

Lexi banged the gavel, signaling the end of Nick's time. "Senator. Will you yield?" asked Lexi. Before he could do anything, the next Senator, Wilcox, an Opposition Senator from Montana, leaped to his feet.

"Madame President, I yield my time to the Senator from Colorado." Lexi looked annoyed at this breach of protocol and there were murmurs amongst the other senators at this unusual display of impromptu bipartisanship.

"Very well. I recognize the Senator from Colorado for an additional five minutes."

"Thank you, Senator Wilcox," said Nick with a nod of his head. "Enemies who seek to tear down America and what we stand for surround us. These Fascists, Communists, anarchists, religious fanatics, take your pick. They all would love nothing more than to see this exercise in government by free citizens, ruling themselves, fail. So it would never rise again, anywhere. We are playing right into our enemy's hands. I will dip into Mrs. Smith's speech one last time to highlight her last point. Again, I quote." *'Today our country is being psychologically divided by the confusion and the suspicions that are bred in the United States Senate to spread like cancerous tentacles of 'know nothing, suspect everything' attitudes. Today we have a Democratic administration which has developed a mania for loose spending and loose programs. History is repeating itself…As an American, I am shocked at the way Republicans and Democrats alike are playing directly into the Communist design of 'confuse, divide, and conquer.'…. As an American, I condemn a Republican Fascist just as much as I condemn a Democrat Communist. I condemn a Democrat Fascist just as much as I condemn a Republican Communist. They are equally dangerous to you and me and to our country. As an American, I want to see our nation recapture the strength and unity it once had when we fought the enemy instead of ourselves.'*

Nick allowed Senator Chase-Smith's words to sink in.

"Today, Americans are more divided than ever. Why? Are we really that different? I suspect we all just want to be left alone. Free to earn our wage, raise our family, and live according to our own values. We want to worship however we please or not at all. To choose our orientation, and to have it be our choice, free from persecution. To choose what goes in our body, safe from government mandates and forcible coercion. We want to keep a majority of what we earn, but will pay a reasonable tax for roads, schools, police, fire, and other necessities to benefit all. We want to be safe and to provide a safe environment in which to lead our lives and raise our families. We'll give up some freedom to enable this. As long as the laws are fair and apply equally to all." Nick now spoke in a conversational tone.

"We expect our schools to educate our children. Graduating kids who know how to add, form a sentence, read, and fill out a job application. Morals, ethics, and values come from us, the parents, to be reinforced in schools. Above all, we love our country. We trust our elected President and Congress to have the best interests of the people, and the country at heart. To defend us against our enemies," said Nick, glancing around again to see everyone sitting up and listening to the tale he was weaving.

"This is not where we are today. Today, our politicians, amplified by a militant and compliant media, shout at the top of their lungs and digital voices, claiming there is only one way, my way and if you differ you are not only wrong, you're an enemy of the state," Nick stopped, staring down at the lectern, thinking.

Raising his head, his eyes showing a fierce determination as he looked out. "We are so much smarter than every predecessor and we are facing unprecedented issues, or so we say. Why is it that Mrs. Smith was saying the *same* things about similar issues back

in 1950? The times are not unprecedented, but the response is.
Today, we do not denounce the anarchy of Antifa and other anti-
racist league organizations. We claim they are legitimate protests
and should be allowed to destroy property and commit violence
without prosecution, because we agree with their cause. Yet others
who protest with less or no damage and less violence are persecuted
and imprisoned as insurrectionists. Held accountable for breaking
the same laws, Antifa and ARL factions were not. Because their
opinions differ from the view of our Party, most media, and certainly
this administration. This double standard is insidious, and unequal
application of our laws is dangerous to our survival as a country."
Nick's voice rose as he continued.

"Yet here we sit today, considering the removal of this last
safeguard against the tyranny of the majority. The tyranny of *our*
majority. I think this is not only wrong and reckless, but it would
also speed up the end of our democratic experiment, in rule by free
citizens, and not despots. Removing the filibuster is the last barrier
preventing the creation of at a minimum, an authoritarian regime,
and at worst, one sliding into totalitarianism, cloaked in the mantle
of a fake democracy." Nick paused while the Senate chamber held its
breath, astounded at the political suicide playing out in real time in
front of them.

"I feel for families struggling to counter the indoctrination their
children receive at school. Instead of learning to read, write and add,
they are being taught Critical Race Theory. How everything before
them is tainted with racism. Worse, they are being taught to hate
their parents and their classmates. To push back against any morals,
ethics and values their parents are trying to instill. To instead look to
the 'village of the state and the teacher's union' to tell them what is
right and what is wrong. They are being taught segregation is not only
right, but the only path to equity. We teach them to deny the science
of biology. That they can wait and decide what gender they are, with
no help or guidance from their family, but to trust their teachers
to help them through this. They are being taught not to think for

themselves, but to simply obey. As for the parents, their voice has no weight. I ask, where has common sense gone?"

Nick's voice went up in tempo and power as he approached his finish. "This is as bad as living in Soviet Russia, Communist China, or Nazi Germany. I used to teach history. I suggest all of you check out a library book on the history of these regimes and how they got started. Read a book by William Shirer on the early years of Nazi Germany or Alexander Solzhenitsyn about life under the Soviets. This, despite what my colleagues and the talking heads and anyone else say, is not what the Opposition is proposing. Sadly, it is instead exactly what big tech, big media and the progressives within my Party have, and are, implementing. At this moment, I am not proud of what my party is proposing. Remember, those who shout the loudest about other's transgressions are usually the worst offenders themselves. I ask my colleagues how many of *you*," said Nick, pointing over the assembled senators on the Party side of the Senate. "Are voting because you fear losing your power, or having the reputation destroying tools of big tech, big media and our leadership turned on you out of fear of not following their lead?"

At the end of this question, several senators shouted to be recognized.

"Madame President, I take offense at the implications of the Senator's accusations," said Majority Leader Fontana.

"Senator Turner, if I may remind you, it is against the rules of the Senate to impugn the reputation of another senator. Please refrain from any further accusations against your colleagues," ordered Lexi. "Continue quickly, please."

"Thank you, Madame President. It seems my question was perhaps a bit too pointed in its accuracy. For this, I will not apologize. I'll conclude, as the reaction I have received is demonstrative of exactly that of which I and Mrs. Smith spoke. Intolerance. My request is for all of you to listen to what I am saying. *Don't give up*. Wake up, find your voice, and do not allow them to crush your hopes and dreams. This too shall pass if we don't give up on this experiment. On our constitutional republic, with its glorious design of checks and balances, like the legislative filibuster. For all the denigration we have heaped on our founders, they envisioned this and built-in safeguards to prevent us from destroying *ourselves*. Removing them assures our destruction and the end of voluntary self-rule. Ensuring we shall end up in totalitarianism and rule by the elite, at the expense of the masses."

Nick looked out over the Senate. Several of the Opposition were nodding and smiling at Nick's speech, sensing they may have yet again dodged the bullet. He looked into the gallery of people watching. "I'm not a politician, but I am an American and a patriot. I do not fear what they can do to me personally. Obviously, standing up here and speaking the truth won't be allowed. I'll face the ire of all the Party can throw at me. If that sacrifice helps wake up the rest of America to the actions and the intentions of one-party rule, without minority representation. Then it is a small price to pay. One I'm certainly willing to risk and pay the price. I'm a veteran, I'm a teacher, I am *not* a politician, but I *am* a concerned American citizen." Nick finished in a resolute voice as many in the gallery cheered and clapped.

"Order," demanded Lexi banging her gavel.

"Madame President, I yield the floor."

As he walked away, several senators stood asking to be recognized by the Vice President. She recognized the Majority Leader, Sal Fontana. Sal walked slowly to the lectern. He turned and surveyed the Senate chamber, letting his gaze flow over both the Party and Opposition sections before he fixed his eyes on Nick, who had taken his seat at his desk in the upper circle on the Party side.

"Madame President, my fellow Senators. We have seen many spectacular speeches and actions in this room, what we just witnessed was neither. The Senate comprises highly principled and, in most cases, highly skilled servants of the republic. Most of us have worked for years to achieve our positions. Learning the ways of government, the procedures, the tradeoffs, and most of all, the consequences of our actions. We don't take any task lightly and we most certainly do not decide solely on a partisan basis."

Nick leaned forward in his desk, silently laughing on the inside while smiling on the outside, shaking his head.

"We hold the preservation of the Republic and the safeguarding of the rights of our citizens foremost in all our activities. It's these same rights that allowed my esteemed colleague to express his inexperienced opinion and commentary, after his, what is it now, eleven months of service in the Senate?"

Opposition Senate Minority Leader Sheldon Cobb stood. "Madame President, I object to the personal attacks against our colleague by the Majority Leader."

With reluctance, Lexi acknowledged the Minority Leader, turning to Sal. "Senator Fontana, please observe the rules of the Senate decorum and refrain from personal references to any Senate colleagues in a demeaning manner."

With a smile on his face, Sal nodded. "My apologies to all my colleagues. It was simply my intent to state the Senate is supposed to be the body of wisdom and experience. Lack of these can lead to impetuous actions and consequences unforeseen. Further, I would site, quoting a speech from 1950, underscores the inability of our collective Congresses to solve the problems that were indeed occurring before most all of us were born," this last aimed at Senator Banks, sitting in the first row of desks on the party side.

"As we have pointed out in countless speeches and in the mounds of supporting facts, the filibuster, when used properly, is a tool for the minority to get a say in legislation. However, that's not how the filibuster is being used today. They have weaponized it to prevent the duly elected majority from passing bills discussed and proposed to the voting public, who voted their approval, by electing our majority. The idea that removing the filibuster is the 'end of the republic' is patently false and is, in fact, exactly the opposite. Without the removal of the filibuster and this immoral obstruction of our ability to pass these majority approved bills, we are putting our country at risk. Preventing this much needed legislation from being implemented is truly criminal. It is for the protection of all our citizens, those in both the majority *and* the minority. I think we can forgive passion and ignorance as long as it doesn't impede progress and majoritarian desires. Madame President, I yield the floor," finished Sal.

At this point in the proceedings, the Senate Pro Tempore, Melissa Jenkins, asked to be recognized by the chair. "The chair recognizes Senator Jenkins," said Lexi.

"Madame President, I request the Yeas and Nays."

Lexi stood. "The clerk will call the Yeas and Nays."

For the next ten minutes, the clerk called each senator, and they announced their vote in favor of, or against, removing the filibuster.

"Senator Turner," announced the clerk of the Senate.

"My vote is Nay," answered Nick.

There were audible gasps in the gallery and lots of conversation. Senators turned to their colleagues with scowls on the faces of the Party and smiles on those of the Opposition, at the unexpected events, turning a sure Party victory into defeat. As the tally continued and the clerk finished, the count was 49 for, 50 against, with one absent. Before the clerk could read off the final tally, another clerk handed the Vice President a note. She stood announcing, "the vote will remain open for the full fifteen minutes before we read the final vote into the record."

This highly unusual announcement caused many of the senators to look around to see if someone was not present or if someone was being strong armed into changing their vote. No one was approaching or talking to Nick, the logical recipient of any strong arming. He sat, awaiting the announcement of the final vote.

After two minutes, there were audible gasps on the Opposition side and cheering from a group of Party Senators. Entering the chamber was Senator Fontana pushing Senator Johnny Wilhelm in a wheelchair with an IV bottle hanging on a stand attached to it. A nurse attentively watched as Fontana wheeled him to near his desk.

Senator Wilhelm was not a well man. His skin was hanging on his cadaver like frame with sunken cheeks and eye sockets. Clearly, he had little time left on this earth. His time in the medically induced coma had not helped him heal.

Lexi stood up clapping and the remaining Party senators who were not standing stood and started clapping for the return of their colleague on the Senate floor. Nick stood as well, along with the Opposition Senators, out of respect, but did not clap.

"If you could call for a vote from the Senator, please," ordered Lexi, to the Senate clerk.

"Senator Wilhelm," announced the clerk.

In a shaky voice, a stark contrast to the usual forceful tones of the Senior Senator from North Carolina, a "Yea" could be heard above the murmur. The Party let out a cheer. Lexi gaveled them into silence and turned to the Senate Clerk.

"Please announce the tally."

"Madame President, the Yeas are 50 and the Nays are 50."

"As the Senate rules state, I cast my vote of Yea, in favor of Senate Bill 15. The Yeas are 51 and the Nays are 50. Senate Bill 15 is hereby passed."

The Party senators started cheering and patting each other on the back, shaking each other's hands. From the gallery, supporters initially drowned out a chorus of boos. Soon it reached a louder and louder tone until the Vice President pounded her gavel.

"We will have order in the chamber, please," commanded Lexi. The boo birds did not stop and started stomping besides booing. "You will please clear the gallery. This session is adjourned."

The Capitol Police ushered people out of the gallery and the Senators toned down their celebration as they filed out. Senator Wilhelm was whisked away as quickly as he had arrived.

Nick continued to sit in his seat. Senator Banks slowly climbed the steps out of the Senate well. At almost ninety-five, he was both the longest serving and second oldest senator in history. He stopped next to Nick's desk, leaning heavily on his cane, and catching his breath.

"Senator, may I help?" asked Nick, rising and offering an arm.

"Thank you, Nick. I'll take you up on your offer. This exciting day has worn this old body out," remarked Banks in his pleasant southern drawl as he leaned heavily on Nick's arm. "I should switch to a desk up here, but then I wouldn't be able to see the speakers. It is always something."

"I'm happy to swap, Senator," laughed Nick. "My desk will be open soon anyway, I think."

"Son, there is nothing wrong with speaking what you believe, especially if it's the truth."

Nick raised an eyebrow at the last bit, looking into the sparkling blue eyes of the Senator, who held eye contact, before looking down to navigate the next step.

As they reached the top of the Senate Chamber, Banks disengaged his arm with a sigh as Hobson came to his side.

"I thank you Senator, and now I get to go down the capitol steps for a photo op, oh dear," observed the Senator, sighing.

"You are welcome. Enjoy your moment," nodded Nick.

"It is your moment, too. I served with Mrs. Smith; she would be so proud you used her speech. I think it was quite effective. Good day *Senator* Turner."

Nick turned away and watched Banks, the 'bulldog' of the senate, shuffle away. As he walked, several cable news reporters shouting questions accosted him.

"Senator Turner, how do you feel now that the bill passed despite your 'No' vote?" asked Lauren Bergamo.

"I respect the votes of all of my colleagues and applaud the bravery of Senator Wilhelm to do his duty."

"Senator, you clearly don't agree with the Party position, nor the leaders or the President? How do you expect to work with your Party colleagues?" asked Lauren. Nick bit off his immediate response, staring at the beautiful face of the eager reporter.

"Did you hear my speech? Clearly not. We're allowed to have different opinions and to agree on some things and disagree with others. That doesn't mean we can't continue to work on good legislation. I'll continue to call out legislation I feel is unconstitutional," responded Nick, noticing Chuck was filming the encounter with his phone nearby.

"Are you saying the bill that was passed is unconstitutional?" asked Lauren, not giving up as Nick was turning away.

"It's the right of the Senate to remove the filibuster. That's granted in the Constitution," noted Nick, walking away with Chuck, who was pulling on his arm and steering him free from the reporters.

As Nick walked away, Lauren shouted a last question.

"Senator, do you still think of yourself as a Party member after your act of betrayal?" she asked. Nick stiffened, turning he shook loose of Chuck, and headed back to confront her.

"Would you mind asking that question to my face instead of the back of my head?"

Lauren shrank a bit, but straightened up and asked her question again. "Senator, clearly your speech was against the stated position of the Leadership."

"Miss Bergamo, with all due respect," this last bit drawn out in an exaggerated finish. "That's not what you asked." Nick looked at her cameraman. "I assume you filmed what she said the first time, so I expect this answer to be shown with your original questions when you show this. That is, if you have an ounce of journalistic integrity," Lauren's face reddened as Nick continued.

"You accused me of betrayal. Is having a position that differs from someone or some group a betrayal? How is upholding the Constitution and the checks and balances put in place by the founding fathers a betrayal? How is making sure that every voter who voted against the Party, or this administration, and standing up for the minority, a betrayal? As someone who has risked life and limb for his country, frequently, I do not take lightly to being called a traitor, especially by a journalist. When you have an actual question worthy of discussion, please let me know and I'll be happy to discuss. Until then, I look forward to seeing *all* this footage on ANC tonight," challenged Nick, who turned, and this time walked away.

Chuck, smiling slightly, ended the recording on his phone, as he turned and caught up with Nick, walking away at a brisk pace. As they exited the Capitol, Senator Fontana, Vice President Smythe-Thomas and the 48 other Party senators gathered on the capitol steps for their photo op with a brief statement from the Vice President and the Majority Leader. Senator Wilhelm was nowhere to be seen. Nick and Chuck walked in the opposite direction, toward the Hart building.

"That should make for some interesting television."

"Chuck, apparently that is the sole purpose of the Senate anymore. Sound bites to talking heads on TV and rubber-stamping legislature that makes the country less safe." Nick swept his hand toward his colleagues on the steps. "Legislation directly violating the spirit, if not the law, of the Constitution. In the words of my fearless Majority Leader, what is the fucking point?" fumed Nick.

"Well, I'd tell you the Senate is supposed to be where cooler heads prevail. That is no longer the case since they became beholden to the people instead of the states and since the speeches started being televised," agreed Chuck.

"The problem is they originally televised it for transparency and now it is only about building personal brands. Between the cable news shows and the senate speeches, my fellow congressmen are simply setting themselves up for a big payday. The system is clearly broken," said Nick, disgusted by the entire process.

"What do you think you accomplished today, other than ruining a potentially fabulous career of righteous congressional service?"

"I'm just trying to make a difference. Some of this will at least get on EXN and maybe the social networks. If I can cause a few people to understand what just happened. To question if they trust the Party and specifically the Progressives in charge. To understand their goal of remaking the country, with wholesale change and the destruction of the Bill of Rights. If I can wake a few, then it was worth it."

"Do you think you made that much of a difference? Enough to justify destroying your career?" asked Chuck as they crossed Constitution Avenue between the Capitol and the path in front of the Hart Senate Office Building.

"Not as much as I thought. How'd they get Wilhelm out of his coma? That was a surprise. I thought I had actually stopped them. Now nothing can. Did I make a difference? Apparently not. So, I ask again, what is the point of all of this? If supporting this kind of shit is what it takes for a career, I'll go back to teaching, or at worst, I'll hole up in my cabin in the mountains waiting for the zombie apocalypse."

"That's certainly an uplifting outlook. You have a plan. What happens to the rest of us?" asked Chuck

Nick turned and looked at Chuck as they walked into the Hart building. "You're fucked," he said in a deadly serious tone.

Chapter 41

A smiling Lexi led Fontana, followed by both of their chiefs of staff, into her office in the Capitol. Sal went to the bar and started pouring drinks. He handed one to Lexi and then to Mel and his own chief of staff, Ben. They each stood in the center of the office, smiling.

"We fucking did it," said Fontana, lifting his Waterford crystal highball glass in a toast to his companions, who matched his motion.

"To the filibuster, good riddance," toasted Mel.

"I never thought this day would actually come," admitted Lexi, walking to the couch in her office.

She kicked off her heels and tucked her legs up under as she sat.

"It almost didn't," this from Fontana's chief of staff Ben, pacing around the luxuriously furnished office. "So, what are the next steps?" he asked, not looking at either Fontana or Lexi, but at Mel.

Mel looked at his watch, as if expecting something.

"First, we have to deal with Turner. Then Morris for nominating him. Now we need to push the legislation through quickly. Lexi, we probably have a month, maybe six weeks, before we need to get serious about the primaries. We have the holiday break and then we need to come out of those swinging in January. Our useful idiot competition will hang in just to keep it interesting and to make you look good in the debates. They all know the roles they need to play for their cabinet posts. We seem to have prevented any of the radicals from mounting a grass-roots campaign this time. We shouldn't have any surprises," lectured Mel.

"Good," agreed Lexi, beaming as she sipped her drink.

"You should wrap up the primaries in February, super Tuesday in March at the latest. Then you can look presidential, shepherding more legislation through Congress with the filibuster gone. This will be in stark contrast to the zoo the Opposition will put up. They have no front runner, and they'll all be at each other's throats trying to be 'make America great again, again' or whatever other racist slogan they use to rouse the right. Whatever it is, it won't work. We've seen to that," continued Mel.

"Who do you think will be the candidate?" asked Sal.

"Jack Wilson," blurted out Lexi. "My money is on him."

"Could be Wilson, could be Garcia, hell they could even go with Chandra-Miller to run a minority woman against you," mused Mel. "Honestly, I think it will be Blackbird from South Dakota. I don't think any of them can draw enough support to put up a significant fight. We just have too many advantages now. Demographic changes, mail in ballots, ballot harvesting and our grass-roots organizations to make sure we have the votes where we need them," ended Mel.

"Plus, we have DOJ, CIA, FBI, Homeland and NSA," laughed Sal, as he poured another full drink. He didn't notice the hateful stare this last produced from Mel. "Hollywood, social media, cable news, and our new friends in the black hoodie brigades," continued Sal, when he noticed the look on Mel's face.

"Come on Mel, let's call a spade a spade. They do what we tell them to do, or rather, what *you* tell them to do."

Lexi, sensing a pissing contest again, interjected.

"What about Turner? We need to discredit him without it looking like we are picking on him too much. He *is* a national hero, after all."

Mel glanced at his watch again. "We'll see. Even heroes can go too far. Maybe this was that time. I admire his conviction, but he almost screwed up forty years of effort to remake the Constitution and get rid of that filibuster when WE can take advantage."

Lexi's cellphone vibrated on the couch. She glanced at it, intending to let it go to voicemail, but seeing who it was, she answered.

"Mr. President," said Lexi. "Oh hello. What?" said Lexi in a shocked tone. "When? Of course, Sal is with me. He will give a statement." She hung up the phone. "Wilhelm died in the ambulance on the way back to the hospital. That was Amy," said Lexi, referring to the President's communications director. Sal and Ben both stood up, shocked. Lexi glanced at Mel and thought she saw a smirk on his face before he, too, appeared surprised at the news.

"What happened?" Sal asked.

"Apparently the drugs they gave him were just too much for his system combined with the physical activity. He had a heart attack in the ambulance when they were taking him back to the hospital. They tried to revive him, but pronounced him dead on arrival," said Lexi.

"Sal, you need to get out there and tell them how brave Wilhelm was. How he sacrificed to allow the future to happen," commented Ben, scribbling on a notepad. "We can point out none of this would have been necessary if Turner hadn't betrayed Colorado and the Party."

"Good, I like it; we can hang this around Turner's neck," remarked Sal, rubbing his hands together gleefully.

"Just be careful. I know you dislike him, but we need to walk a fine line. Go after him too hard and you make him Joan of Arc," reminded Mel.

"I hear you, but he deserves to be blamed for some of this," growled Sal.

"We still need his vote to ensure we pass legislation," noted Ben.

"Not anymore. With Wilhelm gone, Governor Grayson will appoint a replacement. That will give us 50, even if Turner goes against us. Lexi can break those ties all day long and it makes her look presidential," explained Mel. "Actually, Wilhelm, in a coma, would have made it harder to capitalize on this vote."

"How about naming the amendment after Wilhelm? We can gather sympathy and ride this into a windfall in fundraising," suggested Lexi.

"I like it. I'll go make my statement for the press. Let's get our talking heads out there bashing Turner," said Sal, rubbing his hands.

Sal and Ben left the office. Once the door shut, Lexi returned to her perch and took a sip from her scotch while staring at Mel.

Mel was at the bar refilling his drink. He sat down in the easy chair opposite the couch.

"What?" asked Mel, answering the questioning look from Lexi.

"Do I want to know?"

"Know what?" answered Mel with an arched eyebrow.

Lexi took a sip. "With Turner a wildcard, we needed Wilhelm's vote to pass all the bills we have tee'd up. Wilhelm dying was very convenient."

"We didn't come this far, only to be stopped from crossing the finish line. Either Wilhelm was going to survive and stay awake, or he was not," shrugged Mel. "We knew the risks when we gave him the drugs. Don't get squeamish on me now."

Lexi let out a laugh. "Hardly. I just knew him. He was one of my mentors when I first got to the Senate. Took me under his wing and showed me how to maneuver people into corners to get what I wanted."

"If we play this right, we might even get Turner back in the fold. I think he actually has a conscience," asserted Mel.

Lexi laughed again, "only because he hasn't been here long."

"He is going to feel bad about Wilhelm and may even blame himself because his not voting our way forced Wilhelm to make that trip. If we can use this to get him to realize what we're trying to do, really is best for everyone, maybe he'll get back on the bandwagon."

"I'll be honest. I don't like him," admitted Lexi. "When he looks at me, I feel like he's looking right through me. He's so intense."

"Why don't you just sleep with him?"

Lexi didn't even bat an eye. "I would if I thought it would help and if I thought he would take me up on it. Somehow, I think I would strike out and you know how much I hate losing."

"Really? I didn't know that about you," retorted Mel sarcastically as Lexi flipped him off.

"There is something about him. I don't think we should underestimate him. He's a man of action, not like these spineless jellyfish surrounding us up here. Just keep an eye on him and keep Sal from going to war with him. We don't need it," ordered Lexi. "What do we really know about him?"

"Not much more than everyone else. I have some folks looking into his background once he made his little speech at that committee meeting. I don't like surprises," confided Mel. "I also suggest we pull some media heads together and discuss *their* first amendment rights," finished Mel with a sneer.

"Good idea. Probably time to remind them of the consequences of not following our lead," Lexi said with a ruthless edge.

"Especially with the filibuster gone. Our threats now have teeth and are no longer theoretical." Mel merely nodded, thinking ahead to the next moves on the chessboard of the Great Game.

Chapter 42

Several interns and aides immediately accosted Nick and Chuck as they walked into his office in the Hart building. Waving call slips and asking how to respond to various requests. Nick looked around.

Everyone he could see was on the phone. He smiled, hearing a lot of, 'of course the Senator will call you back when he has time'. As Nick entered his office suite, Chuck stopped in the hallway, corralling the staff, trying to get to him. He turned to Chuck.

"Go on. Let me grab Margie, Greg, and Jenny," stated Chuck.

Nick nodded and headed into the office. Everyone stared as he went. Margie stuck her head out of her office and made to shout after the Senator, but a glance at the shaking head of Chuck stopped her. Chuck headed into her office. Greg and Jenny followed.

Nick went to his fridge, grabbed a water and stood in the center of the room surveying the lack of warmth, character, or any distinguishing item. The place was sterile. It was as if he knew all along he wouldn't be staying. He sat on the edge of his desk, sipping his water, contemplating, raising his head at the sound of a knock.

"Come in."

Chuck walked in, followed by Margie, Greg, and Jenny. They sat down in various places, waiting for Nick to start.

"First, make sure everyone knows I won't think less of them if they want to move on from this office after my little show today."

Chuck laughed. "Sometimes…" he said, shaking his head. "You really know nothing about people. No one is going to quit because you took a principled stance. Next."

"OK, I feel like I just disappointed my teacher in class," he commented, looking sideways at Chuck perched on the arm of a chair.

"Actually, you did. You should know these people are here because they believe in you. Now enough of the pity party martyr shit. What do we do next, Margie?" asked Chuck.

"We have requests from everyone except Sesame Street for you to appear. I would expect none of them to be friendly except for Tommy. He'd love to trot you out," announced Margie.

"Recommendations?" asked Nick.

"Well, I think we need to take a tone of 'you were just following the wishes of your constituents, fresh off your visit home and felt you needed to vote the way they felt'," suggested Margie.

"Do *Tommy,*" this was from Greg, who interrupted her.

"Excuse me?" questioned Margie.

"No really, go all in. You're right. This is against the founders and the Constitution. It violates the exact idea of checks and balances. Go try to educate the public on why this is a bad thing."

Nick made an exaggerated gesture of looking around the room.

"Anyone seen Greg? He seems to be missing. Turning to Greg, he held out his hand. I'm Nick Turner. You are?" he asked, smiling.

That made everyone in the room laugh and lessened the tension. Greg looked animated, as if he had suddenly found a calling and was ready to go door to door to sell it.

"What you said made sense to anyone listening. You were right, and they knew it. Fontana didn't stand up and pick you apart on anything you said. He couldn't. And he was smart enough to know it. Instead, he violated decorum and made his point by saying you were young, inexperienced, and simply emotional. The decisions needed to be handled by career politicians like him. But he missed the mood of the nation. They *hate* politicians like him after years of these so called 'elder' statesmen screwing things up," explained Greg. "Now is the chance to drive the point home. Do Tommy's show. He'll probably give you the entire hour if you want it. We need to double down."

Nick turned to Chuck and Margie. "What do you think?"

"He has a point. It probably can't get worse, so trying to appeal to conservatives, moderates, and independents may help. Your kind of screwed anyway, right Jenny?" asked Chuck.

Jenny nodded, joining the conversation. "If I were Fontana, I'd look to strip you of a few of your committee assignments. Maybe not all of them. Rules or Armed Services for sure, to punish you. Could be temporary. You can also forget about any of our bills getting attention. Don't think he would look to censure you, since that would just give you more time on the floor. Also, I doubt he'll give you a chance for any more grandstanding during debates. You'll just be going through the motions now. Greg is right, your only real choice to stay relevant is TV," declared Jenny.

"Margie? You're pretty quiet. What do you think about *Tommy*?"

"Depends on how combative you want to be."

"Any of them actually give me a chance to speak?" asked Nick.

"Not ANC or FLCN for sure. They would just scream at you and then point out how you betrayed the cause. You might try *NewsRight*, but that'll just make Tommy mad," offered Margie.

"Networks?"

"Only morning shows. Not worth your time if you ask me. You want to hit the most, do EXN's morning show again. More people watch them now than the network's morning shows."

"I'm not afraid of them. I can handle it."

"Why kick the hornet's nest at this point?" questioned Chuck.

"If that's what you both think, OK," shrugged Nick.

"Let's stay off tonight. Schedule *Tommy* for tomorrow night. Let them have their moment of triumph. If you go on, it'll look like you are attacking versus just taking a principled stance. You can explain your position and why you felt you needed to vote the way you did. It's not a betrayal, but an attempt to keep the checks and balances in place as the founders intended," urged Chuck.

"Just call me Jimmy Madison," said Nick.

"Way too tall. He was a shrimp. Maybe Washington would be better. You're about his height or even Lincoln," suggested Greg, looking up at Nick.

"It was a joke. Jeez, all of you need to lighten up. This is the first time I've enjoyed the job in a while."

"Well, if this is having fun, I'd hate to see what the party is going to look like," smiled Jenny.

"I guess time will tell," answered Nick, smiling as well.

"Speaking of which, we haven't gotten the skinny on Dolly's. Was your tux a hit?" asked Jenny, slyly.

Before Nick could answer, Chuck chimed in.

"Oh yeah, he stood out. Then again, I saw little of him. He was too busy dancing with the hostess," said Chuck with a wink.

Jenny and Margie both laughed, and Jenny gave a little clap.

"Success," she said, raising her hands.

"I don't know what you're all laughing about, at my expense I might add," grumbled Nick. "Yes, the tux was fine, the party was nice, and Dolly is a wonderful dancer. It was the jitterbug that got me, though. I couldn't move all weekend."

"Jitterbug?" asked Margie in surprise.

"Oh yes, you should have seen it," spilled Chuck. "Our fearless leader went upstairs to the ballroom, where all the young staffers were swing dancing and doing a jitterbug. Once the youngsters saw Nick, they all wanted to meet him. They dragged him out, intending to show him a few moves. Next thing I know, he has a pretty young redhead in tow and is flinging her around his head. It appears we do not know our boss as well as we thought. Ladies, he can dance, and his jitterbug wasn't half bad," said Chuck in an accusatory tone.

"Hey, my so-called dancing skills are of little consequence in the senate," disclosed Nick, shaking his head.

"He danced with Dolly for forty-five minutes." Chuck enjoyed his boss's discomfort.

"No way! Holy Crap," said Jenny, looking at Margie, grinning.

"It's no big deal. She wanted to dance, and I danced a few waltzes with her." Nick just shrugged.

"*Forty-five minutes*. Nick, it is a big deal. Dolly avoids entanglements with everyone. It's why she can stay bi-partisan and keep her galas civil. I've been to every one of them. She has *never* danced with anyone, *ever*. Including heads of state," explained Chuck.

"Maybe nobody asked?" offered Nick, holding his hands up.

"Must have been the tux," nodded Jenny with a mischievous laugh. "I bet you looked like James Bond."

"More like Humphrey Bogart," added Chuck, earning a rude hand gesture from Nick.

"Rick from Casablanca? He got Ingrid Bergman. That would work as well," grinned Jenny.

Chuck made a show of turning his head to look at Nick's profile.

"What the hell are you doing?" asked Nick, perturbed.

"Just checking to make sure you got all the lipstick off."

"*Lipstick?*" Jenny and Margie said at the same time.

"Don't worry, she wiped it off his lips, just left her territory marked on his cheek," shared Chuck, as Nick smiled.

"I thought Dolly's parties were secret. What would happen if I told her you were gossiping?" threatened Nick in mock seriousness.

"Nick, there may not be any pictures, but I guarantee you all those youngsters have told all their friends how cool you are. That they actually got to meet you and shake your hand. That redhead would've probably had your baby," confided Chuck with a laugh.

Nick was about to retort when there was a knock at the door.

"Come on in," Nick shouted. Carla walked in. "Senator, you should look at ANC," while handing him a stack of messages.

"Also, lots of calls. Some seem to be important. One from Governor Morris and one from Senator Banks. I put them on top."

"Banks?" questioned Nick. "Thanks Carla."

Greg had been turning on the TV as Carla delivered the messages and shut the door on her way out.

"Breaking news. We are just learning that Senator Wilhelm has succumbed after complications from several strokes. As many of you know, the Senator made a courageous trip to the Senate chamber earlier today to cast the deciding vote to pass Senate bill 15. Apparently, on his trip back to the hospital, he suffered a heart attack in the ambulance. They pronounced him dead upon his arrival."

"Shit," Margie said snarling. "They're gonna blame you for this."

The talking head on ANC continued. "We have a statement from the President expressing his admiration and gratitude for the forty-four years of public service from Senator Wilhelm including his commitment to leave his hospital room for this final vote of his tenure in the Senate." The commentator raised a hand to her ear.

"Hang on, we have the Senate Majority leader," said the ANC host. The image shifted to Senator Fontana outside his office.

"It is with a sad heart that I announce the loss of one of the true icons of the Senate. After bravely making his way to the Senate chamber to help us pass this groundbreaking legislation, the Senator has passed as a result of his declining health. We all, the entire nation, owe a debt of gratitude to the Senator for making the ultimate sacrifice to ensure the future of the Republic with his final vote. In his honor, we will rename Senate Bill 15 the Wilhelm Amendment, to celebrate his sacrifice. I ask everyone to keep Senator Wilhelm in their prayers and to pray for his family. Thank you."

"There you have comments from the Senate Majority leader, praising the efforts and career of Senator Wilhelm. The filibuster bill will now be remembered as the Wilhelm Amendment. For comment, we bring in Jamal Abraham. Jamal, your thoughts on these events? You've worked for Senators and Presidents. What went on here?"

"What went on here is nothing more than outright betrayal. Senator Turner tried to screw the Party and the majority of Americans who supported our key legislation. Voting with the obstructionist Opposition just showed his contempt for his constituents. For decades, we have been trying to remove these filibuster rules, which are archaic and designed for an entirely different time in our history.

The minority has used them to prevent the majority from rightfully capitalizing on winning elections."

"We finally reached a point where we could pass this, and Senator Turner tried his best to stop it. I'll call him 'Benedict Turner' from now on, as his attempt to stop this was no less a betrayal of his country than that of Benedict Arnold in the Revolutionary war. I cannot say enough about the courage shown by Senator Wilhelm, ultimately giving his life for the cause."

"Yes indeed, Senator Wilhelm's bravery and courageous sacrifice made all of this possible. They will remember him as the man that made all this progress reality. What are the next steps?" asked the ANC commentator.

"For what? Senator Turner or legislation now that we have removed the filibuster?" asked Jamal.

"Well, both I guess," said the ANC talking head.

"If I were the Majority Leader, I would punish Senator Turner for his betrayal. Especially considering the death of Senator Wilhelm directly results from Senator Turner's reprehensible antics. At a minimum, kick him off committees, kill his bills, and censure him. As for the legislation, as you know, we have been trying to get comprehensive gun control passed for years. Then there is the Supreme Court expansion, additional states, voting rights, student loan debt forgiveness, re-codifying *Roe* and affirmative action, plus a host of other items to fight against injustice and racism promoted by the opposition party and the bigoted Supreme Court. The gloves are off. We will fight, as the people have repeatedly asked us to," said Jamal righteously.

"It is indeed a great day for justice and fairness, but tinged with sadness. It's unfortunate that a hero like Senator Turner used his celebrity and position to fight against the people who put him in his role. Does he have any election prospects?" asked the ANC anchor.

"None as far as I can see, at least not in our party. If the election wasn't in a year, I'm sure Governor Morris or others in Colorado would start a recall campaign, they may still."

Nick sighed. "Please turn it off. Benedict Turner, that's clever."

"You can expect more of the same. They're going to ride this for sympathy and make Wilhelm a goddamn hero," promised Chuck.

"There are plenty of empty pedestals where Lincoln, Grant, and Washington once stood. They can put up a statue of him, or more likely Fontana," fumed Nick, dripping with sarcasm.

"We need a plan," declared Margie. "You have to get out there with a statement or make an appearance to refute some of these accusations and reiterate your principles for the vote. I know you won't apologize or fall on your sword, so we need to highlight your reasoning for voting no."

"You know me. Rule number 6. Never apologize,"

Chuck laughed nervously. "Oh, good God. Your credo cannot be based on a TV character."

"Why not? It worked for Gibbs on *NCIS*," said Nick in all seriousness.

"Please don't quote him while you are on TV," pleaded Margie. "Where do you want to go? TV or a press conference?"

"I think I'll stay off mainstream media. Before Wilhelm passed, I would have relished the idea of taking on the talking heads, but now, it is all going to be how do I feel now that I am responsible for his death. I can't win that argument. I guess *Tommy* is my only hope for a chance to tell my side."

"Agree," said Chuck, looking at Margie, who was nodding her head.

"Do we need to do a press release as well or just an appearance on *Tommy*?" asked Nick.

"I think *Tommy* is better. You speak with a passion we cannot get across in a press release. Let me see how much time I can get from him tomorrow night and we can work on points to make," replied Margie.

"Sounds good. The best defense is offense. Let's attack. I don't want to back down at all," announced Nick.

"I'm glad you had a good time at Dolly's party," remarked Jenny, sighing.

"It seems like a lifetime ago now."

Chapter 43

Chuck knocked on Nick's office door.

"Bergamo did a real hit job on you last night on ANC," shared Chuck. "As you figured, she selectively edited the conversation and made it seem like you were threatening her."

Nick sighed. "Why are they so predictable? You have your recording, right?" Chuck nodded. "Good, maybe I'll show it on Tommy's show tonight. Serves her right, accusing me of threatening her. I mean, come on, she or her cameraman knew we were filming."

"Well, you were pretty steamed. I was worried."

"Really? I was just pissed a reporter would question my patriotism and imply I was a traitor."

"From her point of view, as a liberal, you betrayed *their* cause, and you are six-four and what, 220? You can be a *bit* intimidating," noted Chuck.

"So, you think she was right?"

"Of course not, but there is always perspective. You need to put yourself in other people's shoes before you jump to conclusions. It only gets you in trouble if you don't."

"So, I overreacted? She does a hit job on me on ANC and I'm the bad guy? I didn't see this coming," he said, looking at Chuck.

"Do what you want," commented Chuck, holding up his hands in frustration. "But going full attack dog on her is what got you in trouble the first time. Might not be the best look. I'll send you the footage and you can decide."

Nick got up to get a cup of coffee and looked at Chuck, who raised his own to say no.

"210," corrected Nick. Chuck looked at him questioning.

"You said I weighed 220. I'm 210. Ten heavier than when I arrived, sadly."

He sat down in the chair behind his desk and sipped his coffee. "ANC is attacking me, Bergamo is claiming I threatened her, the Party thinks I'm a traitor and an accessory to the death of Wilhelm. The phone calls today have been all about how I need to resign, kill myself, or, at a minimum, apologize. Got any good news?"

"You're making tons in donations. That's the best sign it's not as bad as you think or as bad as the leadership and media are making it out to be. Who knows, this could benefit you if you decide to run. You need to decide. Especially since they might primary you now."

"God Chuck. Why does anyone voluntarily choose to do this job? You have to sell your soul and any integrity."

"Well, if you play the game, it can be a pretty nice life. If you don't, your expiration date is pretty short. You have to decide what you want to do. Not all those praising your principled stance were from Colorado. Hopefully, that gives you something positive."

Nick nodded. "Thanks. I'm not feeling much appreciated right now. Here, it always seems to be a choice for the lesser of two evils. I'm really questioning my ability to make any difference by staying."

"Only you can make that decision," mused Chuck.

"Thanks. It's pretty sad when I can expect a conservative talk show host to treat me better than my party," lamented Nick.

"Welcome to Washington," explained Chuck, leaving the office.

Chapter 44

"Tonight, I welcome back Senator Nick Turner. As you know, the Senator showed great courage yesterday, as he has done time and time again for his country. Voting his conscience, rather than voting with the rest of the Party to silence the minority. He stood against the Party's goal of destroying our Constitutional system of checks and balances," said Tommy Charles from his perch on his EXN show.

Because of his short stature, Tommy's side of the stage behind the curved desk was six inches higher than his guests. For most guests, this made him taller. Nick still towered over Tommy.

"Thanks for having me back."

"Senator, you are being accused of all but pulling the trigger on Senator Wilhelm. How do you respond?" asked Tommy seriously.

"Every Senator voted in that chamber. We all had our reasons for how we voted. I didn't administer the drugs to wake up Senator Wilhelm from his coma. Nor did I load him into the ambulance to drive him to the Capitol. I didn't wheel him into the chamber to vote and I didn't watch him die in the ambulance back to his hospital," said Nick, counting these points out on his hand, as he continued.

"Somebody did. I think the proper blame should go to those folks. Any of my fellow members could have shown the same courage I did, or that Senator Wilhelm did, to vote their conscience."

"True," agreed Tommy.

"I'm disappointed so many of my colleagues, many of whom are on record defending the filibuster when we were in the minority, suddenly decided it was no longer as critical as they once felt and said it was. This is the height of hypocrisy. They are just blaming me because they had to wake up Senator Wilhelm to complete their goal.

He died in the process, because of their actions, not mine." Nick leaned back in his chair.

"Senator, that's quite an accusation. Do you have evidence to back up the claim?" begged Tommy.

"Tommy, do I need evidence other than common sense? He was in a medically induced coma for six weeks. The only way you wake up from a medically induced coma is to give the patient drugs to wake them up. Clearly, I didn't do that, now did I? Does anyone have evidence I'm responsible for his death? 49 other senators voted to preserve the filibuster too. Are any of the others being accused? I think not. I'm perfectly content with the reasons for my vote and accept the consequences of those actions."

"Well said Senator. You have my thanks and those of conservatives, independents, and moderates everywhere. Now what are you going to do? Do you still consider yourself a Party member?"

"Tommy, we all swore an oath to uphold the Constitution and the laws and rules within, regardless of the party allegiance. You know, I once thought the Senate to be the part of Congress where cooler heads would prevail and put a stop on any mob rule. It was intended to stop 'the tyranny of the majority', represented by the House elections every two years." Nick raised his hands in air quotes.

"The feeling was you could have a popular crusade sweep in a majority in the house who would pass a bunch of legislation for emotional reasons. The Senate was supposed to stop this and protect the livelihood of citizens," said Nick, leaning in again as he spoke.

"You mean like the populist PW4C and the progressives?"

"Indeed, Tommy, the radical ideas of some in the house would qualify as populism against which the founders sought protection in the Senate. They designed it to not be beholden to the popular vote. They could make the unpopular, but necessary decisions, and keep any radical legislation from violating the Constitution."

"Most people don't realize this is why House members are elected every two years. To represent the people. Their state government appointed the Senators for six-year terms. This was so they didn't have to worry about pissing off the people or currying favor to win a reelection vote. Does anybody remember this?"

"Senator, I doubt it. I keep forgetting you taught history once. Please continue the lesson. Many of our viewers may not know this and I think it's important," encouraged Tommy.

"As you can imagine, the Senate rarely did what the House wanted. Often it stopped presidents from getting their radical agendas passed as well. They stopped agendas of both political parties, I might add," said Nick, getting into his story.

"Along came the first leader of the Progressive movement in America, a former college president and governor of New Jersey. He wrote a dissertation for his PhD on how the Constitution was holding back progress. His name was Woodrow Wilson."

"To be fair," Nick continued, "Teddy Roosevelt was also a progressive. Wilson presided over three major changes, all of which altered our country in ways they couldn't imagine. First, they passed the income tax in his first year; before 1913 there was no income tax. Imagine that," said Nick as Tommy interrupted.

"Until 1913, there was no income tax?" asked Tommy.

"Nothing permanent. They needed guaranteed income from the citizens to pay for all the professional bureaucrats Wilson was about to start creating. The administrative state was born under Wilson. These 'experts' now make up over 3 million unelected workers in our country's biggest business; our Government. Keep in mind that number does not include the armed forces or the state bureaucrats."

Tommy shook his head. "Senator, I doubt there are more than a handful of our viewers and certainly even fewer of the Party voters who know what you just said. This is truly depressing."

Nick nodded in agreement. "The second piece of legislature was making the Senate elected by the people and not appointed by their states. This seemed like a good idea at the time because a few senators were corrupt and appointed to their role by state legislatures, paying back favors. State congress also often took a long time to agree on an appointee, leaving a state unrepresented in Congress."

Nick continued his lecture, varying his tone, using his hands and emphasizing his keep points to keep his audience engaged, just as he had for so many freshman history courses at Colorado State.

"A Senator appointed by the state government is accountable to them. They have to be focused on what is best for the state to continue serving. The state congress are the ones beholden to the state voters for bad appointees. With this amendment, the state government now has no representative in Washington. Senators get money and power in Washington, voting with their party, not for their states. In one fell swoop, one of the biggest checks and balances in the entire Constitution was eliminated. The Senator's ability to make unpopular decisions was gone," revealed Nick.

"Again, let me make sure our viewers are getting this," interrupted Tommy. "Woodrow Wilson was the father of the Progressive movement. Passing both the Income Tax and making the Senate beholden to the people instead of protecting states' rights, correct?"

"More or less, it started before Wilson, but both passed soon after he became president. Today, thanks to Wilson, there is really no difference between the two branches. Why do we even have two of them? This was a case where the Constitution was amended in the dark of night with little fanfare. They quickly took advantage of public opinion and huge Party majorities. The consequences of electing senators and permanent income taxes should have been debated and a national referendum with three-fourths of the country's state legislatures required to vote yes for this monumental change."

"Just like the ERA amendment, which could never get a majority to vote for it in three-fourths of the states," explained Tommy.

"Yes. They bribed the state governments to not fight losing their representatives in DC, with the prospect of having nationally collected tax dollars directed to them. To gain the people's support, just like today, they claimed the rich would pay 99% of the income taxes and the working man little, if any."

Tommy laughed. "I see nothing has changed. You quote a speech by a Senator from 1950, and the soak the rich tax story was used by the Party in 1913. Wow."

Nick smiled in reply. "It worked then, too. One more quick note. Today we have all these foundations, set up by the uber rich families. Care to guess when these were created? That's right, just before this law and guess where all that wealth from so many other well known 'philanthropists' went? Into these foundations where they are not subject to the new income tax," explained Nick.

"Unbelievable," said Tommy, shaking his head.

"The income tax of 1913 was never designed to tax the rich. It was meant to tax everyone else to fund the bureaucratic state. And it worked. Let's also still remember, even with the foundations, the top 1% still pays over 50% of the income tax."

Tommy was shaking his head at these revelations.

"I would add one last test. In response to the next tax the rich tirade, I think we should have everyone in Congress and the Senate show their net worth when they entered Congress and what it is today. Spouses and family too. We will find out just who is getting rich and buying multiple multi-million dollar beach houses. On only a government salary," finished Nick.

"An interesting concept, senator," laughed Tommy as Nick continued.

"Today was just the culmination of 110 plus years of effort by Wilson to neuter the Constitution. He has finally won," said Nick in a disgusted tone, once again leaning back.

"You believe the end of the filibuster is as bad as I have been saying? The end of the 2nd amendment, more Party states, packed Supreme Court, voter suppression, Critical Race Theory mandated in all our schools and worse?" asked Tommy.

"Anything is possible as long as the Party keeps a majority. Tommy, think about it again. How things might have been different if senators were still appointed? States wishes would trump Party or Opposition policies if Senators wanted to get reappointed. There would no longer be rubber stamp votes where everyone voted Party because they need reelection funds from Party war chests among other reasons. We would already be more bipartisan. Because it would focus states on what is good for their state, not just for their party," said Nick, trying to settle down.

"Senator, you have that right. Not something most of us even considered. The states are constantly arguing they should handle most decisions in their states. The President, Congress, and the bureaucrats all say they are in charge of these decisions, not the states."

"Tommy, they educate very few people on how the government is supposed to work. The Masters of Media easily manipulate all. The suppression of alternate opinion is near complete. Only a few dissenting voices, such as your own, are still allowed to exist solely to be pointed to as an example of freedom of speech. While they cancel others for having an alternate opinion. This serves to coerce people into keeping their feelings and opinions, which may differ from the Progressives, internalized," said Nick, with passion.

"This is exactly how Nazi Fascism, Soviet and Chinese Communism, and Iranian and other repressive regimes stay in power. Orwell wrote about this in 1984. I find it hilarious that my Party constantly brands the Opposition as the party of big brother when they are the ones using the tools and state-run organs of power to suppress and persecute alternate opinions. It's a master class in gaslighting, perfectly executed by our media and the Party."

"Amen to that, Senator," said Tommy, in violent agreement.

Nick's voice became more animated, also using his hands.

"If I hear one more of my colleagues claiming some Opposition member is Hitler, I may just lose my dinner. They need to look in the mirror to see the true authoritarians. The destruction of the filibuster was one of the last bastions of protection remaining from the Constitution to prevent America from becoming a totalitarian state," finished Nick aggressively. His phone started vibrating in his pocket. He knew it was Chuck sending him a 911 to tone it down.

"Those are pretty brave words, Senator. Something we're not used to hearing, especially from those needing to win the approval of voters," said Tommy. "Especially from a Party senator."

"Well Tommy," replied Nick, slowly, trying to calm down. "Maybe the people need to hear a bit more truth and understand what happens when they put people in power who couldn't care less about them? Removing the filibuster hurts conservatives, moderates and it is going to hurt liberals too. They just have the blinders on. Totalitarian regimes only have two classes. Elites holding the power and everyone else who is simply a serf, a peasant, a drone, a slave. Call it what you will."

Tommy nodded his head in agreement. "True."

"Supporting their policies won't shield you or your children from getting a crappy education or your local police being defunded or you having to protect your home with a 9 iron because only the criminals have the guns. Or keeping your job from being shipped off to Mexico, China, Vietnam, or wherever human rights violations are not prosecuted," spoke Nick, getting animated again.

"Senator, there are few times when I'm speechless," said Tommy with a nervous laugh. "This is one of those. I have nothing to add to what you are saying. I agree one hundred percent. This is definitely a first and I think you answered my earlier question, even if you don't know it yet. You, sir, are no longer a Party member."

"That may be true. But I'm not a conservative either. I simply support upholding the Constitution and common sense."

"Senator, you said three things earlier?"

"Right, even worse than the Income Tax and elected Senators, the genuine triumph of Wilson's removal of the Constitutional checks was the creation of the Federal Reserve banking system. I know you are running out of time. We'll save it for another visit. Maybe when I am no longer in office," smiled Nick.

"Senator, I sincerely hope you are joking about being out of office. I only have another minute. I have one more question. Yesterday, Lauren Bergamo went on air with some footage showing a confrontation between you two after the vote. She is claiming you tried to intimidate her to keep her from asking tough questions."

"Tommy, I have footage of the entire ambush from Miss Bergamo. It would contradict her narrative and show that she selectively edited the interview to make me look bad. But you know what?" said Nick, leaning back in his chair. "I don't give a shit. It's just another example of the press lying to advance a false narrative. Miss Bergamo, in fact, impugned my character and suggested I wasn't a patriot. Because I didn't vote in lockstep with the Party. Instead, I used my brain and made my own decision. I think people who think for themselves already know I'm the last person in the world who would betray my country. My actions have shown that. I'll leave it at that, Tommy," ended Nick.

"Don't you want to air the footage, Senator? Maybe it would be better to get it out?" pleaded Tommy, wanting to show the tape.

"Tommy, this is the problem. Everything is sensationalism and designed to change the conversation. I have nothing more to say. Embarrassing Miss Bergamo is unnecessary. There is nothing to gain by doing it. I'll just let them continue to play their games of personal destruction. It just further demeans journalism when facts aren't shown to let folks make their own decisions," remarked Nick.

"Well, there you have it. Senator, I think that may be more potent than showing the footage. That's all the time we have. Thank you again, and good luck in the future dealing with the fallout."

As the show ended, Nick removed his microphone. "Man, you're in a heap of trouble. You have a death wish?" whistled Tommy.

"Not following? I'm just telling it like it is," said Nick, standing.

"And I'm George Clooney. If you think they won't retaliate, you're more naïve than I think. You know they're going to blast you," said Tommy, walking next to Nick as they headed out of the studio.

Nick smiled but said nothing as Tommy continued.

"Why the smile? What do you have to gain? Wait a minute, you want them to come after you, don't you?" Nick just kept smiling.

"Not sure what game you're playing, but keep coming on," laughed Tommy. "I bet most of my audience knew nothing about what happened under Wilson. I hope they are googling him."

"Education, even more than guns, is the only hope the republic has if we are to survive," said Nick, standing at the elevator. "My mission is to force people to learn and think for themselves. Hopefully, they'll start acting in their best interests instead of doing what others tell them to do. Thanks for giving me so much time."

"Until the next time," said Tommy, shaking Nick's hand.

Chapter 45

Several weeks and Thanksgiving passed. As predicted, they removed Nick from many of his committees. There was even talk of an official Censure vote. Until they replaced Wilhelm, Fontana couldn't guarantee it would pass. Governor Morris of Colorado was also making noises to start a recall campaign, but with an election in less than a year, it was not likely to amount to much.

Lexi was using her ability after the filibuster vote to clear the Party's path to passing all the thwarted legislation. Using this win to hammer her primary opponents. She was quickly running away with the nomination in all the polls, with only a couple of opponents registering even double digits. In most state polls, she was ahead by thirty to fifty points.

Senator Wilhelm's body laid in state in the North Carolina capital. The Vice President and Majority Leader delivered statements at the funeral. Each again alluding to both the bravery and courage of Wilhelm in making his way to the chamber to vote. Both included not-so-subtle digs at Nick, for showing neither bravery nor courage in his dissenting vote.

The President had even bestowed on the Senator, the Presidential Medal of Freedom, posthumously. Chuck's prediction came true. They made Wilhelm a hero of the Republic.

Nick continued to be vilified by the press. Benedict Turner memes were all the rage on social media. Yet his appearance on Tommy earned the highest ratings ever for the show. In contrast, Nick slipped to the lowest approval rating in his short tenure. Only 37% of Coloradans approved of his work, in polls by the local NWN station.

On a lark, Chuck ran a national poll. 62% of respondents approved of Nick's principled stance. An interesting revelation was he did equally well with Party, Opposition, and independents. At these results, Nick had just laughed. "Polls are useless," he'd opined.

Eventually the stories died down as the media moved on to more mass shootings, inflation, Chinese provocations, the first Trans balloon character in the Macy's parade, and football scores.

Early in December, Nick was in his Senate office, reviewing the proposed amendment to expand the Supreme Court to fifteen seats, something he was vehemently against but knew he could not now stop from becoming reality, when his desk phone rang.

"Senator Turner. Sure, I'll hold."

"Senator, this is Harlan Grayson," said the voice on the other side in a slow southern drawl, oozing with charm.

"Governor, first, let me offer my condolences for the loss of Senator Wilhelm."

"He was a fine senator, a fine North Carolinian, and a friend. He's also why I called. They killed Johnny. And he had no choice. They gave him drugs to force him out of his coma, the bastards."

"Governor, do you know that for a fact?" asked Nick, sitting up straighter, making sure his recorder was on.

"I do. Johnny had a private nurse besides the hospital staff. She was in the room when some guy came in with the doctors. They were very nervous as they administered the drugs. The man told them not to worry, it was all approved. The nurse told me it couldn't have been approved, because *she* had the medical power of attorney. When she asked what they were doing, the man explained to her it was a matter of national security and she needed to stand down or risk being arrested for obstruction of justice."

"Once the Senator woke up, she understood what had happened. As they got him ready for the trip to the Capitol, she called me and asked what she should do. At that point, there was nothing she could do, so I told her to just stay out of the way. When she tried to accompany the Senator, they said she couldn't. He would get the care he needed from their staff. That was the last she saw him until she was told he died in the ambulance on the return trip."

"I'm so sorry Governor, this is all my fault. I thought my plan would work and never even contemplated anyone bringing Senator Wilhelm out of his coma. Maybe they're right. I am responsible for his dying," suggested Nick, trailing off.

"Son, Johnny may not have supported the bill either, but he was in congress for 44 years. They had plenty to hold over him. He had lots of kids and grandkids they could threaten to ruin for not toeing the line. He was dying and probably would never have come out of the coma on his own. You didn't kill him. They did."

"Thank you, Governor, but I'll still carry this burden. It appears my vote and his life couldn't stop them from dismantling the Constitution."

"Senator, this is how the game is played. Tomorrow, I'll announce the Party's chosen replacement for Johnny. When you have something to lose, and compromise your principles, as I have so many times in the past, they have you. Family, reputation, honors, children's livelihood. Then you're in the belly of the beast. It's a slippery slope and one where once you go down it, no matter how hard you try, you can't climb back out. Remember this."

"I now realize it too, Governor. I see it all around me. It wasn't what I was expecting," laughed Nick bitterly.

"What did you expect? Honesty? Integrity? Patriotism? Son, there is too much money involved for any of these to survive in politics. I'm old. I was a North Carolina congressman for 45 years, and I have been the Governor for almost 12. You just keep telling yourself you're doing more good than harm. Sadly, I fear this is no longer true. The dirty tricks used to win elections, and keep fraud alive, is the only thing allowing them to stay in power in Washington. There is a storm brewing in the states," said Grayson, pausing.

"Governor, I understand, believe me. I know what I threw away with that vote. I chose not to go down that slope," confided Nick, accepting Grayson's confession.

"God bless you, Nick. For what you did and for preserving your soul. I believe a majority of good folks do not agree with how things are progressing. But they have no way to stop them, and now with ballot harvesting and mail in voting the norm, only a giant majority or a revolution can stop them. The first is not likely to happen with everyone assuming they no longer matter. The latter may be the only choice the average person will have. I fear for my children and grandchildren," Grayson concluded in a resigned voice.

"Earlier this fall, I rode around on my motorcycle in Colorado. I have to say I agree with you. There is resentment and a lack of trust. No one knows what they can do, but they aren't happy with the direction. We must give them hope. I see votes like this, and I see how the talking heads on cable claim we're making progress. My colleagues go on TV as well, promising to help. Then they do nothing to change things for the regular folks," revealed Nick.

"Don't let them get you down. Benedict Turner, hah, more like George Washington. You are one of the few showing actual bravery in Congress, as you have in life. To call you, of all people, a traitor or a coward! How many people were standing around when you acted and took down that terrorist in New York? How did he get into the country in the first place? Our so-called intelligence agencies aren't keeping us very safe."

"I appreciate the kind words. I intend to keep telling the truth, representing the average person, and pointing out corruption wherever I see it. If that makes me the enemy of the elite, it makes me the champion of the common."

"Senator, that sounds like a campaign slogan," laughed Grayson.

"You know, you may be right. I'll have to keep that in my back pocket when I run for the school board or city council. About my only prospects for the future."

"You'll have my vote. Nick, don't give up. Fight. Thank you for what you tried to do. And quoting Margaret Chase Smith was glorious. I knew her when I served as a freshman congressman back when compromise was the rule of the day. She was principled. This last bit with poor Johnny, he deserved a better end than being carted off as the sacrificial lamb on the altar of their progressive agenda."

"I appreciate the support and the kind words and sage advice. I promise you, I will never give up, if only to honor the true memory of Johnny Wilhelm."

"Thank you, son. The founders surely shudder at what we've done with their gift," finished Governor Grayson.

"Of that I have no doubt," agreed Nick.

Chapter 46

Nick's Uber driver dropped him off outside Senator Bank's estate
in the twilight. He walked up to the ornate front gate surrounding
the house in an old, well-established neighborhood in Chevy Chase.
He admired the architecture and the manicured grounds behind the
wrought-iron fence as he pressed the intercom.

"Yes, may I help you?" answered a clipped British accent.

"Hello Hobson, it is Nick Turner to see Senator Banks."

"Ah yes Senator, please come on through."

Nick walked through the gate as it buzzed. He walked toward
the massive wood and glass double entry doors. As he approached,
Hobson, in a proper English waistcoat, opened one side to greet him.

"Good evening, sir. Nice to see you again. If you would follow me,
the Senator is in his library."

"Thanks Hobson, lead the way."

Nick followed him through the house, noticing the rich wood
paneling, high coffered ceilings, and antique furnishings as they made
their way to the library. Hobson led Nick through another set of
ornate wooden double doors into Senator Bank's library.

Banks sat in an old-world European style, well-worn leather chair,
wearing pajamas, slippers, and a cardigan sweater. An inhaler in one
hand and a brandy snifter in the other.

"Come in, come in and have a seat, pardon me. This damned
COPD will be the end of me," groused Banks, puffing on his inhaler
and setting it on an end table. "What will you drink, Senator? Scotch,
bourbon, cognac?"

"I might try a bit of what you are having. Cognac, I suspect?"

"Indeed, good choice. Hobson, if you would please," said Banks, waving at the bar in the library's corner.

Hobson handed Nick a cognac as he sat in the comfortable leather chair opposite Banks.

"If that is all, sirs?" asked Hobson.

"For now, I will ring when the Senator is ready to leave. Thank you, Hobson," responded Banks.

"Thanks Hobson," added Nick as well, as he took a sip of his cognac. It went down like butter, with a hint of tobacco and chocolate. "Wow."

Banks smiled, "Good, isn't it? Too bad it doesn't cure COPD. But I keep trying."

Nick laughed. "I'll say. The chairs are comfortable as well."

"The cognac is almost as old as the chairs."

Nick stood up and wandered around the perimeter of the library, glancing at books, and swirling his cognac, increasing the aeration. The shelves stretched up eleven feet with an ornate ladder on a brass rail circling the room to access the upper shelves.

"Quite an impressive library and house as well. I suppose this is the reward for a lifetime of public service," remarked Nick in a more cynical tone than he intended.

"Hardly. It's family money. Daddy was from a long line of plantation men and briefly a diplomat. Mother was the granddaughter of a lesser branch of a German Rothschild. You'd have to cheat on a pretty grand scale to achieve all this," revealed Banks, waving his arm around from his seat, watching Nick as he paced.

"I see."

"Do you? I'm guessing you aren't liking Washington much?" asked Banks, continuing to watch Nick as he paced.

Laughing, he turned to Banks. "Whatever gave you that idea?"

"Did you enjoy it? Sticking it to them?"

"I have to admit there was some satisfaction. Kind of like the euphoria the jumper supposedly feels *before* they hit the pavement."

"The problem I hear is the pavement shows up all too quickly," said Banks dryly.

Nick nodded and sipped his smooth cognac.

"They want to throw you out. Bunch of blowhards and cowards. Not a stiff spine among the bunch."

Nick shrugged. "Not too surprising. You don't feel the same?"

"I've been here a long time. Believe it or not, there was a time when this was an honorable profession. Before TV, social media, cable news, and frankly before the money made it a popularity contest. We all had passion, and we *believed* what we were doing was indeed the right thing for the right reasons. That has all been replaced by focus groups, analytics, polls, and what has the best optics," explained Banks with a snort.

"Nick, there was a time when being in our Party was an honest moniker. We cared about the working man and stopping exploitation of the weak and less fortunate by the cold-hearted hand of a capitalist society. Where money and power ensured wealth and ease built on an endless supply of nameless, faceless workers. Chewed up, spit out and disposed of to be replaced by younger models with strong backs and weak minds."

"These were *our* people. They were our charge to defend and help. I sense in you that old time classical liberal streak. One long since banished from this town and certainly *our* Party. Today, both parties are all cut from the same cloth. We are the perfect congress for an uncaring capitalist society. Motivated by only money, power, and perpetuating these through more control over ensuring those in power never lose it."

Nick sat down, leaning forward, his elbows on his thighs, listening to Banks, surprised at his candor. "Senator, if what you say is true, it's pretty depressing and frankly reprehensible."

"I don't seek absolution. Our society has been in decline for a long time. Some say since LBJ, others since Roosevelt. I agree with you, it started with Wilson. He did more to unmake our founders' efforts with his bureaucratic super state of rule by faceless, unelected 'so-called experts', rather than the whims of the people."

"And he did it with glee. Those 'people' he disenfranchised. Whom he despised. The modern day 'bitter clingers', could be, and often were wrong, but by God, at least they got the chance to fix their mistake every two years by voting the bums out. A bumbling or corrupt bureaucrat never faces their victim, nor the angry mob affected by their decisions."

Nick listened intently to the man many called the Professor.

"In recent times, we have had one who accelerated it because he couldn't keep it in his pants. He made the Presidency base and common, like a TV sitcom or one of those stupid *Bachelor* reality shows. He forever removed any thought a president was someone better, more qualified, or nobler. Not that it deserved any lofty consideration since he did nothing others before him weren't also doing. He just got caught. They elected and re-elected him, anyway. Did you know I was a congressman when JFK was assassinated?"

Nick shook his head, not wanting to interrupt the story Banks was weaving.

"I've seen a lot in my time. A lot of good and a lot of bad. Lots of good intentions. Our Party has always been the party of good intentions. Often misplaced and not always right. Unfortunately, wishing for good outcomes is the stuff of fiction. Power and greed are the enemy of these and there are too much of both in Washington. You can never have enough. Sorry, I bet you're wondering why I asked to meet with you. Certainly not to hear my confession."

"I have to admit to being a bit curious. Despite your words in the chamber, I can't imagine my little tantrum meets with your approval. It didn't exactly fit the decorum of the Senate."

Banks started to answer, interrupted by a coughing fit instead. Nick got up and got a glass of water from the table. Banks stopped coughing, pulled out a handkerchief, took a sip of the water, and replaced it back in his cardigan pocket, after carefully wiping his mouth.

"My apologies, I am not a well man, but at my age I cannot complain," he said. "I saw your interview with that vile man on EXN. You need to be careful. To him, you are only ratings. It was obvious there, you have decided politics is not for you?"

"It was not my intent, but it just built up and came out. Not being a professional politician, I guess I'm missing the disingenuous gene. No offence intended," apologized Nick with a wry smile.

Banks raised a hand weakly and smiled. "None taken. I think what you did is what a lot of your colleagues would like to do. They, however, are all entangled in the Washington game and can't afford to piss off their sources of money. They're not leaders, and they're not risk takers. To survive and thrive here, you take orders, you don't take risks. In many ways, we're as bad as the lowest civil servant. We claim to represent our constituents, we take their money, we make promises, and we come here and take orders from a handful of special interest and other hidden voices," Banks paused holding Nick's gaze.

"A far cry, from what did you quote, 'the world's greatest deliberative body'? Good ole Maggie. She was a firebrand," finished Banks, now staring wistfully into space, remembering.

"Hidden voices?" queried Nick, perking up.

"Senator, there are many forces in this world. Some are nationalistic and some are globalist. Some mean well and some just mean to take what they want. All these forces wield tremendous power in various ways. If Dante were here today, he'd have to create a 10th circle of hell for modern politicians."

"And the punishment would be?" queried Nick.

"To swim in and have to eat their own excrement endlessly. Seems a fitting fate," said Banks with a croak, as Nick laughed louder.

"How appropriate Senator. I am sure you have done more good than harm. One thing I have learned, is politics is all about tradeoffs," offered Nick.

"You've been in combat and you're clearly a man of action, as witnessed by your exploits. You're not afraid to speak your mind or risk the results. In short, you have nothing to lose or are willing to lose it if your actions fail. Do you agree?"

Nick cocked his head in thought and shrugged. "Not sure I'd put it exactly that way, but I tend to follow my heart when I should pay more attention to my head," said Nick with a half-smile. "I'm not afraid of what the Majority Leader can do to me if that's what you mean. If you want to kick me out of Congress, I'll survive. This isn't the end of the world."

Banks stared at Nick for a few seconds, looking down into his nearly empty cognac glass. "Unfortunately, I do believe it may indeed be the end of the world."

"Getting kicked out of the Senate may be the end of your world, Senator, but I can assure you it would not be the end of mine," said Nick, standing as if to go.

"Please sit. You misinterpret my meaning," said Banks anxiously, waving Nick back in his chair.

He sat back down. Banks continued, "I believe the end of the world or at a minimum the end of our experiment in democracy is imminent. If we go down, freedom in the rest of the world goes with us. I apologize for sounding melodramatic, but I've seen and lived the consequences of a lifetime of poor decisions."

"We are reaping the constant deferment of the hard decisions in favor of the short-term success. We're on the brink of the destruction of the Republic. I know things. Things about our enemies and our friends, or rather, so-called friends. This isn't a simple issue of killing the filibuster or guaranteeing Party majorities in Congress. This is about freedom or slavery. About living a life of our choice or one of obedience," said Banks, a fire in his eye unlike anything Nick had seen previously.

"We have failed in our stewardship of the system. Betrayed the sacrifices of Washington and Lincoln. All the sons of both sides in the Civil War, and my father storming the beaches on D-day. We took their gift and allowed our greed for power and desire for money to cloud our judgment. We have squandered the blood, treasure, and sacrifice of our forefathers, letting what they left us fall through our hands like grains of sand," Banks said with force as he sat on the edge of his seat.

"Sorry, Senator, but you sound like so many other pundits. All claiming the latest decision on the topic du jour will be the end of civilization as we know it. Why are you telling me this? Hell, I agree we are going down in flames and the last vote just speeds it up," agreed Nick.

"We're at the tipping point. The brink. A point of no return. Either the ship turns, we catch a breeze and sail back upstream to new lands, or we go over the falls to die on the rocks below," predicted Banks.

"OK, don't disagree. Once again, why are you telling me? I just sabotaged my career. Shortly, I will return to obscurity and any chance I had to make a difference is long gone. You've been here for almost seventy years, and if you beg my pardon, why didn't *you* stop it? You have way more power than I ever will," accused Nick.

Banks held Nick's eyes before looking down. "You said it yourself. The Constitution limits the ability to make massive changes quickly and spreads power among a large group of representatives in multiple branches. This kept any of us from radically changing anything. But remove the Constitution and what do you have? An opportunity to implement massive change on a grand scale, quickly. This is where we are. Once the Constitution ceases to stop dangerous policy, you're on the way to one party rule. At best anarchy, at worst totalitarianism, socialism, or communism, it doesn't matter which. The result is the same. The end of freedom as we know it. Once this happens, the barbarians are at the gates and the guards are gone. This happened to Rome, and it is happening to us," said Banks emphatically, once again kicking off a coughing fit.

After Banks finished coughing and took another puff of his inhaler, Nick responded. "So, you think our colleagues who control the Senate, the House and the Presidency are about to throw away the Constitution and open the gates and let who through? The Russians, the Chinese? The Mexicans, Afghans, Guatemalans, Hondurans, and Haitians? Seems like we have already done all this. The filibuster and the Opposition didn't stop any of it," prompted Nick, challenging Banks.

"They won't do it willingly, but they're too naïve to understand their pet projects and policies are being driven by outside forces. The goal of these powers is beyond national borders. Our enemies have been playing the long game. Thinking and planning for decades. Slowly weakening our defenses, lulling us into thinking we're on the same side trying to solve the same problems, when they're just playing us. Distracting us with silly ephemeral priorities while they maneuver for concrete advantage."

"Senator, forgive my impertinence, but why are you telling me this? And why in riddles?"

"What I saw gave me hope. What you said, did you believe it, or did you just say it because you knew it would piss off our Party leaders?" asked Banks, leaning forward, scrutinizing Nick's answer.

"What do you think? You think I could have faked those feelings? I'm not that good," responded Nick with a laugh.

"That's what I thought. You have nothing to gain. It's not like the Opposition would welcome you either," mused Banks aloud.

"No one likes a rebel. I'm a man without a party."

Banks smiled. "Maybe in Washington, but everywhere else, they love you for what you say and what you *do*."

"Excuse me?" inquired Nick, looking at Banks.

"I may be old and social media baffles me, but I know *many* people who know these things. They tell me what you did is generating a lot of interest, way more than it should. It's all about the right time, right place, right message, and you are hitting all three," said Banks.

"More like slowing down to look at the wreck. They call all that attention online 'going viral'. It's like a disease," laughed Nick.

"It's the content of your tirade, the delivery of the message, the people who are looking at it, and how long they watch I'm noticing. This means they're not just looking at the wreck, they're reading and listening to the content, digesting what you said. I'm told 'Wilson' was the most searched term for the *week* after your interview with *Tommy*. People are thinking about it. More people understand the filibuster and what it means to have it gone, thanks to you. You can inspire and lead. I believe you can unite people," said Banks.

"The Senate is about to pass a resolution to censure me. I have no hope for re-election. What can I possibly do?"

Banks shrugged. "Movements have started with far less auspicious starts. You have momentum. Sometimes forces pull you in ways you least expect. Who says you can't win re-election? You can make a difference, because you are on to their game."

"You said it yourself, my Party hates me, the Opposition, while happy I helped, are no friends either. My polling is lower than ever in my home state. Independents are mere novelties."

"True, historically. But you said it yourself. There is a group of people who dislike what is happening. What if they are looking for someone to offer a choice between the parties?" offered Banks.

"That is an enormous task."

"Nick, how do you think Washington felt when he took over the Continental Army? He decided his job was not to win battles. Rather, to keep his army intact. Keep the idea of independence alive, long enough for the British to tire of the fight," explained Banks.

Nick contemplated the statement. "He believed in the fight for independence. He figured better to die trying than sit idly by."

"Precisely. Face it, you're not meant to sit 'idly by' on the sidelines. Your place is on the battlefield. Do not despair. I know about some of your other antics. Now is the time for you to come up with one of those brilliant plans," said Banks, a twinkle in his eye.

"Senator, I have no idea what you're talking about," lied Nick, smiling. "But thank you for the advice and the wonderful cognac."

"My pleasure *Senator*. God speed."

Chapter 47

Nick spent an hour in the morning meeting with a group of Colorado Rotary members in town for a conference. He spent the rest of the morning taking and making calls to constituents back home. It was one of his best days as a senator.

He heard from small business owners, housewives, teachers, medical doctors, college students, and even lawyers. Nearly all of whom agreed with his statements on *Tommy* and his vote. They were all universal in their condemnation of media outlets trying to imply Senator Wilhelm's death was Nick's fault.

He looked up from his seat in his office conference room at his pollster Jer, standing in front of the table pointing to slides he was showing on the big screen in the corner.

"Jer, what are the polls telling us?" asked Margie in an excited voice.

Jer showed a series of slides with bar charts and rattled off statistics about sample sizes and margins of error in the surveys. Others around the table smiled at Jer's obvious pleasure in slicing and dicing the numbers.

"Just net it out, Jer," said Margie, smiling at him.

He reddened a bit at Margie's attention.

"Basically, we're kicking ass," said Jer, with a smile on his nerdy face.

"That's a statistical term, right?" asked Nick, getting a laugh from the room.

"Sorry," said Jer. "The email, phone, and social media trends are all up. Some are as high as 4 to 1 favorable. None are less than 60/40 in our favor."

"The only people upset are the party leaders and their lapdogs in the mainstream media," stated Chuck, leaning back in his chair and turning to face Nick. "It seems they may have overplayed their hand going after you, especially on Wilhelm's death."

Nick looked around at the eager and smiling faces of his staff.

"We got another $1.5 million since the Thanksgiving break. That's more than $5 million since the vote," said Greg. "Keep it up, boss. Most of it isn't from within Colorado. Guess that is your answer, Chuck."

"I hate to break up the love fest, but legislatively, we are screwed," said Jenny, throwing her pen on her notebook and leaning back.

"How so?" asked Nick.

"As you suspected, they are removing you from the rest of your committee assignments and I've been told our legislation for the wildfire relief won't get a vote," she answered.

"Well, that sucks. Not unexpected," said Nick, thinking. "I really don't care so much about the committees, but the wildfire relief is important. Can we see if Jacobson in California or Cooper in Oregon would take over?"

"I can make some calls; it is worthy legislation, so somebody will pick it up," answered Chuck.

"Good, what else? There may not be much for us to do if they freeze me out? I guess we can find a picket line to join somewhere," laughed Nick.

"Well, the phones are ringing off the hook. Lots of groups want to visit and meet with you and not all from Colorado, just as Greg said on the fundraising," added Margie. "After EXN, you are being asked to come on a few networks and weekend shows, no doubt to be roasted."

"I'm curious, anything from Bergamo? Any comment directly or appearances on TV? Any other comments on what I said about her or didn't do on *Tommy*?" asked Nick.

"Just a few mentions about you questioning journalistic integrity and whether you actually have the footage, but nothing from her or her network directly," replied Margie.

"It surprised me I didn't have to fight my way through feminist groups to get to the office after the break. To hear them tell it, I all but clubbed her over the head with my intimidation tactics. I thought I showed amazing restraint," offered Nick. "Plus, I gave her a chance by not totally embarrassing her on TV. Oh, well."

"The other things you said have drawn some less than kind words from your colleagues in the Senate and our brethren in the House," remarked Margie. "I guess they decided it was easier to attack you on than the treatment of a reporter. The Speaker of the House and the Majority Leader both weighed in on your rampant disregard for the voters of Colorado and the trust placed in you by the Governor to follow in the footsteps of the Senator you succeeded," finished Margie, reading from her notes.

"They, of course, reiterated your selfishness and blatant disregard for loyalty. Making a couple more digs about you being the reason Wilhelm left his medically induced coma. Leaving his hospital room to stay alive only long enough to vote before conveniently dying so they can replace him with a living Party appointee. That last bit is me paraphrasing," ended Margie in a disgusted voice.

"Hmm, nothing about court packing, gun grabbing, expanding the Senate, or anything else I said they would do now that the filibuster was gone?" wondered Nick.

"Not a single denial, not even a halfhearted one."

"I know they are prepping the bills. They intend to ram these through before the primaries kick off," announced Jenny.

"As soon as Wilhelm's replacement is sworn in. They may even vote to Censure you, but some of that initial talk has died down. I think there are a few in the Party who wouldn't vote for that. The Opposition continues to praise your moment of bipartisanship," explained Chuck.

"Wonders never cease. Given our suddenly empty agendas, I understand if I need to write any recommendations for staff who want to jump ship," said Nick in all seriousness. Before Chuck could admonish Nick again for his lack of faith in his team, Greg broke in.

"Jer, can you shift over to TV and put it on EXN, please?"

The screen came on and showed Governor Harlan Grayson of North Carolina standing at a lectern. Behind him and to his right stood former Opposition Senator Betty Crawford.

"HOLY shit," said Chuck, standing up. "Is he nominating Crawford to fill out Wilhelm's term?"

"That's what the crawler says," said Jenny excitedly.

Nick just leaned back and smiled while everyone turned to look at him.

"You knew?" accused Chuck.

"I knew nuthing," said Nick in his best Sergeant Schultz accent.

"Crap, I would love to be a fly in Fontana's office right now. This changes *everything*," laughed Chuck.

Chapter 48

"What the fuck!" shouted Sal Fontana as he leaped to his feet, holding the phone. He reached for his remote and turned on the TV. Governor Grayson was speaking about how, "at this critical time in our country, it is necessary to put politics aside and nominate an experienced and principled person to the Senate. There is no one more qualified than our former Senator, Betty Crawford, who served honorably for three terms before retiring to tend to her ill husband. May he rest in peace. Senator Crawford has graciously agreed to jump into the fray once again and nobly represent North Carolina until the election next November," said Governor Grayson.

Lexi came charging into Fontana's office, followed by Ben and Mel. Even before the door fully shut, she was screaming at Fontana.

"Can you not control any of these fuckers?"

Sal turned, holding out his hands as if to fend off an attack by Lexi.

"I swear, just yesterday he told me he was going to nominate Jerry Broadhunt, who we recommended."

"He played you," said Lexi in disgust, her pretty face now a twisted mask of rage.

"You think he decided this on his own or you think he had help? I mean, he's ancient. He's got nothing to lose, and he needs nothing from us anymore," remarked Ben.

"That is exactly why we should have been worried. No leverage," answered Mel, standing in a corner, hand under chin, contemplating the next steps. "He can change his mind, knowing you have nothing to hit him with. In North Carolina, it is all his decision who to appoint. We can't stop him."

"So there go all our 'wins' before the primary, hell before the election. We'll get nothing the President promised done. This can't be happening," wailed Lexi, circling the room, throwing her hands in the air in frustration.

"We could try to win over Turner, maybe offer him a role in the new administration if he plays ball," suggested Ben.

"He's a fucking boy scout. My people could find nothing on him. He's also a fucking hero. He foiled a terrorist attack on US soil, his military record is full of medals, and he has no political track record to attack," said Fontana, now holding his hands up in defeat as he made these points.

"Everyone has a past; we just need to find it. Something they care about," said Lexi menacingly, as she sat in a chair.

"He doesn't even have a dog we can kill. No girlfriend, no ex, no kids, no siblings, no parents," said Sal, now leaning on the edge of his desk but keeping his distance from Lexi.

"He's never married. At his age, gay?" asked Mel.

"Don't think so. He's had girlfriends. Most ended OK. Seems to have a fear of commitment. Last one made him choose between her and flying. We know how that worked out. She's bitter but nothing else. He moves around a lot, no real roots. He seems to have settled in Colorado, now. Owns his house and has a cabin up in the mountains. Actually, I'm glad he isn't gay. Wouldn't look good if we were attacking a gay given our support for the LGBTQ community," said Ben, reading notes from his phone.

"Fellas, he's definitely not gay. I saw him dancing with Dolly. Trust me, those sparks were real," noted Lexi, annoyed as they flailed about.

"Has he ever posted anything or visited any shady sites?" asked Sal in a hopeful voice. "We can get NSA to go through his phone or FBI through his web surfing."

Ben laughed. "Way ahead of you. You'd think this guy was your age, Sal. He has no presence on social media. Never has. He has no internet record either. The only thing any of the agencies could ever find was research on history. Must have been a book he was working on or research when he was teaching," finished Ben, looking up from his phone.

"That's it. Surely there is a college student we can get to claim he harassed her or made advances. Even if he didn't, we must be able to find someone we can pay to say something. Some racist comment, a gay slur, something," said Mel, pacing at one end of the office, also keeping his distance from Lexi. He was well too aware of her vindictive nature. She would lash out at someone, and Mel intended it to be Sal.

"I'm telling you, any students we talked to loved him. It's almost as if he was there to build a background of nothing controversial. If that was the case, it worked," informed Ben. "Plus, there isn't enough time to mount a recall campaign and get him removed from office with the election in a year. We already looked into it."

Lexi sat silently fuming, "I don't really care what we do or how we do it, but we need to keep him from getting any more attention. Turn off the attack dogs. He's getting way too much coverage. We screwed this up once before, thinking we were hurting somebody and all we did was give him billions in free campaign coverage. Turner is a nobody. Talk to our friends in the media and make him a nobody again. Keep him off TV."

"You know we don't control EXN and some of the other smaller ones," replied Ben, not reading the room as Lexi stared daggers at him.

"Ben, we can put the pressure on them. We have friends at EXN too. He can keep going on *Tommy*, but we can put a stranglehold on their advertisers. That guy that does their Sunday interviews. He's on our side. He can do a hit job when we need it," offered Mel.

"Can we accuse him of something? Just get it out there and make him respond? Plant some kiddie porn on his laptop or something," asked Lexi, in an exasperated tone.

"It didn't work on the last few Supreme Court nominees. We tried the whole rape and religious fanatic angles. Thank God we had COVID, both times, and mail in ballots to fall back on. That sped up our alternative voting methods," said Mel with a smile. "The opposition is getting smarter. They don't immediately resign any longer. They take a page from our playbook and wait for it to blow over. We really haven't tried it on one of our own, but I don't think it would work," finished Mel, shaking his head at Lexi's suggestion.

"I want no more surprises." Lexi got up and stood in front of Sal, towering over him in her heels. "Get this under control, or else," she threatened, stalking out of the office.

Mel stayed behind and looked over to Sal. "What the fuck happened? We had Governor Grayson under control?"

"I literally talked to him last night, and he assured me it was going to be Broadhunt. Hell, I already had a speech ready welcoming him," said Sal, holding up some papers with handwritten notes he made a show of dumping in the trash.

"How bad does this hurt her?" asked Ben.

"It hurts us all; you know we've been whipping up the radical leftists and they're counting on us to deliver on the Supreme Court, police defunding, reparations, critical race theory, student loan relief and on and on. We can't count on the Chief Justice to keep helping us with everything. If we passed these bills, they were and are sure to be challenged in the court. We need the court first. Without this, it looks worse to do it and lose," said Mel, still sitting in front of the fireplace while Ben and Sal paced.

"Thankfully, the right is fragmented, and on the defense," voiced Sal, using his hands to make his points. "Surely, they can't mount a good campaign against us. So, we win back the Senate and expand our hold on the House. Our mail in ballot machine is only getting bigger and better and the same with harvesting laws becoming more and more prevalent. We killed the threat of voter IDs. We fought them off last election. It was their best chance to overtake us. Now we have the safeguards in place. We should be fine," said Sal. "We just have to wait until after the election and then we can implement all this. Lexi can still campaign on it and use it as a rallying cry to keep the coalition together."

"We'll see," worried Mel. "The people in flyover country are getting desperate. People everywhere are getting restless. It's like dry grass. Just waiting for a spark to ignite. We need to make sure we don't provide it."

Chapter 49

Lexi walked away from the Majority Leader's office toward her own Capitol Office. As she entered, her aide, Anastasia, handed her a stack of call notes. She entered her inner office, pulling the door shut behind her in Anastasia's face, making it clear she needed to be alone. She pulled out a secure Sat phone and dialed a number.

"I want to know who got to Governor Grayson. I want to know who he called and who called him," commanded Lexi, listening as she moved behind the desk and sat down in her chair.

"How are you doing on the other stuff?" asked Lexi, listening intently to the reply.

"Good. You have something on all of them? Great," she said.

"I want you to build one on Turner, too. If you need me to get Rhett involved, I can. Look into his overseas duty. Look into his staff. We know Robinson's background. Get me something to squeeze on those around him if we can't find anything on him."

"I don't care. You have the whole NSA. Use it. This is a national security concern," growled Lexi, listening. "Why? Because I said so!" shouted Lexi into her secure satellite phone. "Rhett has the CIA use it. FBI, DOJ, IRS, use the fucking Postal Service. I don't care," said Lexi, drawing each of the words out slowly and making her point very clear. "I want results, and if you want to keep your job in a year, I had better have them," she finished in a threatening tone.

She listened intently to the other side of the conversation.

"Don't worry, I have your back, just like we did on the Russia shit," said Lexi, hanging up the call. A knock at the door almost set her off before realizing it was probably Mel.

"Enter." Mel walked into the office and closed the door.

"We need to put more pressure on Turner, turn up the heat. If he won't play ball, let's get him on the defensive. I want people on every cable channel saying he killed old Wilhelm with his selfish actions."

"Lexi, you just said don't talk about him. We've already tried that. Like I said before, it's not working. We tried to embarrass him with Bergamo. That didn't work either. He's very good. By not showing the footage, which we didn't know he had, he defused the situation and turned it in his favor, *and* he didn't even have to show it. In women's eyes, this made him even more honorable because he didn't show up Bergamo. Hell, maybe he doesn't even have the footage. Remind me to never play poker with this guy," said Mel, taking a seat in a comfortable chair in Lexi's office.

Lexi listened intently, looking at Mel.

"You want a date with him?" She asked with a sneer. "I don't care about giving him exposure. I want him destroyed. He screwed up all our plans. What are we going to do now? We won't deliver all the promises we made, and all the other stuff we were going to do during the campaign to ensure I win in a landslide?" said Lexi with visible frustration.

"We'll deal with it," answered Mel calmly, trying to get her to settle down. "I have honed our machine to a sharp edge. Your opponents are all feckless and for show. The Opposition is fragmented, disunited, and their supporters are afraid to speak out publicly for fear of losing their jobs. We just resort to the same old playbook and make sure we win the same way we won last time."

"This was supposed to be different. It wasn't even supposed to be close. It's getting riskier. More and more people believe the elections aren't on the up and up," said Lexi, glaring at Mel.

"We'll continue to cancel them and call them out as conspiracy nut jobs intent on overthrowing the government. They can't get any traction when we control most of the media outlets. We have the military going woke. The corporations are spending billions on diversity training and suppressing any contrarian opinions as being racist, sexist or homophobic and a risk to further employment. We are strangling the corporations' funding unless they focus on their DEI initiatives to raise their ESG scores. With them on our side, doing the work of keeping people in line, we control the message and most people's livelihoods who work for others. We continue to make life miserable for the small business entrepreneur with tons more regulations and hoops to jump through and less funding at higher costs. We have a hold on everyone in some form," said Mel, stalking around the office, counting off these points on his fingers, encouraging Lexi to consider their position.

"The schools are ours. Every year we churn out a new generation of ill-prepared, pampered, woketivist children with limited skills and poor work ethics. Easily cowed peasants indoctrinated to do what we want, when we want it, at the slightest encouragement. Now with AI everywhere, we are dumbing them down even more. We control the algorithms, so they only see what we want them to see," Mel continued gleefully.

"The universities continue to do our bidding, in their idealistic simplicity, thinking their anti-capitalism is righteous, while simultaneously licking the boots of the Chinese to get their research grants. We now have everyone under the age of 40 fully immersed in our cultural rot. They do not have the backbone of the depression and cold war generations who could rally to the flag."

Lexi looked at Mel. "You always make it sound so easy. Yet it never works out that way."

"Lexi, times have changed. We fought a war for 4 1/2 years to avenge Pearl Harbor. Our comradery lasted a week after 9/11 and our good old buddies in the defense industry showed they were only in Afghanistan, Iraq, and Ukraine for the money. We are primed for an existential collapse. From the ashes you can rebuild and lead us into a better, kinder communal civilization where the tech oligarchs and the uber rich no longer get to live like kings on the backs of the people," said Mel.

"Thanks. Would you get me a coffee, please?" asked Lexi.

She sat back in her chair, staring into space, contemplating their situation. Lexi felt this could only end in Armageddon. Nuclear or otherwise, when the wrong people got hold of the wrong weapons and used them to punish these successful capitalists.

She believed it was her destiny to lead America and the world from the brink. To a place where more people have something, and fewer people have everything, instead of the vast majority having nothing.

As Mel arrived with the coffee, Lexi said. "Remind me to not have you write my acceptance speech. Unfortunately, we cannot be that honest with the people. They'll have a hard time understanding why not buying their next Range Rover would feed 10,000 people in Central Africa for a year," said Lexi.

"Back to Turner. I'm not worried about him. What can one man do? He had his five minutes of fame. Fontana is working on kicking him off the last committees. His legislation is dead. We have our hacks publishing stories in the local rags in Denver and Boulder blaming his antics for keeping the wildfire legislation from passing to help his state. We'll throw in some other items about him being in favor of base closings and things sure to rile up the Party base in Colorado. If he runs, we will primary him and cut off his money. Politically, he's done," said Mel with certainty. "Let us handle this. You just keep running the country."

Lexi sat studying Mel pensively. "I don't know. You said it yourself. None of our attacks so far have landed a punch. He seems to dodge and turn them into pluses. We either need to leave him alone or take him out of the picture, permanently," mused Lexi aloud.

"Permanently?" asked Mel.

Lexi leaned forward and put her hands on her desk. "Oh, come on Mel, getting soft on me? After Wilhelm? This is certainly not the first time. People disappear all the time. People have accidents."

"True," said Mel, "but a healthy sitting US Senator is on a whole different level, from a dying one in a coma."

Lexi shrugged. "Somebody did it to a president and nobody got convicted except the patsy."

"Well, I don't think Turner poses *that* level of problem. If that is your solution, you can *execute* that plan at any time. Let's focus on trying to discredit him and picking someone we can count on this time for the Senate in Colorado," said Mel, using emphasis and trying to dissuade Lexi from doing something she might regret.

"Agree. We need to kneecap Morris in Colorado. He put us in this position so he could help his reelection efforts. Now he is hurting mine. If he thinks he is joining my administration, he is sadly mistaken. And Grayson. He may not care, but put the screws to his kids and their kids. I want him to understand you don't fuck with us," laughed Lexi menacingly. "What else is on the docket?"

\#

Once again, the conversation was being recorded and encrypted. It was then sent out over a series of secure communications lines to various places around the world.

Chapter 50

Lauren Bergamo came into the conference room in the National Press Club where Senator Turner was giving his press conference. She stood at a seat in the second row, next to a distinguished looking gray-haired man.

"Adam, this seat taken?" asked Lauren with a bright smile.

Adam Mullen glanced up at the pretty auburn-haired reporter. Lauren wore a midnight blue dress and beige high heels, the form fitting dress accentuating her beauty.

"Be my guest, Miss Bergamo," he replied, frostily.

"Miss Bergamo? Why so formal, Adam?" Lauren asked with a smile as she sat.

"Well Lauren, what you did to Turner wasn't right. Call me old school. I still believe in facts and letting people form their own opinion. I don't feel it's my job to tell people what to think. That's why I got fired from ANC," revealed Adam.

"And ended up at EXN, where nothing but facts are reported?" asked Lauren sarcastically.

"At least we try with our news to report the facts and let people decide, unlike every other network, where every news show is also an opinion show," retorted Adam.

"Somebody got up on the wrong side of the bed this morning," responded Lauren. "Maybe I'll find another seat."

"Fine by me."

As Lauren got up and turned to go, several other news reporters looked away, pretending to not be listening to their exchange.

"Just for the record," she said, looking down at Adam. "I did want to show the whole tape of my conversation with Turner. My producers wouldn't let me, and they edited it the way they did."

"That's not okay, Lauren. It doesn't let you off the hook. It just perpetuates the problem. The people have lost faith in *all* of us. They know we're lying to them. That we're trying to tell them what to think. Episodes like yours, especially when there's evidence showing someone edited it to mislead, make it harder for all of us," said Adam in a raised voice, gesturing with his hands.

"What was I supposed to do, quit?" asked Lauren, still standing next to Adam and looking down at him with a fire in her eyes.

"Lauren, all you have is your integrity," shrugged Adam.

The reporter behind them pointed to the lectern where Nick was standing. Lauren blushed deep red, quickly sitting down.

"Don't let me interrupt, it was just getting good," said Nick, smiling as others also laughed, while Lauren turned even redder.

Adam hid a smile. Lauren looked like she wanted to crawl under her chair. "My apologies Senator."

"Accepted. After all, I'm supposed to be the news here," said Nick in a conversational tone. "Let's get started."

"First, I want to say how grateful and honored I am to represent the good citizens of Colorado. I take this job seriously and I believe it is my duty to all these citizens to do the best I can and to act honestly and call things as I see them. For that I make no apology."

A reporter behind Lauren whispered to his neighbor, "You owe me $20. I told you he was going to resign." His seat mate whispered back, "He ain't done yet." Lauren glanced at them disapprovingly.

"Lately, I've made some statements and perhaps a vote or two that have ruffled a few feathers," deadpanned Nick, as the room laughed.

"Seriously though, I've been in Washington for a year. It has certainly been an eye-opening experience. I know there are a lot of folks expecting or hoping I'm here to apologize or admit the error of my ways. I've done a few things in my life. Aspiring to public office was never one of them. Yet here I am," Nick paused. He saw the bank of cameras in the back, all broadcasting his speech live. He had his audience.

"As you also know, I am a veteran and swore an oath to protect the Constitution and the people of the United States. I know what it takes to defend the Constitution of this country against enemies, foreign and domestic. The risks and the sacrifices made every day, countless times by our fathers and mothers to allow us to live the way we choose. Yet I'm serving again, for the same purpose, and even though the bullets aren't flying, this is still a battlefield. One of words and ideas, rhetoric and lies, and money, power, and control. I can tell you; this battlefield is every bit as vicious as anything I saw in Iraq or Afghanistan." Nick heard murmurs in the crowd at his revelation.

Nick let his statement sink in. "I won't apologize for what I said. It was from the heart and is what I see daily. I don't mean this to be disrespectful, but it reiterates what I said. I believe it was truthful and I stand by it fully. Nor am I going to resign. I took an oath to serve and defend and I'll continue to do so."

"Out of respect for my Party colleagues, I can no longer serve as a member of this Party. My personal beliefs, feelings, and outlook about how government should run, following the guidelines of our Constitution, conflicts with the goals of Party leadership."

There were audible gasps in the audience. Looking over the crowd, Nick could only imagine the texts. Saying he was joining the Opposition. "However, as I don't agree completely with the Opposition view on governing, I won't be joining their party either."

"I believe it best to become an independent member of Congress, not part of either party and free to vote in the best interests of my constituents, free from party pressure." As Nick paused, reporters started raising hands and shouting questions.

Nick raised his hand. "Hang on, while I know you have a lot of questions, I'm not done."

"I believe I'm here, at this moment in our time, for a reason, just as I was in New York. I truly believe this," said Nick in a forceful tone.

"I believe in fate, and I believe equally in faith. Between these two, I think there is a reason for everything."

"With the freedom to fail and the freedom to succeed. There has been no greater result in history than what we have achieved while living under the framework provided by the Constitution, ratified 250 years ago. We've made mistakes, but we could also acknowledge and fix them. My intent is to use my remaining time in office to educate all who'll listen about how we've lost our way. How greed for money and power corrupted this society our forefathers built," explained Nick.

He looked out over the fifty reporters seated in the room, at the TV cameras in the back of the room with their blinking red lights, and at members of his staff standing around the perimeter, all smiling encouragement as he made eye contact. Kevin, one of his interns, even gave him a thumbs up. No reporters jumped in at this pause, sensing he was still not done with his statement.

"Given the fact I have destroyed my political career, seemingly before it has begun, I feel there is only one logical step," continued Nick with a wry smile. "Today I formally announce I'll run for President of the United States as an Independent, not seeking the nomination of either party."

This elicited gasps of astonishment from the reporters assembled. "What the…" said the reporter behind Lauren, handing a $20 bill to the reporter next him. "You win," he said, laughing. The other reporter took the twenty. "I didn't see that coming, but I'll take your money."

Several reporters asked questions. Nick once again held up a hand. He glanced at Chuck in the back of the room, wishing he had a camera to take a picture of his dumbfounded chief of staff's face.

"A few more things and then I promise I'll answer questions."

"While some may feel this is a publicity stunt, I assure you it is not. Like some before me, I've concluded our government, as it is today, is ineffective and, in many cases, hopelessly corrupt. Our institutions are compromised and beholden to outside influence and, most of all, to big money elites. Whether it is big business or sovereign nations, we have lost sight of the fact that America is a shining beacon on a hill. Something to inspire joy, hope, and the promise of a better life. Today, it no longer represents that to so many."

"I used to teach history, not the revisionist history taught today, but actual factual history. History does repeat itself. Very little happening today cannot also be found in some historical context. This also includes the ability to know and understand the consequences of those decisions. We are ignoring this at our own peril. Allowing our society and our fundamental principles to erode to where we can no longer preserve the freedoms that made us the greatest and freest society the planet has ever seen," declared Nick, as reporters were busy scribbling notes on pads and phones.

"My candidacy will focus not on making promises to curry favor with big money donors, but on educating the people who suffer the most; the Americans who go to work every day trying to provide for their family. Hoping for a better life for themselves, their children, and grandchildren. The people forgotten in Washington or taken for granted and only catered too every four years to cast a vote."

"I believe our challenge is voters who are uninformed. I'll provide them with facts. Enable them to ask the right questions of their candidates. Why they make the decisions they make and who benefits from each of these? In the end, everything in Washington comes down to money and power. We need to cut through the bullshit, find out who gets the money, and with that, the power to spend it to help their friends. You can be sure they don't spend it on *you*. Once voters find this out, watch out! They're going to be pissed."

Nick took a deep breath and continued, "I want to have some honest conversations with everyday Americans. To understand what issues they face. To help them understand how the government is supposed to work. How it used to work, and the truth about what has happened. I want to teach people stuff no longer taught in school. Civics and responsibility. About the social contract between citizens and their government. Of the importance of trust and faith in their neighbor, a higher power, and the need for morals and ethics."

"I want to show people how to think for themselves. Not tell them what to think. Actions have consequences, but inaction has consequences as well. Do not sit on the sideline. Get smart, understand what needs to change. Question those claiming to have the answers and force your candidates to live up to their promises. At the end of all this, I want people to cast an informed vote, one they make based on facts and research they do themselves. Not what is fed to them by newspapers, cable channels, social media, and Hollywood. To hold those they vote for accountable."

"*Think for Yourself.* That is my campaign slogan and the purpose of my candidacy. To help everyone free themselves from the enslavement of misinformation in the media. I have faith in all of you out there. Once you do this, you'll make the correct choice for yourself, for your family, for your community, and ultimately for this country," said Nick, finishing.

He looked out over the sea of stunned reporters, eagerly holding up hands to fire questions at him.

"Fire away," said Nick. "Adam?"

Adam Mullen of EXN stood up. "Senator, I think I speak for my colleagues here. This is *not* what we expected." The audience laughed at Adam's understatement. "That being said, my first of many questions would be, how do you expect to continue in the Senate with your obvious disdain for both parties?"

"Good question Adam. There are well meaning Party and Opposition members in both chambers. I believe party politics has trumped the good of the people and replaced it with the good of the party. The good of both parties' big donors and *their* agenda. This causes block voting on individual issues. Places where moderates on both sides might be inclined to find a compromise decision are no longer permitted. This goes by the wayside because it does not fit the party narrative when both sides work together. Of course, it would limit their funding and potential lucrative work after public office if they compromised." Nick paused, standing tall behind the podium.

"Since I expect neither of those, I can be honest. What people seem to have forgotten is we sent them to Washington to work together. Not solely to pass partisan legislature and make sure the other side gets nothing they want. This is not a football game. There shouldn't be a winning and a losing side. As an independent Adam, I intend to be just that. I'll support and vote for legislation I believe is in the best interests of Colorado, and the country, and oppose what I believe isn't helpful to the wellbeing of all Americans."

Nick pointed to a woman in the front row. "Beverly."

"Senator, running for president is not something one does on a whim," this from Beverly James from NWN news. "The last presidential race saw each of the candidates spending a billion dollars or more. They started building organizations and raising money long before they announced. As far as I can tell, you have neither."

"You make a great point. While I haven't been planning to run for President my whole life and haven't been working my way up through local politics to mayor to state office to governor or congressman to senator and raising the corresponding war chest, I still feel it is appropriate. There are several reasons. First, while not coming up the traditional way, I haven't had to make and pay back favors to achieve my position. Trust me, Governor Morris didn't expect to be paid back in this manner," the audience laughed.

"On a more serious note, I am also not beholden to anyone. Have no markers to be called. I haven't taken money from big media, or tech, or sovereign wealth funds. Nor do I have a PAC. I don't intend to start now either. Second, I also do not have a record of decisions. I won't have to contradict prior votes and explain why I was for something once and am now against it to appease a new donor or activists whose favor I am trying to curry. I think both are advantages, not disadvantages."

Lauren had her hand up, trying to get Nick's attention. He glanced at her, made eye contact, and chose the person behind her.

"Senator Turner, since you're not running for either major party's nomination, how do you intend to reach people?" asked a reporter from *Reuters*.

"Grass roots. I just came back from a tour I took of Colorado. I stopped in small towns and sat down with everyday Americans. No cameras, no entourage, no sound bites, and no staged pictures. Just me alone and them. It was eye opening. Mostly, what we're focused on here on the Hill is nowhere near the top of the average American's priority list. Before you ask, yes, I spoke to people of all races, gay and straight, old, and young and from all parties. Jobs are number one, followed by education for their kids and safety for themselves, their property, and their country. I intend to talk to as many people as I can everywhere I can. I make no promises other than to listen to what they have to say and use common sense to get back to the way our founders expected us to be. To trust our neighbors and work with them to build a community built on mutual trust and mutual benefit," explained Nick.

"Senator," said *Reuters*, following up. "No offence, but what you're saying sounds pretty naïve. You have no money. No local organizations. No Presidential Election committee. You have no campaign manager. This seems like an emotional decision. I get you're unhappy with how things work in Washington. You may not fit in, but announcing a run for President is a bit spur of the moment."

"Maybe you're right. But this *is* America. You can be whatever you want. Not being a swamp creature is a good thing. I could be wrong. In which case, I'm sure you'll use up gallons of digital ink, pointing this out. I feel there are many people on all sides of the aisle who are upset with our government. Upset with both parties, our media and how the elites get richer as the working class keeps working harder and harder to stay afloat. Don't get me wrong, I'm not a socialist. I don't believe in redistribution. I don't want to seize what the rich have and give it to the poor."

"What I want is equality of opportunity. I want to remove their hands from the levers of power or cut the puppet strings they hold.

Use whatever analogy you would like. Free markets and unlimited opportunity enabled America to achieve what we did before we lost our way. I don't intend to penalize those with a work ethic and a willingness to do it. In fact, I would hope to instill it in more folks. By the same token, China has achieved their success, not through freedom, but through coercion, intellectual property theft, suppressing their people with threats, taking advantage of other's weaknesses, including America. We cannot blame them for taking advantage of us if we willingly let them and, in fact, encouraged it. So no, I don't consider myself naïve, just not corrupted by Washington."

Lauren waved her hand again while Nick called on another.

"Senator, why not switch to the Opposition party? What you're saying today seems more in line with their platform?" asked the *Washington NewDay* reporter.

"I thought about it. After about 10 seconds, I realized it would be no different. Since I have pissed everyone on the Party side off, I might as well do the same to my colleagues on the right. The Party is unified and almost always vote as a block, regardless of topic. Leadership says jump and they dutifully say how high. This is how you get money for reelection campaigns, get on committees, and get influence in the Party. It is the party of conforming to leadership wishes. Obviously, I don't follow well. I have to vote for all the folks back home and sometimes it's different from what the Party leaders want. I know it's an alien concept," Nick smiled at the last part.

"The Opposition seems happiest when they're in the minority, like now. Raising issues, making noise, and complaining, but never really accomplishing anything. I don't mean to be so critical and as I have said, there are individuals on both sides who are well-intentioned and honest people. But they too have become 'corrupted' by Washington and the need to keep getting reelected. This changes everyone who gets here. They came in, like me, full of ideas, and then they decide they really like everyone deferring to them and the 'so called' power they think they have. I wouldn't be happy or useful there either. The Opposition talks a great game, but in the end the Party wins. They show up at the fight with a knife, bat, gun, bazooka. The Opposition shows up and asks to be shown to their seat in the stands. It is not a fair fight," said Nick, shaking his head.

At the pause, Lauren blurted out a question without being called upon. "Senator, you're painting with a broad brush, accusing all your colleagues of being ineffective and corrupt without proof."

Nick stared at Lauren for a moment. He ignored her question, calling on another further back in the room.

"Senator, you sound like all the other candidates and their sound bites at town halls and on cable shows. Why should people believe you are any different?" asked a reporter from *People's Voice*, cynically.

"You know, *that* is a wonderful question," said Nick, giving a glance to Lauren. "Let's think about this for a moment. Have you heard any of them telling you the truth and their own opinion like I have today? Seen anyone stand up for their convictions, not just on a cable show, but on the floor of the Senate like I did, and buck their party? Have you seen anyone get a witness at a committee hearing to tell the truth and get off script like I did? My campaign will be honest. It may not win me votes, but it will be an honest dialogue with the people I talk to. It will not be sound bites and empty promises designed to not make anyone mad while taking their money. I think people can expect something entirely different," said Nick in a determined tone.

"Senator, every candidate says that," responded the reporter.

"Then I guess you'll just have to watch and see if I keep *my* promise," replied Nick. "I hope you'll report it when I do, but frankly, I expect you'll get pressure not to. It would definitely be counter to your marching orders from the Party leaders," accused Nick.

"Senator, I can assure you I don't get orders from anyone," replied the reporter.

"I'm not here to argue with you, but I think the collective actions of most of the mainstream media reveal a bias in favor of the Party's platforms and against anything else. I don't know if it is consciously directed or simply like-minded. I say this as someone from inside the Party who has seen this in action," responded Nick, once again holding up his hand. "There is no need to defend yourself or your publication. Actions are speaking way louder than denials. This is another reason I just can't stay in the Party. There is a general disregard for what the people think and a belief that only the leadership has the intelligence to understand what needs to be done. The mainstream media is *generally* their willing propaganda arm."

The reporter was shaking her head in disagreement.

"You may agree with their position's, and you may think you're being unbiased, but look at the polls. No one trusts you. Take heart. They trust Congress only slightly more than you. You're not alone at the bottom of the popularity and trust chart," revealed Nick.

"The truly sad part is you squandered your franchise. People relied on you for facts and information. When you were more subtle, you could still manipulate folks to follow where you led. Then others started offering programming countering your narrative, other sources, other takes on the facts. You panicked. Suddenly, subtlety went out the window. Your efforts became overt, manipulative, and one-sided. Misinformation and lies masked as truth. Best of all, the politics of personal destruction aimed at anyone with a differing opinion. You did this to yourselves. *This* is why no one trusts you."

"Senator, I don't know how presenting facts can be called lying or propaganda?" replied the *People's Voice* reporter.

"The true facts no longer matter. Only the view of the facts as you see them. Parsed as you want them to see it. Omit a sentence to change the context. Cut a piece of the video to remove a clarifying statement," said Nick while looking at Lauren, who met his gaze defiantly. "Your profession broke that trust and now you're paying the price. We're all paying the price of not having news organizations dedicated to presenting just the facts without bias. Now we're all tribes, only listening to what matches our beliefs. We no longer look at issues from multiple sides or, God forbid, debate," explained Nick.

"Senator, this sounds like QAnon stuff," said a voice from the back of the room.

Nick looked up, trying to see who shouted out the question.

"Who asked that please?" said Nick, looking around the room. No one held up a hand or claimed to have asked it.

"Typical. And so, it begins," laughed Nick, shaking his head and looking at his watch. "You guys work fast. This is exactly what I expected. Twenty minutes into my campaign, some Party operative from the crowd shouts out the provocative question, anonymously, and flees like a coward. Folks," Nick looked into the camera, "get used to this. What did I just say? Speaking the truth is dangerous. They'll do anything they can to keep you from listening. From thinking for yourself, from forming your own opinion. Get ready for attacks on me and my character and my beliefs, cast as some sort of kook fringe ideas, leading the country to ruin. Well, that is exactly why I'm standing here. Look at that, ANC just turned off their camera. And there goes FLCN and NWN," said Nick, laughing.

"For the cameras still on and brave enough to show this footage, I don't and am not part of any QAnon, nor do I support it. I'll say this: we have a problem. We elect 535 congressmen and one president. While many of the 535 are looking out for themselves and their big donors. The problem is hundreds of thousands of unelected career bureaucrats running the country. Party or Opposition, it doesn't matter to them. This is the swamp, deep state, global elite. Call it what you will. These unelected bureaucrats run the country and they are not beholden to any of you. This should concern you, regardless of the party. It affects your life." No one tried to interrupt Nick this time as he paused.

"You must get smarter about how Washington runs. Think about it, we have seen the Intelligence agencies politicized. There are thousands of others in the FDA, State, FCC, Commerce, HUD, Education, Transportation, EPA, and many other executive agencies. Sure, the president appoints the leader, but the management and the staff stay the same, year after year. They make policy. They implement and enforce policy. You and Congress really have no say in this. Just something further to concern you; there are now over

75 armed agencies. The number of armed federal agents and officers in these agencies outnumbers the Marines. Think about that. Your bureaucratic, unelected officials have at their disposal an armed force larger than the United States Marines."

Nick continued. "You don't have to believe in QAnon to worry that a collective group of anonymous staffers in these organizations are making laws and policies that affect your life, sometimes significantly, with no visibility or accountability. Who is giving them their direction? You guessed it. Big money lobbies. You may not know this, oh hey, there goes another camera," said Nick, pointing, "but congressmen do not write their own bills. Lobbyist and staffers do. You remember affordable healthcare, and the famous 'We need to pass it to find out what was in it' statement by a former Speaker of the House?"

"She said the quiet part out loud. Whoops! The bills are often open-ended and leave the last details to be worked out by staffers and lobbyists. What the rules are and how they are enforced are usually written to favor these big money lobbies and enrich their principals. There is too much money available, and it is too easy for them to dip their snouts in the trough."

"For those willing to listen and to cover," said Nick, waving at the cameras. "This, and many like it, will be the conversations I'll have with Americans on the campaign trail. Trying to educate them on how Washington works and how they can go about fixing it. Thank you for attending. It will be interesting to see who shows what, and how this is reported. We'll make the entire speech available on social media, at least until they ban me," laughed Nick, as he turned to leave the podium.

Lauren Bergamo commented loudly, "I guess my question was too tough to answer?"

Nick stopped and turned back. Chuck, who had recovered from his shock and was back at his side, grabbed his arm to continue to steer him out of the room. Nick calmly removed his arm and turned back to address the now standing crowd.

"Miss Bergamo, you have something to say?" asked Nick, as the others in the room turned, sensing a confrontation about to happen. The EXN camera kept running and several others turned their equipment back on.

"Only that you appeared unwilling to answer my earlier question," accused Lauren.

"You mean the question you blurted out without being recognized?" said Nick in a slightly condescending tone. "I simply expressed my opinion that Congress is beholden to big money. No one has an honest opinion, or rather, will express an honest opinion publicly for fear of retaliation or dishonest reporting of the facts," stated Nick, staring at Lauren, who blushed a bit at the last part.

"Senator, do you not think you are betraying your governor, your constituents and that you are partially responsible for Senator Wilhelm having to travel from the hospital in his delicate state, indirectly leading to his death, as many say?" countered Lauren.

"You are tenacious. I'll give you credit." Nick shook his head. "Miss Bergamo, I am a thinking person, not a puppet. I apologize to the Governor if he thought he was nominating a mindless drone to this Senate seat. One who would do as the Party leadership and media demand, out of fear. I won't apologize for having a mind, a conscience, and using both to vote against legislation that hurts my constituents and country." Nick stopped, hesitating before continuing, and then kept talking.

"As for Senator Wilhelm's tragic death, if you and your other shameless cohorts in the media see fit to blame me for his death, I cannot stop you. It's yet another example of the abuse of the trust the country should place in your profession to tell the truth. It isn't something you and your network are concerned with. The blame for Senator Wilhelm's death lies with those who woke him from his coma and drove him to the Capitol to vote for this legislation. I'm sure you can watch my unedited comments from *Tommy* online."

Nick took a deep breath and continued in a now calm voice.

"You want justice or someone to blame? Do the research and expose that decision process that led to him being brought to the Senate chamber. Ask Governor Grayson. Evidently, he too believes the treatment of Senator Wilhelm was less than compassionate, as witnessed by his choice of replacement. The Governor also believes in the Constitution and the need to preserve the minority's rights in congress." Nick now faced the camera and looked directly into it, rather than at Lauren.

"Perhaps, in retrospect, the question one should ask is to the Majority Leader and the Vice President. If their efforts to get Senator Wilhelm, especially in his condition, to the chamber to vote, was worth his life? Did he even know what he was voting 'yes' to? I suspect one does not wake from a coma with all faculties immediately intact. Did he even know he was casting the deciding vote to destroy the Constitution? I'm not a medical professional. Ask those questions and broadcast those answers and it will impress me. Good day Miss Bergamo," said Nick, this time turning and walking away as a barrage of questions were hurled at the back of his head.

As the reporters stood and collected their things, typing and talking on phones to producers and news desks, Adam turned to Lauren.

"What is with you?" he asked. "You trying to get a book deal or get on a network news desk?"

"He drives me crazy. I didn't choose to air the footage the way it was done, like I told you."

"Let me give you some advice. He's winning. Every time you question him, he's making you look less and less credible. When you attack him, you give him a chance to turn it back on you. Like he just did. Unfortunately, this last bit is what they will show, or selectively edit instead of anything else he said, at least on ANC."

Lauren just gave him a look of desperation. Adam felt a moment of pity. A lifetime of being in the arena, covering the White House, had left him jaded and cynical. He couldn't help but feel sorry for the lovely young woman standing before him, confused and angry. But in time, she would learn the same lessons. The hard way, just as he had.

"It's just going to give him more ammunition because he's going to claim, rightfully, once again, that 'we' are lying about what he said. He'll be right. We're helping him make his point and he is manipulating us into doing it willingly. I wouldn't underestimate this guy. He's very good, and is speaking from the heart. None of what he said was rehearsed or memorized. It was all ad lib. If I were Smythe-Thomas, I'd be worried," finished Adam.

Lauren looked exasperated for a second, not sure what to say. "What am I supposed to do? Every time I ask him a question, he's going to attack me, all because my producers showed what they wanted. I can't help that."

"Lauren, I'd try to get a private audience and explain to him you didn't decide on what to show from that clip in the Senate. He may or may not believe you, but if you don't, he is going to consider you public enemy number one and use you as his example every time he wants to point out the dishonesty of the media. I guarantee you right now *your* producers are making this feud between him and you, *the story*."

"Shit," said Lauren, looking around in frustration. "Thanks for the advice, Adam, but I think my chances of getting a private audience with him are zilch."

"Good luck, but heed my warning. Your producers will be happy to sacrifice you on the altar of ratings if they think they can use you to get him to blow up in front of the cameras. It's your choice to choose to let them use you this way or not."

#

As they left the press conference, Chuck almost sprinting to keep up with Nick's fast walking. "Thanks for the heads up. Much appreciated," finished Chuck in an out of breath and frustrated voice.

Nick glanced at him, smiling.

"Didn't want to give you a chance to talk me out of it."

"I'll schedule a press conference tomorrow where you can tell them all you are off your meds and claim temporary insanity," responded Chuck in all seriousness.

Nick just smiled back as they continued their walk to his office, surrounded by smiling and exuberant staff.

"You *were* kidding, right?" asked Chuck, as Nick returned his look and laughed.

Chapter 51

Lexi and Mel were sitting in her office drinking tea, watching Nick give his press conference.

"So, he isn't going to resign. Too bad," remarked Lexi.

"You really didn't think he would do that, did you? Especially with the Opposition at fifty, with Wilhelm's replacement. He isn't going to let us get back to 50/50 so you can break the tie."

"One can hope. Maybe he'll have a stroke and die."

"Unlikely. He is without a doubt in the best physical shape of anyone in the Senate, probably the House as well," laughed Mel.

They continued to watch and sip their tea.

"Fuck," said Lexi in an unladylike tone, reaching for her phone.

"Get your ass over here!" shouted Lexi into the phone. "Now."

"Well, that was certainly unexpected," stated Mel calmly.

"Unexpected? That's all you can say?" asked Lexi, fuming.

"It doesn't really matter, Party or Independent, he is still against us. At least he didn't switch parties. That would have been worse optically," said Mel.

"Why can't he just shut up and write a book or something?" said Lexi, gritting her perfect teeth.

There was a knock at the door. Mel got up and walked to the door to let the Majority Leader and Ben into the office.

"President? Who is he kidding?" laughed Sal, with his phone in his hand, having just seen Nick make his announcement.

"I don't like it. Can we do a recall campaign?" asked Lexi.

"Not much reason to do that, since there is an election in less than a year," answered Mel. "Would just look vindictive on our part and a waste of people's time and money. The Opposition can't pass anything either since we own the House. We get more gridlock for a year. We'll use this as a hammer to hit the Opposition candidates over the head, and Turner if he becomes relevant."

"What about Bergamo? She sure seems to get under his skin," asked Lexi as she continued to watch the press conference and see Nick purposely ignoring Lauren.

"We might be able to use her. She's a climber and ambitious. Trying to make a name for herself," agreed Mel.

He dialed his phone and spoke a few words. No one else could hear from a corner of the room where he stood.

Continuing to watch the press conference, the screens went back to commentators at the QAnon question.

"What the hell," complained Lexi. "Sal, put it on EXN."

"I told them to cut away if he bashed us anymore," noted Mel.

They looked at the press conference on EXN and watched as Nick accused the media of being a mouthpiece of the Party. They also witnessed his last exchange with Lauren.

"If some investigative reporter starts nosing around, like he suggests, they are going to find out who 'did' give the orders to wake up Wilhelm, we'll have a problem," Sal said, concerned.

"Don't worry about it. We have it covered," assured Lexi.

"I hope so," worried Sal. "I know he had a private nurse."

Lexi ignored him. "Let's definitely see what we can do to use Bergamo as his foil. She likes to push his buttons. Maybe we can get him to screw up on camera and say something we can use."

"I'll make some calls," nodded Mel. "Make sure she is on the ANC team covering him."

"Do we want to make a statement about him switching parties or his claims about Senator Wilhelm, or any of the other provocative statements about everyone being corrupt? There are so many angles," asked Fontana's chief of staff Ben, speaking for the first time.

"Ya, we'll hit him with both barrels, the little putz," gloated Sal.

"Don't think you want to say that to his face," laughed Mel.

"I ain't afraid of him."

"You should be. He has already screwed up our legislative plan and our campaign strategy. He is catching on fast," stated Mel.

"I disagree. Let's stomp on him like the ant he is. I want 24x7 hate. I don't care if you make it up. Discredit him," ordered Lexi.

"Lexi, you made me your campaign manager for a reason. We made this mistake before. We cannot make this guy the story. It's a mistake. I say we ignore him as much as possible. Starve him and keep him off TV. Off social media. He'll have to rely on EXN and alternate sources. It's not enough and if he keeps it up, he's going to piss off the higher ups at EXN too. My advice, ignore him."

"This doesn't seem like you?" mused Lexi with a sideways look.

Mel stood up. "Think about it. He has nothing, just like they said. He has no money, staff, expertise, no state or national organization, and he won't get exposure during the primaries and those debates. If he is still in it when we get to the debates, we set the rules and we can keep him out. I doubt he lasts that long anyway. His staff are all neophytes except Robinson, and he can't do it all."

"You have fourteen Party and twelve Opposition candidates running. No chance any of the good campaign managers are going to jump ship to work with him. They know they'd never work on a legit campaign again," said Mel. He was using his hands as he lectured to his audience, just like his Harvard days. "He has no local networks, no campaign offices, no fundraising team, no infrastructure, no call lists, no mail lists, and nobody who can even begin to understand how to raise the kind of money it will take to compete."

"Once he gets his free press for this, the networks will give up on him and he'll lose access. We'll see to that. Strangle his access to money, social media, the web, and networks. With none of this, he can't survive. By the time we run the first primaries, he'll be broke and out of the picture. Just a memory by Super Tuesday."

"Let's make sure we keep him off TV. Sal, no time on the floor. Don't give him a chance to grandstand," ordered Lexi.

"Got it," nodded Sal. "We already removed him from his committees, and now that he is independent, we don't have to give him anything. I suppose the Opposition could, but jeez, after what he just said, he isn't making any friends there either. What is up with this guy? He is trying to piss off everyone. And succeeding."

"OK, if you think that is the best approach, Mel, fine. I don't agree, but as you say, I put you in charge. Alright boys, operation ignore starts now."

As the men made to leave Lexi's office, Mel stopped.

"Oh, and by the way, in case you didn't hear, Senator Wilhelm's private nurse was tragically killed in a hit-and-run accident this morning on her way to a lawyer's office."

"How unfortunate," remarked Lexi as Sal snickered, leaving Lexi alone in her office.

Chapter 52

A tall and slender, but powerfully built man with dark hair, an oiled black mustache and beard approached Maksim Pavlovich. He stood in front of the desk in the library, in the military at ease position.

"You summoned me?" asked Roland Gill, tensing as he saw a damaged military pilot's helmet on the desk. He recognized it.

"How is Paris?" asked Maksim with a sly smile.

"Still chaotic after the bombing. They are making all kinds of concessions to the immigrants and the yellow vests to get them to stop agitating. It'll work long enough to get Chaumont elected in a few weeks. But he too, like all the others, will fail. They are too French," said Roland with a shrug.

Maksim nodded. "And too white. They will never allow equal status for their immigrants. America is much more integrated than a country like France or any other country, no matter what the agitators say. Visit a slum in Mumbai, London, Sao Paulo, or a *banlieue* in Paris and see true government supported segregation. The poor in America would be middle class or higher in most of these countries. These other countries have multi-generational segregation and poverty down to an art form," opined Pavlovich shaking his head.

Roland merely nodded as Maksim continued.

"Your plan worked brilliantly. I admit I had my doubts as to the stability of your 'soldiers'," admitted Maksim.

"Not all are suited to the task, but there are plenty to choose from. The autistic are not treated well in France. The parents usually send them to special orphanages once the level of care required sinks in. Soon the visits drop off and the child grows up a ward of the state. It is easy enough to convince the caretakers to release them to our care. Contributions to their general fund buy silence. I observed our soldier during the rally. He remained calm, no doubt repeating his mantra."

Maksim nodded as Roland continued.

"However, we'll have to work on this. Had this not been short notice, I believe the police would have picked him out, as he wasn't demonstrating or responding to the speech like those around him. I have instructed the Doctor to consider other ways to ensure compliance but still allow for some level of normalcy. I cannot confirm this would work again, unfortunately. Certainly not in the United States. To many observant citizens," finished Roland.

"Any chance they discover you loaded up an autistic man with a suicide vest and used him as a living bomb?" asked Maksim.

"Unlikely. Even if they have retrieved his DNA, it won't be in any database. They'll assume it is from someone in the crowd," said Roland. "Luc Gauthier has involved himself though."

"Oh really? Our old friend Luc? Is he making any progress?"

"There is nothing to find. But I believe Chaumont brought him into the case when the local authorities found nothing. There are no leads to pursue. No one claiming responsibility. That has to be driving him crazy. Who goes to the trouble of killing a National President and doesn't take credit for such a spectacular success?"

"True. Watch Luc. He is like a dog with a bone and never relents. He no longer has a family we can threaten to dissuade him."

Roland merely shrugged at the last.

"I will monitor his progress."

"Good," he nodded. "Roland, I am concerned. You understand I dislike uncertainty."

"Yes, I'm aware of your ire when things don't go as planned," said Roland, rubbing a hand over a scar on the right side of his face. A thin line, from under his eye across his cheek to below his ear.

"I did not give you that scar," commented Pavlovich, noticing Roland's reaction and his quick look at the helmet.

"No, you did not. But I got the job because my predecessor became detached from his head. I believe something uncertain occurred on that occasion as well," said Roland.

"You cannot believe every rumor. Our young Mr. Turner is causing us problems. Who would have guessed this?" said Pavlovich in a surprised tone. Picking up the helmet and turning it in his hands.

The helmet had seen better days. The visor was cracked with a starburst pattern from either a bullet impact or shrapnel. One side had a decal of the 190th Fighter Squadron. Yellow and black circles with a skull in profile. The opposite side had a decal of Captain America's star shield. This side of the helmet also had a large dent and fracture, from a significant impact. Pavlovich turned the helmet back and forth, looking up at Roland.

"He was simply a target of convenience when our friends captured him after he crashed his plane," Maksim remembered.

Roland rubbed his hand on the side of his face again as he answered. "I would be happy to send Turner to hell," said Roland with a snarl.

"Now, now, this is not personal. Turner may be useful to our plans. He serves as a poster child for what happens when one dares to buck the system. He has destroyed any chance of a political career and running for President as an Independent. In America? Pure silliness," laughed Maksim. "We can just keep using him to help discredit the Constitution, and the people trying to protect it. No, you leave Turner alone. You think he would recognize you?"

"No, I wore a balaclava the whole time. He would not recognize me, nor my voice. I was speaking Arabic," said Roland.

"Well, just in case, get in your American character and hide your accent in case you run into him by happenstance."

"Where are you sending me?"

"I want you in the Vice President's campaign. I'll make some calls and get you on her campaign security team. On the inside, making sure they are not making mistakes. If you think they are, let me know. We cannot afford another setback."

"Seems a bit of a waste of my particular talents."

"Have no fear, my friend. We will make good use of your Mossad skills at the right time and place. I need you to ingratiate yourself to her and earn her trust. I don't trust her chief of staff. He is a little too cagey for me. I think he thinks he can outwit me," said Pavlovich to himself rather than Roland.

"When do I meet with them?" asked Roland.

"Soon. Be ready and I will arrange the meet. After the new year. In the meantime, get established in Washington. Study up on the situation in America. Spend some time researching Turner."

"With pleasure," said Roland with visceral hate.

"What bothers you more? That he gave you that scar or that he escaped? You knew the plan was always to let him go after we captured him. The Americans never leave comrades behind. He was just a soldier we were trying to extract intelligence from."

"True, but it was supposed to be on our terms. We didn't get any intel, and as you know, that cost us dearly. Your money and my people. Yes, it bothers me he escaped on his own and caught me off guard. He should have killed me. He could have, but he didn't. I want to know why," said Roland. "Especially after what we did to him. Who doesn't take their revenge when they have that chance?"

"My friend, they nickname you *Daboia* for a reason. The Viper waits patiently, waiting for the right moment, the opening, and then strikes to kill. You will promise me now, you will not strike until I decide the time is right. If you do not, you will not leave alive," said Pavlovich in a sinister tone.

"You know me better than that. I serve you and promise to abide by your wishes," said Roland, bowing slightly.

"Good. Go," said Pavlovich.

Roland turned to leave, shutting the door to the study behind him. Maksim watched him leave the estate on a closed-circuit camera. He was concerned *Daboia* could not contain his anger and hatred over his humiliation at the hands of Turner. He chuckled, thinking of Turner having *Daboia* stalking him without even knowing, or why.

Turning the helmet in his hands, he looked at the back. Between the decals was another stating the helmet belonged to Lt. Col. Nick 'Cap' Turner. This meant little to those who had captured him. How different things might be. If only he knew then what he now knew about Nick Turner. Pavlovich sighed, setting the helmet down. Things might be different indeed.

He pulled out his phone, dialing another number. He quickly spoke in perfect Arabic to the person on the other end of the line.

"Yes, America. No orders, just activation and stand by. Of course, the regular fee," he responded to a question. "I'll provide the target when the time is right." He ended the call. Sinking back in his chair. As he had every so often during his unusually long life, he contemplated if fate existed. If man truly had free will or if events were pre-destined. Turner reappearing right in the middle of his schemes. When he could so easily have snuffed out his life before. He reflected on his disdain for fate and faith. He pressed a button and his nurse dutifully appeared with his elixir of life.

Chapter 53

An orange light began flashing on a desk phone. The occupant of the office reached inside a hidden compartment in the drawer in the desk. Pressing a button caused panels to come down over the windows, shuttering the view and the light from the windows. There were audible snaps as locks engaged, securing the office and other sounds as it projected white noise at a barely audible hum.

Once the room was fully secured, the orange turned to green, and it projected a holographic image above the desk. There was no body or face, only a symbol from the Chinese zodiac, a Rat projected on the screen. The viewer knew his own image was being shown as the Chinese zodiac symbol of a Dragon.

A disembodied mechanical male voice came through on a hidden speaker. "Did we know this was coming?" asked the voice with the Rat symbol.

"No," said the man in the room represented by the Dragon.

"Why is that? Do we not have assets everywhere?" Rat asked in an annoyed tone, audible through all the voice washing technology.

"This appears to have been spontaneous. There was no pre-planning, no leaked intentions, no outreach," disclosed Dragon.

"How disappointing."

"Not really. It shows a lack of planning, poor execution, and inability to take advantage of the one chance to get a point across before we could censor or stop it. It was, frankly, an amateur move by an amateur," declared Dragon.

"You know we dislike surprises. This is the reason we spend so much money and effort to cultivate all those in the second circles. Members of the media, government, and business. They are our eyes and ears. Our unwitting accomplices. This is their role in implementing what we tell them to do and to prevent what we do not want to happen. We cannot fail again," said Rat.

"Agree, we need to find more ways to ensure we know what he is thinking. We thought we had it handled, but he still does things seeking no additional council," explained Dragon.

"We need to ensure he does not do that in the future. Make sure they understand this." The threat in Rat's statement was clear.

"Understood. I will ensure our operatives are aware of our displeasure at their failure."

"Do we need to prove our point?" asked Rat.

"No. Even though he moved without our knowledge, he has no organization going forward. We will make sure we are represented to help direct and ensure they achieve our wishes."

"We are placing our trust in you."

"Again, understood."

"How badly are our plans affected? Do we need to engage any contingency plans?" asked Rat.

"The filibuster is gone. But we have lost our leverage in the US Senate to push through the agenda. It will be delayed for a year. We can continue to lay groundwork, as we have in the past when plans were thwarted, but we are close to completion," explained Dragon.

"This is what we said before, going back generations now. The United States has been the sole stumbling block to our plans for too many years. We put faith in *your* plans this time. You have failed to deliver. How should we react?" asked Rat.

"You should give me time to finish. If you recall, I did not choose the prior candidate. I also counseled against how the opposition coverage was handled. This is a temporary setback, as we have experienced before. We continue to advance our plans. Police are being marginalized. Crime is rampant. Laws are ignored. The criminal justice system is ineffective. Public perception of Congress and the media are at all-time lows. Unemployment remains high, inflation is through the roof, a majority of citizens now rely on some form of government assistance. Socialism continues to gain support in the polls, especially among those under forty."

"We continue our efforts to erode the fabric of American society. Religion is all but banished. People are forming tribes and pulling back from community. Addiction and pornography are at all-time highs as well. Drugs are more and more prevalent. Marijuana use is widespread among the young. They're addicted to social media and easily manipulated. The inroads our AI initiatives are making in schools and corporations ensure both instability and further control points for us," Dragon's metallic voice continued as he described the outcomes of their plans and efforts at destabilization.

"We are all set to destroy America from the inside out. Our open borders strategy is tearing the fabric of middle America apart. They will no longer band together to fight off anything. They'll welcome a benevolent government promising to take care of them forever. To protect them from the chaos and anarchy, we've unleashed," finished Dragon.

"You make it sound so inevitable. She said the same thing. Remember what happens to those who fail. You've done well to accomplish what you have. We need to finish the project, taking American exceptionalism off the chess board permanently," observed Rat.

"Agree. In eleven months, we'll have what we need when Alexis Smythe-Thomas is elected president along with a compliant US Congress. Once this happens, there are no more obstacles."

"We shall see," concluded Rat, ending the conversation.

The End

What Can One Man Do?

Writer's Note

It is true, this is fiction. Nick Turner is a fictional character. The actions described in this story did not happen. Yet. But, consider for a second, that it is instead history. Told from our future. Just contemplate that I am writing this sometime in the near future, say 2044. Starting around now and telling what happened in the years between. George Orwell predicted a bleak future in *1984*, writing in the years following World War II to warn future readers. To show us a potential future, we could still prevent from becoming a dystopian reality.

I too sit contemplating our future, writing from a view of what could happen, looking backwards towards today. Contemplating what has transpired in our not-so-distant future. Offering a view of actions and consequences. Writing about what is about to happen for the rest of us. As a result of the consequences of these actions, or inactions, we contemplate today.

That is the task I am undertaking. To weave a tale about what has happened in my fictional world, in the hope it will not happen in the real world. To give us that 'what if' look at what could happen. Every action has a reaction. Every decision a consequence. Some good, ending as intended. Many more not good, and unfortunately, ending in both unforeseen and unintended results.

This fictional history I write is full of both. It is up to us to study this as if it is history and a potential future reality. Recognize the good and avoid the bad by seeing what can happen.

Only we can decide this future by standing up, thinking for ourselves, and choosing our own path. Each of us must take responsibility for our choices. It is a blessing and a responsibility we all share and should own rather than squandering it by neglect and allowing others to choose for us. Wake up, Stand up, and Think for Yourself (WST4Y).

Connect with the Author

- Author website: www.ejriceauthor.com
- Facebook author site: https://www.facebook.com/ejriceauthor
- Substack Blog site: https://ejriceauthor.substack.com/
- Twitter account: https://twitter.com/EJRiceauthor
- Instagram account: https://www.instagram.com/ericriceauthor
- TikTok: https://www.tiktok.com/eric.rice.author